"Will remind readers what chattering teeth sound like."
—*Kirkus Reviews*

"Voracious readers of horror will delightfully consume the contents of Bates's World's Scariest Places books."
—*Publishers Weekly*

"Creatively creepy and sure to scare." —*The Japan Times*

"Jeremy Bates writes like a deviant angel I'm glad doesn't live on my shoulder."
—Christian Galacar, author of GILCHRIST

"Thriller fans and readers of Stephen King, Joe Lansdale, and other masters of the art will find much to love."
—*Midwest Book Review*

"An ice-cold thriller full of mystery, suspense, fear."
—David Moody, author of HATER and AUTUMN

"A page-turner in the true sense of the word."
—*HorrorAddicts*

"Will make your skin crawl." —*Scream Magazine*

"Told with an authoritative voice full of heart and insight."
—Richard Thomas, Bram Stoker nominated author

"Grabs and doesn't let go until the end." —*Writer's Digest*

I

BY JEREMY BATES

WORLD'S SCARIEST LEGENDS: VOLUME 1

Mosquito Man & The Sleep Experiment

Jeremy Bates

Ghillinnein Books

WORLD'S SCARIEST LEGENDS: VOLUME 1

MOSQUITO MAN

PROLOGUE

1981

You would think a missing person case would be a pretty straightforward affair.

The person goes missing. They either turn up alive, or they turn up dead.

If it's the former (which is usually the case), you can get all the answers you want straight from their mouth. If it's the latter, you can piece together what happened to them with a combination of investigative work and forensic evidence. The woman who embarked on an evening run and ends up half naked and dead in some park bushes: rape. The kid who didn't come home for dinner and whose body parts are discovered beneath cement in the neighbor's dingy basement: pedophilia. The gambler or drug addict whose wasted body is found decomposing in an alleyway Dumpster: bad debts. The hiker whose skeleton is uncovered in the spring thaw at the bottom of a gorge: misadventure.

Yet it's when the missing person never turns up that things get tricky.

Because now you're not only dealing with the relatively straightforward questions of why they ran away, or who took them, or what happened to them. Now you have to start exploring a plethora of other possibilities. Were they being held against their will? Were they alive? Were they going to be alive for much longer? Were they in an accident? Were they suicidal? And so forth and so on. The questions chain ad infinitum, and until you have a body, be it warm or cold, they are unanswerable.

These were the thoughts going through Chief of Police Paul Harris' mind on a wet August night in 1981, as he sat inside his beat-up Crown Victoria out in front of the Chapman's log cabin that overlooked Pavilion Lake, British Columbia.

Two hours earlier, Troy and Sally Chapman's seven-year-old boy, Rex, had been picked up on Highway 99 by the local pest and rodent expert, Shorty Williams. Shorty had been coming back from an extermination job in Cache Creek. Rex had been walking barefoot along the shoulder of the highway, fifteen kilometers from Pavilion Lake and forty from the town of Lillooet, to which it appeared he'd been heading. He was white as a ghost and mute as a fish. When Shorty dropped off the boy at the police station, Paul's wife, Nancy, fixed him a bowl of chicken noodle soup and a glass of warm milk, but he wouldn't do anything but stare hauntingly at his hands in his lap. Wouldn't say a word to Nancy either, who was about as threatening as a permed Cockapoo, or to Paul himself, who had a friendly Good Cop way with kids. So Paul got in the Crown Vic and cruised down Main Street until he spotted Ed Montgomery, his volunteer and sometimes sober deputy, eating dinner at the picnic table at the Esso gas station, and together they drove out to the Chapman's place to see what was up.

Given the spooked state of young Rex Chapman, Paul had expected to find Troy and Sally in the midst of some nuclear domestic dispute, cussing and shouting and slamming doors, perhaps Sally bloodied and beaten. Or the worst case scenario: both of them, along with Rex's older brother, Logan, dead in a double murder-suicide.

Yet what he and Ed found was...nothing. Not a thing. The

cabin was in perfect order. No toppled furniture, no broken tableware, no blood, nothing to indicate anything sinister had taken place.

So what had driven Rex to flee barefoot to the highway?

Where had Troy and Sally and Logan gone?

Was an outside party involved? Had he kidnapped the family, with only Rex escaping? But who would do this? And why? And where would he take them? And were they still alive? And were they going to be alive for much longer?

All those damn missing person questions.

Paul shot a Marlboro from his pack and lit up, winding down his window a few inches to let the stuffy air out of the cab.

Ed wound down his window too and said, "Car doesn't stink enough of cigars? You gotta add cigarette smoke to it?"

Paul's father and the previous Chief of Police of Lillooet had smoked three cigars a day for most of his life. One after lunch, one after dinner, and one before he went to bed. He was a man of habit and almost never varied from this routine. Paul's mother had forbidden him from smoking the stogies inside the police station or the constable quarters above it, where they lived, so he smoked them in the patrol car, where he could relax while listening to whatever baseball game he could pull in on the radio.

Paul had believed from a young age that it was his birthright duty to follow in the footsteps of his father. So when he turned nineteen earlier that year, he "applied" to become a deputy. Getting the job had been as easy as it had been during the days of the American frontier, when all you had to do was show up at the sheriff's office with a revolver and an impressive mustache. Paul had neither the facial hair nor the six shooter, but with the chief being his dad, he had only to fill out the required paperwork and that was that. He received a uniform, boots, handcuffs, a portable radio, a weapon, and ammo—along with the sage advice to try not to shoot anyone.

When his father died unexpectedly two months ago at the age of fifty-two due to a stroke, Paul also got the beat-up Crown Vic with 250,000 kilometers on the odometer.

"I don't mind the smell," Paul said, staring straight ahead through the windshield at the black night. "Sort of grows on you."

"Maybe they went for a walk?" Ed said, referring to the Chapmans. Ed Montgomery was sixty-nine, hawk-nosed, and gray-headed, and still as randy as a man thirty years his junior. He'd been an acclaimed chef when he was younger, and had worked at some of the top vacation resorts in British Columbia (in the summers) and Florida (in the winters), where he spent almost as much time orchestrating romantic trysts with the guests as he did cooking meals for them. Nowadays he liked to remind people to call him "Monty," a nickname Sean Connery had allegedly bestowed upon him during a round of golf at a Tampa Bay country club. Nobody in the Lillooet Country believed this to be true, and so nobody called him Monty. Paul wasn't an exception. The old coot was, and always had been, Ed to him. Just plain old Ed.

"A walk?" Paul said thoughtfully, streaming a jet of smoke out the window. "Where are they going to walk, Ed? It's forest in every direction. And don't forget about the boy. You don't get all shook up like that because your family goes for a walk without you."

"I'm not forgetting about him, Paulsy. I'm just throwing out ideas here. They obviously didn't drive anywhere. Car's right there." He tipped his head to the wood-paneled station wagon parked ahead of them on the driveway.

"Troy was some sort of middle manager, wasn't he?"

Ed nodded. "Ayuh. In a Canadian Tire. The one time I had a drink with him at the sports bar—he was buying—he wouldn't stop talking about how good his goddamn pension was. So what?"

"Middle management isn't a seasonal job. He wouldn't be up here for the summer. Probably just up for the weekend to visit the missus and kids."

"So what?"

"Maybe they had two cars? One for Troy, one for Sally."

Ed was silent as he thought about that. "Maybe. But I've never seen Sally in town driving anything at all. And a Canadian Tire middle manager with two kids and a wife that doesn't work, I can't see a man like that affording two cars."

"He can afford a cabin on the lake."

"Nu-uh. That's something else we talked about at the bar. He inherited it from his pa. It's been in their family since it was built back in the Gold Rush days."

"So maybe he inherited money to buy a second car too?"

"Then what the fuck's he doing middle managing a Canadian Tire if he's got all this fucking money? C'mon, Paulsy. Let's not get carried away with speculating here."

Paul tapped some ash from his cigarette into the ashtray, took another drag, then snuffed the thing out. "So they didn't go for a walk in the woods. They didn't drive off anywhere. You think someone took them, Ed?"

"I'm not saying that. 'Cause you have something like that happen, you have a struggle, don't you? But there was no struggle. No sign of one, at least."

"Not inside," Paul said. "So maybe they were outside. Someone comes by when they were all already outside. The struggle coulda been outside. We won't know until we can look around properly tomorrow morning in the daylight."

Ed grinned. "Hey, Paulsy, maybe you got some of your pa's thinking inside you after all. I reckon that's a possibility. Someone got 'em when they were outside." Ed shifted his body a little so he could reach a pocket in his jeans. He produced a red apple and offered it to Paul. "Wanna bite?"

Paul frowned. He'd seen a bowl of fruit on the Chapman's Formica kitchen table. "Did you take that from inside, Ed?"

"So what?"

"It's evidence."

"Evidence, right. It's just a fucking apple." He took a loud, crunchy bite. He began chewing almost as loudly. Sinking back into the seat, he closed his eyes and kept chewing. Around a full mouth he said, "Wanna know what's messed up? When you close your eyes, you're still just staring straight ahead. Like right now, my eyes are closed, but I'm still just staring straight ahead. My eyeballs are just staring."

"It's time we get going, Ed. Get an early night. We'll come back tomorrow morning—"

A loud bang on the driver's side window made Paul jump. Ed choked, coughing out a pulpy piece of the chewed apple.

"Shit!" he gasped, slapping his chest hard.

Paul wound down the window all the way. A grizzled, bearded face peered in at him. A moment later the lone-wolf face of an Alaskan Malamute appeared next to its master's, its pink tongue lolling out of its mouth.

"How you doing, Paulsy!" Don Leech said. Squinting past him, he added, "You okay, Ed? You having a tough time eating over there?"

"You scared the shit out of me!" Ed sputtered, wiping his mouth with the back of his hand. "I'm sixty-nine, for Christ's sake. You trying to kill me? I oughta sue your ass for attempted murder, that's what I oughta do."

"Can't sue someone just 'cause you can't eat properly, Ed. It's a simple concept, really. Food goes in and down. You're doing it all backwards."

"What's going on, Don?" Paul asked, scratching the dog between the ears.

"You tell me, Paulsy. If you and Ponch are on a stakeout or something, you're not being too discreet about it, parked right here in the driveway like you are."

Paul explained.

"Oh, jeez." The banter left Don's demeanor. "Is little Rexy all right? I just seen him the other day playing down at the lake. Him and his brother, Loge. I can see them from my dock."

"He's okay," Paul said. "Physically, that is. But he's not saying what happened. Did you hear anything, Don? Any shouting or…anything?"

Don frowned. "Don't think so. I mean, I'm five hundred meters down the road. You can't hear much from that distance. Sometimes I hear some things, sure. The boys shouting in play. Their mom shouting at them. But how do you know that kind of shouting from serious shouting from that distance?"

"Did you hear any of that earlier today?"

"Serious shouting? No, don't think so. Well, yeah. Maybe I heard Sally. I was dozing, and I remember thinking she better not wake me up with her yelling. But I thought she was just yelling at her boys again."

"How long was she yelling for? Did you hear anything specific?"

"Nah, it was just noise. I can't remember much, t'be honest. I was in that halfway place, you know, between sleeping and being awake, and I was trying hard at not being awake."

Ed threw his apple core. It flew past Paul's face and over the head of the malamute. The dog disappeared to track it down.

"Your aim's as bad as your eating," Don said.

"I wasn't aiming at you or your big dog, you twit," Ed snapped. "I was just getting rid of the apple. It was making my fingers all sticky. And you know what—maybe it was you."

Ed blinked, his tea-colored eyes confused. "Me?"

"Maybe you got Troy and Sally and the boy tied up over at your place. What do you think, Paulsy? Should we go check?"

Don snorted. "You're crazier than a bag full of raccoons, you know that, Ed?"

After dropping off Ed Montgomery at his meticulously kept

bungalow at the end of Murray Street, which had unobstructed views of the back of the Chinese restaurant on Main,
Paul returned to the century-old police station a few blocks
away. He locked the front door behind him, which had one
of those speakeasy-esque peepholes at a little lower than eye
level, so you could see who was knocking. His office was in
the back of the building, in the same room as the three stone
holding cells. He spent the next hour on the phone before
he climbed the stairs to the second-floor constable quarters.
The Bob Newhart Show was playing on the color TV. Rex Chapman sat in Paul's leather club chair, his knees pulled to his
chest, his arms wrapped around them. He was facing the TV,
but Paul didn't know if he was watching the show or staring
off into his own thoughts. Paul's wife Nancy was on the rose
loveseat reading one of her mystery novels.

Setting the book aside, she got up, took him by the arm,
and led him to the kitchen.

"How's he doing?" Paul asked in a semi-hushed voice.

"How he's always been doing since he got here. Hasn't
said a word yet." Nancy had a cheerful, almost childlike face
framed by chestnut hair and straight bangs. He'd known her
since kindergarten but had barely said more than a handful
of words to her over the years until he'd screwed up the courage to ask her to their high school prom. They were married
two summers later, and now she was six months pregnant
with their first child, the baby bump clearly visible beneath
her luxe knit sweater. "Did you talk to Troy or Sally?" she
asked. "What happened? Are they coming to pick him up?"

Paul shook his head. "They weren't at the cabin."

She frowned. "Weren't there?"

"Nobody was."

"What do you mean nobody was there? Somebody had to
be there. They wouldn't just leave him."

"There was nobody there, Nancy," he said patiently. "I
just spoke to the captain of the RCMP's Whistler detachment. They'll be sending some crime scene guys out here

tomorrow. I also got hold of Troy Chapman's brother. His name's Henry. If Troy and Sally don't turn up anywhere, he'll drive up from Vancouver in a few days and take custody of Rex for the time being." He shrugged. "There's nothing else more I can do right now."

Nancy appeared disturbed. "This isn't good, is it, Paul?"

"It'll work itself out," he said. "Just go on and take the boy to bed. He can sleep in the spare bedroom. I need to get some sleep myself. It's going to be a helluva day tomorrow."

Nodding hesitantly, Nancy returned to the living room, while Paul continued down the hallway to the master bedroom without bothering to stop in the bathroom to wash his face or brush his teeth. He changed into a pair of striped pajamas and was asleep before Nancy slipped beneath the covers next to him.

Sometime later he woke to a shrill, piercing scream.

Leaping to his feet, he rushed to the spare bedroom and threw open the door and flicked on the light.

Rex was sitting up in the single bed, his face a pale mask of terror, his eyes shiny and bulging, his mouth still open, still screaming.

Nancy burst past Paul into the room. She plopped down on the edge of the bed and pulled the boy against her breast, rocking him, hushing him. His scream became a moan, then a breathless sob, then nothing. He wiped the tears from his cheeks and laid back down, curling into a fetal position, facing the wall.

"You go on," Nancy said to Paul softly. "I'll stay with him."

"Do you want me to turn off the light?"

"No, I think we should leave it on, don't you?"

Paul returned to bed then, more bothered than ever by the boy's state of mind. As he drifted off to sleep for the second time that night, he wondered what answers tomorrow would bring—unaware that it would not be tomorrow, or the next day, or the day after that, but another thirty-eight long years before the monstrous truth of what happened to the Chapman family would come to light.

1

38 years later

"**A**nnddddd...." Rex Chapman stretched the conjunction several seconds as they crossed the imaginary boundary line separating the towns of Blaine, Washington, and Surrey, British Colombia, before adding with exclamation, "We're in Canada now!"

Bobby said from the back seat in his small five-year-old voice, "It doesn't *feel* any different."

"Well, there's nothing really to feel that's different, bud."

From next to him, Ellie, also five going on twenty-five, said, "Nothing *looks* different."

Tabitha, Rex's girlfriend of six months, turned in the front passenger seat of the sporty Mazda sedan to face the kids. "Nothing's going to feel different or look different, guys, because the United States and Canada share the same landmass. What will be different will be cultural things like —"

"Where are all the bears?" Bobby asked. "Dylan from school says there are lots of bears in Canada."

Rex glanced in the rearview mirror but could only see a golden cowlick sprouting defiantly from the top of Bobby's head, and to the right of him, the tips of Ellie's jet-black

Sailor Moon hair buns. Bobby was his; Ellie, Tabitha's.

"There are bears in the States too, bud," he said, "especially in states like Washington."

"Are there owls here too? Owls are my favorite birds."

"Yup, owls too. But I doubt we'll see any. They're nocturnal."

"Owls aren't turtles!" Ellie said, giggling.

"I didn't say that. I said—"

"Where are the Indians? Are we going to see an Indian?"

"I'll let you field that one," Rex said, glancing sidelong at Tabitha. Turning forty next month, she was five years younger than he was. She had the same jet-black hair as her daughter, though hers was cut into a more mature jaw-skimming cut. Beneath her bold brows, her eyes were bright violet, her skin as smooth as porcelain. Despite the Elizabeth Taylor-esque look, she saw herself only as a working single mom operating on too much stress and too little sleep, and if you told her that her beauty matched that of any Hollywood actress, she would most likely tell you where to stick it.

"Do you guys want to play I-Spy?" she said, sidestepping her daughter's questions.

"That's so boring!" Ellie complained.

"Why don't you watch something on your iPad then, sweetie?"

"Fine..." Music began to play. "Ugh. Jonas Hill again. He doesn't have many friends, does he?"

Mario music began to play also, indicating Bobby had gone back to his handheld Nintendo Switch.

Seeing the upcoming traffic light turn yellow, Rex accelerated through the intersection. He wasn't an impatient driver, yet they'd already been on the road for three hours since leaving Seattle, plus an extra half-hour wait at the border crossing, and they still had another three or so to go. So the less number of reds they had to sit through, the better.

It was late afternoon. The October sky was a washed-out

blue, filled with fluffy clouds rimmed white that deepened to a slate gray in the center. Having been born and raised in the Pacific Northwest, Rex knew it wasn't a question of if it would rain but when. Being mid-October, it was the beginning of the rainy season on the coast, which meant they wouldn't be seeing much in the way of weather variation other than rain, fog, and moody skies for the next six months.

"Looks like it might rain," Tabitha said, as if reading his thoughts.

"Hope it's just a drizzle," he said.

"You know it doesn't drizzle around here."

"You're right. It's going to be a downpour."

"A downpour that comes in sideways with the wind."

"A *torrential* downpour that comes in sideways with the wind."

"Umbrella-killing gale-force winds."

"Death and destruction all around."

"And we're going to be in a little cabin in the mountains." She smiled. "Sounds cozy."

"Sounds suicidal," he said.

"If you don't like the rain, you live in the wrong part of the world, mister."

"It's not the rain. It's the grayness. Everything's always gray. November to June. Gray. Don't you ever get tired of that?"

"Jeez, you're sounding glum."

"Yeah, Dad," Bobby said from the back, "stop being so *glum.*"

"I'm just saying, some vitamin D sometimes would be nice."

"Don't listen to him, Bobby, he's just being the devil's advocate."

Bobby didn't reply, and Rex wasn't surprised. The boy didn't speak to Tabitha unless it was absolutely necessary. He was taking his mother's absence pretty badly, and from his erroneous perspective, Tabitha was to blame for the absence.

The silence in the wake of Bobby's pointed lack of reply lingered in the car. Rex rested a hand on Tabitha's thigh. She covered it with hers.

"What's a devil's abby cat, Mommy?" Ellie asked abruptly.

"It's someone who argues with you just to argue, hon."

"Why?"

"They just like to argue, I suppose."

"But why?"

"They just... Are you being a devil's abby cat right now, sweetie?"

"No!" she replied.

"I think you are."

"Devil's abby cats are stupid!"

"Totally," Tabitha agreed.

"Hey, are you calling me stupid?" Rex said.

"Yes!" Ellie said.

Rex zipped through another intersection in the nick of time and felt absurdly proud of this accomplishment. On the left, a Tim Horton's coffee shop slipped past, followed by a Best Western with a neatly manicured garden of alpine flowers, and an auto repair shop hidden behind a phalanx of old tires. Surrey was one of Vancouver's southern suburbs, and like most suburbs, it consisted of wide roads, ample trees, a network of telephone poles and their corresponding wires, commercial shops, and pleasant houses, none of which were too big nor too small.

It took them roughly an hour to get through Vancouver before they were once again surrounded by raw nature.

"Any idiots out today, Dad?" Bobby asked out of the blue, with a confident nonchalance that made him sound ten years older than he was.

Tabitha laughed. "Does your dad call a lot of drivers idiots, Bobby?"

He didn't answer her.

Rex said, "Haven't run into any yet, bud. Hope it stays that way."

The Sea-to-Sky Highway continued north along the shore of the steep-sided Howe Sound, a network of fjords populated with small islands, and up into the Coast Mountains, where it cleaved through forested slopes and clung precariously to cliff walls, all to the backdrop of majestic ocean vistas.

While Tabitha and the kids oohed and ahhed at the sights —even catching a glimpse of a circling bald eagle hunting for its next meal—Rex remained focused on the road. With all the twists and turns, driving demanded his full attention. Still, every now and then his eyes meandered to the rugged backcountry, and he had the same thought each time: there wasn't another freeway in North America, not even the I-70 through Colorado or the I-80 over the Sierra Nevada, which matched this remote, pristine beauty.

After another hour or so they reached the charming mountain town of Squamish, a haven for the outdoorsy types and renowned for its gushing waterfalls, stomach-dropping suspension bridge, and the Stawamus Chief, a huge cliff-faced granite massif towering seven hundred meters into the sky. Rex filled up the Mazda at a gas station, bought some candy bars for the kids to nibble on, and then they were off again.

"I want the Snickers!" Ellie said when he told them what he had.

"Can I have a Twik?" Bobby asked.

"You mean Twix, bud."

"No, I only want one."

He passed the Snickers and Twix back over his shoulder, then said to Tabitha, "Got a Mars and Kit Kat left."

"I'll pass," she said, patting her stomach. "Got to stay trim for this guy I'm seeing."

"Lucky guy, him. But I'm sure he'd like you just as much

no matter your weight."

"He *is* a sweetheart."

"Eww!" Ellie said around a full mouth. "You guys are gross."

"Someday you're going to have feelings for boys too, sweetie," Tabitha said. "Just so you know."

"I already do have feelings, Mommy. I hate them."

Leaving the waters of Howe Sound behind and heading inland now, the Sea-to-Sky Highway continued its ever upward ascent, snaking through hilly meadows, dense old-growth rainforests, and extinct volcanoes. It was a roller-coaster ride, the turns steep and sudden with some gradients approaching ten degrees. Rex had dreaded this part of the journey as a kid, not only because of the sickening blind corners and dizzying elevation, but because rockslides or accidents had been a regular occurrence, often trapping his family on the road for hours, which had always seemed like an eternity.

When they passed a turnoff to the ski resort town of Whistler Blackcomb, Tabitha remarked she would like to visit there someday, and Rex made a mental note to plan such a trip on their one-year anniversary, if they made it to that point, though he couldn't see any reason why they wouldn't, given how smoothly their relationship had progressed thus far.

Thirty minutes onward they entered the rustic town of Pemberton, which wouldn't have been out of place in an Old West movie, a consequence of its ranching and mining culture during the gold rush era.

"A McDonald's!" Bobby said.

"Can we stop?" Ellie asked.

Rex glanced at the McDonald's on the right: with its quaint cedar façade and covered walkways, it resembled a saloon from the 1920s. "We got our own stuff to make hamburgers, guys," he said. "Besides, we have a schedule to keep. Don't you want to reach the cabin before it gets dark?"

"Are there bears there?" Ellie asked.

"Well, yeah, but they won't come near us. They're more scared of you than you are of them."

"I'm not scared of them," Bobby said defiantly.

"Yes, you are," Ellie said. "Everybody's scared of bears."

"I'm not!"

"Are too!"

"Am not!"

"Guys—enough!" Tabitha said.

They drove through farmland for a number of kilometers before climbing once again into the snow-capped mountains for the final, and most treacherous, leg of the journey. Coniferous trees prevailed here, the blend of fir and pine in the lower elevations gradually giving way to spruce and aspen the higher they got. Nearly ninety white-knuckle minutes after this, they arrived at an intersection of deep gorges in the lee of the Coast Mountains where the tiny community of Lillooet was located. They crossed a wooden bridge over the Seton River, a tributary of the Fraser, and were immediately greeted by a totem pole carved from an enormous western red cedar. Bobby and Ellie yapped and pointed. Rex pulled to the side of the road so they could all have a gawk.

"It's huge!" Bobby said, pressing his nose to his window.

"It was there when I was a kid," Rex said, noting that it was even taller than he remembered, perhaps fifty or sixty feet top to bottom.

"Why are the faces so scary?" Ellie asked, leaning toward Bobby's side of the car as far as her seatbelt straps would allow.

"They're just animals," Bobby said.

"One's a beaver," Tabitha said. "See its teeth?"

"The top one's a bird!" Ellie said.

"Looks like an eagle," Tabitha said.

"What's that one with the big nose?" Bobby asked.

He was referring to the face carved into the bottom of the

pole.

"It's a mosquito," Rex said.

"I hate mosquitas!" Ellie said. "They bite!"

"Everyone hates them," Tabitha said. "That's why that one's at the bottom."

"That's not exactly true," Rex said, putting the car in gear and pulling back onto the road.

"You like mosquitos, Daddy?" Bobby asked.

"What I mean is, a lot of people think that the most important figure on a totem pole is placed at the top. But it's actually the reverse. The most important one is at the bottom to support the weight of all the others atop it. That, and it puts it at eye level with the viewer."

"I didn't know you were such a connoisseur of Native American art," Tabitha teased him.

"My father told me that one summer."

"What did grandpa do, Dad?" Bobby asked. "Was he a pilot like you?"

"No, he was a humanitarian."

"What's a human-tarian?"

"It's like a vegetarian," Ellie said assuredly. "But they eat humans instead of vegetables."

"Not quite, honey," Tabitha said. "It's somebody who helps others less fortunate than themselves."

They crossed the old CN railway tracks that served the Lillooet Railway Station, then made a right onto Lillooet's Main Street—and Rex was immediately clobbered with a myriad of nostalgic memories. The big Swiss-looking hotel that greeted them. The old pizza parlor with its hand-painted sign. The mom-and-pop convenience store, where he'd often spent his weekly allowance on gummy bears and sour keys. The House of Jade Mineral Museum, the Royal Canadian Legion where "EVERYONE IS WELCOME," and the Esso gas station. There was also the cinder-block supermarket where Rex had always checked the slots of the gumball machines for forgotten change. The pub that was still reminding people with its signage that it sold "Ice Cold Beer," and where his dad had always bought his cases of Labatt 50 and Coors Light. The I.D.A. pharmacy, the Canadian Imperial Bank of Commerce, and next to the post office with its Canadian flag flapping in the wind, the iconic Goldpanner Restaurant, which used to offer a weekend buffet, and perhaps still did.

In general, everything was as he recalled. Nothing had really changed. It was almost as if the tired community had remained locked in a time bubble for the last thirty-eight years—

"I knew there were Indians here!" Ellie blurted suddenly.

Rex had no idea what she was talking about until he spotted four men standing in the parking lot of a budget inn, smoking cigarettes. They wore jeans and plaid lumberjack shirts. Their Native American heritage was evident by their dominant coloring, smooth features, and straight, dark hair.

"You shouldn't call them Indians, Ellie," he told her.

"Huh?" she said.

"They're called Aboriginals."

"Abo-what?"

"Aboriginals. That means they're the original inhabitants of this land."

"Abodidinal."

"Yes, that, or Native Americans. So try to use one of those instead. Okay?"

"Okay."

"Thank you."

Rex caught Bobby mumble, "You're so stupid," under his breath, which prompted Ellie to reply, "Like you knew! You're the stupidest stupid head in the world!"

The north end of the town deteriorated into a grungy industrial zone, which included an A&W restaurant that had been a teenage hangout when he was a kid, and a relatively new open-air strip mall he hadn't known had existed until now.

"I need to go to the bathroom," Bobby said.

"Can't it wait, bud?" he said. "We're almost there."

"I really need to go!"

"He's going to pee his pants!" Ellie said.

"Am not!"

"Are too!"

"Am not!"

"Ay yi yi," Tabitha said with a sigh.

Rex was thinking about doing a U-turn to head back to the A&W when, ahead on the right, he spotted a rickety old A-frame house that, if his memory served him correctly, was a mining museum that also doubled as a tourism center.

He made a right into the parking lot, which was empty of any other cars. "Should be bathrooms in here if it's still open," he said, stopping before a maple tree resplendent with fall leaves. He killed the engine. "But let's not dally, okay?"

Everybody got out of the Mazda, four doors slamming in quick succession. Rex breathed in the cool, fragrant air, which was redolent with pine needles and wood smoke from a burning fire. He led the way to the log building that had VISITOR INFORMATION CENTER hand-carved into a thick slab of wood above the front door. A signpost next to the porch bristled with arrows indicating the distance to everywhere from Bangkok to Paris.

"Hey, isn't that cool?" Rex said, indicating the post. "How far does it say Seattle is, Bobby?"

"I *really* need to go, Dad."

"Okay, okay, just hold on a bit longer."

The steps up the porch creaked loudly beneath his feet. A sign hanging in the door's mullioned window read CLOSED, though the lights were still on inside.

Rex rapped on the door and waited.

"Dad..."

"I know, Bobby. Hold on."

He rapped again, and the door opened a moment later. An

elderly woman dressed in a brightly-patterned dress stood on the other side of the threshold. She was tall and delicately built with a short-cropped white perm, ski-jump nose, and sagging jowls. Bright red lipstick contrasted garishly with her sun-weathered leathery skin. Kind eyes probed Rex from behind tortoise-shell eyeglasses. "I'm sorry," she said, offering an apologetic smile, "we've been closed for a little while now. We'll be open again tomorrow morning—"

"My son just needs to use the restroom," Rex said. "Would that be possible? We've been driving all day."

"Oh, I see." The woman glanced at Bobby, who was cupping his genitals in dramatic fashion, and her smile became genuine. She gathered the fabric of her dress around her thighs and stepped back to allow them to enter. "Come in, please."

The interior of the museum/tourist center was one large dilapidated room with raked ceilings from which depended three antique brass fans. A smorgasbord of glass display cases contained all sorts of metals and minerals. Others held old mining tools, surveyor's instruments, and black-and-white photographs depicting life at the turn of the last century. In one dark corner stood an eerily life-sized exhibit of two haggard prospectors panning for gold over a creek bed. Nearby, a fire burned warmly in a stone fireplace.

"Restrooms are right over there," the woman said, indicating a set of doors at the end of a log counter stacked with tourist brochures.

"There you go, bud," Rex said, ruffling his hair with his hand.

Bobby took off.

"Mind you, there's no toilet seat!" the woman added.

Bobby hesitated at the door with the MENS decal, glanced back.

"It's okay, bud," Rex said. "Just don't fall in."

Bobby slipped inside and closed the door behind him.

"Wow!" Ellie said, staring up at the wall where an eight-point stag mount presided over them. "A deer head!"

"Ran right into the museum, that one did," the woman said with a lopsided grin. "It wasn't suicidal. Deers are rarely suicidal, you know. So it must have been real dark. But that's how I found it in the morning, head sticking through the wall, just like that."

"Was it okay?" Ellie asked, concerned.

"Dead as a mackerel," the woman stated bluntly. "So I lopped off the body on the other side of the wall and that was that. Been up there ever since."

Ellie was speechless for the first time all day.

Rex was too.

Crouching before Ellie, so they were at eye level, the woman continued, "But never-mind that. How do you like our little town so far, lovely?"

Ellie said, "We saw some Abodidinals."

"Aboriginals? Very good. A lot of young people often mistakenly call them Indians, but that's not correct. A long time ago, you see, Christopher Columbus set sail for what at the time everybody called India, or the Indies. But then he accidentally landed on an island in the Caribbean instead, which is just south of the U.S.A. Thinking he was in the Indian Ocean, he called the people Indians, and the name stuck for all the different native people in North America."

"I knew they were Abodidinals because T-Rex taught me that."

"T-Rex?"

Ellie pointed at Rex. "That's T-Rex, my mom's boyfriend. And that's my mom. She looks like me when I get bigger."

"Oh—oh my, I see." The woman glanced up at Tabitha, who was blushing, then at Rex, then at their denuded ring fingers.

"I'm Rex," he said, not knowing what else to say. "This is my partner, Tabitha."

"Call me Barb," she said. Then to Ellie, "And you, little princess, are absolutely right. There are a lot of Aboriginals in Lillooet. In fact, just over half the town are St'at'imc. Do you know why?"

"Why?"

"You've seen the big river outside?"

Ellie nodded.

"That's the longest and most important river in British Columbia. Several streams converge with it right around here, making this area a great fishing spot. Aboriginals have been coming here long before Lillooet was called Lillooet, some archeologists think for thousands of years, specifically to catch migrating Chinook salmon."

"Huh," Rex said. "I didn't know that."

"Sure," Barb said, nodding her head sagely. "They also believe it's one of the oldest continuously inhabited locations on the continent."

Ellie scrunched her nose. "I don't like salmon, and I don't like mosquitas."

"Mosquitos?" Barb said. "No, not many people do, do they?"

"Abodidinals do."

Barb raised an eyebrow. "Do they now?"

"Because they made the mosquita face on the big totem pole, and T-Rex says the most important face is at the bottom, so that means they probably like mosquitas."

"Rex—or T-Rex, I should say—is exactly right. And you are too, in a way. The Aboriginals don't like mosquitos how you might like a cute puppy, with affection, I mean, but they certainly hold great respect for them."

"Why do they respect them?"

"Ellie," Tabitha said, "that's enough questions for now, I think. I'm sure Barbara has better things to do than—"

"Oh, not at all," Barb said. "I'm honored to have such an inquisitive young lady in my museum." To Ellie, "Would you like to hear a story, lovely?"

"Yes!"

Barb took Ellie's hands in hers and said, "A long, long

time ago, long before there were white people in Canada, and when Lillooet was just a longhouse village, some of the St'at'imc were out on the river in their elm-bark canoes—"

"Fishing for salmon?" Ellie said.

"That's right," Barb said. "Fishing for salmon. Only on this morning they didn't get a single bite in their usual spot, so they tried a new stream. They didn't get any bites there either, and so they paddled farther and farther into uncharted territory. Suddenly along the tree-lined bank there was a loud rustling sound and then"—she made an astonished gesture— "something thin and tall burst through the thick vegetation and snatched one of the men!"

Ellie covered her eyes with her hands. "Did it eat him?" she asked, peeking through her splayed fingers.

"Nobody knew what happened to him," Barb replied. "But back at the longhouse village, the chief wasn't happy. So the next morning he sent his best warriors to track down the creature."

Ellie lowered her hands reluctantly. "Did they find it?"

"They did. But they weren't strong enough to kill it. Instead, it took another one of the men and injured several others, who quickly fell sick and died over the next few days."

"Oh poo!" Ellie said, frowning in despair.

Rex cleared his throat. "Maybe we should pause the story there for now—"

"But I want to hear what happened!" Ellie protested, looking up at him with pleading eyes.

"I don't want you having nightmares tonight."

"I won't," she said. "I promise."

Rex glanced at Tabitha. Her daughter, her call.

Tabitha shrugged. "Ellie's a big girl. She can make her own decisions."

"Well," Barbara continued, picking up from where she had left off, "the chief wasn't just angry anymore. He was scared. What was this creature that could defeat his best warriors with such ease? He decided to send messengers to the neighboring St'at'imc villages to warn them about the creature—and much to his amazement, the other villages already knew about it. In fact, they had a name for it too. *Zancudo*. That means long-legged."

"Were there more like it?"

"Nobody knew. Nobody knew much of anything about it. Not where it came from, nor how many of them there were, if there were indeed more than one. Only that it was very dangerous—and that the attacks kept happening. So after much worrying and consulting, the villages decided to work together. They organized the biggest hunting party yet. With their bows and arrows, war clubs and hunting knives, dozens of warriors tracked down the Zancudo, overwhelmed it with their sheer numbers, and chopped it up into pieces."

"They killed it?" Ellie said.

"They did indeed. But while they were celebrating, the strangest thing happened. Tiny little insects appeared in the Zancudo's spilled blood. Swarms of them took to the air, turning the sky black. Buzzing and biting, they attacked the warriors, killing many and driving the rest back to their villages—and returning every summer thereafter to seek their revenge." The old woman smiled. "And that, little princess, is the origin of hateful mosquitos, and why the St'at'imc people have a grudging respect for them."

Ellie scrunched her nose. "Is that true?" she asked skeptically.

"It's what the St'at'ime people believe."

"Is it true, Mommy?"

"You heard the woman, honey," Tabitha said.

"Little mosquitos came from a big one?" She chewed on this. Then, "Do other big ones still exist?" she asked worriedly.

"I have never seen one—"

The door to the men's restroom opened, and Bobby

stomped out, fiddling with his belt.

"All good, Bobby?" Rex asked, happy that they could finally get going. There was something about Barb that bothered him in a vague and undefined way, almost as though she were in on a joke they knew nothing about.

"Yup!" Bobby said, coming over. "It was just me and my penis."

Rex cleared his throat. "A bit too much information there, bud. Now thank this lady for letting you use the bathroom."

"Thank you," Bobby said shyly.

Barb stood. "Where are you staying in town, if I may ask?"

"We're not," Rex replied. "I have a cabin on Pavilion Lake."

Her eyebrows went up in surprise. "Is that so?"

"I spent summers there as a kid. Haven't been back since."

"Rex... Rex *Chapman*," she said, her disposition changing in a heartbeat—and in her face...something like fear? Her eyes went to his prematurely white hair for just a moment. "Your parents were Troy and Sally Chapman."

Rex nodded tightly. This was the last conversation he wanted to have right then.

"I was in my twenties then," Barb said. "I remember... well, I don't remember too much. I heard..." She cleared her throat. "I never saw you after your family... They took you away..."

"Where did you go, Daddy?" Bobby asked.

"It's time we get going, guys," he said, placing a hand on each of the kids' shoulders and turning them toward the door. "Last one to the car's a rotten egg!"

Yelping and clawing at one another to gain the advantage, they bolted through the door and down the porch steps.

Rex placed a hand on the small of Tabitha's back and directed her outside after them.

"Mr. Chapman?" Barb's voice rose behind him, striking a

concerned note. "Are you sure it's a good idea to go back to that cabin? Perhaps we could talk in private, please? Mr. Chapman? *Rex*?"

Without replying, Rex unlocked the Mazda with the remote key and slipped behind the wheel. When everyone else was buckled up, he turned on the ignition. The engine cranked and started, purring loudly.

Tabitha frowned at him. "Are you okay, hon?"

He nodded, clicking on the headlights. "Fine," he said, though he felt far from fine.

"Did that woman know you, Daddy?" Bobby asked from the back seat. "When you were a kid like me?"

"I suppose," he said lightly. "Everybody knows everybody in a small burg like this, bud—and they all have long memories."

"But you don't remember her?"

"No," he said, pulling out of the parking lot and turning right onto Moha Road, into the darkening shadows of dusk.

2

Paul Harris, who had become known affably by the townsfolk as Policeman Paul over the years, was not only the Chief of Police of Lillooet, but he was also the township's patrolman, detective, traffic cop, crime-scene investigator, and search-and-rescue guy. He had assumed all of these roles not by choice but by necessity.

He was the last man standing on the now one-man police force.

This had not always been the case. Paul's first deputy had been his father's old friend, Ed Montgomery, who had lived behind the still-standing Chinese restaurant. Since then Paul had gone through a handful of different deputies, the last one being a spunky mother of four named Fiona Marshall. Paul had gotten along great with Fiona. He would have liked to have kept her, but she moved with her husband and kids to Saskatchewan two months back to be closer to her sisters.

A few people interested in filling Fiona's role had approached Paul, but he hadn't made any decisions yet. He didn't want to choose hastily. Besides, it wasn't like Lillooet was drowning in major crimes. His duties were pretty mundane. He performed firearms inspections to ensure farmers were storing their guns according to regulation. He enforced traffic and attended collisions. He searched for hikers, mostly tourists, who ventured off the official trails and became lost in the wilderness. The two most serious offences over the last six months had been an illegal lighting of a fire during a fire-danger period and an opportunistic burglary.

Of course, Paul also dealt with all the day-to-day interpersonal drama that came with policing a township of less than three-thousand people. Concerned mothers and fathers telling Paul to "have a word" with boys they didn't want their daughters dating. Bitter wives urging him to lock up their no-good alcoholic husbands. Those same husbands bitching to him about how their ungrateful wives were lazy cows that didn't lift a finger around the house. Others wanting him to settle boundary disputes with neighbors, or gambling debts with former friends, or God knows what else. It was always something or other. And it never seemed to matter that "parent" or "marriage counselor" or "surveyor" or "fixer" weren't in Paul's job description. As the only cop within a hundred-kilometer radius, he had been nominated, whether he liked it or not, as the town's jack of all trades. So he listened politely to everybody's concerns, offered whatever support he could, and most importantly, remained objective in his actions. *Be friendly but not a friend* his father had once told him, and it was a mantra he now lived by.

Nevertheless, it would be nice to have a deputy along again for those domestic violence call-outs, Paul thought. These usually involved the same two or three families in town, mind you, who were generally more belligerent than violent...but you never knew. Sometimes it was the most ordinary folks who turned out to be the craziest in the head. Take Chad Burnett, for example, a charismatic sheep farmer on fifty acres a few kilometers north of town, who had also served as mayor between 2008 and 2012. He had been respected by everyone young and old, Paul included, so it was to Paul's great surprise when he gave his pretty wife Hula two black eyes, three cracked ribs, and a broken foot after she hid the TV remote because she believed he was watching too much pay-per-view porn. And let us not forget Maggie Williams, fulltime muckraker and grandmother of four who once tripped out on a cocktail of anti-psychotic meds and Chardonnay and terrorized her neighbors by banging on their windows and tearing up their garden. She'd nearly taken off Paul's head with a steel-toothed hand-rake before he and Fiona were able to cart her off to jail.

Maybe I should *start looking a bit more seriously for Fiona's replacement,* Paul mused as he rolled down the Crown Vic's window and lit up a cigarette

Inhaling deeply, tobacco crackling in the still air of the cab, he returned his attention to the sprawling hotel across the street. Two weeks ago, after Troy Levine plowed his Ford pickup truck through the pioneer cemetery out in front of the old Anglican Church, Paul had decided it was time to crack down on the drunken driving that he had mostly turned a blind eye to over the years. So last Saturday—the first of the month when the welfare checks came in and you couldn't find an empty seat in any of the town's licensed establishments between noon and midnight—Paul had staked out the same hotel he was now watching, which ran the town's largest and busiest pub, and busted a few patrons over the point-oh-eight threshold who attempted to drive home. Word had clearly gotten around, because today the parking lot was only half full.

Paul took another drag on the cigarette, which set off a series of phlegmy coughs. A tickle in the back of his throat kept the coughs going for a good ten seconds.

The price you paid for smoking a pack a day your entire adult life, he supposed.

The back door of the hotel's pub opened, and a man beneath a cowboy hat emerged, his face hidden mostly in shadows, though he appeared unsteady on his feet. He disappeared around the west side of the building, and Paul figured he was either taking a leak or walking home, when he returned a short time later in the saddle atop a chocolate Quarter Horse.

"Oh, for fuck's sake," Paul mumbled, flicking the cigarette

out the window. He put the cruiser in gear and eased up behind the horse. He blurped the siren. The man glanced over his shoulder, and Paul recognized Sammy Johnson of Fraser River Meats.

Sammy reined the horse to a stop.

Putting the cruiser in Park, Paul got out and flanked the steed. "Evening, Sammy," he said, looking up at the bleary-eyed butcher.

"Didn't see you out here, Paulsy," Sammy said, slurring his words. "Where you been hiding?"

"You been drinking, Sammy?"

"Had a couple, maybe."

"You want to blow into this for me?" He raised a small handheld breathalyzer.

"I got a medical condition that don't—"

"Hell you do, Sammy. Now let's just get this done with."

Scowling, Sammy leaned toward the device—and for a moment Paul feared he was going to topple head over heels to the ground. But he kept his balance, placed his lips on the device's mouthpiece, and blew.

"Harder," Paul said.

Sammy blew again.

After several seconds, Paul checked the digital readout.

"One-point-three, Sammy."

"Those things ain't accurate, you know that."

"Accurate enough. You're going to have to come to the station with me until you sober up."

"But I ain't even driving a car! It's a horse! And a *sober* horse at that!"

"I suppose technically that's only half a DUI then, but I still gotta take you in."

"Come on, Paulsy. We went to school together."

Paul got this all the time. "It's a small town, Sammy," he replied. "Everyone went to school together. There's only one damned school."

"Can't you just—"

"No. Now enough bullshitting. You're coming with me."

Paul helped the drunk butcher down off the horse, then tied the reins to the top rail of the fence that ran parallel to the sidewalk. He would come back later for the animal.

With Sammy in the back of the patrol car, bitching and moaning about his constitutional rights being violated, Paul drove the half klick to the police station, pulling over at the curb out in front of it.

Built the same year Winston Churchill was born, the original wooden structure had burned to the ground in 1926. The stone building that stood there now rose in its place, along with the iron-clad stables, long since demolished, and the constable quarters, which were still there, and which have housed every officer and his family since.

Paul led Sammy up the flagstone walk, stopping to pick up his grandson's bicycle, which had been abandoned on its side, kickstand be damned. The three stone holding cells were located in a room at the back of the building that also served as his office. Paul opened one of the barred doors and gestured for Sammy to enter.

"How the hell long do I have to sit in there for?" Sammy asked, though he nevertheless entered the six-by-eight-foot cell without protest and flopped down on the bed.

"A few hours, I reckon. Just try to get some shuteye. It'll be morning before you know it."

"You wanna call the wife for me then? Tell her you locked me up and I won't be home for supper?"

"I can do that."

"And, hey, Paulsy—you got any food?"

"Just get some rest, Sammy."

Paul closed the cell door, which deadlocked automatically. He went to his desk and sat down. By the time he had looked up Sammy's phone number in the white pages, and had spoken with his missus (who took the news of her husband's incarceration with bitter amusement), Sammy was already asleep and snoring loudly.

Hanging up the phone, Paul sighed while stretching his arms above his head. On his desk sat three plastic-framed photographs of his grandson. The boy had short black hair and dark, cynical eyes like Paul's (cop's eyes, Paul always told him proudly), as well as the Harris nose, which some would say was so big it distracted from the other facial features, though Paul had always considered a large nose to be distinguished rather than obtrusive.

A knock sounded at the front door.

Paul glanced at the wall clock: 6:12 p.m. His official hours might be nine-to-five like everybody else's, but he was unofficially on duty 24/7.

His sigh turned into a groan as he heaved himself out of his chair, returned to the front of the station, and answered the door.

Barbara McKenzie stood across the threshold, her craggy features bathed in the sepia tones of dusk. She pushed her tortoiseshell glasses up the bridge of her sharp nose and smiled at him.

"Evening, Paul," she said.

"Evening, Barb," he said. "Let me guess. Vandals again?" Kids had been spray-painting menacing-looking stickmen on the trunks of some conifers in the vicinity of the museum.

"No, no, not that. I wanted to tell you I had some interesting visitors at the museum just now."

"Oh?" he said, already thinking of an excuse to get out of the conversation tactfully.

She nodded eagerly. "It's about...well, you told me...this was a number of years ago...but you told me to let you know if I ever heard of anybody going down to Pavilion Lake."

"Oh?" he said again, his half-formed excuse immediately forgotten.

"You won't believe who it was either."

"Who, Barb?"

"*Rex*," she said with an uncertain smile. "*Rex Chapman*."

A sudden wash of unreality struck Paul like an open-handed slap. "That kid..." he said, frowning.

Barb nodded. "He's not a kid anymore..."

"Are you sure it was Rex Chapman?"

"Of course I'm sure! His hair was still as white as a snow-flake. Not to mention he told me his name. He was with a woman—not his wife, I should mention—and two of the most adorable little children you have ever seen."

Paul ran a hand over the stubble surrounding his clenched mouth, the August night in '81 returning to him in a jumble of rusty images. After Rex Chapman was found wandering on the highway, he stayed overnight with Paul and Nancy, in the guest bedroom. Not that he'd done much sleeping. He'd woken up every hour, screaming at the top of his lungs. And by morning, his previously blond hair had turned completely white. Every goddamn follicle.

Paul had interviewed Rex a half-dozen times over the following two days, but the boy didn't remember anything, not what had frightened him so badly, nor what had happened to his parents and older brother, none of whom had ever been heard from again.

Barb was saying something.

Paul looked at her without comprehension, his mind still fogged up with the past.

"Paul?" she said. "Did you hear me?"

"What was that, Barb?"

"What are you going to do? You can't let them stay on the lake. Not with everything that's happened up there. The other families that've gone missing. The Petersons and—"

"The Ryersons. But, hell, that was a dozen years ago now. Nothing's happened since—"

"Because everybody else moved away!"

"Keep your voice down, Barb."

"Sorry, Paul," she said, casting a wary glance at the stairs leading to the second floor. "But it's just...I just...*you* were the one who told me to tell you if I heard of anybody going up to the lake."

"More than a decade ago, I did," he said, lowering his voice as well. "But whoever was down there, Barb, whoever was responsible for whatever happened to the Chapmans and the Petersons and the Ryersons…that person's gotta be at least my age now. He's long gone—"

"But—"

"Or more than likely he's dead. There's nothing to get all worked up about—"

"But what if someone *is* still up there?" she said. "What if something *does* happen? Those kids, Paul…"

He shook his head in frustration. "What do you want me to do, Barb? It's Rex's cabin. It's his right if he wants to go there."

"He probably doesn't know better. He hasn't been back since he was a kid. At least he hasn't been seen in town, or spoken to anybody from town. So you have to at least tell him what's happened since he left."

Paul placed a hand on the door with the intent to close it. "I need some time to think this through, Barb. Thanks for bringing it to my attention." He started to close the door.

She held it open with both hands. "You have to go up there, Paul."

He sighed. "Yeah, I guess I do."

"Tonight."

"Let me think about it, okay?"

"Tonight."

"Yes, fine, tonight."

Barb sagged with relief. "Thank you, Paul. Maybe I'm overreacting. I know I'm probably overreacting. But I just keep thinking about those adorable little kids…"

"You go home now, Barb," he said. "Everything is just fine."

She stepped back, nodding, and then started away.

He closed the door halfway. "Barb?" he said.

She turned back toward him. "Yes?"

"Let's keep this between you and me for now. Can we do that?"

"Well, yes," she said. "That's probably a good idea. When are you going to go—?"

"Soon," he said, and closed the door all the way. Standing with his back to the wood, staring down the long hallway that led to the holding cells, Paul felt the skin over his skull and arms tingle and tighten, as if it was suddenly one size too small.

"Paul?" Nancy's voice floated down the stairs. "Who was that?"

"Barbara Moore from the museum."

"What did she want?"

"Nothing," he said, before adding, "At least nothing important."

3

"That lady was strange, Mommy," Ellie said.

"Who are you talking about, honey?" Tabitha asked. They were passing through the northern stretches of Lillooet, looming foothills to the left of them, white-siding houses with wood-picket fences and scrub-filled lots to the right.

"The mosquita story woman."

"You mean Barbara? Why was she strange?"

"She just was."

Bluntly put, but Tabitha didn't disagree. Barbara's heavy-handed presence and melodramatic storytelling had been a bit over the top. A simple, "The restrooms are over there," would have sufficed just fine.

"Did the mosquito story scare you?" she asked her daughter.

"A little," Ellie admitted.

"You're not going to have nightmares, I hope?"

"No…"

"You're a scaredy cat!" Bobby said.

"Am not!" Ellie replied.

"Am too!"

"Am not—"

"Guys!" Tabitha said sharply. "Enough. Can't you think of something else to say?"

"Like what?"

Tabitha shook her head. They were five years old. They each had maybe a two-thousand-word vocabulary. How articulate did she expect them to be?

"Just...give it a rest," she said.

"What are you watching there, Ellie?" Rex asked.

"The Wiggles!" she said. "They're from Austwalia."

"Bobby?" he said. "How's your game? Kicking some Goomba butt?"

"Huh?"

"That's what those little brown mushroom creatures you stomp on are called."

"Goombas?" Bobby said doubtfully. "Are you sure?"

"Believe it or not, bud, *Super Mario Bros.* was around when I was a kid."

"Computers didn't even exist when you were a kid!"

"How old do you think I am?"

"Twenty-five?" Ellie guessed earnestly.

"Thanks, Ellie," he said, "but no, I'm a tad older than that. Forty-five."

"Forty-five!" she repeated, impressed. "So soon you'll be fifty. And after that, you'll be dead."

"Anyway, Bobby, I'm telling you the truth. My dad bought me a Nintendo when they first came out in 1985. They even came with a gun back then."

"A *real* gun?" he asked.

"No. It shot ducks."

"*Real* ducks?"

"No...Goombas... What was I saying?"

"I don't know, Dad."

"Me either," Ellie said, with exaggerated exasperation.

"Tough audience," Tabitha remarked.

"Tell me about it," he replied, chuckling.

They drove on in silence for a little. Roughly a kilometer outside of town they crossed a bridge over the Fraser River and reunited with Highway 99. The two-lane road passed through a gentle meadow with a meandering creek before switchbacking into a jagged gorge bordered by rugged peaks. Road signs warned drivers on a regular basis to slow to thirty kilometers an hour around the tight bends, and to be vigilant of rock slides.

"How much longer, Dad?" Bobby asked eventually.

"Not too much longer, bud," Rex said. "Just hold tight."

"I'm bored," Ellie said.

"I'm super bored," Bobby said.

"I'm boreder than you."

"Guys!" Tabitha said.

"What?" Ellie asked.

Closing her eyes, Tabitha tried tuning them out. When she was their age, she had been no less quarrelsome with her siblings. She was the youngest of three sisters. The eldest, Beth, was Rex's age now, and a dentist in Portland. Ivy was thirty-seven and a sex therapist on a radio station that broadcasted out of Olympia. Although Tabitha didn't visit as much as she would have liked, she had a good relationship with both of them.

Which hadn't been the case when they were kids. All she seemed to remember from those days was a lot of name-calling, hair-pulling, pinching, and double-crossing.

Long car trips had been especially...adventurous...with each sister valiantly defending the invisible borders of their seat space from errant thighs or elbows.

One car trip in particular stood out in her memory. It had been to Astoria, a three-and-a-half-hour drive from Seattle. There had been all the aforementioned sibling infighting on the way there, but as only children under a certain age were capable of, all was forgiven and forgotten as soon as they arrived at the campground where they were staying, which had featured a bouncy pillow, a playground with fast slides, a King Tut-themed mini-putt course, and a video game arcade. They ate lunch at a café/bakery that sold bread so fresh all it needed was butter. They stopped by the Goonies' house from the namesake movie, which had just been released the previous summer. They went swimming at Cannon Beach, explored the shores around the famous Haystack Rock, and when darkness fell, they cooked wieners and s'mores over a campfire.

I should really try to get in touch more with Beth and Ivy, she thought. Once or twice a year really wasn't enough. Beth's two boys were growing up so fast. And Ivy was six months pregnant with her first. *Maybe I'll drive down to Olympia and surprise her next week*, she decided. *Ivy would like that. We'll go to that Italian restaurant she likes out on…where is it? No matter, I can google it…*

Tabitha opened her eyes and was surprised to find herself drowsy and disoriented. She had nodded off.

She blinked the sleep from her eyes. The half-tones of dusk muted the landscape. Shadows pooled in the nooks and crannies of the foothills. Streaks of vermillion and cotton-candy pink colored the sky.

"Welcome back, sleepy-head," Rex said.

She stifled a yawn. "How long was I out?"

"Half hour."

"That's all? Feels like hours."

"Perfect timing." He pointed out her window. "Should be just around this bend…"

"Oh my," she said when the lake came into view. It was glass-smooth and perhaps a half-mile in diameter. Its mirrored surface, tinted red from the setting sun, reflected the forested slopes rising steeply from its far bank. "It's beautiful. Kids—"

"Wow!" Ellie said.

"Are we here?" Bobby asked.

"Just about, bud," Rex said.

A few minutes later they reached the northern tip of the lake. Rex turned off the highway onto a dirt lane, which followed the shore east. Almost immediately they were bumping up and down so violently to elicit gasps and cries from the kids.

Rex stopped the car. "The road was never this bad," he said, frowning.

"Looks like it hasn't been used in years," she said. "Yours isn't the only cabin on the lake, is it?"

"No, there are another half-dozen others..." He shook his head. "I wonder if they built another road in?"

"GPS is showing only this one," she said, consulting the navigation system in the center console.

He sighed. "Guess we're going to have to walk." He turned in his seat. "Sorry, guys. There's a little problem with the road. Are you okay with a short nature walk?"

"Do we have to?" Ellie asked. "My feet hurt."

"You haven't even walked anywhere yet!"

"They still hurt."

"Well, we can sleep out here in the car..."

"Can we?" she asked excitedly.

"No, sweetie," Tabitha said. "And we're not arguing the point. So pack up your bag."

"How far is it, Daddy?" Bobby asked.

"Not too far, bud," he said. "We should still get there before dark."

Tabitha placed her hands on the small of her back and twisted her torso. The stretch felt good. How long had they been on the road? Five hours? Six?

Her gaze settled on the dirt lane that snaked away from them into a stand of impressive old-growth trees consisting of birch, Douglas fir, whitebark, pine, and spruce giants. The road was torn up with ruts and potholes and lined with knee-high grasses and weeds. The sight filled her with an undefined, uneasy dread. Nobody would let their road fall into such disrepair, which meant nobody likely lived, or even vacationed, out here anymore.

Why not? It was God's country, pristine and beautiful.

Rex noticed her frowning and said, "Shouldn't take us more than twenty minutes to get there."

"It's not that," she said. "It's just..." She shook her head. "Nothing. Ellie? Are you ready?"

Her daughter was trying to stuff her iPad into her pink Hello Kitty backpack. "It doesn't fit!"

"I'm sure it does."

"Bobby," Rex said. "No Nintendo. Leave it behind in the car, please."

Bobby looked like someone had just cracked an egg on his face. "But I want to bring it!"

"There are plenty of other things to do out here than play video games."

"Like what?"

"How about I take you fishing in the morning?"

"Really?"

"Sure."

Reluctantly, Bobby placed the Nintendo on the back seat.

"That's a good point," Tabitha said. "Ellie, I'd like you to leave your iPad behind too."

"Mommy, no!"

"I'm not arguing, sweetie."

"Mommy, I'm not joking, I'm not kidding, and I'm not playing. I *need* my iPad."

"No, you don't *need* it, Missy. Like Rex said, there are plenty of other things to do out here."

"I don't even want to go fishing! I hate fish!"

"Put it in the car, Ellie," Tabitha said. "I'm not going to ask you again."

Huffing, she tugged the tablet from her bag and tossed it onto the back seat. She didn't have to worry about damaging it as it was wrapped in a mango-orange shockproof case.

"Thank you," Tabitha said. Then, to Rex, "Does this apply to us too?"

"Why not?" he said, digging his phone from his pocket.

Tabitha produced hers from her handbag. "I need to make a quick call first—check on everything at home." She dialed her eldest daughter's cell phone number. It rang four times before going to voicemail. "Surprise, surprise," she said. "Vanessa's not answering."

"On purpose, you think?" Rex asked.

"That phone doesn't leave her person, ever. Definitely on purpose."

"She's having a party!" Ellie crowed.

"Better not be," Tabitha grumbled.

"Here." Rex passed her his phone. "She won't recognize my number."

"You don't think she'll find a second call right after the first suspicious?"

"Probably. But it could be a boy she likes. Would she risk not answering that call?"

Tabitha accepted the phone and dialed her daughter's number again.

"Hello?" Vanessa answered on the second ring.

"Hello, sweetie," Tabitha said.

"Mom!"

"What?" she said innocuously.

"Who's phone are you using?"

"I just called you from my phone less than a minute ago. No answer."

"I didn't get to it in time."

"I'm glad that's the case and you simply didn't want to talk to me."

"So who's phone are you using?"

"Rex's," she said.

"I should have known," Vanessa quipped. Vanessa, like many teenagers, could be at times selfish, rude, rebellious, and most of all, emotionally fragile. When Tabitha had first begun dating Rex, Vanessa had acted as if he were the devil incarnate and had done her best to make him uncomfortable whenever the two of them came face to face. Rex, to his credit, took the insults and snide remarks with remarkable poise, and he could usually turn the awkward situations into merely uncomfortable situations with self-deprecating wit. Eventually this humor won Vanessa over, and she was now on the record as admitting he was "an okay guy." Having said this, Rex was still the "boyfriend," and Vanessa could often and easily fall back into the I'm-not-supposed-to like-him mindset.

"Anyway, sweetie," Tabitha said, "I'm just checking in to make sure everything is okay."

"It's like six o'clock. Why wouldn't everything be okay?"

"It's a little past seven."

"Is it? So?"

"What time does the party start?"

Silence. Then: "What? What are you talking about?" A bit panicky.

"Ellie thinks you're having a party."

"Tell Ellie to mind her own damn business—and change her diapers while she's at it."

Tabitha glanced at Ellie, who was bent over a wildflower, sniffing it, perfectly content in the moment, and Tabitha felt a pang of sadness. Vanessa had once been equally innocent. When had she changed? When would Ellie change? When would she stop being "her little girl?"

"I was serious when I told you no parties," Tabitha said. "You know the rules when I'm away."

"Dad would let me!"

A dial tone.

Sighing, Tabitha handed the phone back to Rex.

"Sounded all right," he said.

"You only heard my end of the conversation."

"She wasn't happy?"

"She hung up on me."

"Is Ness having a party?" Ellie asked.

"That doesn't concern you, honey."

"I bet she is."

"She's not."

"How do you know?"

"Ellie, enough."

When all the electronics were deposited in the Mazda, Tabitha grabbed her shoulder bag, which contained the toiletries, while Rex retrieved four bags of groceries, leaving the heavier two bags behind. They would come back for them and the remaining backpack tomorrow morning. Then he locked the car with the remote key.

"Are we all ready then?" he asked.

"Why are there so many holes in the road, Daddy?" Bobby asked.

"It hasn't been taken care of."

"Why not?"

Rex shrugged. "When I used to come up here as a kid, your grandparents paid a fee to keep the road serviceable. All the families with cabins along the road did. But it seems everybody's stopped paying that fee. So the rain and snow have caused all that damage."

"Why did everyone stop paying? Did they run out of money?"

"That I don't know," he said.

"Ow!" Tabitha said, and swatted her bare left bicep with her right hand. "Mosquito."

"Unfortunately, they don't go away until first freeze."

"Ow!" Ellie said. "One got me too!"

"Ow!" Bobby said. "Me too!"

"We better get moving then," Rex said, "or we're going to be eaten alive."

Following a little distance behind T-Rex and her mom, Ellie was trying to figure out what she was going to do for two whole days without her iPad. All her *stuff* was on her iPad: her songs, her movies, Peek-a-Zoo, Elmo's Monster Maker,

Hungry Caterpillar. All the pictures her mom let her download from the internet. Her sticker album. *Everything.* She might only be five, but she had collected a lot of stuff in her life so far, and it wasn't fair for her mom to not let her play with that stuff.

"I hate fishing," she told Bobby, who was trudging along beside her.

"Huh?" he said.

"I'm not going fishing with you tomorrow."

"So?"

"Your dad's going to make me."

"No, he's not.'"

"He will, and I hate fish."

"You can help me catch bugs."

That sounded sort of fun. "What kind of bugs?"

"I dunno yet. Whatever I find. Probably a lot of ants."

"I like butterflies."

"They won't fit."

"Fit where?"

Bobby dug an empty Tic Tac container from his pocket. "My dad gave it to me. He brought it all the way back from Gurmamy."

Ellie frowned. "Where am I going to put my butterflies?"

"Dunno. But you can't use my case. They won't fit."

"Mommy!"

Her mom glanced back over her shoulder. "Yes, honey?"

"Where am I going to put my butterflies?"

"What butterflies?"

"That I'm going to catch."

"Oh...well, we can figure something out. We'll have a look around the cabin for something when we get there."

"It has to be big so they have room."

"Okay. We'll have a look."

"My mom's going to help me find something better than your case," Ellie told Bobby happily.

He shrugged. "Your mom sounded mad before."

"When?"

"When she was talking on the phone."

"That's because my sister is having a party, and she's not allowed to have parties." Ellie thought of something. "Why don't you like my mom?"

Bobby shrugged again. "I never said that."

"But you never say anything to her."

"So?"

"So…why don't you like her?"

"I never said that."

"You already said *that*."

"Stop talking to me."

"I can talk if I want to."

"I'm not listening anymore."

"You're a stupid sad head."

"I'm not sad."

"You're going to cry, and your tears are going to drown us."

"Dad!"

Rex turned around. "What's going on, guys?"

"She's teasing me!" he complained.

"No, I'm not!" Ellie protested.

"You two are going to have to start to learn to get along better—"

"But Bobby's a stupid head—"

"I know I am but what are you?"

"You're a stupid head!"

"I know I am but what are you?"

"A stupid head!"

"Ha! You're a stupid head!"

"Am not!"

"Am too—!"

"Guys!" Rex bellowed.

Ellie clamped her mouth shut. She knew when she "went too far," something her mom would often tell her she'd done, and by the angry look on T-Rex's face, this was one of those times.

◆ ◆ ◆

Bobby knew his dad wasn't really mad at them. He was just pretending to be so Bobby and Ellie would stop arguing. Still, he lowered his eyes to the ground and tried to look like he was sorry, which he was. He didn't like making his dad angry, regardless of whether it was real anger or make-believe.

When his dad and Ellie's mom started walking again, Bobby followed, though he kept his distance. He even let Ellie get a little bit ahead of him, so they wouldn't have to walk side by side, and so she wouldn't call him any more names.

He hated her. She was so mean to him all the time. He wasn't sad. Well, that wasn't true. He was sad inside his head sometimes. He was sad that his mom was gone. She'd been gone for so long now he almost didn't remember what she looked like unless he looked at one of his pictures of her. But he still missed her.

His dad told him that she was only going to be away for a short time. She wasn't dead, which was good, so he would be able to see her again. But the "short time" seemed like a real long time. Bobby had been in preschool when his mom left, and he was in kindergarten now.

Why didn't she come home for a visit? Why didn't she Facetime him?

Did she not love him anymore? Did he do something wrong? He might have. He was just a baby when he was in preschool, and his memory wasn't as good as it was now. So he might have done something to scare her away. But what?

He asked God every night when he said his prayers to send his mommy back. But God was really busy, and he never re-plied to Bobby's prayers. Bobby was probably at the bottom of his list, just like Chris Zukowski was always at the bottom of Mrs. Janet's list at school when she called out everybody's name.

And maybe Ellie's mom was praying to God too, asking him not to send back Bobby's real mom so she could stay around as his fake mom forever. She probably was, because she liked Bobby's dad. This was why Bobby didn't like her. She was blocking his real mom from coming back.

Bobby would be really happy if everything was like it had been when he was in preschool. His mom and dad loving each other and living together. Ellie and her mom going back to their house on Mercy Island or whatever their island was called and never coming back to Newcastle, where his house was. That would be *rad*, a word that Dylan from school had taught him. Then he would have his mommy back, and he wouldn't have to listen to Ellie making fun of him all the time either.

God, he thought, squeezing his eyes shut as tight as possible to make the wish stronger, *if You're still listening, can you please do that? Make everything go back to how it was? I promise I'll be really good. I promise I'll love my mommy and daddy as best as I can. Just please send my mommy back.*

"Bobby?"

Bobby opened his eyes. It was his dad calling his name. Bobby must have been walking slowly, because everybody was way ahead of him now.

"Yeah?" he called back.

"You're dawdling, bud! Let's pick up the pace a bit."

"Coming!" he said, and began to run, all thoughts of his moms, both real and fake, forgotten.

When Bobby caught up to them, Rex dropped to his knees and told his son to climb on his back. Bobby latched on, and Rex stood.

"How's the view from up there, bud?" he asked.

"Go faster, Daddy!"

"No can do. This is my top speed. The groceries are heavy. You don't want me to slip and fall. I might land on top of you. And you know what that would make you, don't you?"

"A pancake?"

"A *squashed* pancake."

"Am I next?" Ellie asked, tugging at Rex's pant leg. "I want to be next!"

"You let Bobby have his ride, sweetie," Tabitha said, taking her daughter's hand and leading her away. "You're doing a good job walking on your own."

"But I want a piggyback too!"

"You heard me."

"Poop head," she mumbled.

"Excuse me, young lady?" Tabitha said sternly. "What did you call me?"

"Poop's not a bad word."

"As a matter of fact, it is a bad word when you use it as an insult, like you just did."

"I didn't. I said… *snoop* head… Like Snoopy."

"Now you're fibbing, and that's getting you in even deeper trouble."

"I'm not fibbing!"

"She's going to cry," Bobby said into Rex's ear.

"Stay out of this, bud," he replied.

"You're fibbing about not fibbing," Tabitha continued. "That means there's no dessert for you tonight—"

"No!" And now the tears came.

"You know better than to tell fibs."

"I didn't!" she wailed.

"Keep it up, Ellie, and you can go to bed early too."

Ellie's face had gone red, and her wet eyes simmered with indecision: remain combative or submit to her mother's authority.

Reason prevailed. She sniffed resignedly and wiped an arm across her eyes.

"That's better," Tabitha said.

Ellie took off ahead of them.

Tabitha sighed and followed. Rex did a couple of circles, making Bobby squeal in fear and delight, and joined her.

The road wound into the dense rainforest, pushing deeper and deeper into the thick vegetation rife with moss, lichen, ferns, and epiphytes. They passed a towering cedar twice as thick as the other cedar and spruce and hemlock around it, and Rex was amazed to discover he had a childhood memory of it, of asking his father why it was so big. He didn't recall what his father's answer had been, but the tree remained as impressive now as it had been then.

All around them warblers, finch, and sparrows sang their late afternoon songs, and Rex inhaled the mountain air deeply. He felt good. The best he had in a while, and that was saying a lot, as he was currently experiencing one of the most trying periods of his life.

Last month Rex had caught the flu and had called in sick to work on the morning of September 14. It proved to be a fateful decision that would save his life, because on that same evening, at 11:36 p.m., nine hours into Flight 2026's journey from New York to Frankfurt, Frederick Johnson, his First Officer of five years, began an unscheduled ten-minute descent that concluded with the Airbus A320 colliding into a mountainside in the French Alps, killing Frederick and all one hundred and fifty-nine souls on board. When crash investigators recovered the cockpit voice recordings, a chilling suicide speech by Frederick blamed depression for his final and barbaric act.

Investigators uncovered email correspondence between Frederick and the airline's Flight Training Pilot School a number of years earlier in which Frederick had requested time off due to an episode of severe depression. Per protocol, the flight school should have kicked Frederick out of the program. Instead, they allowed him to resume his training to obtain his pilot's license, eventually issuing him a medical certificate confirming his fitness to fly.

Consequently, the airline was now facing charges of criminal gross negligence, which could result in criminal prosecution. To save their asses, the top brass went looking for a fall guy, and that guy turned out to be Rex. The argument was that Rex, having worked with Frederick for so many years, had been derelict in his duty as Captain for not observing and reporting any suicidal tendencies that his First Officer, in light of the magnitude of his depression, must have surely exhibited at one point or another.

In any event, while the investigation and litigation played out, Rex had been grounded, and his distinguished twenty-five-year career was now at best tarnished with a stain that could never be completely cleansed, and at worst in jeopardy of being irrevocably destroyed in one fell swoop.

To get away from all the bullshit, Rex had decided to come up to Canada for the week, to visit the old family cabin he hadn't been to since his childhood, even if it meant confronting an entirely different closetful of ghosts. He had originally planned to bring only Bobby with him, but Tabitha had the weekend off and insisted she and Ellie come as well, to which he happily agreed.

His back and arms starting to ache, Rex set Bobby down on the ground. "Looks like Ellie has found something, bud," he said, referring to the fact she was kneeling in the middle of the road thirty feet ahead of them. "Why don't you go find out what it is?"

Bobby obeyed, running in that silly, uncoordinated way kids do.

"Hope it's not some animal's...poop," Rex said lightly, and laughed.

Tabitha frowned at him. "You think I was too hard on her?"

"Nope. I think you did exactly the right thing."

"She's not like Bobby, you know. He's so well-behaved. Ellie's like a female version of Dennis the Menace sometimes."

He shrugged. "She's just mature for her age."

"You know her school sent me a letter the other week informing me she said poop in class?"

He arched an eyebrow. "She called someone a poop head?"

"The letter didn't specify the context. When I asked Ellie, she said she used the word when she asked the teacher if she could go to the bathroom."

"What does the school expect her to say? *I need to defecate, Miss.*"

"That's what I thought. Her teacher was just being hyper-liberal. But now…maybe Ellie did direct the word at another student. That would better justify the letter. So what concerns me is not Ellie's language, exactly, but whether she's lying to me. She's five. Do other five year olds lie? Vanessa never did. She had been an angel—well, until she reached her teens, that is."

"Like I said, Ellie's mature for her age. That means typical five-year-old rules don't apply to her. She thinks she can get away with things others her age couldn't. That includes manipulating others."

"Great, so she's not just a liar, she's a manipulative liar."

"All liars are manipulative, by definition. But what I mean is, look, it's not a bad thing. Not at her age. She's just… smart, I guess is what I'm saying."

"That definitely has a better ring to it than manipulative liar."

When they approached the kids, Ellie spun around and said, "Mommy, look! A baby squirrel."

Rex and Tabitha bent over for a better look. It was a chipmunk, Rex noted, not a squirrel, and it was just lying there, barely moving.

"What happened to it?" Tabitha asked.

Rex glanced at the branches crisscrossing the sky above them. "It must have fallen out of a tree," he said.

"Can I keep it?" Ellie asked.

"Definitely not," Tabitha said. "It's a wild animal. It might bite you."

"But it's just a baby! *Please.*"

"I think you should leave it right there."

"But it will die."

"Everything dies, sweetie. And chipmunks aren't exactly an endangered species."

"It's not a squirrel?"

"Chipmunks are smaller than squirrels, and brown, with a stripe down the back, like this one."

"Do they still eat acorns?"

"They love acorns."

"More than human food?"

"They *hate* Mexican food," Rex said lightheartedly.

Ellie eyed him suspiciously. "Well, I love chippymunks just as much as squirrels. So can I keep it?"

Tabitha said, "I've told you—"

"I promise I'll take care of it!"

"I'm allergic to chipmunks, honey. At least hamsters and gerbils. So probably chipmunks too."

"You can sleep outside."

Tabitha rolled her eyes and looked at Rex.

He shrugged. "She's right. It's going to die out here. I think a turkey vulture already has an eye on it." He nodded at the sky, where he'd spotted the large bird circling.

Tabitha saw the vulture too. "I guess maybe we can take the chipmunk to the cabin," she relented. "And if it lives until Monday, we can take it to a vet in town. But," she added quickly, holding up a finger. "And this is a big but, sweetie. It stays with the vet. It's absolutely not coming back to Seattle with us. That's the deal."

"Deal!" Ellie said, reaching for it.

"Whoa, hold on," Rex said. "Not so fast. I don't think chipmunks carry diseases, but it's best not to touch it. Here." He shrugged off his windbreaker and carefully scooped the rodent into it.

"Can I carry it?" Ellie asked.

"Be gentle." He passed her the jacket and its cargo.

Ellie held the injured creature against her stomach as if it was the most precious thing in the world. She started walking, Bobby in lockstep, peeking over her shoulder, asking excited questions.

"I wouldn't be surprised if the poor thing dies of a heart attack with those two ogling over it like that," Tabitha said.

"One summer up here," Rex said, "I found a baby bird. I nursed it back to health before letting it go again. I felt pretty proud of myself as I watched it fly away. This might be a good life experience for those two if they can do the same for that chipmunk."

"You mean chippymunk."

"Right."

The road rounded a bend, and on their left, hidden behind a phalanx of hemlock, pine, and Douglas fir, was a brown-painted cabin with white trim and green shingles on the roof. The mailbox leaned drunkenly askew. The driveway was more weeds than gravel.

"That was an old couple's place," he said, pointing it out. "The McCleods."

"Good memory," she said.

"I only remember them because Mr. McCleod—I never knew his first name—was a crazy bastard who once sicced his little…Yorkshire terrier, I guess it was…on Logan and me when we came down this way."

"You were scared of a Yorkshire terrier?" she teased.

"I was five or six. Any yapping dog regardless of size is terrifying at that age."

"Why'd Old Man McCleod do it?"

"No idea. Loge and I never really left the immediate vicinity of our cabin. There was no reason to really. With the lake, we had everything we wanted right there. But one day we went 'exploring.' Ten minutes down the road was pretty far for us. We saw Mr. McCleod out in front his place using a broom to get rid of spider webs or something around his eaves. He yelled at us, saying," —Rex assumed a crackly voice — "'What are you up-to-no-good-kids doing down here? I know your father. I'm going to tell him you've been snooping!' At least, it was something along those lines. Then he said, 'Blixy? Blixy?'"

"The Yorkshire terrier?" Tabitha said.

Rex nodded. "The dog came roaring around the cabin, and then Mr. McCleod was telling it, 'Go get 'em, girl! Get 'em!' I'd never run so fast in my life."

"What an awful old man," she said. "I thought Canadians were supposed to be polite."

"Not him."

"Why did your parents decide to buy a place up here in the first place?"

"My great-grandfather jumped on the gold-mining train in the eighteen hundreds. He worked a claim on Cayoosh Creek for a decade and found a fair bit of gold. When the claim was exhausted, he retired in Lillooet. You might not guess it now, but at that time Lillooet was considered to be the largest town in North America west of Chicago and north of San Francisco—which was maybe why my great-grandfather ended up building the cabin out here. A little place to get away from everybody. I don't know what happened to his place in town, but the cabin got passed down to my father."

In the distance, Rex thought he heard a car engine. He stopped and listened. Yes, a motor, approaching from the highway.

"Guys!" he called to Bobby and Ellie. "Move to the side of the road! A car's coming."

He watched them move to the margin. "A little more."

"We'll be in the woods!" Bobby said.

"Better than road kill!"

They stepped back farther.

The engine grew louder, then a rusty old pickup truck came bouncing around the bend—the high axle allowing it to traverse the ruts and potholes that scarred the road.

"Maybe it's Mr. McCleod?" Tabitha kidded. "Come back from the dead?"

"Blixie's revenge."

But Rex could see into the cab of the truck now. The driver was a middle-aged man with a long beard and a Stetson hat pulled low over his face, keeping his eyes in shadows. In shotgun was a younger woman with blonde hair. She waved at them as the vehicle crunched by.

Rex and Tabitha returned the gesture. Bobby did too, while Ellie kept both hands securely cradling the chipmunk against her chest.

Then the truck was gone around another bend.

"Well," Rex said as the sound of the motor dwindled, "at least now we know we're not the only people out here."

4

They arrived at the cabin just as the sky began to spit small and icy droplets of rain. The cabin stood twenty feet from the road, surrounded by a variety of mature evergreens and deciduous trees, the leaves of the latter blazing fiery colors.

In an age of pre-fabricated building material where everything was perfectly square or symmetrical, the idiosyncrasies of the cabin afforded it an old-world charm: the stacked logs with their rough axe cuts and corner notches, the slapdash gray chinking to seal the spaces between the logs, the hand-peeled porch railings, the crumbling stone chimney.

Tabitha clutched Rex's arm. "Oh Rex, it's lovely."

"Amazing what you can do with a broad axe and mallet," he said.

"Can we go inside?" Ellie asked.

"That's the plan," he said.

They swished through a carpet of browning leaves to the covered porch. The wood planks moaned loudly beneath their footsteps. Rex stopped before the door and tried the cast-iron handle. It turned with a rusty gargle, and the door swung inward.

"Glad it's unlocked," he said. "I don't have keys."

"You're kidding?" Tabitha said.

"I haven't had anything to do with this place since I was

seven."

"What would you have done if it was locked?"

"Broken a window, I guess."

Rex stepped inside the cabin. He scrunched his nose at the dank, musty odor.

"Ewww," Ellie said, pushing past his legs. "What's that smell?"

"It will go away when we open some windows, sweetie," Tabitha said.

Rex glanced around the room, surprised by how familiar it was to him. The teak sofa upholstered in drab earth tones; the Edison-style light bulbs in the brass fixtures; the rocking chair where his mother had read him C.S. Lewis's *Prince Caspian* on a particularly rainy weekend; the wood-paneled television set, which had required bunny ears to pull in its only channel. The pair of antique ice block tongs he'd once taken off the wall and used to terrorize Logan. The little tin sign that read AN OLD BEAR LIVES HERE WITH HIS HONEY.

A hand-carved bookcase held a number of foxed paperbacks and hardcovers bookended between art deco flying geese. On the uppermost shelf were three silver-framed photographs. The first was a studio shot of his parents, his mother's auburn hair fashioned into a perm, his father's parted neatly down the side and the same rich brown as his mustache. The second was of Logan wearing a Gobots tee-shirt and smiling to reveal the gap between his front teeth. And the third was of Rex who, with his blonde hair and blue eyes and dimples, bore a more-than-passing resemblance to Bobby.

Swallowing tightly, Rex looked away.

"Where can I put my chippymunk?" Ellie asked, stopping in the center of the room.

Rex retrieved a hand-painted wooden box from next to the sofa, dumped the stack of dusty magazines onto the teak coffee table in front of the television, and set the empty box next to the magazines. "That should do," he said.

Ellie gently set the chipmunk into the box, then passed Rex back his windbreaker. He hung it on a wall-mounted coat rack fashioned from a barn-red bucksaw.

Ellie studied the rodent closely. "Is she going to be okay, Mommy?" she asked.

"How do you know it's a 'she?'" Tabitha asked.

"Because boys are dumb, and I want it to be a girl like me."

"I think she'll be okay for now. Once we're settled in, we'll get her some water and a little bit of food to nibble on."

"Where's my bed?"

"There's a small second floor," Rex said. "You and Bobby will sleep up there."

"Where're the stairs?"

"In the next room."

"Beat you to them!" Bobby said, darting around the afghan hanging in the doorway that separated this room from the next.

"No fair!" Ellie said, giving chase. "You got a head start! No fair!"

"Be careful!" Rex called after them. "The stairs are steep!"

Tabitha dumped her shoulder bag on the floor. "This place is perfect," she said. "It really is."

"Can't believe it's just been...here...unoccupied for so long." He shrugged. "Better take the groceries to the kitchen."

The adjoining room featured a stone fireplace, a roughly hewn timber staircase that led to the attic, and a seventies-style kitchen complete with linoleum floor tiles, Formica counter tops, and an ergonomic dining table complete with four tubular steel stools. As far as appliances went, there was a harvest-gold Kelvinator refrigerator, a stove the same horrid color with a stacked-stone backsplash, and an avocado-green toaster.

"Whoa," Tabitha said. "I wasn't expecting Carol Brady's kitchen."

"I remember my father doing the 'upgrades,'" Rex said.

"He and my mom had been pretty proud of the finished product." He set the groceries on the table and opened the cupboard above the sink. It was stocked with plates, bowls, and glasses, though these were all littered with mouse droppings.

"Good thing we bought paper plates and plastic cutlery," Tabitha remarked.

Rex tried the sink tap. Not a drop of water.

"I'm guessing there's no electricity either," Tabitha said, opening the fridge door with a sticky pop of the gasket seal. She immediately spun away, a hand going to her mouth.

Rex caught the stench a second later and glanced inside the fridge. It was filled with all sorts of different shaped items—everything covered with a layer of putrefied mold and mildew.

He slammed the door shut.

"Gross!" he exclaimed, then, seeing the green look on Tabitha's face, couldn't help but laugh. "Guess we're not having leftovers."

"It's not funny!" she said. "I hope I didn't breathe in any of those spores."

"We're going to have to lock up the fridge somehow so the kids don't go opening it."

"I can still smell that stench. It's like..."

"Maybe it's time to air out the place."

They spent the next few minutes opening all the windows, letting the stale air out and the fresh alpine air in.

"Much better," Tabitha said, inhaling deeply.

"After we light some candles, we'll be all set."

"Dad!" Bobby yelled from the attic.

"What is it?" Rex asked, facing the staircase.

"Which bed can I have?"

"There are only two. You choose."

"This one!"

"I want that one!" Ellie challenged.

"I called it!" he said.

"I called it first!" she said.

"Did not!" he said. "Dad!"

"If you two can't work it out, then you'll have to flip a coin."

Silence. Then their voices lowered as they entered serious negotiations.

Tabitha said, "I'm a bit scared to ask, but if there's no water, what do we do for a toilet?"

"Right." Rex scratched his head. "Well, water used to get pumped up from the lake. But the pump needs electricity. There's a big old diesel generator in the shed we used to use for electricity. Hopefully it will fire up. I was going to have a look at it tomorrow. For now, I'll go fetch a couple of buckets of water from the lake. Pouring it slowly into the bowl should make the toilet flush."

"And if I can't wait...?"

"You really need to go that badly?"

She nodded. "I should have gone when Bobby did at the tourist center."

"In that case, there's an outhouse not too far away..."

She groaned. "I was worried you might say that." She tugged free the KittenSoft toilet paper from one of the grocery bags, tore the plastic packaging open, and grabbed a roll.

They went outside. The sky was still spitting, though the droplets didn't have enough weight behind them to be anything more than a cold nuisance.

Rex pointed. Fifty feet away the outhouse loomed rickety and ominous in the gathering dark.

"Inviting," Tabitha said.

"You can go behind a tree," he said.

"I love having a choice."

"I'll be back up in a few."

Holding her arms in front of her to deflect branches from her face, Tabitha made her way through the trees toward the outhouse. It was a fair hike from the cabin, she thought, but the location made sense. You didn't want a stinking hole in the ground near your residence, did you?

Tabitha experienced a sudden swelling of warmth in her chest—for Rex, for the cabin that time forgot, for the opportunity to be here with Ellie and Bobby for the weekend.

Getting away from the city was not only what Rex needed, but what she needed too. The untangling of her life from her ex, Jacob, had been taking an enormous emotional toll on her, to the point where the stress of it had caused her to break down in spontaneous tears on more than a few occasions of late.

When Tabitha and Jacob had first met, Jacob had been a software developer for Microsoft and had often traveled to conferences around the country. In the early days of their relationship, Tabitha had missed him terribly on these occasions. Then the weekends away turned into three or four days away, then full weeks at a time. Jacob told her the increase in travel was due to a promotion he'd received, and she bought that for a while. But then his attitude toward her began to change. He became aloof, easily annoyed. Communication seemed an effort. Tabitha was convinced he was having an affair, and she confided this to Cindy Chew, a friend she'd known since college. Cindy ended up asking her husband Danny if he had any dirt on Jacob, because Danny also worked at Microsoft's headquarters in Redmond, though in a different department. The dirt relayed back to Tabitha had been heartbreaking and mindboggling: Jacob was a notorious womanizer who had hit on half the women working in his department. The mindboggling part: several of these women had filed sexual harassment suits against him, and he had been fired more than a year ago now. Tabitha confronted him that evening, they fought, he became violent, and she left with the girls, fearing for her safety. The following day she hired a divorce attorney—and in the process of sorting through their financial situation, she learned Jacob had been manipulating their books behind her back, and they were effectively broke.

Tabitha had always suspected Jacob had a gambling addiction (though he'd done well to hide or downplay it over the years), and she instinctively knew it was this addiction that had swallowed their life savings. However, knowing something and proving it in court were two very different things. The judge overseeing the custody litigation wanted evidence, not accusations, and that evidence was proving to be frustratingly circumstantial and elusive. Tabitha had retained the services of a private investigator in the hopes of tailing Jacob to one of his gambling dens, but either Jacob was aware of the tail, or at least suspected it, and he was refraining from gambling in public, or he had moved his habit online, which he could do in the privacy of wherever he was living these days.

Currently the investigator was combing the accounts of multiple online bookies and gambling operations. So far he'd found no links to Jacob, and if this didn't change before the divorce proceedings began in a fortnight, Jacob could win joint legal and physical custody of the girls, which would throw their lives into chaos—

No, Tabitha thought angrily. *I'm not going to think about this now. I'll deal with everything in a couple of days when I'm back in Seattle. Not now. This is my time with Rex and Ellie and Bobby.*

Jacob isn't going to ruin that.

Tabitha stopped before the outhouse. It was a humble and utilitarian structure that appeared to be one push away from falling over. Horizontal wooden planks had been nailed, Band-Aid-like, over gaps where vertical boards had fallen away.

After a brief hesitation, Tabitha creaked open the door,

which featured a star cut-out to allow ventilation and light into the stall. Cobwebs dusted the dank ceiling and walls, but a perfunctory glance did not reveal any eight-legged creepy crawlies. The toilet seat was nothing but a piece of wood with a hole in the middle of it. She peeked down the hole into the pit latrine. There was no smell, as any untreated waste would have decomposed years ago.

Did she really have to sit over that? But what other option was there? Go behind a tree like Rex suggested? That was almost preferable...

Carefully, Tabitha laid out toilet paper on the seat. She undid her belt and pushed down her jeans and underwear. She couldn't hear her urine hit the bottom of the pit, which made her wonder as to the depth of the hole.

What if some animal was down there? A family of raccoons or rats? What if she was peeing on them? What if they climbed up and...?

What? Bit her in the butt?

Suddenly and alarmingly, a sharp crack sounded outside the outhouse, the distinct sound of a branch splitting in two.

Her bladder froze.

"Hello?" she said.

Nobody replied.

"Rex?" she said, knowing he wasn't out there; if he was, he would have announced his presence.

An animal then?

Would have to be a pretty large animal...

A bear?

God, she hoped not!

She finished her business, yanked up her jeans, and secured her belt. She inched open the door a crack and poked her head out. The forest was dark and cold and silent. The gray sky continued to spit rain. She looked to the left, the direction where the sound had originated.

Nobody was there. No animals either.

But she hadn't imagined the sound.

Folding her arms to ward against a chill that had nothing to do with the foul October weather, she hurried back to the cabin.

◆ ◆ ◆

After collecting two plastic buckets from the shed behind the cabin, Rex picked his way down the pine needle-covered hill to the lake, following a path that was no longer visible but that he remembered vaguely from his youth. The massive conifers he passed beneath eclipsed the darkening sky and made him feel small and unimportant, a reminder that they had been standing here long before he had been born and would remain long after he had died.

When he emerged from the last of the saplings and sagebrush, he stopped to take in the view of the still lake, which, in the dying minutes of dusk, spread away from him like a narrow black abyss. A dock supported by pontoons had once floated on the water a little way out. Now it was gone, likely destroyed by the ice that scabbed over the lake in the wintertime. The only indication it had ever existed were the skeletal remains of the gangway pilings that had linked it to the rocky shore.

In the distance, the haunting wail of a loon echoed over the dark water, sounding eerily like the howl of a wolf. A different wail answered it a moment later, though this one more closely resembled the crazy laugh of a hyena.

Man, I've missed this place, he thought to himself as a kaleidoscope of memories rose to the forefront of his mind. All the summer afternoons he had spent down here as a kid with Logan on inflatable rafts and tires that always seemed to lose their air. Snorkeling with their ill-fitting rubber fins and cheap K-Mart scuba masks, the head straps of which had all snapped so you had to rely on air pressure keeping it suctioned to your face. Fishing for sturgeon and trout, char and steelhead. And just goofing off in the sun doing kid stuff while their mom watched on from beneath a rainbow-colored parasol.

Pushing aside the nostalgic images before they overwhelmed him, Rex continued to the lake where he filled both buckets with ice-cold water. He scanned the rocky shore to the west until he spotted where the pump's black intake pipe emerged from the water. He followed it with his eyes to the pump house twenty feet or so inland. He went to the small structure, pleased to note it appeared to have weathered the years well, keeping its four walls and shingled lid intact. He set the buckets on the ground and opened the lid. His optimism that the pump might be serviceable went up in smoke. The pressure tank and valves and pipes were so covered in rust they looked like they might have been salvaged from the *Titanic*. He tried a valve, and it snapped off in his hand.

Guess nobody's going to be showering this weekend, he thought with a sigh as he picked up the buckets of water and returned up the hill.

He found Tabitha sitting with Ellie in the front room of the cabin, both of them studying the chipmunk.

"How's it doing?" he asked. "Sorry—*she*?"

"She won't eat," Ellie said. "We gave her some banana and peanut butter, but she won't eat. She won't drink her water either."

"She's probably just a bit overwhelmed by everything that's happened to her. Imagine if a family of giants picked you up and brought you to a strange place."

"Come on, Miss Chippy! Get it together!"

"Whoa there, sweetie!" Tabitha said. "Cut the little critter some slack. One of her legs might be broken. Each time she tries to get up, she falls over on the same side."

Rex had a look at the chipmunk. It was flopped on its belly. "Broken leg's not good," he said. "But the vet should be able to do something about that."

"Do we *have* to give her to the vet?" Ellie asked.

"We had a deal, Missy," Tabitha said pointedly.

"But if we give her away," Ellie complained, "I won't ever get to see her again. But if we let her go here, then she'll be here when we come back again, and I can be friends with her every summer until one of us dies first."

"I hope it's the chipmunk that dies first," Rex remarked amusedly.

"I hope it's me," Ellie said, "so I won't be so sad when she dies."

"Don't say that, sweetie," Tabitha said with a note of motherly concern in her voice. "You're going to live much longer than a chipmunk. And you're being a bit presumptuous to think that Rex will want us to come up here every summer. He might never want us to come back."

Tabitha kept her attention fixed on the chipmunk, but Rex sensed the statement was for him as much as it was for her daughter.

"Of course I'd like you guys to come back," he said.

"That's good news!" Tabitha said playfully. "Isn't that good news, sweetie?"

"Do we have to wait all the way to next summer?" Ellie asked. "I'll already be six by then."

"To be honest, I haven't really given it any thought, Ellie," Rex said. "But if that's too long to wait...how about Christmas?"

"Really?" Tabitha said, looking up at him.

"Why not? The fireplace would heat the place. We could bring up some portable gas heaters too, if we needed to make it extra toasty."

"But will Santa be able to find us here?" Ellie asked skeptically.

"Don't worry about Santa Claus, sweetie," Tabitha said. "He has a list with the addresses of every child in the world. He'll find us."

"Does he use Google Maps?"

"His list is much better than Google Maps."

"Okay!" she decided. "Then let's have Christmas here! We can even use a Christmas tree from right outside."

"Let's not get ahead of ourselves, hon. Christmas is still a couple months away. It's not even Halloween yet."

"Can we have Halloween here too?"

"You've opened Pandora's Box," Tabitha said to Rex with a smile.

"My bad—do people still say that? Oh—and now for some genuinely bad news. The generator looked fine in the shed. I think it should fire up tomorrow. But the pump down at the lake has gone kaput. Which means we'll probably have electricity, but we won't have any water except what we lug up from the lake in buckets."

"So I don't have to have a bath tonight?" Ellie asked happily.

"Or tomorrow," Rex said.

"Yeah!"

"But that also means when you need to use the potty," Tabitha said, "you're going to have to pour your own water into the bowl to make it flush. I'll show you how before bedtime."

"Speaking of toilets," Rex said, "how was the outhouse?"

"Ugh," she said. "However, I did appreciate the star cutout in the door. Bit of a change from the usual crescent moon."

"Ah," Rex said, holding up a finger, "here's something that might come in handy on your next trivia night…"

"Our resident armchair polymath," Tabitha remarked.

Rex would consider himself more of a humble trivia buff than an armchair polymath, but in any event, he did love learning, and one of his favorite studies of interest was how mundane things people took for granted in the present originally came into being. He said, "The tradition of carving symbols into the doors of privies began in the early eighteen hundreds, because back then most of the population was illiterate."

"What's illyate?" Ellie asked.

"Illiterate," Tabitha said, "means you can't read or write."

"I'm not illyate. I know uppercase *and* lowercase."

"A sun was usually used on the men's door," Rex went on, "and a moon on the women's. But over time, when restrooms with plumbing began to replace outhouses, the outhouses that were first to be torn down were the men's, because they were never as well kept up as the women's. Eventually the only outhouses left were women's with the moons on the doors. These became unisex—and the reason why the crescent moon is the symbol for all outhouses today."

"Where do you read this stuff?" Tabitha said, shaking her head.

"Gotta read something on the long-haul flights. Like everybody says, planes fly themselves these days."

"So you have yourself an original gem out there?"

"The outhouse? I suppose so. Maybe I should put it up on eBay? Where's Bobby?"

"He's upstairs in bed," Ellie said, her attention once again on the chipmunk. "He doesn't like being here with just my mom when you're not here too."

"*Ellie*," Tabitha said sharply, color rising in her cheeks.

"I'll go check on him," he said.

Rex went to the next room and climbed the steep staircase, deciding that he'd block off the top with cushions from the sofa later on, so the kids didn't inadvertently stumble down them if they got up during the night.

The attic was an oblong triangular-shaped room. A window at each end allowed light during the daytime. The hodgepodge collection of furniture included a chest he knew was filled with children's books, an old dining room set in a corner, a rocking horse in another corner, a metal filing cabinet, and a small dresser. A threadbare red rug of Native American design covered part of the floor.

Bobby lay on his belly in one of two handmade beds, the LED flashlight he kept on his single-key keychain clutched in one hand, the bright beam illuminated a book open before him.

Rex crossed the room, bending so he didn't smack his head on the exposed beams of the pitched roof. He sat on the edge of the bed.

"What're you reading, bud?" he asked.

Bobby showed him the cover. "Sesame Street."

"Good?"

"So-so."

A few other books from the chest were beside him. Rex picked up the top one. *The Secret of the Old Mill.* The 1950s-illustrated cover showed Joe and Frank Hardy peeking between a gap in the floorboards of the eponymous old mill —and if Rex's memory served him correctly, the plot had something to do with counterfeit money.

"Isn't it a bit early to be up here in bed?" he asked his son lightly.

"I'm not sleeping," Bobby said. "Daddy?"

"Yeah, bud?"

"Why do my little things hurt when I squeeze them? My intesticles? They're not even attached to my body."

Rex blinked. That certainly hadn't been the question he'd been expecting. "Well, first of all," he said, "I think you're mixing up your testicles and intestines. Your testicles are down by your penis, while your intestines are inside your stomach. As to why your testicles are so sensitive, I don't really know. Maybe it's your body's way of telling you not to go get them all banged up, because they're important in making babies."

"Do you have to kiss a girl to make babies?"

"You have to do a bit more than that, bud. But let's leave that discussion for another time. Ellie and Tabitha are trying to feed the chipmunk downstairs. Do you want to come back down and feed it too?"

"No," he said simply, and lowered his eyes.

Rex considered giving him another lecture about his

mother, how she would be coming back soon, how Tabitha wasn't taking her place and never would. But instead he said, "Want to see something cool?"

Bobby perked up. "What is it?"

"It's a surprise. It's outside."

"*What is it?*"

"I'll show you. C'mon."

Rex led the way back downstairs to where Ellie and Tabitha were still fussing over the chipmunk.

"He eating yet?" Rex asked them.

"No," Ellie said despondently.

Bobby pulled on his shoes. "I'm getting a surprise!" he said.

"What is it?" Ellie asked, alarmed she wasn't in on the know.

"My dad's going to show me something *cool*."

"I want to see too!"

"This is only for Bobby now, Ellie," Rex said. "You can see it tomorrow."

"That's not fair!"

"That's enough, Ellie," Tabitha said. "You can stay here with me. Rex said he'll show you tomorrow."

"But I want to see it *now*."

"We won't be long," Rex said, retrieving from his overnight bag the Maglite flashlight he'd packed. "And when we get back we'll roast some wieners over a fire. How does that sound?"

"Poop head!"

"*Ellie!*" Tabitha said, stunned.

"Come on, bud," Rex said softly, ushering Bobby outside to escape the inevitable melodrama that was about to play out.

He closed the door just as Tabitha told Ellie she had lost her iPad privileges during the car ride home, and Ellie shrieked in indignation.

Rex took Bobby's hand and led him away. It had stopped

raining, and a damp heaviness weighed over the forest.

"Is she going to cry again?" Bobby asked gleefully.

"That's not for you to worry about."

Playing the flashlight beam ahead of them, Rex picked a path through the dense growth of trees, the ghostly trunks of which all looked the same in the black of night. He thought he was heading in the right direction, but after a hundred paces or so, with each step taking them deeper into the woods, he began to second-guess himself.

Then he saw it.

"There!" he said, aiming the yellow beam at the wreck.

"What is it, Daddy?" Bobby asked.

"Let's go have a closer look."

"A car!" Bobby exclaimed as they drew closer. "It's a car!"

It was indeed a car—some type of Ford, according to the hood ornament and badge, and one probably dating back to the 1920s or 30s.

The years had certainly not been kind to it. Rust had eaten large holes through much of its body, which appeared to have once been painted tan. At some point someone had taken its four tires, so it sat flat on the axles and black fenders. The fifth wire wheel remained mounted to the trunk. Only tattered scraps remained of the canvas convertible top.

Rex hiked Bobby into his arms so he could see inside the car—though there was little to see save for the aged steering wheel and the brown seats spilling their guts of foam and springs.

"What do you think, bud?" he said. "Pretty cool, huh?"

"How'd it get way out here?" Bobby asked, clearly in awe.

The story Rex's father had told Rex and Logan went something like this: The car belonged to an old prospector named Barry White. Barry had amassed a small fortune during the Cayoosh Gold Rush, but his wealth had turned him paranoid over time. Believing his partner was planning on robbing him, Barry invited the man over for dinner one evening and sunk an axe in his back. Barry dumped the corpse into the trunk of his car and went looking for a spot to bury it. Unfortunately for him, he drove off the road and crashed into a tree. Injured but alive, Barry left the wreck where it was and resumed his life as normal. And to this day —cue the *dun dun dun*—the remains of his partner could still be found in the trunk of the car.

Unsurprisingly, the Legend of Barry White had given Rex and Logan nightmares for the rest of the summer, and Rex wasn't going to make this same mistake by passing on the story to Bobby, so he simply said, "There used to be a road —more of a dirt path—through the forest. The driver of this car crashed into a tree and left it right here. Over the years the woods grew up around the car and the road disappeared."

"Can we open the trunk?" Bobby asked.

Rex frowned. "Why would you want to do that?"

"Maybe there's gold inside?"

"Oh, well—no. We don't need to do that. The metal's all sharp and rusted. If it cuts you, you could get tetanus—"

Something loud and large crashed through the under-growth perhaps fifty feet away. Rex whipped the flashlight left and right in alarm, throwing yellow ribbons through the night.

"Daddy?" Bobby said, worried.

Rex barely heard him.

A deer? A bear? A cougar?

Jesus Christ, where did it go?

"Daddy!"

"It's okay, bud," he said in a harsh whisper. "It was just a deer. But we should probably start back now."

Holding Bobby tightly against his chest, Rex heeded his own advice, resisting the urge to run.

5

T abitha had set the Oscar Meyer wieners and buns out on two paper plates on the kitchen counter, and she was dicing onions and tomatoes when Rex and Bobby returned.

Bobby burst past the afghan into the room, saying, "We saw a deer!" When he found only Tabitha in the kitchen, he clamped his mouth shut.

"Ellie's having a Time-Out right now," Tabitha said.

"Can I come down?" Ellie called from the attic.

"Are you going to be polite?"

"Yes!"

"Then I suppose so."

Footsteps darted across the ceiling, then down the stairs. Ellie skidded to a stop before Bobby. "You saw a deer?" she asked excitedly. "Like Bambi?"

"We didn't actually *see* anything," Rex said, pushing past the afghan. "We *heard* one."

Tabitha frowned as she remembered the sound outside the outhouse. Was that what she'd heard too? A deer? The same one? But wouldn't it have made more noise than the snapping of a single stick?

"It was real noisy!" Bobby said, as if in answer to her thoughts. "It was like..." By the expression on his face, he didn't seem to know how to replicate the sound, and instead he ran in circles around the room, mimicking the sound of a motor by blowing air through his pressed lips.

"So—the deer was the surprise?" Tabitha asked, confused. How did you organize to hear a deer in the wild?

"No, there was a car—" Bobby said before realizing to whom he was speaking.

"A car?" Ellie said.

Tabitha looked questioningly at Rex. He nodded. "It's been there for close to a hundred years. You guys can see it tomorrow. But right now let's get cooking. It's stopped raining, and I'm starving."

Rex carried the wieners and buns outside, Tabitha the onions and tomatoes and condiments. They set everything on the ground next to a ring of weathered stones that would serve as the fire pit. Rex collected the stringy shavings from the bark of a nearby cedar, which he rubbed quickly between his hands to create a small fluff ball. He used this as tinder, as well as the papery bark from a birch, to encourage a few nascent flames into existence, over which he added scavenged twigs and sticks for kindle, as well as larger deadwood. Ten minutes later they were sitting around a decent-sized fire, roasting wieners impaled on sticks.

"Smell that air, guys," Rex said. "How fresh is that?"

Ellie sniffed exaggeratedly. "Smells like the beginning of the world," she said straight-faced.

Rex and Tabitha laughed.

"What?" Ellie asked.

"You're beyond your years sometimes, sweetheart," Tabitha said.

"Can I have some Coke?" Bobby asked.

"I left the bottle in the car, bud," Rex told him. "It was too heavy to carry with all the other groceries. I'll go back and get it tomorrow."

"Can we roast weenies tomorrow night too?"

"That's the plan."

"What's for lunch tomorrow?" Ellie asked.

"Tuna fish sandwiches," Tabitha said.

"Do we have pickles too?"

"No pickles."

"I think your wiener's done, Bobby," Rex said. "Better pull it out or it's going to fall off."

Tabitha snickered at the double entendre. Bobby carefully removed his stick from the flames, but before he could get the wiener to his paper plate it slipped loose and fell to the ground.

"Oh no!" Bobby said, a look of devastation on his face.

"It's okay," Rex said quickly. "Have this one." He lowered his wiener over Bobby's plate. "Just pluck it off with your fingers. But be careful. It will be hot."

"Ow!" he said.

"I told you it will be hot."

"Yuck!" Ellie blurted, making a face.

"What's wrong?" Tabitha asked.

"I don't like that mustard!" She pointed to the bottle of Dijon mustard on the ground next to the regular mustard.

"That's adult mustard, honey. It's a bit stronger, that's all."

"I-I-I hate it," she sputtered, her cheeks coloring, her jaw setting, her eyes glowering—all the telltale signs of one of her temper tantrums. "And now. My life. Is ruined."

To avert a total meltdown, Tabitha said, "Guess what we have for dessert, guys?"

Silence.

Bobby was clearly curious but wouldn't speak to her.

Ellie seemed torn between curiosity and defiance, but finally put her concern over her ruined life temporarily on hold and asked, "What, Mommy?"

"S'mores! They're a kind of marshmallow sandwich."

"There's no such thing!"

"There sure is, sweetie. I had them all the time when I was your age."

"When were you my age?"

"A long time ago."

"When you were just like me but smaller than now?"

"That's right. Anyway, make a new wiener with the normal mustard, and I'll go fetch the ingredients we need."

While the kids finished up their dinner, Tabitha went inside and collected the graham crackers and marshmallows. Returning outside, she recalled she had banned Ellie from having dessert, but she decided to turn a blind eye to the punishment. This night was special for everybody.

She was just approaching the fire again when Ellie cried out, "Ewww!" She pointed at Bobby. "He's letting it bite him!"

"What's going on, bud?" Rex asked him.

"I'm letting the mosquita have dinner too." He held forth his right hand proudly to reveal a mosquito, plump with his blood, stuck to his wrist.

"Flick it off, Bobby," Rex said.

"Do I have to?" he said.

"You heard me."

"But I want to keep it as a pet."

"You can't keep a mosquito as a pet."

"Ellie got the chipmunk!"

"Not for keeps."

"I can put it in my Tic Tac container."

"How are you going to feed it? They only eat blood."

"I can give it mine."

"You're not a human blood bank, bud. Now flick it away."

Reluctantly, Bobby nudged the insect with his finger. It didn't move.

"It's too fat to fly!" Ellie crowed.

"Just give it a good flick," Rex said.

Bobby tried again. This time, however, he accidentally squished the bug flat, staring in surprise at the smear of blood it left behind on his skin.

"Gross!" Ellie said.

"And the moral of this story," Tabitha said, "is to not be greedy."

"Or risk getting struck down by a..." Rex trailed off.

Tabitha looked where he was looking and saw a light bobbing amongst the trees.

"Who could that be?" she said, frowning.

"Probably the neighbors," Rex said. "Must have heard us and are coming by to say hi."

"But the road... Do people still come out here?" She remembered the pickup truck. "That couple who passed us...?"

"Maybe," Rex said.

It would be an innocuous encounter, surely—this wasn't the city; people in the country were friendly—but Tabitha nevertheless felt a shiver of unease. "Kids," she said, "I think it's time to call it a night."

"But we haven't even had the S'mores!" Ellie said.

"We'll save them for tomorrow night."

"But you promised!"

"What did I promise? You can have the S'mores tomorrow, or none at all."

"Oh, crud!" she said, kicking at dirt. "Tomorrow's *forever* away."

"The faster you go to sleep," Rex said, "the faster it will come."

"Is that true?"

"One hundred percent."

Ellie relented. "I guess I'll go to sleep really fast."

"That's a very good decision, sweetie," Tabitha said. "Now say goodnight to T-Rex."

"See you later, alligator," she said.

"In a while, crocodile," he replied, reciting their old joke.

"C'mon, guys, let's go brush our teeth." Tabitha looked at Rex. "I'll be back out shortly."

"Sure," he said. "I'll be here."

Rex fussed with the fire, stoking the ashes with a stick to reinvigorate the winnowing flames, all the while keeping an eye on the foreign flashlight beam, which continued to move in his direction. He wasn't concerned by the neighbor's unexpected arrival. Inconvenienced was more like it. He wanted to spend the evening with Tabitha, not strangers.

When he could make out the silhouettes of two people, he rose from his crouch and faced them. It was indeed the couple from the pickup truck. The blonde woman wore a blueberry quilted jacket over a black turtleneck, tight jeans, and white high tops. The man had exchanged the Stetson for an oilskin mesh-back trucker cap. Despite the fact it couldn't have been any warmer than forty degrees out, he wore neither jacket nor sweater, only a black Metallica tee-shirt that revealed beefy biceps. A black belt that featured a flashy silver buckle held up stonewashed jeans. He gripped the flashlight in one hand, a tallboy can of Molson Canadian beer in the other. He had been limping, and now he stood with his weight favoring his left leg.

"Hi," Rex said, extending his hand. "I'm Rex."

"Hi!" the woman said, shaking. "Daisy." Her skin was icy cold.

The man made no effort to set aside either flashlight or beer can to shake. "Tony Lyons," he said simply, almost a grunt. His eyes were bright blue and serious.

"Saw you guys on our way in," Rex said. "Didn't know the road was going to be so bad. Forced us to leave the car behind and walk."

"It's been like that for years now," Daisy said. "Nobody comes out here nowadays."

"They don't like the view?" he said lightly.

She chuckled. Tony's face remained impassive.

"Are you next door?" Rex asked. "The place with the big deck...?"

"No, no," Daisy said. "Do you know the Williams' cottage? It's about two klicks down the road."

"Fair walk to get here," he remarked.

"We wanted to meet the one and only Rex Chapman," Tony said, smirking.

Rex hadn't told the man his last name, but he figured anyone who grew up in Lillooet would have heard about Rex —or more specifically, what happened to his family. Small towns talk, and remember. "Are you from around here?" he asked, guessing the man to be roughly his own age.

"Around," Tony said, draining his beer. He crushed the can in his fist and tossed it onto the fire, which irked Rex, as he would be the one picking the can out of the ashes tomorrow. "Spent a lot of time with the oil and gas companies up north. Tough as fuck work. People get injured. Some die. You living in Vancouver now, I bet?"

Rex studied Tony. The man's barb had been perfectly clear. He may as well have said, "You're a fruitcake office-worker, I bet?"

"No, not Vancouver," he said.

"City boy?"

"You don't like cities?"

"Don't care much for the people from 'em. Pussies, most of 'em."

So the gloves were off, Rex thought. The question was why. What was this guy's problem?

He looked at Daisy. Her smile had faltered. He decided to remain pleasant for her sake. "And you? Are you from around here too?"

She nodded. "Lived all my life here."

"So you're friends of the Williams?"

"No, I never met them actually."

Rex frowned. "But you're staying at their place?"

"They're dead," she said with a shrug. "Been dead for a long time now. Their place just sits there empty, so sometimes we come down here for a bit of a vacation, I guess you would call it."

"You're *squatting*?"

"Oh, we don't stay long or nothing," she insisted. "We just come down for the night usually. We leave in the morning. We stayed at the Starr's place once. They're not dead. They just don't come out here no more. But we like the Williams' place the best. It has a fireplace and is practically right on top of the water. Don't worry though. We've never stayed here in yours!"

Rex was baffled. "Given the condition of the road," he said, "I figured people didn't come out here much anymore. But *never*?"

"Never ever," Daisy said. "Except us, course. You're the first person we've seen since we began coming…" She looked at Tony. "How long now, babe? Four or five years?"

"What do you do?" Tony asked him.

"I'm a pilot," Rex said, caught off guard by the abrupt change of conversation.

"You fly one of those commercial things?"

"An Airbus 380."

"I got me a single-engine Cessna. Use it to get to the oil and gas fields. You have to actually fly a Cessna. No autopilot bullshit."

Rex had had enough of the jerk's condescending attitude. "What is it?" he asked. "A 172?"

Tony nodded. "172RG Cutlass. Four-seat, single-engine."

"One-fifty, one-sixty horsepower?"

"One eighty," Tony said proudly. "Got the more powerful O-360 in her."

"Nice," Rex said appreciatively. "But not quite the same as having four eighteen-hundred-horsepower Rolls-Royce engines under you, is it? That's what? Eight thousand horse-power all told?"

Tony's eyes darkened.

"So—anyway!" Daisy said, intervening. "We just wanted to say hi. Meet the famous Rex Chapman! We knew right away it was you." She pointed to her head.

It took Rex a moment to realize what she meant. His white hair.

"Famous?" he said, unimpressed by the crass choice of an adjective. Did losing your family in a boating accident grant you celebrity status?

"Well, you know, because of everything that's happened," Daisy said. "You were the start of it."

Rex was dumbfounded. "What are you talking about?"

She seemed equally stunned that he was in the dark. "You mean...you don't know?"

"Don't know what?"

"Hey, Rexy," Tony said. "You gonna offer your guest a beer?"

"I don't have any," he said.

"Don't got no beer?"

"I don't drink beer."

"Ah, right. You a wine man?" That smirk.

"As a matter of fact, I don't drink at all."

"That so?"

"That's so."

"What you hiding?"

Rex blinked. "Excuse me?"

"All the teetotalers I know, they don't drink 'cause they got issues. They drink, and it all comes gushing out. All the tears and shit and everything. They just come fucking apart."

Rex had quit drinking after a night out in university. He'd drunk so much spiced rum at a frat party he woke in the bushes behind the house with no memory of the preceding few hours. He'd been covered in vomit and knew if he'd passed out on his back and not on his front he likely would have choked to death. During the three-day hangover that followed this epiphany, he'd decided alcohol wasn't for him —and he'd simply never imbibed any more since.

Rex wasn't going to tell Tony this, of course, and so he returned his attention to Daisy. "What don't I know?" he asked.

"Everything that's happened since you left! The guy who...who got your family...he got—"

"The guy who got my family?" he said, incensed. Deciding he was the butt of a bad joke, he added: "I don't know what the hell you two are getting at, or what rumors have been spun about my family over the years up here in Hicksville, Nobody Cares, but nobody 'got' my family, and I think it's in extremely bad taste to come onto my property spreading such nonsense. They drowned in a boating accident. Now I think we're done here. You should both leave."

"Oh Rexy," Tony said, shaking his head. "How naïve do you think we are? Drowned?" He barked a laugh. "Where did the bodies go if they drowned? Pavilion Lake ain't the Pacific Ocean. They would've washed up eventually."

Rex frowned. The bodies were never found? He hadn't been aware of this. He'd only known what his Uncle Henry had told him when he came to Lillooet to take Rex back to Vancouver all those years ago. *They drowned, Rex. I'm sorry to have to tell you that, and I don't want you thinking too much about it. There's no point thinking about what you can't change. You got a new life now to focus on.*

"If my family didn't drown," Rex said tightly, fighting the thick air of unreality washing over him, "do you want to tell me what happened to them? Who's this guy you mentioned?"

"We don't know exactly," Daisy said. "What I meant was, whoever got your family must have been a guy, a man. That's all I meant. No woman could, you know, make so many families just disappear."

Rex almost fell over. "Other people have gone missing too?"

She nodded. "That's what I was trying to tell ya. A whole lot of other people. I was only two years old when you left, so I don't recall anything that happened with your family and everything. I mean, I don't have *my* memories of that.

Just what people told me when I got older. Like your hair and stuff. But I was eight when the Petersons disappeared. And I remember *that*."

"The Petersons?" Rex said, his heart pounding. They had been friends of his parents and had stopped by occasionally for cocktails. He seemed to recall Mrs. Peterson always having a cigarette in her hand.

"They were from Vancouver," Daisy said. "They only came up here in the summers. Always hosted a game of bridge on Friday nights. But one Friday they just weren't home. Car was there and everything, but they just wouldn't answer the door. Friends got concerned and called Paulsy who had a look around—"

"Paulsy?" Rex said.

"The police chief. He was still just a kid then. Didn't find any clues or nothing of what happened to the Petersons, and that got everybody talking. You know, because of how your family just disappeared six years earlier. Even the TV was talking about it. I remember everybody on my street going to one of the neighbors' to watch a story about it on the six o'clock news."

"There were no suspects?" Rex said. "No theories?"

"Suspects, no. Theories? Yeah, everybody had their own theory."

"You got a theory, Rex?" Tony asked him.

"Me? My uncle told me my family died in a boating accident. I was seven. I believed him. And to tell you the truth, I'm still not sure everything I'm hearing right now isn't a big load of bullshit."

"We're not messing with ya," Daisy said. "It wasn't just the Petersons in '87 either. The Ryersons went missing in 1998. Rick, Sue, and their two teenage daughters. That time it was different. People actually heard them screaming. Paulsy found the front door wide open. Kitchen window was open too. Nobody knew if this was due to someone trying to get in, or the family trying to get out. Blood everywhere. In any event, all four of them were never seen again. And that was the tipper, I guess. When everyone decided to get the hell out of Dodge. One family disappearing, okay. Two families, well that's just weird, but it can happen, maybe. But three? Three families in what? Less than twenty years? On a lake that only a handful of people live on? That you can't ignore. That's getting into Jason Voorhees territory. The next summer every cabin out here went up for sale, but there were no takers. Not with what happened, and the rumors. A crazy mountain man. Ghosts. Bigfoot. Pavilion Lake got a reputation. A bad reputation. And, well, that hasn't changed. People just don't come here no more."

"So tell us what you know, Rexy," Tony said.

Rex clenched his jaw. "I told you—"

"Out of all the families that have been attacked and gone missing, nine people in total, you're the only one to have been part of that and survived. You want us to believe that's just one big coinky-dink?"

Rex was incredulous. "You think I killed my own family when I was seven and have been coming back here to murder other unsuspecting families ever since? You're a fucking lunatic."

"I never said it was *you*. But I reckon you know who's responsible." Tony took a step closer and said in a threatening tone, "What did your pop say to you the night he killed your family?"

Rex was too shocked to speak.

"Come on, Rexy," Tony pressed. "You were there. Your hair turned white. That didn't happen 'cause you witnessed people drowning. You watched your pop kill your mom and brother, didn't you? Then he made you swear to never tell anyone what happened."

"Get the fuck off my property."

"It's the only thing that makes sense—"

Rex shoved Tony, hard. The bigger man shuffled backward two steps before regaining his balance. Rage flashed in his eyes, and he made to lunge for Rex, when Daisy grabbed his arm.

"Tony!" she cried. "Stop it!"

He tried to shake her off, but she held on.

"I'm sorry," she said to Rex, tugging at Tony. "We shouldn't have come."

Rex had balled his hands into fists. They were trembling.

Finally Tony let himself be led limping away, casting a final, furious glance back at Rex, who remained where he stood, sick to his stomach, his world suddenly turned upside down.

Holding up an apple cider-scented glass candle she'd brought from home, Tabitha peeked out the attic window and recognized the people speaking to Rex as the man and woman from the pickup truck that had passed them during their walk in. She felt relieved. She didn't know what had made her so skittish at the sight of the flashlight earlier. She supposed it had something to do with the fact it was after dark, and they were in a very isolated place.

Tabitha crossed the room to the two beds. Ellie was in the closest one, on her back, a white wool cover with candy cane stripes pulled to her chin. She'd folded her hands behind her head so she resembled a sunbather soaking up rays on a beach.

Bobby, in the adjacent bed, was scrunching his eyes shut the way he always did whenever Tabitha tucked them in.

She sat on the floor next to Ellie's bed so she was at eye level with her daughter. "Did you pick a story for me to read?" she asked.

Ellie produced a book from behind her head with a flourish. "This one!" she said.

"Were you hiding that?"

"Yes!"

"I was wondering why you were in such a silly position." She took the book and studied the cover. "...*I Love You, Broom Hilda*," she said, reading the title doubtfully. She thumbed through the pages of the thin paperback. "This isn't a novel, sweetie. It's a comic strip."

"But she's a green witch!"

"Who chain-smokes cigars and drinks whiskey, by the looks of it."

"*Please?*"

"We'll give it a shot, I guess. Can't be too bad if it was up here in the first place."

Tabitha spent the next twenty minutes reading to Ellie, and admittedly developing a soft spot for the cantankerous chubby witch and her eccentric friends.

When she closed the book, Ellie asked, "Can I be a witch like her when I grow up?"

"Absolutely not."

"How come?"

"Do you have a bent hat and striped socks?"

"No..."

"Well, that's why then." Tabitha kissed her daughter on the forehead. "Now try to sleep."

"Do I have to go fishing tomorrow?" she asked as she rested her head on the lumpy pillow.

"Not if you don't want to."

"T-Rex isn't going to make me?"

"When has Rex ever made you do anything you didn't want to do?"

"He made me come to this house."

"He did not. I asked him if we could come. You don't like it here?"

"It's okay."

"Just okay?"

"It would be better if I was allowed my iPad."

Sighing, Tabitha stood. "Good night, sweetie. I love you."

"I love me too."

"Goodnight, Bobby."

At the sound of his name, Bobby scrunched his eyes together even more tightly, no doubt convinced he was pulling off an Oscar-worthy performance.

Tabitha returned downstairs and found Rex on the sofa in the front room. He'd lit the other three jar candles they'd brought, and the small flames filled the room with warm light and jittery shadows.

"That was a short visit," she said, referring to their company.

"Oh, hi," he said. He had been deep enough in thought he hadn't seemed to notice her standing there.

"Everything okay?" she asked.

"Yeah, sure," he said, and although she couldn't read his expression in the poor light, his voice sounded uncharacteristically melancholic.

"Did they want something?"

"Who?"

She frowned. "The couple you were talking to outside."

"No. They were just saying hi."

Tabitha wasn't sure she believed this, but Rex had always been very open with her, which meant there was likely a good reason for his reticence. She wasn't going to pry. "I'm going to get changed," she said. "Be back out shortly."

"Sure," he said.

Tabitha retrieved her shoulder bag and carried it to the small bathroom. Setting the jar candle and bag on the counter, she stripped down to her underwear and bra, unzipped the bag, and withdrew the pieces of her neatly folded flight attendant uniform. She pulled on the fitted navy skirt and matching jacket, and tied the colorful scarf around her neck, fussing with each end to perfect the bow. She studied her candle-lit reflection in the mirror and thought she looked pretty darn good for a forty-year-old mom of two. Despite the fact Rex was a pilot, and she a flight attendant, they rarely saw each other in their uniforms because they neither lived together nor worked at the same airport. She hoped he appreciated this little surprise.

She returned to the front room quietly so as not to disturb the kids. The last thing she needed was for Ellie to call for her, or worse, come downstairs.

Rex still sat on the sofa. His eyes were closed now, his feet up on the coffee table. *Such a handsome man*, she thought, starry-eyed. Handsome, kind, patient, gentle, caring, successful. How had she ever gotten so lucky meeting him?

It had been a chance encounter. Her friend Leena had set her up on a blind date. She was to meet the date at a popular pub in downtown Seattle. Tabitha was punctual to a fault, and she showed up early. She went to the bar and ordered a gin and tonic. Rex was a few barstools down from her, drinking water. When she overheard him mention to the bartender he was a pilot, she told him she was a flight attendant. They started talking shop. Which airline do you work for? Which flights do you fly? This quickly devolved into what pilots and flight attendants liked discussing amongst each other best: gossip. You couldn't escape this when you worked in one of the most hardcore customer-service jobs in America. So they exchanged their favorite stories, like the time when Tabitha had to inject a passenger with a sedative after he'd dropped ecstasy and began dancing in the galleys, or when severe turbulence turned the cabin into a mosh pit, causing luggage to rain down from the overheads, or when a woman on a red-eye flight had too much to drink and vomited her dinner everywhere, which had the domino effect of causing the entire last two rows of passengers to follow suit.

Rex, however, trumped all her stories with a truly terrifying tale. When he'd been ten seconds from landing at JFK one winter, he was forced to pull up at the last second to avoid colliding with the tail of a Boeing 747 that had crossed into his landing path without permission. He'd told her the disaster had been averted by a matter of feet.

"My God, Rex!" she'd said. "Were you scared?"

"I would have been screaming along with everybody else, but I was pinned to my seat with such force I could scarcely breathe."

In retrospect Tabitha didn't believe that modest statement. Rex was too calm, collected, unflappable. More than likely he would have exhaled deeply when the danger had passed, made a wisecrack to his First Officer about air traffic controllers getting too little sleep, and apologized over the loudspeakers to the passengers for the severe maneuver.

In any event, Tabitha and Rex had been getting along so well that evening that when her blind date eventually showed up, she huddled close to Rex and pretended to be together. Her date didn't look twice at them.

"Keep your eyes closed," she said now, adding a good dose of huskiness to her voice.

"Huh?" Rex said, turning.

"Eyes closed!" she said.

He kept them closed.

She stopped before him and cleared her throat. Was she about to make a total fool of herself?

"Okay, you can open them," she said.

He did—and stared in surprise.

"Well?" she said, striking a pose like a game show model and turning in a circle. "Do I compete with all those young flight attendants you work with?"

"Compete and defeat," he said, and grinned.

"Good, because I feel like an idiot."

"You look stunning," he said, and she could tell he meant the compliment.

Stepping over his stretched legs, she straddled his groin. She leaned forward and nuzzled his neck, breathing in the spicy scent of his aftershave. She nibbled his earlobe. "We're going to have to be super quiet."

He kissed her on the cheek. She pressed her lips to his— but could tell right away he wasn't into it, which was a first in their relationship.

"Hey?" she said softly, pulling back. "What's wrong?"

"I'm just—I've got something on my mind."

"Those people... What did they...?" She shook her head, thinking of the boating accident that had taken his family. "It doesn't matter. Can we cuddle?"

"I'd love nothing better," he said.

She shifted off his lap and curled up on the sofa next to him, her head resting on his shoulder. "If you want to talk," she said. "I'm here."

"Thanks," he replied, but he said no more.

Tabitha closed her eyes, telling herself she would get up in a few minutes to take out her contact lenses and brush her teeth and make a proper bed on the foldout couch...but the long day quickly caught up with her, and almost immediately she drifted into a dreamless slumber.

In the quiet dark of the night, the only sounds were the susurrate whistle of wind on the other side of the cabin's sturdy log walls and, barely audible, the deep and regular rhythm of Tabitha's breathing.

Rex wrapped his right arm around her shoulder and pulled her more closely against him. She murmured but didn't wake. He pressed his nose into her hair, which smelled faintly of pears, and kissed the top of her head.

He would tell her in the morning about the conversation he'd had with Daisy and Tony. He needed some time to first digest what he'd learned, to try to make sense of it, or to debunk it, he didn't know which.

As he had been doing for the last while, he continued to scour his brain for memories of his father. Yet it was proving frustratingly difficult to recollect anything more than a foggy face and a few inconsequential impressions. He had been too young when his father had disappeared to conjure anything more concrete.

Which made it much easier to recast the man as a family-slaying monster.

The ease of which Rex could accept this possibility, at least theoretically, was frightening but not all that surprising. Because evil people existed in the world. They did horrible things to other people every single day. Somewhere some sick bastard was doing something unspeakable to someone right now.

So if Rex were to remain objective in the face of Tony's allegations, and not let his emotions cloud his impartiality, there was no valid reason for him to rule out that his father could not be one such sick bastard, innocent until proven guilty be damned.

Some humans were psychopaths.

Rex's father was a human.

Ergo, Rex's father could be a psychopath.

That was the syllogistic argument anyway, and if Rex were to go with the wild conclusion—and he was, for the time being, if only to prove it false—what then might have occurred up here in the summer of '81? Did Troy Chapman have too much to drink one night and pick a fight with Rex's mother, Sally? Did the argument spin out of control, and did he kill her in the passion of the moment? Did Logan and Rex witness this and try to flee? Did their father catch Logan and kill him to keep him silent? Did their father get rid of the two bodies so there would be no physical evidence of his crime if he were ever captured and charged? Did he disappear into the mountains to live the life of a hermit? But what of the other families? The Petersons and the Ryersons? Why kill them? Did he return to Pavilion Lake in 1987 to stock up on supplies? Did he play Goldilocks in vacant cabins? Did the Petersons catch him red-handed in theirs? Did the same thing happen eleven years later in 1998 with the Ryersons...?

Rex massaged his temples with his thumb and middle

finger, plying the skin in small circles. *This is ridiculous,* he thought. *Sitting here, thinking about this, playing Sherlock Holmes, turning his father into some murderous mountain man, ridiculous.*

The bottom line was that Rex didn't have any proof, Tony didn't have any proof, nobody had any proof of what happened to his family, to the Petersons, and to the Ryersons. Not one iota of proof. Whatever *did* happen would likely never be known, as was the case with the vast majority of unsolved murders—

Murders? he thought. *There I go again. Tony's poisoned my mind. Because without any bodies, who's to say a single murder was ever committed? Mom, Dad, Logan, the Petersons and the Ryersons, they could all be living in some backcountry utopian commune, sharing chores and clothes, husbands and wives—*

Something slammed into the cabin door, seeming to shake the entire room.

Rex shot upright. Tabitha, wide-awake, seized his arm in a vice-like grip.

BANG! BANG! BANG!

Someone was trying to get in.

6

Paul Harris climbed the staircase to the police station's second floor. The spacious constable quarters included a living room, kitchen, dining room, two bedrooms (which had originally been a single space filled with bunks for the unmarried troopers), and a large bathroom. Most of the building's original architectural features remained intact, such as the stone walls and chimney, double-hung sash windows, hardwood floors, and high mansard roof. In the 1950s, an east-facing bay window was added in the living room to capture the morning light. More recently, the kitchen and bathroom received modern facelifts, with the latter getting a small laundry.

Paul stuck his head in the living room, expecting to find his wife, Nancy, curled up on the rose loveseat reading one of her mystery novels. She wasn't there. He continued down the hallway and heard water running through the bathroom pipes.

That woman has more showers than anybody else, Paul thought to himself. One in the morning, one at night, sometimes one in the afternoon if she was bored and wanted something to do. Perhaps she had been a fish in her past life?

For his part, Paul had little interest in water in general, aside from drinking it. When he took the family to Joffre Lakes to soak up the wilderness on a warm spring or summer day, he would remain on shore, or in the canoe if they brought it, while Nancy and their grandson, Zephaniah, splashed around in the shallows.

Why get wet? What was the point? You just had to dry yourself off again. One shower in the morning was enough for him. One every other day in the wintertime when the temperature dropped below zero.

Paul had clearly been no fish in his past life. Likely something from a temperate or tropical climate. An orangutan, maybe, or an armadillo. Yes, maybe an armadillo, from a South American rainforest. That sounded like the good life. Forage in the mornings, catch some Zs in the afternoon, forage a little more in the warm evenings...

Paul stopped outside Zephaniah's bedroom door. Zephaniah's father—Paul's forty-three-year-old son—had been in and out of jail since he was twenty, and he was now serving three years in a medium-security penitentiary for smuggling firearms across the border for a convicted felon. Zephaniah's mother died when he was two from a drug overdose. Consequently, Paul and Nancy had agreed to take custody of Zephaniah until his father was released from prison—though they were now planning to request permanent custody of the boy on the grounds that his father was an unfit parent.

Paul knocked on the bedroom door.

"Yeah?"

"Can I come in?"

"Yeah."

Zephaniah was seated at his desk, playing a video game on the computer. Paul pulled up a chair next to him and sat down. "What game's that?"

"Halo."

"Looks fun."

"It's boring."

"Then why play it?"

"This computer is really old. It can only play really old games."

The computer was a Dell Dimension from the late nineties. It had served Paul fine, as he had only used it for word processing. He had considered buying something better for Zephaniah to use, but had been hesitant, not wanting to turn the boy into one of those zombie kids that sat inside all day and night, eyes glued to a screen.

"How was school?" Paul asked.

"Fine," Zephaniah said, pausing the game.

"That was polite of you."

"What was?"

"Pausing the game."

"I'm not good at multitasking."

"Me either."

"That's not true. You're good at everything."

"I'm flattered, Zeph. But, no, I'm not. Don't you ever wonder why only your grandmother cooks?"

"You can make pancakes."

Paul nodded. "I can do that." He shifted his weight on the chair. "I spoke with Mr. Jenson today." Mr. Jenson was Zephaniah's grade-five teacher.

Zephaniah looked down at his lap.

"Hey, you didn't do anything wrong," Paul said gently. "It was those boys who did the wrong thing. What are their names?"

"Steve Kozlow and Clay Parrish."

"They're older than you?"

He nodded. "They're in grade six."

"What were they teasing you about?"

"It doesn't matter."

"I'd like to know."

Zephaniah shrugged. "My nose."

Paul raised his eyebrows. "Your nose?"

"They called me a shoebill."

"What the hell's a shoebill?"

"It's a bird that always falls on its face because its beak is so heavy. Steve showed me a video on his phone of it falling over. Then they tried pushing me over too."

Paul clenched his jaw. "Did you push them back?"

Zephaniah seemed surprised. "Am I allowed to do that?"

Paul thought it over for a moment, then decided what the hell. He wasn't going to stand for his grandson being bullied. "Usually I don't condone violence," he said. "But bullies are the exception to the rule. They need to be taught a lesson. It's the only way they learn."

"But they'll just push me back harder, won't they?"

"Maybe. But I'll tell you something else about bullies. They're usually big wimps. It's true. They're scared of a fair fight. That's why they go after kids smaller than themselves. So if those boys tease you again, you know what I want you to do?" He held up a fist. "You pop them one right in the mouth."

Zephaniah's eyes widened. "Really?"

Paul nodded. "That'll teach them."

"I won't get in trouble?"

"Not by me. And I'm the law."

"Cool! Thanks, Grandpa." He twisted his hands in his lap. "Can I ask you something?"

"That's what I'm here for."

"Can I get a nose job?"

Paul chuffed. "Get real, son."

"But then nobody will ever tease me about my nose again."

"What's wrong with a big nose? Look, I have one too." He turned his head to profile. "It runs in the family. You'll... grow into it."

"But I don't want a big schnoz."

"Schnoz?"

"That's what Clay Parrish called it."

"He's just jealous of it. You know why? Because if you have a big schnoz, you don't ever have to worry about your sunglasses falling off."

Zephaniah rolled his eyes. "Grandpa..."

"And you'll never lose a photo-finish race."

"Grandpa!"

"Okay, okay. But look, Zeph. All I'm saying is there's nothing wrong with having a big nose. It makes you look distinguished."

"I just want to look normal."

"You do look normal. Don't ever think you don't."

Zephaniah nodded. "Can I play my game again?"

"Go for it." Paul messed the boy's hair, got up, and left. He found Nancy in the bedroom, wrapped in her housecoat, searching the closet for something to wear.

"Why do you like water so much?" he asked her.

"Excuse me?" she said, glancing back at him. At fifty-six, Nancy was still as beautiful to Paul as the day she'd accepted his invitation to the prom. A few more wrinkles, sure, some gray in her chestnut hair, but the same lively eyes and childish face.

"You take two or three showers a day."

She selected a pastel blouse and slacks, tossed them on the bed, and went to the dresser, where she rifled through her undergarments drawer. "I like being clean."

"You're clean after one."

"You're cleaner after two."

"What do you do here all day when I'm at work? Roll around in the mud?"

"When I'm not getting hot and sweaty with the milkman." She turned, holding a red bra and matching underwear against her body. "What do you think? Will he like them?"

"I think the milkman stopped delivering the milk in the sixties, when you must have been, oh, five or six."

"You're right. My mistake. I meant to say the pool boy."

"We don't have a pool."

"Maybe we should get one—you know, considering how much I like water and everything."

Paul laughed. "I have to go out for a little, so you and Zeph go ahead with dinner without me. What are you making?"

"Spaghetti Bolognese," she said. "Are you going to be sitting outside that bar all night again?"

"No, something else has come up."

Nancy frowned. "Something to do with Barbara McKenzie?"

"Sort of. Do you remember Rex Chapman?"

"Troy and Sally's boy?"

Paul nodded. "The one and only. Barbara said he stopped by the tourist center earlier. He was heading out to Pavilion Lake with a woman and two kids."

"Rex Chapman..." She shook her head. "My, my. He hasn't been back here since...well, why *is* he back?"

"No idea. I guess I'll find out when I speak with him."

"Why do you have to speak with him?"

"I don't *have* to. But he likely doesn't know what happened to the Petersons, or the Ryersons. Barb thinks I should give him a heads up."

"But that's all... It must be twenty years since the Ryersons disappeared!"

"Twenty exactly," Paul said, nodding. "Anyway, I better get a move on it." He clapped his peaked hat onto his head. "I still have to find somewhere to stable a horse for the night."

7

Bobby lay on his back in bed, looking up at the inky black ceiling. His nose and cheeks were cold, but the blanket, pulled up to his chin, kept his body warm. The blanket smelled funny, like his grandma's house, where he stayed when his dad had to fly to different countries.

Bobby wished there was a nightlight up here in the attic like there was in his bedroom at home. It was too dark. He couldn't see much except the rafters above him and the shadowy outline of the furniture around him. Ellie told him there was a monster hiding under his bed, and if that was true, it might be thinking about coming out and grabbing one of his feet. He would scream if it did that. He didn't want to. He wasn't a baby anymore. But he would. His dad would come running up the stairs and fight the monster. Bobby couldn't picture this scene in his head. Maybe because he didn't know what the monster looked like in real life.

"It has big claws and big teeth," Ellie said from her bed a few feet from his.

"No, it doesn't," Bobby replied, and now he *could* picture the monster, and it made his stomach twist.

"Yes, it does," Ellie insisted. "And it's going to bite your head off."

"I'm going to tell my dad."

"Don't be a baby."

"I'm not a baby."

"You still suck your mom's boobies!"

"Do not!"

"Do too! And you always want your dad."

"You always want your mom."

"Not *all* the time."

Bobby swallowed and listened carefully. He didn't hear anything under his bed.

Should he turn on his little flashlight and look? But what if Ellie was telling the truth, and the monster grabbed him? What if it pulled him under? She probably wouldn't help him. She would be glad if a monster got him.

"I think it's gone," he said hopefully.

"No, it's still there," she said. "I heard it."

"I don't believe you."

"It's going to eat you."

"Shut up.

"*It's going to eat you.*"

"It will eat you too."

"No, it won't, because I'm almost six."

"I'm almost six too."

"But I'm older."

Bobby was getting frustrated—and scared.

"It will still eat you too," he said.

"Monsters only eat little kids."

"You're little too."

"I told you, I'm almost six. I can do anything."

"No, you can't."

"Yes, I can."

"Do a headstand."

Ellie was silent.

"See?" Bobby said happily. "You *can't.*"

But then he heard Ellie pushing off her blanket. He looked over at her. She was on all fours. She planted her head on the mattress, then kicked with her feet. She went straight up— and came straight back down.

"I did it!" she said happily, pushing hair away from her

face.

"That doesn't count," he said. "You have to stay on your head for longer."

"How long?"

"One minute."

Ellie sighed and tried again. She came down just as quickly as before, only this time she fell sideways off the bed and hit the floor. Bobby laughed.

"Hey!" Ellie's mom called from somewhere downstairs. "What's going on up there?"

"Nothing!" Ellie replied, hopping back into her bed and slipping beneath the blanket.

"Go to sleep!"

Bobby remained perfectly silent, but when Ellie's mom didn't say anything more, he whispered, "Why do you always wear yellow?"

"I don't always," Ellie said.

"All your clothes are yellow. Your dress today was yellow. And your pajamas are yellow."

"I like yellow."

"Is your underwear yellow?"

"No!"

"What color is it?"

"I don't know." She checked. "It's white. What color is yours?"

"I'm not telling."

"I told you mine!"

"So?"

"Mommy! Bobby's not telling me what color his underwear is!"

"What?" her mom's voice came back.

"I told him mine, but he won't tell me his!"

"Don't make me come up there!"

"She's mad," Bobby whispered.

"We better go to sleep," Ellie replied.

"What about the monster? If we go to sleep, it can get us."

"I think it's gone to sleep already."

"You're sure?"

"Yeah."

Bobby was relieved. He closed his eyes, not tightly like he did to trick Ellie's mom into thinking that he was sleeping, but just normally. He thought about going fishing tomorrow morning with his dad. He had never been fishing before. He wondered if he would have to put the worm on the hook himself. That would be gross. And what would he do if he caught a fish? Would his dad make him eat it? That meant he would have to kill it, and he wasn't sure he wanted to do that. Maybe he would just let it go again.

Bobby kept thinking about fishing until he found himself thinking about bears. They lived out here in the woods. What if one came to the cabin? What if it busted down the front door? They could do that. He saw it happen in a movie. His dad had been on a date with Ellie's mom, and Ellie was having a sleepover at his house. They watched *Shark Tale*, but before it finished, Ellie and the babysitter fell asleep. Bobby watched TV on his own way past his bedtime and found the bear movie on a channel he usually wasn't allowed to watch. The bear was going around killing people in the woods. It even knocked the head off a horse with its paw. So it could easily get through the front door of this cabin, no problem. It might have a hard time getting up the stairs—it would be fat and the stairs were narrow—but it would get his dad and Ellie's mom. He would cry if it got his dad, and he would probably even be a little sad if it got Ellie's mom...

Bobby slept. He dreamed he was wandering alone in the woods, and a bear was following him. He couldn't see the animal, but he knew it was there. It was a smart bear, and it was waiting for him to lead it back to the cabin, so it could eat not just him but everybody else too. Then somebody was shouting—

Bobby came awake. His dad and Ellie's mom were speaking quickly and loudly, and they sounded scared. Bobby knew right away what was wrong.

The bear had found them!

"Dad?" he cried. "*Dad?*"

◆ ◆ ◆

Rex jumped to his feet. "Jesus Christ!" he said, staring at the door in the candlelight.

Tabitha was beside him. "Who is it?"

"I have no idea." He thought immediately of Tony, but why would the guy be banging on the door at...what time was it anyway? Was he pranking them? Giving them a scare? Rex didn't think so. Tony was an asshole, but he was an adult. He wouldn't resort to juvenile games.

Tabitha said, "Is the door locked?"

"Yes."

"Are you sure?"

"Yes!" He clearly remembered engaging the deadbolt. Locking the door at nighttime was a habit he'd acquired from living in big cities his entire life.

"Dad?" Bobby cried. "*Dad?*"

Ellie called for her mom a moment later.

"Go upstairs and stay with the kids," he said.

"What are you going to do?" Tabitha looked panicked. "You can't go out there! We're in the middle of nowhere. It's nighttime. Someone just pounded on the door. That wasn't a polite knock."

"Maybe they need help?"

"Have they knocked again?"

The kids were shouting more loudly now.

"Go upstairs," he repeated. "Tell Bobby and Ellie everything is okay. Tell them to stay up there, then come back down."

"Don't go outside until I'm back."

"I'm waiting. Now go!"

She grabbed a candle and hurried into the other room.

He heard her ascend the stairs rapidly. He glanced around for a weapon of some kind. The ice tongs on the wall? Too unwieldy.

He spotted a golf club in one corner. He grabbed it. A nine iron, the head rusted, the shaft wooden. His father had used it to chip golf balls off the dock into the lake.

Rex went to the window to the right of the door. He pressed his nose to the glass but couldn't see anything outside except for the black night. His pulse was racing, his thoughts moving as equally fast, playing over everything Daisy and Tony had told him earlier.

"Can you see them?"

He jumped. Tabitha stood behind him.

"Can't see anything," he grunted, his mouth suddenly cotton-dry. "How are the kids?"

"Scared. Do you think it could be the people who came by? That man and woman?"

"No," he said.

"Then *who*?"

An axe-wielding mountain man?

"I'm going to find out," he said, going to the door. "Lock the door behind me."

"Rex, *please*," she said, grabbing his wrist.

He stopped. "What do you want to do, Tabs? Sitting around and doing nothing is going to be one hell of a long night."

"Rex—"

"I won't be long." He thumbed the deadbolt and opened the door. "Oh shit!"

Tabitha screamed.

She's dead. She has to be. Look at all that blood!

Those three thoughts pushed everything else from Tabitha's mind as she stared in horror at the woman lying on her side on the porch. Her purple quilted jacket was slit open horizontally across the belly, which appeared to be where all the blood was leaking from.

Rex dropped the golf club and knelt next to the woman. A moment later Tabitha did so too, recording what she saw in crystalline detail. Wavy blonde hair, no dark roots, recently colored. Pale face, unnaturally so. Eyes closed. Eyelashes too thick and full to be natural. Blood on the left cheek. Mouth ajar. Fillings in the molars and two badly nicotine-stained front teeth. Silver studs in the earlobes. A birthmark on the underside of the heart-shaped jaw.

Tabitha said, "That's the woman..."

Rex said, "Daisy. Her name's Daisy." He patted her cheek. "Daisy? Daisy?" No response. He checked her throat for a pulse.

Tabitha swallowed with difficulty. "Is she dead?"

"Not breathing. CPR, quick."

Rex rolled the woman onto her back. He unzipped her ruined jacket.

Tabitha gasped.

Blood had turned her once white shirt bright red. It had been slit horizontally as had the jacket—along with the woman's flesh beneath. The grisly wound stretched the length of her abdomen, revealing the pink and wormy organs of her gastrointestinal tract.

"Oh fuck," Rex said.

He began CPR. Each powerful compression caused blood to squirt out of the terrible wound. Then the woman's bowels began to slip out too.

"Rex, stop!" Tabitha cried in disgust.

He stopped. His eyes were wide, wild. He felt her throat again for a pulse.

"She's gone," he said woodenly.

"What *happened* to her?" Tabitha said, looking around as if to find evidence of a car accident. Then an epiphany. She stiffened, aghast. "Did somebody *do this*?"

Rex was shaking his head. He seemed haunted.

"Rex? Rex!" she said. "What's going on?"

"We need to get out of here. Go get the kids." He retrieved the golf club and stood.

"What's going on, Rex?" she demanded, leaping to her feet to stand beside him. "Who did this? *Did someone do this?*"

"Get the kids! We're wasting time!"

While Tabitha went upstairs to get Bobby and Ellie, Rex fetched the handmade throw quilt from the sofa and draped it over Daisy's corpse. He knew you were supposed to perform CPR for much longer than he had on a victim in cardiac arrest, but in this case there had been no point. It was clear Daisy was doomed even if she resumed breathing. Her goddamn guts were spilling out of her stomach. Maybe if they'd had a phone he would have kept performing the compressions, because at least then there would have been a chance, however unlikely, of help arriving in time to save her. But they didn't have a phone. It had been his crazy decision to leave them back in the car.

Rex went inside and collected the Mazda keys and the Maglite just as Tabitha and the kids came down the stairs. Tabitha was white as a ghost. Bobby and Ellie were sleepy yet alarmed.

Rex dropped to his knees so he was at eye level with the kids. "Listen up, guys," he said, trying to make his voice as no-nonsense fatherly as possible. "There's been an accident. Someone's had an accident. So we're going to go get help. Which means we have to get to the car. We're going to have to move fast. Maybe even run when we can."

"Who had the accident?" Ellie asked.

"A woman. She's resting right now. But we need to go—"

"Did you cut your hands, Daddy?" Bobby asked.

Rex glanced at his hands, which were wet with Daisy's

blood. "No, I'm okay." He stood and looked at Tabitha. "Should we carry them?"

"They'll be okay on their own."

Rex nodded. "Bobby, Ellie, you two stay right behind me. Tabitha's going to be right behind you. Okay? Okay."

Rex led them outside. The kids yelped in surprise at the sight of Daisy's body, for despite it being covered by the throw quilt, the shape was still clearly that of a person. Tabitha hushed them, saying the woman was only sleeping. Rex scanned the night. He didn't hear or see anybody. He dashed down the driveway, silently cursing the noise his footsteps were making on the mucky ground.

When he reached the road, he waited a beat for the others to reach him, then he started in the direction of the highway, sweeping the flashlight beam back and forth before him. His heart was pounding in his chest, and he felt sick with dread. He told himself they were going to make it, yet deep down he had his doubts.

Three families had gone missing on this lake over the years without a trace.

He had been the only known survivor.

Was fate trying to rectify that mistake?

As she followed Rex down the dark road, Ellie was trying to figure out what happened to the sleeping woman. Why wasn't she sleeping in a proper bed? Why on the porch, without her head showing?

Ellie had tried sleeping like that once when she was allowed to take her afternoon nap in her mom's bed. The bed was huge compared to hers, and she climbed all the way beneath the sheets and covers, holding them up with her head, so she sat in the middle of a little fort. She would have remained there for her entire nap, hidden away from the world with her imaginary friends, but it became really hot and hard to breathe. She remembered when she popped her face back out again how cool the air felt, even though it was probably the same temperature it always was.

She's probably okay with her head not showing because she's outside, Ellie decided. *It's too cold out to get hot beneath the cover.*

T-Rex was moving pretty fast. He wasn't running. He was only jogging, but because he was bigger than she was, jogging for him was like running for her.

She was pretty fast herself. They once had a hundred-meter-dash race at school for all the students. She ran against the other girls in grade one with her, and she had come in third place. Which was good because everybody knew Sylvia Sanders, who came in first, was the fastest girl in their grade, even faster than most of the boys. And Laurie Miller, who came in second, started running before the gun went off, which was why everybody called her a cheater.

Still, Ellie had never tried running *far*—and the car was far. It had taken them forever to walk all the way to the cabin. She didn't think she was going to be able to run fast all that way back to it without taking a break.

Bobby was running right next to her. He was crying, but silently, like when you don't want anybody to know you're crying.

Ellie wondered again what happened to the sleeping woman. Her mom told her the woman had an accident, but sometimes when her mom said "accident" she meant something else. Like when Ellie's real dad came over to the house and broke some things. Her mom and Ellie spent that night at Ellie's grandparents' house. Her mom had a bruise on her face and told Ellie she had an accident, but Ellie overheard her talking to Ellie's grandparents in the kitchen, telling them how Jacob, which was Ellie's dad's name, had hit her.

So did the sleeping woman *really* have an accident? Or did something else happen to her? Ellie wasn't sure what could have gotten her—

The monster under Bobby's bed!

Maybe it had a whole bunch of different doors in its house, and it could go through them to get to other people's bedrooms. After it left the space under Bobby's bed, it went to this woman's bedroom. It bit her or punched her or did something bad to her, and that's why she was sleeping on the porch. She was scared of going back to her bed!

Feeling proud she had solved the mystery all by herself, Ellie concentrated on running fast.

Rex was terrified as he led Tabitha and the kids down the winding road into the unknown. He was terrified he had made the wrong decision leaving the cabin. Because they were now exposed and vulnerable. They had nothing with which to protect themselves save a rusty old golf club. If the murderer caught up to them, and was well-armed, they were as good as dead.

But what could they have done instead? Remained bunkered down inside the cabin? They would have been sitting ducks.

At least now they were moving. It was only another ten minutes to the car.

Yes, that was right.

The car, safety.

Another ten minutes.

The night air on Rex's face and the adrenaline coursing through his veins was helping him to think straight. He began to rationalize the situation, dissect it, and in the process, temper the panic that had until then been dictating his thoughts and actions.

When he had first seen the dead woman on the porch, he had immediately linked her death to the disappearance of his family. The person who had gotten them had returned for Rex and those close to him.

But this was silly, wasn't it? Theoretically speaking, say his father had been responsible for the kidnappings and, presumably, murders, over the years. He had been forty-four years old in 1981. That would make him eighty-three today. If he had spent the intervening decades roughing it in the mountains, living off a meager diet with no medicine or modern accoutrements, his life expectancy would not be ideal. If not already dead, he would be frail. He had not attacked Tony and Daisy.

If someone other than his father were responsible for the kidnappings and murders, someone who had only been, say, twenty in '81, that would put him in his late fifties now. This person could very well have attacked Tony and Daisy.

Nevertheless, as Rex's panic continued to ebb, he asked himself a question that had eluded him until then.

Why did the tragic events of the past have to have anything to do with those of tonight? It had been nearly forty years since Rex's family went missing; twenty since the Ryersons went missing.

There was no connection between past and present.

The much more likely suspect in Daisy's murder, Rex decided, was her boyfriend, Tony. The guy was an asshole, that much was for sure. Did something happen that set him over the edge when they returned to their cabin? Did Daisy get a text message that made him jealous? Did she say something that pissed him off? Disagreed with him in some way? Perhaps an old argument came up, a touchy topic, money or an ex-boyfriend.

And then what? Rex wondered. Tony attacks Daisy with the knife he'd been using to dice onions? Uses it to slice open her gut? Did he take savage glee in this violence? Or did it occur in the passion of the moment? Did he immediately regret hurting her? Was he curled up on the kitchen floor in a puddle of his own tears right now?

No, Tony was a dick. He had too much machismo to ever shed a tear for a woman.

So Daisy fled, hands on her stomach to keep her innards inside, and Tony gave chase. But he had that limp. He was slow. She reached Rex's cabin first. From the time she banged on the door to the time Rex and the others were on the road, on the way to the car, no more than five minutes had passed. The longest five minutes of Rex's life, but five minutes nonetheless. Tony still hadn't caught up.

So where did that put the guy now? Had he just discovered Daisy's body? If so, he would know Rex and Tabitha and the kids had fled. He would be coming. He wouldn't let any witnesses to his crime escape.

And all this was good news.

Because they had a head start. There was no way limping Tony could catch them. Even if he went back for his truck, he wouldn't reach them before they reached the Mazda. They would be zipping down Highway 99 toward Lillooet shortly. They would be at the police station in less than an hour, safe, nightmare over—

A light flashed between the trees.

From ahead.

Rex stopped in his tracks. He felt Bobby and Ellie bump into his legs. Tabitha stopped beside him and whispered, "He's out here!"

"Shit!" Rex said, flicking off his own flashlight, plunging them into darkness.

How had Tony gotten ahead of them?

Rex squeezed the golf club tightly in his right hand. It didn't instill confidence in him. Tony would be armed with something more lethal. The knife he'd used on Daisy. Or maybe even a gun. Canada had strict gun laws on handguns, but anybody could purchase a rifle from their local Walmart.

The light was coming closer.

"Rex?" Tabitha said worriedly.

Should they duck into the forest? No, they would make too much noise, especially with Bobby and Ellie. Tony would surely hear them and catch them.

Which meant the only option was to turn around.

They couldn't return to the cabin. But if they got far enough away from Tony, they could look for a proper spot to hide.

Until when? Morning?

One step at a time.

"We have to go back," he whispered.

Tabitha was totally freaking out as she followed Rex and the kids down the dark and winding road. She clenched her jaw to prevent herself from issuing unwanted sounds as she struggled to comprehend how abruptly her world had been flipped upside down. Just a few hours before they had been sitting around the fire, roasting wieners, happy and unharassed. Now they were being pursued through the night by a vicious killer.

They rounded a bend, and Rex slowed the pace from a stealthy jog to a hurried walk. Tabitha glanced back and could no longer see the yellow light from the flashlight beam. She gave Ellie and Bobby a reassuring shoulder squeeze.

"You guys are doing great," she said, bending over to whisper in their ears.

"Where are we going, Mommy?" Ellie asked in a hushed, conspiratorial voice, almost as if she were playing a part in a movie.

Tabitha wondered the same thing.

Where was Rex taking them?

Back to the cabin?

Tabitha didn't think this was the best idea. The killer knew they were staying there. It wouldn't take him long to realize the woman might have gone there for help.

Perhaps Tabitha and Rex could hide the body, blow out the candles, and make it look as though they were all sleeping, unaware of what the killer had done.

He would leave them alone then, wouldn't he?

No, she decided immediately. He wouldn't. A pool of blood stained the porch. There was no way they could clean that up in the short time they had. There was no way the killer would miss it either.

So did they lock the doors and windows and barricade themselves inside the cabin? Until when? Morning would bring no salvation. Nobody was going to come and rescue them. Almost nobody knew they were there. The woman at the tourist center did. But why would she give them any thought? And all Vanessa knew was that they were visiting Rex's cabin somewhere in Canada. Tabitha and Ellie weren't supposed to be home until Sunday evening. Even then, Vanessa likely wouldn't get worried enough to call the police until Tuesday or Wednesday. That was more than half a week away. They couldn't hunker down in the cabin for that long with the scant food and water they had.

"Don't worry about that now, sweetie," she said in answer to her daughter's question. "Just keep up with T-Rex, and we'll get where we're going soon."

The road continued straight for the next hundred yards through the old-growth rainforest, which had been so alive and green during the day, but which was now silent and ominous. After another hundred yards, Tabitha made out the white, canted mailbox at the end of the McCleod's overgrown driveway. She pictured Rex and his brother Logan as kids running wildly for their lives from a yapping Yorkshire terrier, arms and legs browned from long days in the summer sun flapping madly, mouths pulled into rictuses of fear.

If only it was a toy dog we were running from now.

"Ow!" Bobby cried out.

Rex stopped abruptly. Tabitha did too.

"What is it?" Rex whispered between pants.

"I stubbed my toe. The one that went to the market."

"Do you want me to carry you?"

"I think I'm okay."

"Where are we going, Rex?" Tabitha asked. "We can't go back to the cabin."

"We're not." He hesitated. "We're going to *their* cabin."

"*Whose* cabin?"

"Where Tony and Daisy are staying."

"The guy chasing us?" she said in disbelief.

Rex nodded. "He didn't see us. He doesn't know we're out here."

"He will when he gets to our cabin. And you want to hide in *his* cabin? That's—"

"Not *hide*. I want to take his truck."

She blinked. "His truck?"

"Hopefully he left the keys behind. Then we can drive right out of here."

Tabitha considered this. "What if they're in his pocket?" she asked.

"Do you keep your car keys in your pocket when you're relaxing at home? Anyway, even if we don't find them, we might find one of their phones. We can call for help."

Call for help.

The wonderful warmth of hope filled her chest, and all at once she felt woozy with relief.

They had a way out of this nightmare after all!

Tabitha scooped Ellie into her arms, kissed her daughter on her button nose, and allowed herself the briefest of smiles.

"How far is it?" she asked.

8

The Crown Vic's high beams flashed on the late-model Mazda coupe parked alongside the dirt road. Frowning, Paul Harris pulled up behind it and put the patrol car in Park. Leaving the engine idling and the headlights on, he climbed out, his hand on the butt of his holstered pistol. He walked to the Mazda and peeked in the driver's side window. Empty. He continued a few feet past the vehicle's hood. In the swath of yellow cast by the Crown Vic's high beams, the road was clearly visible, including all of its starkly outlined ruts and potholes. This explained why Rex Chapman had abandoned his car here, if the Mazda was indeed his car, though he couldn't fathom to whom else it might belong.

One mystery solved, Paul thought sardonically. *And one new dilemma.*

Because without a four-wheel-drive vehicle, he wasn't going to be able to drive down the road either.

Tugging his pack of Marlboro's and lime-green Bic lighter from his hip pocket, he lit up, rocked back on his heels, and studied the overcast night sky.

Although the Lillooet Country's boundaries were only loosely defined by cartographers, anyone who lived in the area would tell you they encompassed the land within the Fraser Canyon from Church Creek and Big Car Ferry in the north, to a spot known as the Big Slide on Highway 12 south of Lillooet. They'd probably agree the summit of Cayoosh

Pass near Duffey Lake on Highway 99 was the western "border," if you wanted to call it that, and the summit of Pavilion Mountain Road the eastern one.

Pavilion Lake was located just inside this northeastern demarcator, putting it in Paul's jurisdiction.

Paul had first come up here to investigate the Chapman family's disappearance in 1981, and again to investigate the Peterson's and Ryerson's subsequent disappearances in 1987 and 1998 respectively. Over the years he fished on Pavilion Lake and hiked in Marble Canyon. His most recent recreational visit, however, must have been...well, it was before the Ryersons went missing. So that would make it probably twenty years or so ago. Maybe even twenty-five. He would have been in his thirties.

Jesus Christ, where did the time go?

Paul took a drag on his smoke, his eyes going back to the derelict road.

Pretty much undriveable, he thought. A good enough reason to turn around and head home. Then again, undriveable didn't mean unwalkable. How far was it to the Chapman's cabin? Three kilometers? How long would that take on foot? Twenty minutes? The rain had stopped for the moment, and it was a pleasant enough evening. Walking never hurt anybody. In fact, the exercise would do him good.

Taking a final drag on the smoke, Paul flicked the butt away and returned to the cruiser. He killed the engine and retrieved the Streamlight tactical flashlight from the glove box, which was more powerful than the smaller version he kept in the holder on his duty belt. He clicked it on and started down the poorly kept road. Soon tall conifers and broad-leaf deciduous trees loomed above him, their shadowed boughs blocking out the sky. The air smelled of wet soil and pine needles and wildflowers. Gravel crunched beneath his footsteps, and he did his best to avoid the water-filled potholes.

Tucking the flashlight beneath an armpit, he lit up another cigarette. He would miss his police work when he retired in two years' time, he mused, cold, wet nights included. He would only be sixty years old, but he wanted to spend more time with Nancy and Zeph. Go camping on the weekends. See more of the province. Hell, maybe even more of the country. Travel like that was never an option when you were on duty seven days a week.

Paul would have preferred to spend the rest of his days in the police station's constable quarters. He had lived there his entire life. But the old have to make way for the new; that was how the cookie crumbled. If his son Joseph had followed in his footsteps and became the next police chief, Paul and Nancy might have remained put. But Joseph had not followed in his footsteps. Not even close. He had chosen to walk the other side of the law.

Paul often wondered where he'd gone wrong with the boy. He had been a good father, he thought. Certainly better than some of the other fathers in town whose kids had turned out all right. So why did Joseph turn out so rotten?

Drugs were the easy answer. Joseph got into them after high school when he went to work as a snowboard instructor at Whistler Blackcomb. A lot of partying went on there among the staff, many of whom were backpackers from as far away as Europe and Australia. Most kids experimented with drugs at one point or another in their adolescence. Some decided they weren't for them and steered clear in the future. Some continued to use them recreationally. And some, unfortunately, developed a habit. Joseph got a taste for heroin. Within a year of leaving home he was nearly unrecognizable from his old self. Gaunt, pale skin, puffy eyes, pinpoint pupils. Paul confronted him during the Easter weekend when he came back to visit, which was probably the wrong tactic, because Joseph never returned again. Instead, he turned his efforts to building himself a pretty extensive criminal record. Then he went off the radar for six years before turning up in the news as one of two suspects charged with a string of burglaries in the Okanagan Valley. He was found guilty and spent the following two years in prison. Over the next decade he rose through the ranks of a well-known criminal gang until he was sent behind bars once more for cocaine trafficking, and then again, most recently, for smuggling weapons across the border.

If his son ever wanted to turn his life around, Paul would be there for him, but this seemed like wishful thinking, and Paul had long ago decided he would not waste any more of his time worrying about someone who clearly did not worry about anybody but himself.

A few minutes and another cigarette later, Paul came upon the Ryerson's driveway. It was completely overgrown with weeds and scrub and bush. Paul only knew it was there from memory. He played the flashlight beam over the trees before stopping on a dilapidated white slab of wood nailed to the trunk of a cedar. The black, hand-painted letters spelled THE RYERSONS. He aimed the beam in the direction he knew the cabin to be. He couldn't see it through the thick vegetation.

Ahead, down the road, he spotted a flash of light.

In the next instant it disappeared.

Despite Paul standing statue-still for a full minute, it didn't return.

His imagination? The reflection of his flashlight beam off the lake, or an old road sign?

Someone else out here with him?

Who? Rex Chapman? But why would he be skulking through the woods at this hour?

Paul resumed walking. The Chapman's cottage was still more than a kilometer away, and suddenly he wanted to get this courtesy call over with as quickly as possible.

9

"There it is," Rex said, pointing to the rusty red pickup truck parked out in front of the Williams' dilapidated cabin. They were standing fifty feet away from it, to the side of the road, hidden in the shadows of the trees.

"Are we going to drive it?" Bobby asked.

"If I can find keys, bud," he said.

"It looks scary," Ellie said.

"It's not scary, sweetie," Tabitha said. "It's just a truck."

"It *looks* scary, like a ghost truck."

"You and Bobby are going to stay here with your mom," Rex told her. "I'll go check it out, make sure there are no ghosts. When the coast is clear, I'll wave you over. Got that?"

"Look in the back seat too," Ellie said. "That's where I sit."

"Will do," he said. Hunching over, Rex hurried toward the truck, trying to make as little noise as possible. Nobody should be in the cabin. Only Tony and Daisy had been in the pickup truck when it passed them on the road. There were no other vehicles parked out here. Still, too much was at stake right now not to be extra cautious.

He stopped at the truck and tried the passenger door. It was unlocked! He swung it back with a groan of metal and hopped up on the bench seat. The cab smelled of engine oil and grease. No keys dangled in the ignition. They weren't behind either of the sun visors. He checked beneath the seats and in the glove box with little hope. If Tony had left the keys in the truck, it would have been for convenience's sake. He wouldn't be hiding them, not out here.

Unsurprisingly, all he discovered was an empty Mountain Dew can, the vehicle's logbook, and some tools.

He exited the truck. Looking back the way he'd come, he couldn't see Tabitha or the kids. It was too dark. Regardless, he knew they were there, watching him. He waved them over.

Shadows moved. Then Tabitha materialized, holding kids' hands.

"Did you find them?" she whispered when they reached him.

"No," he said. "They must be inside."

Her face fell as she looked at the cabin. He looked too. It featured a shingled roof, clapboard siding, and an overgrown garden. Candlelight illuminated the windowpanes.

"I'll go get them," he added. "You guys wait in the truck."

Sitting in the front of the pickup truck, behind the steering wheel, Ellie snuggled closer against her mom's warm body, breathing in the familiar smell of her perfume, which made her feel safer.

She wished they had never come to T-Rex's stupid cabin. It had been fun for a bit, but now it wasn't fun at all. She would much rather be back in her house, playing with her Barbie dolls on the carpet in her bedroom. She had just gotten Barbie's Dreamhorse for being good when her mom had to run errands on the weekends and Ness had to look after her. The horse could walk and nod either yes or no when you asked it questions. You could also feed it the carrots that had come in the package (but not real carrots, she'd discovered). And when she got bored of the horsey, she could play with her Lite Brite. Right now she was making a picture of a train, but she was missing some of the pegs to finish it. They might be under her bed. That's where everything that didn't want to be found seemed to go. Last time she had been under there she had recovered two of her black-and-white penguin bath toys.

"I want to go home," she murmured.

"We'll be going home soon, sweetie," her mom said, kissing the top of her head.

"Can I have ice cream when we get there?"

"Sure."

"In a cone?"

"Okay."

Her mom sounded strange, and Ellie looked up. Her face was sad, and she was crying.

"What's wrong, Mommy?" she asked, concerned.

"Nothing, hon." She kissed the top of Ellie's head again. "I'm happy."

"But you're crying."

"It's happy-crying."

Ellie frowned. Happy-crying?

"Like when it rains when it's sunny out?" she asked.

"Yes, like that. You're such a smart little girl."

"Smarter than Bobby?"

"You're both very smart."

"But I'm smarter because I'm older—"

"Ellie!"

"What?"

"You know what."

Ellie didn't. Really, she didn't. But she stayed quiet anyway.

Her mom might start angry-crying, and she didn't want that.

❖ ❖ ❖

When Rex stepped inside the Williams' cabin, he expected to find evidence of a violent struggle in the form of overturned chairs, splattered blood, and a general air of helter-skelter. To the contrary, however, the scene that greeted him seemed perfectly innocuous. A half-dozen candles flickered silently, while embers glowed warmly in the stone fireplace. The sturdy log pine furniture was all upright and where it should be. The rustic décor—everything from the heavy curtains to the well-worn rugs that covered the knotty wooden floorboards incorporated wildlife motifs—appeared undamaged. A bear-sculpture end table held a spread of crackers, cheese, olives, and dips. On the dining table, a bottle of wine chilled in an ice bucket, next to two half-filled champagne flutes and a deck of Bicycle playing cards, dealt into two hands.

All the trappings of a romantic evening, Rex thought—so what the hell happened to change that?

He didn't waste time speculating. Instead, he moved quickly through the room, eyes darting to and fro, each passing second feeling like a knife twisting deeper into his gut.

If he'd been wrong to come here...

If Tony caught up to them...

Shoving aside these thoughts, Rex entered a narrow hallway. The first door on the right opened to a small bedroom. The single bed was neatly made, not slept in. A dated Tom Clancy hardback novel, a bookmark protruding from the pages, sat expectantly on the night table, as if waiting for the absent reader to return and pick up again where he or she had left off.

He didn't see keys or a phone anywhere, so he moved on.

The next room was locked.

Rex drove his shoulder into the door to no avail. He looked up. All of the interior walls rose only three-quarters of the distance to the open rafter ceiling. The unusual architectural decision was likely made so the heat from the fireplace could warm every room in the wintertime.

In any event, it would allow him access to the room.

Rex proceeded to the kitchen. Vegetables waiting to be sliced and diced sat in a bowl on the roughly hewn countertop, along with a package of croutons, a head of lettuce, and a jar of pasta sauce. A glance inside the pot on one of the stovetop burners revealed a clump of cooked spaghetti in about an inch of boiling water.

He clicked off the gas to prevent a fire, then grabbed a chair from the set around the drop leaf table. Back at the locked room, he set the chair against the wall and stepped onto the seat. His head was now level with the top of the partition, though he couldn't see over it. Tucking the flashlight inside his jacket, he hooked his arms over the top beam and tried to hoist himself up, kicking his legs feebly. This didn't work, and he touched his feet back down on the chair seat. On his second attempt he placed one foot on the brass doorknob, using it as a step.

This time his head and shoulders cleared the partition, and he peeked into the locked room.

10

"Hello?" Paul called, sticking his head inside the Chapman's cabin. "Rex? Rex Chapman?" he added, not expecting an answer. Empty residences emitted their own uniquely forbidden vibe, and he was feeling that vibe right now.

Paul turned around, looking down again at Daisy Butterfield, who lay in a pool of thick blood on the porch. When he'd removed the quilt that had covered her a few moments ago, he'd expected to discover the body of Rex Chapman, or his lady friend. Not poor Daisy, who Paul had known since she was a kid selling lemonade from a handmade stand out in front her house on Hangman's Lane. She left Lillooet after high school, earned a teaching certificate from the University of Victoria, and found work in a private school in West Vancouver. When her mother, Darla Butterfield, had a stroke four years ago (widowed a year or so before that when her husband, Joe, died of natural causes in his sleep), Daisy returned to Lillooet to become her fulltime nurse while also teaching at the elementary school.

Paul pulled his eyes away from Daisy and surveyed the wet, black night, fighting the urge to flee back to the patrol car. It wasn't finding the body of someone he knew that was spooking him so badly. It wasn't even that the body had been opened up like a can of beans, though this was certainly unnerving. It was the fact the body was on the doorstep to Rex Chapman's cabin, where Rex Chapman's family had disappeared so mysteriously almost forty years earlier.

Could that be a coincidence? If so, it was one hell of a big one, and a lifetime of policing had made Paul cynical enough to not put much stock in coincidences.

Which left...what?

A sicko playing games?

A copycat killer?

Tony Lyons?

Paul focused on that last thought. *Tony Lyons*. Sure—why jump to outlandish conclusions when nine times out of ten the culprit of a domestic murder was a spited spouse or lover.

Tony Lyons had wandered into Lillooet a little over a year ago, and he'd been keeping company with Daisy for maybe half that time. Paul had taken an immediate disliking to the man. For starters, Tony had one of those bulldog faces that made him look as if at any moment he might hit someone. And his terse personality didn't help his image. Unlike the majority of residents of Lillooet who were more than happy to stop and have a yak with Paul when they saw him around town, Tony never offered a word or even a nod of recognition when they crossed paths. This had led Paul to believe the man might be prejudiced toward cops, perhaps due to a criminal past, and so he ran Tony's name through the National Canadian Police Information Center, discovering he had a laundry list of misdemeanor convictions, as well as three felonies for aggravated animal cruelty, mail and wire fraud, and sexual assault.

Which made him a prime suspect in what happened here tonight.

Moreover, Paul thought, Tony would be somewhere in his mid-fifties, which, in 1981, would put him in his late teens.

Plenty old enough to commit kidnapping and murder.

"Jesus and Mother Mary," Paul mumbled. He set the flashlight on the porch railing and took his cell phone from a pocket. British Columbia contracted policing responsibilities in small villages and rural towns, and even some of the larger cities, to the Royal Canadian Mounted Police. The nearest detachment was in Whistler. They could be here inside of three hours.

Before Paul dialed a single number, however, a whining, buzzing noise from behind the cabin froze him stiff. It sounded like an electrical tool, a circular saw, perhaps, or a drill.

It lasted for maybe two or three seconds, then abruptly stopped.

Swallowing the hard knot of fear suddenly clogging his throat, Paul shoved the phone away and snatched the Streamlight from the railing. Gripping it as you would an ice pick, he held it beneath his pistol so his hands were back to back and the flashlight and weapon were aimed in the same direction—toward the back of the cabin.

"Tony? That you?" he asked, working saliva into his mouth. "It's Paul here. Police. I'm armed. Best thing to do would be to come out with your hands up."

Paul forced his legs to move, taking one cautious step after another. He stopped at the corner of the cabin. He listened. He didn't hear anything aside from his quick, susurrate breathing.

Now or never.

He stepped around the corner, sweeping the flashlight and pistol from side to side.

Nobody there.

He had not imagined that sound—

Bzzzzzzzzzzzzzzzzzzzzz

Looking up, Paul's eyes bulged and he opened his mouth to scream, but a black terror the likes of which he had never experienced muted his voice, and all he issued before the attack came was a pitiful, wheezing, "*No...*"

11

Bobby kept his eyes glued to the pickup truck's window, which looked directly toward the rundown cabin. On other more normal days, he would have found it really weird sitting next to Ellie's mom in such a tight space like the front of a car. In fact, he couldn't think of many times when it was just Ellie's mom, Ellie, and him, without his dad around too. There were nights like when Ellie's mom tucked them in at bedtime, but he didn't have to speak to her then because he always pretended he was already asleep. He didn't have to speak to her now either...but the other really weird thing was that he sort of wanted to speak to her. He felt sick on his inside—not like when he had a cold; more like when he knew he was going to get in trouble for something—and he thought maybe by talking to her, that sickness might go away a little.

He looked down at his hands fidgeting in his lap. "Ellie's Mom?" he said, not knowing what else to call her. He didn't have a nickname for her, like Ellie did with his dad.

"Yes, Bobby?" He felt her eyes on him, though he wouldn't meet them.

"Is Barry coming after us?" he asked.

"Barry? Who's Barry, sweetheart?"

"The man who crashed his car in the woods."

"What man, Bobby?"

"He crashed his car a long time ago. My dad showed me

the car, remember? It's all broken and everything. So maybe Barry couldn't get home and is still in the woods?"

"I think your dad was just telling you a story, Bobby."

"But I saw the car!"

"Didn't your dad say it was close to a hundred years old? That means whoever once owned it—this Barry—died a long time ago."

"Is he in heaven, Mommy?" Ellie asked.

"If he was a good man, yes," her mom replied.

"Is he watching us right now?"

"I don't think so."

"Why not?"

"He probably has other things he wants to do."

"And it's nighttime!" Bobby told her. "He can't see in the dark!"

"Maybe he had special glasses."

"He doesn't."

"You don't know that. You're not God!"

"You're not either!"

"Guys!" Ellie's mom said, sounding more scared than angry. "Quiet!"

"When's my dad coming back?" Bobby asked after a moment.

"Soon, hon."

"What if he doesn't find the keys?" Ellie asked.

"He will."

"But what if he doesn't?"

"We'll think of something."

Bobby tried to think of something himself. They couldn't walk back to his car because Barry—despite what Ellie's mom said, Bobby still thought it was Barry coming after them—would catch them. They couldn't stay in the truck either because Barry would probably check it. Bad guys always found where the good guys were hiding. So they'd have to run into the woods, and this was the last thing he wanted to do. Because bears lived in the woods, and they came out at nighttime, and they might eat all of them, and this was way worse than what Barry would do to them. He might only tie them up and say mean things, like he was going to cut off their heads. But he probably wouldn't do this, because he would go to jail—

Bobby sucked back a breath as a new thought struck him.

"What's wrong, honey?" Ellie's mom asked.

Bobby looked directly at her for the first time. Her eyes were wide, and she looked really pretty, even in the dark. She always looked pretty, and she always smelled nice too.

"Maybe the monster's following us?" he said.

"There's no such thing—"

"It's not!" Ellie said, cutting off her mom.

"Why not?" Bobby demanded.

"Because," she stated.

"Because isn't an answer," he said, using the comeback Marty Phillips from school always used.

"Because it can't live outside from under the bed!"

"You don't know that!"

"Do too!"

"It can live anywhere it wants."

"*You* don't know that—"

"Ellie, *enough*," her mom said.

"But Bobby started it!"

"*Enough!*" She lowered her voice. "We need to be quiet, okay? So…no more talking until Rex comes back."

"What if he doesn't come back for an hour?"

"Ellie, I'm not telling you again."

Bobby heard Ellie huff, like she always did when she got in trouble. But she was smart enough to stay quiet. Otherwise, she might get grounded for a week, or maybe a month. Her mom was a lot stricter than his dad was.

A short time later Ellie said, "Mommy?"

"Yes?"

"What did I earn for being good today?"

"My affection."

"I don't want that!"

"Well, that's what you got."

"Mommy, you're not my friend anymore."

"Ellie, shush—" Suddenly she sat up straight, alarmed.

Bobby heard something too. A loud bang. It came from inside the cabin.

"What was that?" Bobby asked, forgetting that he wasn't allowed to talk.

"I don't know," Ellie's mom whispered. "Shit!"

"Mom!" Ellie said. "You swore—"

"Bobby, open your door. Let me out." She reached in front of him and opened the door. Cold night air blew inside.

She slipped over his lap, stumbled as she climbed out, but then she was standing on the ground, looking in at them.

"Mommy, don't go!" Ellie cried.

Bobby wished the same thing, but he was too surprised by everything happening to speak.

"I'm not going to go for long, sweetie. I promise. I just have to check if Rex is okay. You two stay here. Keep your heads down, below the windows. Keep the doors closed and locked. I'll be right back."

Before either Bobby or Ellie could reply, she slapped the lock knob down and closed the door. Through the window, she pointed to the ground and mouthed the word, "Down."

Bobby ducked his head. Turning it sideways, he saw Ellie was ducked low on the seat as well.

"Maybe you're right," she whispered to him.

"About what?" he asked.

"The monster. It got out from under the bed, and now it got your dad."

Tabitha dashed toward the cabin, instinct dictating her actions, telling her that only two things mattered: helping Rex and protecting the kids. There was no hierarchy to these imperatives. They both simply had to be done.

She burst into the cabin, stealth be damned. Her eyes took in the rustic room in a heartbeat.

Deserted.

"Rex?" she hissed urgently.

"Tabs?" his voice came back from the hallway.

She skirted through the room. Rex stood next to a chair facing a closed door. He appeared shocked and skittish.

"What's going on?" she demanded, some of her fear ebbing at the sight of him unharmed. "What was that noise?"

"That was me," he said. "I'm trying to get into this room."

"What's in it?"

He seemed about to answer, then shook his head. He brought his knee to his chest and drove his foot into the door. The bang seemed to shake the cabin. Wood cracked and splintered.

"Rex!" she said. "Quiet!"

He kicked the door once more.

It burst open in a firework of splinters.

Rex entered the room first, Tabitha following on his heels, curiosity mixing with dread. Two overnight bags sat open on a double bed. A lamp fashioned from snowshoes and garlanded with pinecones stood on a night table. A dresser/mirror combo lined one wall, next to a stiff-looking armchair.

And a body lay facedown on the floor, surrounded by blood.

"Oh!" Tabitha gasped, her hands going to her mouth in surprise.

Rex played the flashlight over the face.

"It's Tony," he said woodenly.

Tabitha's mind spun. "But how…? Then who…?"

"I don't know," he said flatly. He went to the body, careful to avoid stepping in the blood. He crouched and felt for a pulse.

"Is he alive?" Tabitha asked, knowing the answer.

Rex shook his head in the negative. He patted down the rear pockets of the man's jeans. Then, with some effort, he rolled the deadweight body onto its back.

A monstrous incision opened his belly from side to side, nearly identical to the one Daisy had suffered.

Tabitha felt momentarily faint.

Rex rifled through all of the man's pockets, swearing loudly.

"They're not here!" he added, referring to the truck keys.

"They have to be somewhere!" Tabitha said, fighting her ballooning panic. *We need to go, we need to go, we need to go*, she kept thinking over and over while struggling to understand who had been out on the road if Tony had been lying here dead the entire time. "They must be in another room—"

"I've checked everywhere!"

"Phones?"

Rex shook his head, running a hand through his hair. He was about to get back to his feet when something in his demeanor changed. He stiffened and became solely focused on the body. He directed the flashlight beam at the smiling, lipless wound. "What in God's name...?" He extended his hand.

"Rex!" she cried. "What are you doing?"

His hand hovered above the gash for a moment before he plunged it into the bloody tangle of organs.

He's gone crazy! she thought. *He's lost his mind!*

"Rex!" she repeated, though the word was so hoarse with dismay she could barely hear it herself.

Rex removed his hand and held high something shiny pinched between his red fingers.

The truck keys.

12

Rex stared in shock at the bloody keys. Someone was playing with them. Whoever had killed Tony and Daisy, the jackass was playing with them. He knew Rex and Tabitha and the kids were here on the lake. Somehow he'd known they would head to the Williams' cabin. Because the keys weren't for the cops to eventually discover. Why would the cops care about a set of keys to a rusty old pickup truck? The only people the keys mattered to were Rex and present company so they could escape—and the sick bastard knew this!

"What's going on, Rex?" Tabitha asked in a voice near hysterics. "Why would someone do that with the keys? He must know we need them." She was backing out of the room, her face a ghostly white in the backsplash of light from the flashlight. "This is fucked. This is so fucked, Rex. He knows! *He knows we're here!*"

Rex wasn't going to argue that point. He snapped to his feet—and stepped in the puddle of blood. He spun in a pirouette before grappling one of the bed's end posts, reaffirming his balance. "Shit!" Watching where he stepped next, he exited the room. He gripped Tabitha's hand and led her quickly from the cabin.

For a moment his heart seemed to stop when he didn't see Bobby or Ellie in the cab of the pickup truck, but he breathed again when he opened the passenger door and saw them crouched in the foot wells.

"Daddy!" Bobby said, the terror on his face morphing into joy.

"Up on the seat," he said, already rounding the hood.

He slid behind the steering wheel at the same time Tabitha climbed in the passenger door.

"I'm squished!" Ellie protested, as she was pressed tightly between Rex and Bobby.

Rex barely heard her above his pulse thumping inside his head. He jammed the key in the ignition and turned it. The engine coughed, then turned over.

"Are we going home now?" Ellie asked.

"Yeah, honey," Tabitha said, her voice tight with emotion. "Hold tight."

Rex flicked on the headlights, then took a moment to familiarize himself with the truck's controls. He engaged the brake pedal, depressed the clutch, and shifted the stick into first gear. The engine revved and the truck jumped forward. Startled, he let off the clutch. Gears crunched. The truck lurched to a stop and stalled.

"What happened?" Bobby asked.

Rex looked at Tabitha. "Can you drive a manual?"

She shook her head. "Try again! You can fly a jumbo jet, you can drive a silly truck!"

Rex started the vehicle a second time and managed to shift into first without popping the clutch.

"Yay, Dad!" Bobby said as they chugged forward.

"Faster!" Ellie said.

"Shush, guys!" Tabitha said. "Let him concentrate!"

Rex knew he was revving too high. He clutched in and gassed off and shifted from first to second. Gears ground, but not too badly, and then the truck was picking up speed along the dark road.

"Piece of cake!" he said, grinning riotously. He accelerated.

"Not too fast, Rex!" Tabitha cautioned.

He shifted to third. The speedometer needle crept past forty.

With the headlights carving a tunnel through the darkness, Rex kept his eyes glued to the gravel road, doing his best to avoid the worst of the ruts and potholes. Even so, the truck was bumping and shaking on its worn out suspension hard enough to rival some of the worst turbulence he had experienced in the skies.

He eased a little off the accelerator.

"Thank you," Tabitha said, and a quick glance in her direction revealed she was bracing her arms against the roof and the dash. Bobby and Ellie were hugging each other so neither flew off the seat.

Rex slowed a little more.

"Sorry," he said. "Just want to get the hell out of here."

"Let's get out of here in one piece," she said.

Rex realized he was as rigid as a statue. He exhaled and felt his entire body sag.

"You guys okay?" he said casually, wanting to signal a return to normality.

"Yeah," Bobby said, letting go of Ellie.

"Yeah," Ellie agreed, pushing Bobby's legs off her. "But can we change cars when we get to the other one? I like it better."

"In two minutes, sweetie," Tabitha said.

Remaining in third gear, Rex navigated the beat-up road with general success, tapping the brake and gas pedals when needing to avoid the hazards.

"Cabin should be coming up on the left," he said.

A few moments later, beyond a phalanx of gray tree trunks, the cabin came into view—at least the cabin's windows, backlit as they were with the yellow glow of candlelight.

"Watch out!" Tabitha cried.

Rex returned his attention to the road and saw two figures crossing it, one standing, the other lying on his or her side—being dragged? The standing figure spun around just as

Rex swerved hard to the right.

The truck roared into the forest. Vegetation slapped the windshield. The steering wheel spun loose from Rex's grip. He stamped the brake with his foot, though it was too late. The truck crashed into a tree and came to a bone-crushing halt.

◆ ◆ ◆

In his dream Rex was in the Captain's seat of the doomed Airbus 320 that would crash into the French Alps in nine hours' time. As the large aircraft climbed into the sky after taking off from JFK airport, he flicked on the autopilot to allow him to scan for other aircrafts in near proximity. He set the altimeters to standard pressure and turned off the landing lights. After confirmation from the high-altitude controller that no pilots in front of him had experienced turbulence, he switched off the seat-belt sign.

Rex turned to his First Officer in the seat next to his. "Good weekend, Freddy?" he asked.

Frederick shrugged. "Didn't do anything special."

"Jeanne's well?" Jeanne was his wife of close to two years now.

"She's fine." He seemed about to add something, but didn't. "How are you and Tabitha?"

"Good. We're very good, actually."

"She seemed nice."

"She liked you too," Rex said, referring to the time the three of them had a drink at a bar in Sea-Tac Airport.

Below them, New York City disappeared as they coasted out over the Atlantic Ocean. Soon they wouldn't have any ground-based navigation facilities to rely on, so they performed the final checks to make sure the computer was accurately tracking their position.

With this done, Rex was going to phone the cabin crew on the upper deck to bring them coffee when Fred blurted,

"She's leaving me."

Rex blinked. "Jeanne? Ah, shit, Freddy."

"She's met someone."

"I'm sorry, man."

"Some fucking vet. Not even a real doctor."

Rex noticed the First Officer clenching and unclenching his right fist.

"You'll be fine," he said. "There are a lot of other women out there."

"She's kicking me out. She wants to keep the house we bought together."

"There's no working things through with her?"

Frederick shook his head. "She says we don't have anything in common anymore. She says she's bored. She actually told me that. The bitch." He was still clenching and unclenching his fist.

"Hey, Freddy—you okay?"

The First Officer looked at him. "What do you think, man? My wife is leaving me."

"Yeah, but I mean… You want to take some time off to deal with it?"

He barked a laugh. "You don't trust me up here with you?"

Rex shook his head. "I just mean—why not take some time off? Go on a vacation or something. Clear your mind."

"Jesus, Rex. I'm not going to fly the plane into a goddamn mountain."

"Well, I'm here if you want to talk."

"Thanks."

This was the conversation Rex and Frederick had verbatim a week before Frederick took his life, along with the other one hundred fifty-nine passengers on board Flight 2023.

Which raised the haunting question: Had Rex indeed been derelict in his duty as Captain by not reporting this conversation? Rex had asked himself this a thousand times since the crash, and the conclusion he had come to was that, no, he didn't believe so. He didn't know then that his First Officer had suffered previous episodes of depression. In fact, before that day, Freddy had never displayed any odd or depressed behavior whatsoever. To Rex, and the entire flight crew, he had always been a happily married twenty-seven year old doing a job he loved doing. Everyone was entitled to feeling down now and then. Frederick, he'd thought, was just having a down period.

Someone began banging on the flight deck door, shouting to be let in. Suddenly Rex became aware of screaming and pandemonium in the cabin. Then he realized Frederick had started the unscheduled descent that would kill them all. His first thoughts: *It's too early! We're still over the ocean!*

"Fred!" he said, his stomach dropping. "Don't do this!"

"No can do, Captain."

Rex tried to pull back on his yoke to gain altitude, but he found he couldn't move his arms.

"Fred!" he croaked. "Don't do this!"

The aircraft continued its eighty-degree death-plunge, accelerating, corkscrewing, nose rocking. The white clouds parted. The horizon was nowhere to be seen. Just the ocean, sparkling blue, coming at them far too fast.

So this is what it feels like to know you're moments away from dying.

An image of Bobby flashed in Rex's mind, and Tabitha and Ellie, and then—

Ellie's head hurt just as bad as the time she was riding her bicycle without a helmet and lost her balance and swerved into a telephone pole. She not only smacked her head into the pole, but also fell off her bike, skinning her knees and palms.

She almost started crying now, but she knew that probably wouldn't be a good idea. The monster would hear her and eat her. Maybe if she stayed quiet it would just leave her alone and go away.

But what if it didn't?

What if it was coming for her right this moment?

She opened her eyes. She was lying on top of Bobby on the truck's seat. When they crashed she must have hit her head on the dashboard and bounced back onto the seat again. No wonder her mom always told her to wear her seatbelt.

Her mom.

Ellie looked up and saw her mom slumped forward, her head resting against the dashboard.

"Mommy," she whispered. "Mommy, wake up."

She didn't.

Ellie tugged her sleeve. "Mommy!"

Why wasn't she waking up?

Ellie turned and saw T-Rex. He was slumped forward too, his body draped over the steering wheel. The windshield above his head was cracked. It looked like a big spider web.

Ellie didn't think he was going to wake up, so she pushed herself off Bobby and shook his shoulder. "Bobby! Bobby!"

Bobby's eyes opened. He looked at her dazedly. He felt a bump on his forehead and made a face like he was going to cry.

"Don't cry!" she said. "It will hear us!"

Now he saw her, and his crybaby face became worried. "You mean the monster?"

Ellie nodded.

"Did you see it?" he whispered.

She nodded again. "Did you?"

"Not really."

"Me either," she admitted. "Should we check?"

"Check?"

"See if it's waiting for us?"

"I don't want to."

Ellie sat a bit taller and peeked over the dashboard.

The truck's headlights were still on, illuminating the green-black forest. She realized she was facing the wrong direction. The road was behind them. She turned around and looked out the back window. The road was right there, not far away.

And in the red glow of the taillights she saw the monster.

It was crouched over the person lying on the road, unmoving. Ellie didn't know what it was doing, and she couldn't really see anything more than its big black outline, but it frightened her terribly.

"Do you see it?" Bobby asked.

"Yes," she breathed.

"Is it coming?"

"No."

"What's it doing?"

"Just sitting there." She had a new thought. "Maybe it's eating the other person!"

"Let me see!"

Bobby pushed up beside her. He gasped. "Is that person dead?"

"I don't know."

"We need to tell my dad." He shook T-Rex. "Dad! Dad! The monster's eating someone! Dad...?"

"He's sleeping like my mom," Ellie stated.

"Why won't he wake up?"

"I don't know."

Bobby looked back at the monster. "What should we do?"

"We need to help the person."

"How?"

"We need to scare the monster away."

"How?"

Ellie was thinking. She didn't want to get out of the truck, because then the monster might get her and eat her for dessert. She could yell. Tell it to shoo like you do to barking dogs. But it might not listen to her because she was just a little girl.

"Do you know how to use the horn?" she asked suddenly.

"What horn?" Bobby asked.

"The car horn."

They both looked at the steering wheel.

"My dad's in the way," Bobby said.

"You can reach under him and push the button."

Bobby frowned. "What button?"

"The horn button."

"You do it," he said.

"He's your dad!"

"So? You're closer."

Frowning, Ellie stuck her arm under T-Rex's chest. She felt the hard plastic of the circular steering wheel. Wasn't the horn button right in the middle of it? Her hand followed a spoke until she felt a smaller circle. She pressed it.

Beep!

Ellie jumped in surprise.

"It heard!" Bobby said. "Honk again!"

She pressed the button a second time.

Beeeeeeeeeeeeeeep!

"It's standing up!" Bobby said.

"Is it running away?"

"No! It's coming to us!"

"To get us?"

"I think so!"

Ellie pressed the horn again, holding it for several seconds.

T-Rex groaned.

Ellie let go of the button. "Your dad's waking up!"

"So's your mom!"

Ellie glanced at her mom, and she was indeed sitting up, rubbing her head.

"Mommy!" she cried.

"Daddy!" Bobby cried.

With a groan, T-Rex slumped back in his seat. Blood covered his face, and the whites of his eyes seemed very bright in the darkness.

"It's coming, Mommy!" Ellie jabbed her finger at the back window.

The monster had stopped and was just standing there, staring at them.

Her mom frowned strangely at Ellie, like she didn't even know who she was!

"Mommy, look!"

The monster turned and disappeared into the night.

"We need to get to the cabin before he comes back," Rex said quietly but urgently. He had gotten out of the pickup truck and now stood in the forest, peering into the cab.

Tabitha was thinking the same thing. Whoever that man was, he had already killed two people, possibly three, and they needed to return to the cabin ASAP until they figured out what the hell they were going to do.

She shoved open her door, the movement causing pain to flare where she'd struck her head in the crash. Grimacing, she climbed out, her jellied legs nearly collapsing beneath her.

"Come on, Ellie," she said, reaching for her daughter. "Give me your hand."

They met Rex and Bobby back on the road. Rex shone the Maglite on the person lying unmoving on his stomach on the wet mud and gravel.

"Jesus, it's a *cop*!" he exclaimed.

"What's he doing out here?" Tabitha asked. Then with a surge of hope: "Could he know about the maniac? Did he come to help? Are there others?"

Rex didn't reply, and the deep silence of the night seemed to answer that last question.

"Is he dead?" Bobby asked timidly.

"Don't look at him," Rex said.

"Bobby, come here," Tabitha said. When the boy joined her, she turned him and Ellie around so they faced the forest.

"Why can't I look, Mommy?" Ellie asked.

"You don't need to," she said simply.

Tabitha heard Rex roll the police officer onto his back. She glanced over her shoulder. The man was in his late fifties, with a lived-in face and a rather large nose. His Eisenhower patrol jacket, zipped to the neck, had been torn open across the abdomen and appeared to be stained with blood.

Rex checked for a pulse and said, "He's alive!"

Tabitha said, "What should we do?"

"Take the kids to the cabin. I'll be right behind you."

"We're not leaving you—"

"Go! I'll be right behind you."

"Guys, come on," she said, ushering Ellie and Bobby along the road. She could see the candlelit windows of the cabin blinking in and out from behind the trunks of the trees they passed. They had been moving at a swift trot, but when they reached the driveway Tabitha's nerve left her, and she led Ellie and Bobby at a full sprint until they reached the rickety porch. The woman's body, she saw in horror, was no longer covered by the quilt. Thankfully the kids didn't immediately notice this in the dark, and she got them inside before they did.

"What if the monster comes back here too?" Ellie asked, her cheeks flushed.

"That wasn't a monster, sweetie," Tabitha said, trying to catch her breath. "It was just a bad man."

"Do you promise?"

"Monsters aren't real."

"This one was."

"No it wasn't. Now I want you and Bobby to go upstairs and...get under your beds."

"That's where the monster lives!" Ellie protested.

"Ellie, for the last time, monsters aren't real!" Tabitha clamped her mouth shut, knowing this was an argument she wasn't going to win. "Now listen to me, young lady, you and Bobby go upstairs and, well, just get in your beds if you won't go under them. But be very quiet. Because if the bad man does come back here, he might want to hurt you. So the best thing you can do is to go upstairs and not make any noise. Do you understand me?"

She nodded silently.

"Bobby?"

"It's dark up there."

"You have your little flashlight, don't you?"

He nodded, pulling from his pocket his keychain flashlight.

"Good," she said. "You can turn that on if it's too dark."

Suddenly Ellie burst into tears. She wrapped her arms around Tabitha's legs in a hug. "I don't want to leave you, Mommy!"

"Oh, baby, hush, hush," Tabitha said, crouching. "Look, I don't think the man is coming back here. And Rex is with the policeman. And the policeman has a radio, and a gun, so we're going to be okay. I just need you to go hide for me until help comes. Okay?"

Ellie sniffed, rubbing her eyes.

"Okay, sweetie?"

"Okay."

"Good. Now go on. I'll come up and check on you two shortly."

Tabitha waited until she heard the kids clamber up the staircase before she stuck her head out the door and scanned the night. She saw Rex immediately. He was coming down the driveway, bent over, his back to her, as he dragged the police officer by the arms. She went to help him, taking one of the man's arms. Together, they got the body to the porch, up the stairs, and through the door, which they deadbolted behind them.

"Where are the kids?" Rex asked, puffing heavily.

"Upstairs in bed," Tabitha replied.

"Okay," he said, his eyes glinting with concern. "Okay, we need to....we need to secure this place. Give me a hand."

They spent the next few minutes moving the bookcase and sofa and other pieces of large furniture in front of the door and windows. Anyone half determined could still get in, Tabitha knew. But at least they couldn't simply throw a rock through a windowpane and follow through the opening.

Back in the front room, Rex unzipped the police officer's jacket. His navy uniform was shredded and bloodied. The nametag above the breast pocket read PAUL HARRIS.

Rex unbuttoned the shirt's strip of buttons to examine the wound beneath.

"Not as bad as Daisy's," he muttered.

It wasn't, Tabitha noted thankfully, but that wasn't saying much. The police officer's guts might not be spilling out of the leering gash, but it was still an inch deep and at least six inches wide and bleeding freely.

She retrieved a cotton throw pillow they had tossed aside when they'd moved the sofa and said, "I'm going to try to stop the bleeding." She knelt next to Rex, pressed the pillow against the police officer's abdomen, and held it tightly in place.

"Rex! His gun!" she said, noticing for the first time that the man's holster was empty. "Where is it?"

"I don't know," he said, frowning. He engaged the quick release buckle of the police officer's duty belt and slid it free from around the man's waist.

Tabitha glanced at the numerous pouches. "Shouldn't there be a radio? Where's his radio?"

"Handcuffs, spare magazine, keys, flashlight." Rex removed and studied an expandable baton.

"Where's the radio, Rex?"

"He must have dropped it. I'll go have a look."

"Go have a look?"

"Outside."

"You can't go outside! *He's* outside."

"We can't just sit here, Tabs. We need to call for help."

"A phone. Maybe he has a phone."

Rex searched the man's clothing and found only a worn wallet which contained a gold police badge and some bills. His eyes went back to the keys on the duty belt. One of them was for a Ford.

Tabitha knew what he was thinking and said, "He must have parked where we did and walked—

"Oh Christ!" Rex said, cutting her off. "The light we saw on the road," he added, his face drawn. "It was this guy, walking here on foot."

And we turned back, Tabitha thought with a dose of black despair. *We were in the clear, and we turned back. But how could we have known better?*

"What are we going to do, Rex?" she asked, and it was almost a plea.

"Make a break for the car again?"

"We can't! *He's* out there! That crazy, sick..." She shook her head. "He'll be expecting us to do that!"

"Then I have to go look for the cop's radio. If he was surprised, caught off guard, he probably just dropped it. Same with his gun."

"Wouldn't the psycho have taken them?"

"I don't know. But I have to at least check."

"Who is it, Rex? What's going on?"

Rex shook his head. "All I can think is some copycat killer. He heard about what happened to the other families up here, and now he's—"

"*Other* families?" Tabitha blurted. "What other families?"

Rex summarized what Tony and Daisy had revealed to him earlier in the evening. "I swear I didn't know about any of this," he finished. "I've always believed Logan and my parents died in a boating accident. I never would have brought you guys here otherwise."

Tabitha sank back onto her butt, shocked and stunned, and cold, so cold, the sensation seeming to emanate from her bones.

"This is madness," she said in a daze as Rex took over applying pressure to the police officer's wound. "You know that, right, Rex? This is madness. What you're saying happened, what, twenty, thirty, forty years ago? Three families kidnapped and never found? That's bizarre enough. But what's even more bizarre, it's happening all over again, to *us* —"

"It's not!" he snapped. "Whatever happened then has nothing to do with what's happening now. Tonight's a coincidence. Nobody knew we were coming up here."

Tabitha felt as though her world was tearing apart at the seams. This was a nightmare from which she couldn't wake. All they'd wanted was a few days away from the city to relax…

"The kids, Rex," she said. "We can't let anything happen to the kids."

"Nothing's going to happen to them," he said decisively. "Press down on the pillow."

When she did as he asked, he stood.

"What are you doing?" she asked.

"I'm going to find the radio."

"No, Rex!"

"We can't just sit here doing jack shit, Tabs! We're sitting ducks!" He softened his tone. "I'm sorry, but we have to do something. So just hold tight. I'm not going to go far."

13

Rex waited on the porch until he heard Tabitha latch the deadbolt on the other side of the door. Then, armed with the Maglite and a serrated knife he'd taken from the kitchen, he proceeded down the rickety steps. The rain started at the very moment he stepped from beneath the porch roof, increasing to a gentle patter to a hard fall in the space of seconds. The cold drops stung his face and eyes and caused him to squint. He held his hand gripping the knife against his brow in a salute and started along the perimeter of the cabin. The fresh, ozone-laced air filled his nostrils. His ears strained to hear any noise he didn't make. Every muscle in his body seemed tensed to either fight or run.

Rex stopped when he reached the corner of the cabin. He swept the flashlight beam across the ground in front of him, revealing matted pine needles and rivulets of running water and wilted, soggy autumn leaves. He raised the beam, poking the darkness between the crowding, craggy tree trunks. Silent lightning flashed overhead, momentarily stinging the sky purple-blue. In the distance, thunder rumbled menacingly. Wind whistled and moaned and fluttered his clothing.

Rex heard something behind him and spun around. There was nothing there. The sound had been his imagination.

Exhaling the breath that had caught in his throat, he told

himself to keep his cool. He was just about six-feet-tall, fit, and he had a knife. He was likely more than a match for whoever was out here with him. He couldn't allow himself to slip into the mindset of a victim. That's what this guy wanted. Predator versus prey. As long as Rex thought of himself as predator also, then they were on a level playing field.

Maybe I should stalk him? Rex thought suddenly. *Or at least ambush him? I could lie up somewhere with a view of the cabin door. Wait for him to come out of hiding. Sneak up on him. Give the bastard a taste of his own medicine.*

This prospect was appealing. But he'd told Tabitha he would be back shortly. If he didn't return in a few minutes, she would get worried. She might even do something rash like coming outside to look for him.

Best to stick to the plan for now. Look for the cop's gun and radio. If he didn't find either, he would return inside and explain Plan B to Tabitha.

Rex started left along the lake-facing façade of the cabin. Unlike most modern cottages, only a single bay window looked onto the water. As Rex passed it by, he could see orange candlelight seeping between the window frame and drawn blinds, but that was all. He certainly couldn't see the bookcase he and Tabitha had moved in front of it.

The rain continued to pour down in buckets. Rex's hair was already as thoroughly wet as if he'd stepped from a shower. His green bomber jacket was holding up well, but his khaki trousers clung uncomfortably to his legs, and his feet felt clammy in his wet socks and boat shoes.

When Rex reached the far corner, he stopped again. He walked the flashlight beam back and forth revealing only trees, trees, and more trees. Lightning flashed. Through a break between the weeping boughs of two conifers, he glimpsed the briefly illuminated lake. Usually inky smooth, the surface boiled with peaks and white caps.

It was a dark and stormy night... he thought without humor.

Rex started down the back of the cabin. He passed another window shielded by closed drapes (and blockaded with a high chest of drawers in which his mother had kept her good china and silverware). Next came the chimney. It was made entirely of fieldstones and smaller rocks and protruded nearly three feet from the cabin proper. The top of the smokestack had succumbed to the elements years ago, and many of the stones that had composed it were now scattered over the ground.

Rex rounded the next corner so the road was in the trees to his right. Beyond it, the foothills rose steeply up the slopes of the Fraser Canyon to the largely unpopulated inland forests and mountain ranges that stretched for hundreds of miles between here and Alberta.

Anyone could live out there, off the grid, for years or decades, he thought. *And Dad had loved the outdoors. Could he have taken Mom and Logan there? Were they still alive? Could his father have returned to Pavilion Lake now and then in the offseason to raid the cabins for supplies? Had the Petersons and Ryersons caught him red-handed? Had he killed them only to keep his secret?*

But what of Daisy and Tony and the police officer?

How did their attacks fit?

Rex had been so absorbed in these musings he almost walked straight past the pistol lying on the muddy ground. He stared at it for a moment in shock, blinking rain from his eyes. Then he promptly swooped it up.

His heart sung at the sight and weight of it in his hand.

Rex didn't know anything about guns, and it took him a few exploratory moments before he pulled back the slide and saw that the chamber was loaded—though in the process he pulled the slide back too far, engaging the ejector and expelling the round through the breech.

Stupid! he thought, fearful that might have been the last bullet. But to his relief, a second check revealed a new round from the magazine had been loaded in place of the first.

Rex picked up the ejected cartridge and stuffed it in his pocket. Then he searched the ground for the police officer's radio. He discovered the man's cylindrical flashlight, his gold-embroidered cap, and a few popped buttons. But no radio.

"Shit," Rex said. "Shit, shit, shit. *Where is it?*"

Not here, that was all he knew.

Doesn't matter anymore! a voice inside his head told him. *You have the gun! Get inside. Protect the others.*

He obeyed this sound advice.

Rex hung his bomber jacket on the wall-mounted rack, then dumped the three items he'd found outside on the coffee table.

Tabitha, still kneeling next to the supine police officer, applying pressure to his abdominal wound, said, "The gun!"

He nodded. "Have you fired one before?"

"Not for a long time."

"But you have?"

She hesitated. "Yes."

Rex wondered at the pause, but he didn't press the matter. Sitting down next to her on the floor, doing his best to ignore the wet clothing chafing his skin, he said, "I didn't find his radio. No idea where it went. It's pretty clear he was attacked behind the cottage. That's where he dropped his flashlight and gun. So what about his radio?"

"His name's Paul," Tabitha said. "Paul Harris."

"Paul," Rex repeated. Then, to the cop: "So help us out here, Paul. Where's your radio? It would be really nice to know someone was coming out here to give us a hand."

"Someone *will* come," Tabitha insisted. "When he doesn't return to the station, and no one can get in touch with him, other cops will come. And look, I think he's important, like the chief or something." She indicated the rank insignia that adorned his shoulders: a gold crown above three gold pips.

Rex studied Paul Harris. His craggy face was pale and waxy, his eyes closed, his mouth ajar, his cheeks sunken, almost corpse-like.

He probably is the chief, Rex thought. He had seniority on his side. In fact, a place as small as Lillooet probably only had a couple of cops on the payroll. A chief and a lieutenant, maybe. A part-time retiree who volunteered here and there, maybe. But that would likely be all.

So who was going to be missing him at this time of night? His wife? He wore a wedding band on his ring finger. Even so, couples who had been married for a long time often chose to sleep in separate bedrooms. His wife might very well be nestled snug in her bed, visions of sugar-plums dancing in her head, unaware that her husband had yet to return home from his last shift.

Moreover, given Paul's age, it wasn't inconceivable that his wife had prematurely passed on. He could be a widower wearing the wedding band out of obligation, or memory.

The only thing we know for certain, Rex decided gloomily, is that we know nothing for certain. Help could arrive in ten minutes from now, or ten hours, or longer.

Chin up, soldier.

Rex blinked. For a startled moment, he thought Tabitha had spoken those whispered words, but they had been inside his head.

Chin up, soldier.

This was an expression his ex-wife, Naomi, had often used, usually to cheer up Bobby when he was down. A particularly vivid memory struck Rex of the three of them sitting around the dinner table, Bobby in a funk because he knew he couldn't leave the table until he finished the vegetables on his plate, and Naomi ruffling his hair as she carried dirty dishes to the sink, saying, "Chin up, soldier. There are worse things in this world than munching back a few of your mom's delicious veggies."

A not unfamiliar ache rose inside Rex's chest. He had loved Naomi once, and although that love had faded, it had not disappeared altogether. Their divorce had not been poisonous as so many were. There had been no vulgar shouting or scandalous accusations or flying china or behind-the-back disparaging remarks to friends. They had been together for seven years, and despite having a son together, seven years had simply been enough.

Rex's job was largely to blame for their falling out, he knew. His constant traveling had been tough on Naomi. She came to equate his downtime in other countries with mini-vacations while she remained stuck at home dealing with backed-up toilets, car problems, and the like. He tried to paint a more realistic narrative of what he did, along with the downsides to living out of a suitcase, but these efforts were constantly undermined when a co-worker uploaded a picture to social media of him enjoying a cocktail at a hotel bar, or of the sun setting over Athens or Rome or whichever exotic locale his work took him. Moreover, as Captain, he was responsible for every major decision on every flight, which was mentally exhausting. As a consequence, when he returned home he usually wanted to do only one thing: decompress. So when Naomi handed him a to-do list of chores that had accumulated in his absence, he'd often put off doing them. When she made breakfast in the hopes that he'd join her, he'd often opt to sleep in. When she asked him where he wanted to go for dinner, he'd most likely tell her he didn't care (as long as it wasn't McDonald's, which was his go-to airport restaurant).

Although this tension between them over his work had been building for years, the final straw came when Rex got scheduled to fly to London during the family's annual vacation to Hawaii, despite having bid for a different route and date far in advance.

"Maybe I'll just go with Bobby, just the two of us," Naomi said tartly after he explained the change of plans to her.

"Maybe you should," he said sincerely. "Enjoy yourself. You don't need me tagging along."

"No, I don't," she replied in a cold voice. "In fact, I don't think I need you at all anymore, Rex." Her face flushed with anger. "I'm sick of going to Bobby's school functions alone, Rex. I'm sick of falling asleep in front of the TV because it's the only company I have, Rex. I'm sick of being lonely." Her face softened. "You're a good man, Rex, and I love you, but I think it might be best if we go our own ways from here on."

Deep down Rex had known Naomi was right. The only solution to their marital woes would be for him to find a different job, and that would never happen. Like most pilots, he had a passion for what he did, it was in his blood, a part of his identity, and he couldn't change that.

So they quietly and amicably filed for divorce, drafting a parental plan to detail the custody arrangement of Bobby. The boy took the news of their separation rather well, even showing excitement at the prospect of having two houses and thus two bedrooms of his own. But then a month and a half after the divorce was finalized, in October of the previous year, Naomi struck and killed a sixty-five-year-old woman with her Toyota sedan. Too drunk to realize the extent of what she had done, she drove to a side street where she passed out. In the morning she called a body shop to fix her vehicle, telling the owner she had hit a telephone pole. Police, however, recovered a fog-light grill from the scene of the accident and matched it to her car. She was charged with the operation of a motor vehicle causing death, failure to stop at the scene of an accident causing death, and impaired driving causing death. She was released on $100,000 bail. During her court appearance, teary eyed and apologetic, she explained she had been drinking heavily at the time of the accident due to a trifecta of converging events: her mother's death, her father's refusal to continue taking chemotherapy for his cancer, and her divorce to her husband of seven years. The judge, in her ruling, said she took into account these mitigating factors, as well as the fact Naomi had entered a guilty plea and had no prior criminal record, before handing down a five-year prison sentence.

That night, Rex and Naomi explained to Bobby what his mother had done, and that she would be going away for a while. He took this news extremely well also, just as excited at the possibility of visiting his mom in prison as he had been at having two bedrooms. Nevertheless, his seemingly boundless optimism nosedived when Tabitha came into the picture. Her regular visits to the condo where Rex had been renting a unit, combined with Naomi's abrupt departure from his life, caused him to begin viewing Tabitha with suspicion, hence the commencement of the silent treatment he gave her.

For his part, Rex hadn't planned on dating someone so soon after the divorce, but he and Tabitha had immediately clicked upon meeting. As a flight attendant, she understood the rigors of working for an airline, and the baggage that came with the job, so to speak. He could talk to her without feeling defensive about his day, or guilty about providing her with a life she didn't want. For the first time in years he felt young and vivacious and happy.

And now it was all at risk. The new life he was building with Tabitha, Bobby, and Ellie, it was now all at risk of not surviving until morning—

Rex banished these thoughts from his head. He would not dabble with despair.

Wanting a distraction, he retrieved the pistol from the coffee table and flipped it over in his hands, getting a feel for it. The frame was polymer, not steel. At the top of the hand grip was, G L O C K, and above that, MADE IN AUSTRIA. He pressed a button that ejected the magazine.

A series of holes at the back portion of the magazine revealed it currently held six out of a possible seventeen rounds. Rex fished the cartridge from his pocket he'd ejected earlier and inserted it into the top of the magazine, making sure the rounded tip was pointing forward. He reseated the magazine in the hand grip with a satisfying click.

Tabitha was watching him. "Better disengage the safety," she said.

"Where is it?"

She pointed to a lever on the upper back portion of the firearm.

He pushed it down.

"A regular Dirty Harry," she said.

"'Do you feel lucky, punk?'"

"That's not the quote."

Rex returned the pistol to the coffee table. He wrapped an arm around Tabitha's shoulders and kissed her on the top of the head. Then, seeing he was inhibiting her from properly applying pressure to the cop's wound, he released her.

They waited.

Rain drummed on the roof of the cabin. Wind buffeted the sturdy log walls, moaning longingly as if to be let in out of the wet and cold. Thunder rolled across the sky, approaching ever closer.

Tabitha kept the pillow firmly pressed against Paul Harris's abdomen. The slip had been white to begin with. Now it was stained bright crimson. Her hands were sticky with blood.

As the minutes dragged on, she kept her ears pricked for the sound of a car engine approaching in the dark, or distant klaxons, anything that would signal the arrival of help.

All she heard was the damnable rain and wind and thunder.

To keep from totally wigging out, she entertained herself with positive future scenarios. She and Rex and the kids in the toasty warm Mazda, cruising along Highway 99, some cheery pop song on the radio, leaving this little slice of nightmare behind. Or the four of them in a hotel room in Squamish, or Vancouver, sitting by the pool, or eating a buffet breakfast, surrounded by other people, parents and their children, everybody laughing and smiling and enjoying themselves. Or back in Seattle, downtown amidst the bustle of the city, or in her house, or Rex's condo, or in a jet, in the sky.

Oh, what she wouldn't give to be thirty-thousand feet in the air right now!

Black scenarios inevitably crept into this thinking as well, such as one of the cabin's windows suddenly exploding inward, furniture toppling over, and the killer leaping into the room, brandishing a butcher's knife or machete or whatever his weapon of choice might be.

Thank God they had the pistol, she thought. The killer likely didn't know this. He would be surprised, caught off guard. Rex would fire off a volley of shots, and the bastard would be dead before he hit the floor.

And me? she wondered. *Would I be able shoot the man if it came to that?*

Although Tabitha's father had been a Clark Griswold family man on the surface, who liked nothing more than embarking on road trips, barbequing steaks on the grill, and visiting wacky tourist destinations, he was also an avid firearms collector and champion marksman. As a consequence of this, guns had been an integral part of Tabitha's childhood and adolescence. By the time she entered fifth grade, she knew how to field strip, clean, and reassemble several types of revolvers, semi-automatic pistols, and rifles. She knew wadcutters from hollow points. She could distinguish on sight a Browning from a Heckler & Koch from a Smith & Wesson.

One of her earliest memories was of the first time her father had taken her to a gun range. It was a big concrete place with strings of light bulbs lining the ceiling and brass shell casings littering the floor. She couldn't see the shooters in the other booths, so each of their gunshots caught her by surprise, causing her to flinch instinctively, the cumulative effect an unrelenting jumpiness that kept her vividly alert.

After Beth and Ivy had their turns shooting, her father handed her his semi-automatic pistol. She assumed the proper stance, aimed at the paper target, eased her breathing, and relaxed her trigger finger. Then she fired, the gun leaping back up her hands. The spent shell, ejected from the chamber smoking hot, bounced off her bare forearm, shocking her with a quick sizzle. The not unpleasant tang of gunpowder wafted up into her nostrils.

When they got home later that morning, her dad immediately set out cloths, solvents, and oil, and Tabitha and her sisters dismantled the weapons they'd used, wiping the powder residue from the firing pins and the cylinders and pushing solvent-soaked cotton squares through the barrels until they could see the tiny spiral grooves inside. Then, like three little soldiers, they reassembled each gun with speed and precision that belied their young ages, each part joining with metallic clicks and ka-chaks.

Tabitha continued to visit the gun range with her father and sisters throughout elementary school, junior high, and high school. She went to gun shows and participated in shooting tournaments. She read each issue of the NRA's magazine, *The American Rifleman*, cover to cover the day it was delivered to their doorstep each month. When she moved away from home to attend Seattle University, she bought her first gun, a Colt Cobra .38 Special. She kept it in the drawer of the nightstand next to her bed, loaded with five bullets, the firing pin resting on an empty chamber so it wouldn't accidentally discharge. When she heard creaks or strange noises in the house she rented with a handful of roommates, she wasn't afraid. Knowing her gun was within easy reach, she felt empowered and in control.

Then two years ago she had been in downtown Seattle celebrating her thirty-sixth birthday. She and one of her girlfriends, Katy Pignetti, were the last to leave the bar. While they were wandering the empty city streets, looking for a taxi, a man in a hoodie brandished a 9mm snub-nose in their faces and demanded they hand over their purses. Instead of complying, Tabitha gripped the .38 in her handbag and fired three shots through the leather into his chest. She had not thought this action through. It had been an automatic response, as instinctual as looking both ways before crossing a street.

As the would-be robber fell to pavement, mortally wounded, he got off one shot in return. The bullet struck Katy in the chest (Tabitha would later learn it nicked her aorta an inch from her heart). She died minutes later in Tabitha's arms.

Despite the police telling Tabitha she had acted in self-defense, despite her father congratulating her for her quick thinking, and despite her sisters praising her bravery, Tabitha blamed herself for Katy's death. In the days and weeks and months that followed, she suffered severe depression, punishing herself with *if only* questions. *If only she hadn't been so rash... If she hadn't tried to be a hero... If only she'd handed over her purse. If only if only if only...*

Then one day roughly one year after Katy's murder, Tabitha had called in sick to work with the flu. It had been mid-morning. The girls were at school. She'd been in her bathrobe, *Today with Hoda & Jenna* playing on the bedroom television. She'd been planning on drawing a bath, but instead she found herself standing in front of her walk-in closet. She was thinking she could take a belt dangling from one of the plastic coat hangers, slip it around her neck, and hang herself right there. The acidic guilt gnawing away her insides each day would go away. All the shit she was going through with Harry would go away. She would have no more worries.

And she knew—without a doubt—that if it wasn't for Vanessa and Ellie, she would have done it, she would have hanged herself right there and then. Perhaps a bad gene ran in her family, because her grandfather had committed suicide when he was still a young man, as did her Uncle Jed. And her mother very nearly died after passing out one evening after consuming two bottles of wine and far too many sleeping pills (she had always insisted this was an accidental overdose…though what other answer could she tell her daughters?).

So, yes, perhaps Tabitha did indeed have a bad gene inside her, because it would have just been so *easy* to have killed herself that morning.

The seductive and sick thought of taking her life never went away, not fully. It returned every now and then as a passing suggestion—*you could drive right off the bridge, people would think it was an accident* or *you could tip the kayak, drowning would be quick, it might even be peaceful*—and she always shooed it away as quickly as possible in the event it grew roots and became a permanent fixture in her mind.

In any event, Tabitha no longer owned the Colt Cobra. She'd turned it into the police shortly after Katy's death for them to dispose of. And she'd sworn to herself she would never fire a gun again.

But this is different, she told herself now. *This maniac isn't a two-bit mugger. He's a murderer. He's killed two people in cold blood.*

So if he comes after Ellie or Rex or Bobby—hell, yes, I'll shoot him.

I won't hesitate to shoot him.

Rex stood up abruptly. Tabitha glanced at him. He started pacing, rubbing his hand over his five o'clock shadow. "We can't just sit here all night," he said. "He's coming. He knows we're here, and he's coming."

"But he can't get inside. The doors are locked, and we've barricaded all the windows."

"That won't stop him."

"But we'll know he's out there. We'll be ready."

"What if he sets the place on fire? Smokes us out? We'd

run right into his waiting arms. If he has a gun, he could pick us off one by one before we knew where he was firing from."

Tabitha tried not to picture that. "What can we do?" she asked. "Where can we go?"

Rex didn't say anything for a few long moments, then: "I have to get the Mazda."

She stood next to him, alarmed. "You can't leave us, Rex."

"I can be back in twenty minutes. We can be out of here."

"We've already tried that—"

"And would have gotten away Scott-free if we didn't get spooked and turn around."

"He'll know, Rex. He'll expect us to try to get to the car. He'll be watching the cabin. As soon as you leave—"

"You'll have the gun, Tabs. You'll be safe until I get back. Besides, he won't know I've left. There's a root cellar beneath the cabin. The trap door's in the other room, beneath the rug. There's another little bulkhead door that leads from the root cellar to outside, the back of the cabin. I'll leave that way. He'll never know I'm gone."

She considered this. "Let us come with you then. The kids and me. We'll go together."

Rex was shaking his head. "We can't go straight to the road. We have to go through the forest for a bit until we're far enough away from the cabin not to be noticed. The four of us will make too much noise. It's best I go alone. When I reach the road, I'll sprint. I'll be back before you know it."

This plan frightened Tabitha to her core. The last thing she wanted to do was split up. But Rex was right. They couldn't just sit here like bugs beneath a rock, hoping the rock wasn't turned over. They had to do something unexpected.

"He'll hear the car," Tabitha said, even though she knew she had already conceded to Rex's plan, but wanting to exhaust all avenues of argument nonetheless. "He'll try to get us before we get in it."

"I'll drive it right up to the door. You just have the kids

ready. Have the gun ready."

"It's risky," she said. "He could shoot you."

"We don't even know if he has a gun. He probably only has a knife. That's all he's used so far. And how's that going to help him if we're in a car?"

"But he *could* have a—"

"He's just a man, Tabs," Rex said, taking her bloodied hands and squeezing them between his. "We can do this. We can be out of here in twenty minutes. It will be over."

His words were too tempting for her to not believe, or to not *want* to believe, for Tabitha had never desired anything more in her life than for this night to be over with.

She nodded.

14

Rex yanked back the throw rug with the flourish of a magician, revealing the trap door that hid beneath. Even had it not been covered by the rug, it would have been hard to see, as it was flush with the floor and made from the same thick planks of solid timber. There was no handle or latch, so he slipped the blade of the serrated knife he'd taken from the kitchen into the crack between the edge of the hatch opposite the hinges and the floorboards. He pried, and the hatch lifted easily.

Rex clicked on the police officer's flashlight and shone it into the hole. A short ladder descended four feet to hard-packed dirt. Stale, earthy air wafted up, carrying with it the scent of neglect and age.

"There's not much room down there," Tabitha said warily.

"It opens up," Rex assured her. "The ground slopes toward the lake. When you get beneath the front room, you can almost stand."

He shifted onto his butt, dangled his legs into the hole, then hopped down.

"Be careful, Rex," she said.

"I'll be back soon," he said.

Squatting, he swung the flashlight from side to side, scanning the dark cavity that opened away from him. The air was damp and cool. The ground, like he'd told Tabitha, sloped toward the lake, following the natural lay of the land. He crouched-walked forward, using his free hand like a third leg to balance himself, until he was able to stand, though he had to hunch forward so he didn't whack his head against any of the beams or joists that supported the subflooring above him.

Rocks of all different sizes lined the root cellar's walls to help keep the cold air in and the warm air out during mild winter days. Wooden shelves eighteen inches deep protruded from the walls. In Rex's great grandfather's time, before the proliferation of refrigerators and canned food, the shelves would likely have stored apples, sweet corn, potatoes, and perhaps root crops such as beets, turnips, and carrots. Now they held rusty tools, broken toys, musty books, dented paint cans, camping gear, a set of dumbbells, and other miscellaneous junk, all of which was covered with dust, spider webs, and grime.

A lump formed in Rex's throat at the sight of Stretch Armstrong, his once beloved gel-filled action figure, poking out of the top of one toy-filled bucket.

"You okay down there, Rex?" Tabitha called, her voice sounding far away.

"Yeah," he called back.

Pushing aside a life jacket that dangled from an iron hook, which would have originally been used to hang smoked meat, Rex aimed the flashlight beam at the door that led outside. It was made of vertical wooden planks and was about three quarters of the height of a regular door.

He started toward it—and had the scare of his life.

The suddenly molasses-thick air slowed down time and made it difficult to breathe. Rex stared at what lay against the rock wall in shock and dismay as a decades-old memory clawed triumphantly free from the depths of his subconscious where it had been buried for the last thirty-eight years.

Rex working on his Lego castle on the floor of the cabin when the door burst inward and his mother appeared, wild-eyed and ashen-faced.

"Hide!" she told him in a voice so panic-stricken he barely recognized it as her own.

Rex leapt to his feet. "What happened, Mom?"

"He got your Dad," she said, and Rex noticed that her knees, bare below the cuffs of a pair of yellow shorts, were dirtied with mud, and her hands were shaking uncontrollably.

"Who got Dad, Mom?" he asked, his voice rising to soprano level.

"I don't know! We were just walking and he got ahead of me... and he screamed... I didn't see what happened... He was too far ahead. He just told me to run, I didn't see what... I didn't see..."

"Is Dad dead, Mom?" Rex asked, feeling as though his insides had just been scooped out with a giant spoon.

"I don't know, pumpkin, I don't know, I don't know, I don't know." She shook her head and seemed to snap out of the paralysis that had gripped her. "You have to hide!"

"Where's Logan?"

"Logan?" she said, turning in a circle, as if just realizing he wasn't there. "He was with me. He was right beside me. Logan? Logan, baby?"

A moment later Logan staggered through the door. Rex thought he was smiling, perhaps about to burst into laughter (maybe tell him this was all a prank), but then Rex realized it wasn't a smile he was seeing on his brother's face; it was a grimace of pain. And then Rex noticed that Logan's hands, pressed against his tummy, were red with blood.

"Logie?" their mom said. "Logie? Baby? You're bleeding! What happened?"

"I tried to help Dad..." His voice was a whisper.

"Logie!" their mom all but screamed, dropping to her knees. She made to touch his wound, but hesitated, as though fearful to

hurt him. "Is it bad, baby? How bad is it, baby?"

"It hurts," he moaned.

She started to lift his torn shirt. He cried out.

"Sorry, baby, sorry." She stood decisively. "You boys hide. Right now. Hide."

"Where are you going, Mom?" Rex asked.

"Take your brother, Rex, and go hide right now. You boys are good at that."

She went to the door.

"Mom!" Rex cried. "Don't leave us!"

"I have to lead him away." She pushed her dark hair from her dark eyes, which were looking at Rex but didn't seem to be seeing him.

"Hide with us," he pleaded.

Attempting a smile that trembled and became a frown, she left the cabin, closing the door behind her.

Rex turned to Logan, whose mouth was twisted in pain. "Did he have a knife?" he asked.

"It wasn't a person," Logan mumbled, and then he began sobbing.

"What?"

"I'm scared, Rex."

"What was it, Loge?"

"I don't know!"

Although Rex was the little brother, he knew he was going to have to make the decision where to hide. Logan was acting way too weird.

Upstairs under their beds was the first spot that came to his mind. But he quickly dismissed this possibility. That was the first place where people looked when they wanted to find where you were hiding.

In the chimney?

Rex grabbed Logan's hand and all but dragged him into the connecting room. He stuck his head into the fireplace's firebox and looked up. The flue was too narrow. Neither of them would fit. When he pulled his head back out, Logan had already thrown the little rug back to reveal the trap door to the root cellar. Rex and Logan used to play down there. But then at the beginning of the summer their dad found that a family of raccoons had moved in and told them it was off limits, and they hadn't been down there since.

Logan jumped into the hole. "Come on!" he said, his head poking up above the floor.

Rex hesitated. If he went down too, who would put the rug back in place? Someone needed to, or the man who attacked their dad would easily find them (Rex couldn't believe that the person coming after them wasn't a person).

He started swinging the hatch back in place.

Logan stopped it with one of his hands. "What are you doing?"

"I need to put the rug back."

"Where are you going to hide?"

"I'll find a better spot."

Logan held his red-stained hands in front of him. "Am I losing too much blood, Rex?"

Rex shook his head. "I don't think so."

"I don't feel good."

"Just hide. Mom will be back soon."

Rex closed the hatch and pulled the rug back in place. With his heart beating so fast and loud in his chest he could hear it in his ears, he tried to think of a place to hide. In the stove? He was too big. Under the sofa? That was as bad as under the bed. In the closet? No room with the shelves. The bathroom? He could lock the door. No, the attacker would just break it down.

Outside, he decided. There were way more places to hide outside than inside.

Rex left the cabin. It was late afternoon, the sky dull and gray. The forest seemed especially quiet and still. His mind raced through all the places where he had hid before when he and Logan played Hide and Seek—

His mom screamed.

She sounded like she was near the Sanders' place, which was

next door but still far away. Maybe she was going there for help? No, it was late summer, and Rex and his family were the last people remaining on the lake. She understood that. She was just leading the attacker away—

(and he caught her)

Rex grimaced. His first instinct was to go and help her, but he knew he would be too late and too small to help. His second instinct was not to hide but to run. He could try to get to the highway, and then to town. Even though nobody was on the lake, there were always cars on the highway. If he could reach it, someone would drive by and pick him up and—

◆ ◆ ◆

"*Rex?*" Tabitha called. "*Rex? What's happening?*"

Rex couldn't look away from the small skeleton that lay alongside the wall a few feet away from him. It was dressed in clothes he recognized from his childhood. Logan's green KangaROOS sneakers with the zipped pockets where he used to carry his pennies, nickels, dimes, and quarters. Logan's Hawaiian tiki-print jeans cinched around a non-existent waist. Logan's fluorescent green tee-shirt clinging to his sunken chest, outlining the ribs beneath and revealing his denuded arms poking out from the short sleeves.

Perhaps the worst sight, the most ghastly, was Logan's skull. It had turned brown and brittle with age. The skin that still clumped to it was cracked and shriveled. Hair sprouted from the dome. Dried detritus filled the eye sockets. The unhinged jaw gaped unnaturally wide, revealing gaps in the teeth where an incisor or canine had fallen free of the rotted gums.

All at once Rex felt hot and sweaty and sick. He bent over, his stomach cramping, thinking he would throw up.

"*Rex?*" Tabitha called yet again, sounding frightened now.

A deep breath dispelled some of his nausea, and he replied more sharply than he'd intended, "*What?*"

"Why weren't you answering me? Is everything okay down there?"

"Fine," he said absurdly, still focused on the skeleton, thinking, *It's really you, Loge. You've been down here all along. Right down here, in the root cellar, the goddamned root cellar. Dead. Lying here dead for forty years while I've been going about living my life. Jesus Christ, I'm sorry, Loge. I'm so sorry.*

"Rex? What's wrong? Rex? You're scaring me. I'm coming down."

Rex pried his eyes away from his brother's remains and shone the flashlight back the way he'd come. He saw Tabitha's legs dangling through the trapdoor.

"Stay there!" he shouted.

"What's going on?"

"Nothing. I'm at the door." For some inexplicable reason he didn't want Tabitha to see the skeleton. He didn't want her to freak out. But more than that, he wouldn't allow his brother's remains to become a spectacle to elicit horror and pity, like some schlock horror movie prop.

With a final glance back at Logan, telling himself he would mourn his brother properly at a later time, Rex went to the small door. He pushed against it but found it locked. He shoved harder. The latch and mini padlock on the other side of it, which he glimpsed between cracks in the timber, rattled but held firm.

"Come on!" he said, throwing his shoulder into the door. Wood splintered and cracked, and the door swept open. Rex's momentum propelled him into the storm. The driving rain splashed off his head and shoulders. The gale-force winds lashed his exposed face and hands and pulled wildly at his jacket.

Wiping rain from his eyes, Rex scrambled into the dark mass of forest that surrounded the cabin, his feet making little noise on the soggy leaf litter. He didn't think the night could get any blacker, but it did when the towering, swaying trees closed around him.

Moving blindly, he felt his way forward with his hands, pushing water-logged branches and other vegetation aside. He tripped over what he guessed to be a large rock, his arms pin-wheeling. Pain ripped across his forehead as he plowed face-first into a wall of prickly pine boughs. When he shoved free, his fingers probed a fresh wound above his brow. It was tender and bleeding but didn't seem too deep.

Wiping more rain from his eyes, he considered turning on the Maglite so he could see where the hell he was going, but he didn't dare. He was too close to the cabin. Anyone watching it might spot the light and know someone was afoot.

Rex bumped into a large solid structure. At first he thought it was the outhouse before realizing it was the little lean-to where his father had kept a stockpile of split firewood.

On the far side of it, the ground sloped downward, and he descended carefully. Somewhere nearby, where the soil had eroded along the declivity, was an exposed slab of rock that stretched for fifteen or so feet. Rex and Logan had spent countless hours sliding down it atop a patina of leaves and pine needles and moss, challenging each other to see who could go the farthest, or who could climb back to the top the quickest.

There had always been something forbidding about visiting the rock—

Poison ivy, he thought. Both he and his brother had been severely allergic to the plant's oil. It had never seemed to matter how carefully they crept through the poison ivy patch, or what precautions they took to avoid their skin touching the sea of almond-shaped leaves (such as wearing gum boots that went to their knees, or tucking their pants into their socks), they developed an itchy, painful rash each consecutive summer.

During one afternoon visit to the rock, they brought a bucket of water, in the hopes of making the rock's surface especially slippery. They got in a fight about one thing or another, and Rex ended up dumping what remained of the water over Logan's head. In retaliation, Logan plucked some poison ivy plants by the stems, pinned Rex on his back, and rubbed the leaves all over his face.

Rex ran back to the cabin screaming bloody murder. Getting poison ivy on his arms and legs, or between his toes and fingers where the skin blistered and oozed fluid, was bad enough. But on his face!

His mom lathered his skin with Calamine lotion and made him wear a pair of winter mittens she found in the cupboard so he didn't scratch where he would soon begin to itch. Nevertheless, when he woke the next morning, half his face was puffy and inflamed, while one eye was swollen shut. The rash must have lasted three weeks, ruining a good chunk of his summer, and the only silver lining was that he had been allowed as much ice cream as he wanted, which he always made sure to savor in front of his brother.

"Bastard," Rex mumbled quietly to himself, a sad smile ghosting his lips.

He trudged onward, already exhausted from pioneering a path through the dense, wet forest. The terrain flattened out again at the bottom of the small glen. The trees thinned and opened up around him. Yet this slight reprieve lasted for only one hundred feet or so before he found himself climbing the far side of the concavity, struggling with each step to gain reliable footholds in the mud. For every few feet of progress he made, he slipped half that backward. Frustrated but determined, he grasped recklessly at saplings and branches and whatever else he could use to help pull himself up until finally he reached the plateau.

A few paces later gravel crunched beneath his feet, indicating he had reached the neighbors' driveway. Leech had been their surname, if he wasn't mistaken. They had a big Alaskan Malamute that barked constantly most days. Rex was amazed he remembered so many of the lake's summer residents given that as a child he had barely met any of them more than once or twice. But he supposed when you're five or six, and your world is not much larger than the size of your residence, everything in it holds extra significance.

Rex took a moment to orientate himself in the dark. Unless he'd gotten completely turned around, the lake—and the Leech's cabin that sat on a small peninsula visible from Rex's dock—was to his left. Which meant the road was to his right.

When Rex reached the juncture where the driveway met the dirt road, he looked both ways. He saw no flashlight beam bobbing through the dark. If the killer was coming after him, he would be as blind as a mole.

Ducking his head against the storm, Rex hurried north along the road toward the Mazda.

Bobby slipped out of bed, clicked on his keychain flashlight, and padded softly to the collection of old furniture stacked in the corner of the attic. The rain was falling on the roof really fast now, and the thunder was loud enough to probably knock down trees.

"What are you doing?" Ellie demanded from her bed.

Bobby didn't answer her. Instead, he silently examined the furniture—a low table with sewing machine legs, a white cabinet, a yellow dresser, three wooden shelves attached to each other with metal pipes, a turquoise desk on which sat a clunky black typewriter—before selecting a chair with a plastic seat and black legs, not unlike the one at his desk at school. It rested upside-down atop the white cabinet. He dragged it free and carried it back to his bed.

"What are you doing?" Ellie asked again. She was still in her bed, but sitting up now. She was staring at him in challenge, like she did when she thought he might be cheating at a game they were playing (he usually wasn't, but it was hard to convince her of that once she made up her mind on the matter). "If you don't tell me," she added, "I'm going to tell my mom."

Bobby set the chair down on the ground to give his arms a break. "You're a tattletale," he said.

"You're going to get in big trouble."

"*Tattleteller.*"

"I'm going to tell right now."

"You'll get in trouble too!"

Ellie seemed to contemplate this, and when Bobby decided she wasn't going to say anything more, he stripped back his bedcover, lifted the chair again, and plunked it down in the middle of his mattress. Then he pulled the heavy cover over the top of the chair.

"You're making a fort!" Ellie exclaimed.

Nodding, Bobby climbed onto the bed and slipped under the cover. He sat crossed-legged and bent forward so his head didn't brush against the ceiling. He propped the flashlight in his lap and looked around the interior of his fort, pleased with how bright and comfortable it was.

"Can I come in?" Ellie asked, and Bobby heard her hop out of her bed.

"Only boys are allowed," he replied.

"There's no sign that says that."

"I don't need a sign."

Thunder boomed in the sky so loudly and unexpectedly that Bobby flinched and Ellie yelped.

"Let me in!" she said, sounding scared.

"What's the password?"

"I don't know it!"

"What's my favorite TV show?"

"*PJ Masks?*"

"That's *your* favorite show."

"What's your favorite one?"

"*Noddy.*"

"Is that the password?"

Bobby hadn't actually thought of the exact password yet,

but "Noddy" would do.

"Yeah…" he said.

"Okay, let me in."

Bobby lifted the bedcover. Ellie's head appeared a moment later. Her wide eyes sparkled as she looked around, and she was smiling. "Neat!" She climbed inside.

"Don't hit the chair!" he said.

"It's small in here," she said, pulling her knees up against her chest and ducking her head like he was. "You should build a second floor."

"How?"

"With more furniture."

"You can't have a second floor in forts."

"Yes, you can," she replied knowingly. Then, suddenly: "Miss Chippy!" She tugged the chipmunk out of her pocket and held the little animal in front of her face. "Were you biting me Miss Chippy? Naughty chippymunk! Are you all better now?"

Bobby stared at her. "You're not allowed to have that up here!"

"Am too!"

"Your mom said you're not allowed to touch it!"

"No, she didn't."

"You shouldn't lie."

"I don't."

"Yes, you do. You always lie. You're lying right now. You lie more than the devil."

Ellie stuffed the chipmunk back in her pocket. "No, I don't. The devil lies the most in the world. And if you tell on me, I'm going to tell on you."

Bobby frowned. "For what?"

"I'll tell my mom you played with Miss Chippy too."

"But I didn't!"

"My mom will believe me. She always believes me."

But Bobby had stopped listening to her. He was looking at his stomach. "Did you hear that?" he asked. "My tummy is making funny sounds."

"That means you're hungry."

"I *am* hungry."

"I wish we could have popcorn."

"We've already had dinner," he reminded her.

"I know. But sometimes my mom lets me have cockporn at nighttime, if I've been a good girl all day."

"You said cockporn!"

"No, I didn't, stupid head. I said *pop*corn."

Bobby shrugged. Popcorn sounded pretty good to him right then. It was one of his favorite foods along with chocolate bars, potato chips, and ice cream. He was never allowed to have any of these except for on special occasions, like when his dad came home from being away in a different country. "Can you ask your mom to make us some?" he said.

"I don't think your dad bought any at the store."

"He might have."

"He didn't."

"Just ask your mom."

Ellie hesitated. "She's not feeling very well."

Bobby frowned. "Your mom?"

Ellie nodded. "She's scared of the monster."

With all the talk of popcorn, Bobby had almost forgotten about the monster, despite it being the reason he built the fort in the first place. "I think my dad's scared of it too."

"I'm not scared," Ellie proclaimed.

"I'm a little bit," Bobby admitted.

"I'm not," she said defiantly.

"What if it catches us?"

"It can't. It can't get in the fort."

Bobby wanted to believe Ellie that the monster couldn't get in, but he was pretty sure it could if it tried.

Thunder exploded, seeming to shake the entire cabin.

"That was *loud*," Ellie whispered.

Bobby nodded and tried not to think of a tree falling down on top of them. "What do you want to do?" he asked her. "Do you want to play a game?"

Ellie held up her hands, her palms facing outward. "Paddy cakes?"

"I'm not a girl! And it's too noisy. Your mom will hear."

Ellie made her thinking face. "Dares?"

Bobby brightened. Dares were always fun if you could think of a good one.

"When I played with my mom," Ellie went on, "she dared me to crack an egg over my head."

"Did you do it?"

She nodded. "You have to. Or else."

"Or else what?"

"You get punished. My mom made me eat a raw carrot once."

"Yuck," he said, glad they didn't have any carrots around.

Ellie sat straight, her head touching the bedcover above her. "Okay, me first. I dare you..." She put on her thinking face again. "I dare you..."

"What?"

"I dare you to...do a chicken dance!"

Bobby couldn't picture what this might look like. "I don't know a chicken dance."

"You have to! I dared you!"

"But I don't know it! I can't do it if I don't know it!"

"Act like a monkey."

Bobby shrugged. He could probably do that.

"I have to go outside the fort."

He slipped under the cover, then hopped off the bed. Ellie stuck her head out to watch him.

Bobby didn't know how he was supposed to act like a monkey without being loud, but he did his best, jumping from foot to foot, holding his arms funny, like he had a coat hanger in the back of his shirt, trying not to make any sound. Ellie giggled wildly.

"Shhh!" he said.

She clamped her hands over her mouth.

"Okay, my turn now," Bobby said. "I dare you…" He looked around the dark attic. The game would be a lot easier if they were playing in the day and didn't have to be so quiet. He could have made Ellie eat a spoonful of mustard from the kitchen, or walk backwards everywhere with a lampshade on her head, or sing a song in a funny voice. Now he couldn't make her do any of that.

Bobby's eyes paused on the window near the pile of old furniture. When he had his first sleepover after George Papadopoulos's fifth birthday party earlier this year, George's parents let all the kids sleeping over stay up really late watching movies and playing video games. After this, when they were lying in sleeping bags on the floor of George's bedroom, Jamie Stevenson—who had an older brother who knew all sorts of cool stuff—explained that if you looked in a mirror after midnight and said "Bloody Mary" three times, you would see the face of a witch covered in blood. Only George and Jamie were brave enough to try it, and they both said they saw Bloody Mary.

Still looking at the window, Bobby thought it would work as a mirror, because when it was nighttime, you could never see out a window, only your reflection.

"I dare you," he said, unable to hold back a smile, knowing Ellie was going to be too scared-y cat to do it, "to go to the window and say Bloody—" He changed his mind. "And say the monster's name three times."

Ellie frowned. "That's a stupid dare."

"No, it's not." Bobby explained what happened at George's sleepover.

Ellie said, "So if we say the monster's name instead, the monster will appear?"

Bobby nodded. "If you don't do it," he said, "you lose and I win."

She looked frightened. "I don't want the monster to appear."

"You have to! I dared you!"

"I don't want to!"

"Then you have to do the punishment."

"What is it?"

Bobby didn't know and didn't bother to think of one. He was having too much fun seeing Ellie scared. "You're a baby," he said, knowing this always got her angry.

"I'm not a baby!" she said.

"Then go look in the window and say the monster's name three times."

They both stuck their heads out of the fort and looked at the window. It was a grave-black square in the wall.

Ellie slipped out head-first, planting her hands on the floor and somersaulting, before standing up beside Bobby.

"You're going to do it?" he said, surprised.

"We don't know the monster's name," she said.

"We can make one up." Bobby shrugged. "Mike?"

"You stole that from *Monster University*."

"So?"

"That's not scary."

"You think of one then."

"Mike's okay. But you have to come with me."

She took his hand in hers and walked slowly to the window. Bobby couldn't believe they were really going to do this. He wanted to run back to the fort, but he knew Ellie would make fun of him if he did.

I just won't look, he thought. *Like at George's, I'll just close my eyes.*

They stopped before the window. Raindrops streaked the glass, creating zigzaggy patterns. Bobby kept the tiny flashlight aimed at the floor. Ellie stood on her tiptoes so she could look out the window.

"I can only see me," she said.

"I told you," he said, "you have to say the monster's name three times. Then you can see it."

After a moment's hesitation, Ellie spoke, and Bobby squeezed his eyes shut as tightly as possible.

"Mike...Mike...Mike..."

The rain, blown diagonally by the wind, shredded the rainforest's canopy and understory, and churned the road into a bubbling stew. Rex's chest heaved and his lungs burned as he kept up a brisk run, even as the road ascended what seemed like a never-ending slope. He was only a few minutes away from the Mazda now. He'd gotten his second wind. He didn't care that his legs were mush. He wouldn't slow until he reached the car.

Rex still believed fetching the Mazda was the best plan of action, and he hoped Tabitha was holding up okay in his absence. She must be terrified waiting alone for his return. Well, she wasn't alone, of course. She had the kids with her. But their presence most likely only added to her trepidation. She was their sole protector, the one person standing between the killer and them. If he decided to attack before Rex returned—

No, Rex wouldn't think of this. Tabitha was fine. The kids were fine.

The killer was—

Where? Where *was* the bastard?

He'd been dragging the cop across the road when Rex almost ran him over. Why? To bury him in the woods? Where did he flee to? Rex hadn't gotten much of a look at him, but he figured the guy must be fit and strong. After all, Tony had been muscular, no pushover, and he'd locked himself in a goddamned bedroom, apparently fearful for his safety.

Which brought Rex back to the question of what exactly happened to Tony and Daisy earlier in the evening.

They're sitting at the table in the living room, enjoying some cheese and wine, playing cards, when, what—they hear a noise outside? Tony goes to the door and sees the killer. And locks himself and Daisy in the bedroom without bothering to lock the front door first? That didn't make sense. So perhaps the killer strolled boldly into the cabin. Daisy and Tony, seeing that he is armed, run to the bedroom, lock the door. Then what? The killer scales the partition wall, drops down on top of Tony, and delivers the fatal wound across his gut? And Daisy? She escapes out the window while this is happening. The killer catches up to her somewhere along the road and cuts her too. Yet she has spirit, fire, wants to live. She fights back and gets away and makes it to Rex's cabin with the last of her strength before succumbing to her injury...

It's possible, Rex thought. *It all fits.*

But the big question is, Who the hell is this guy?

Not Rex's father, as Rex had previously speculated. His mother, he now recalled, had said she'd heard their father scream, indicating he was not the attacker but the attacked. And Logan had been attacked too, which meant he would have seen the killer. If it had been their father, he would surely have admitted as much.

Far above in the night sky a yellow bolt of lightning splintered into a constellation of frenetic offshoots. A blast of thunder as loud as cannon fire obediently followed. The rain fell harder.

Rex stepped in a deep pothole filled with rainwater and lost his balance. He toppled forward, his knees and palms slamming the ground. A piece of gravel the size of a walnut tore into his left kneecap. Crying out in pain, he rolled onto his side, his hands cupping his knee. One of his fingers slipped through the hole where his khakis had torn and touched the pulpy wound beneath.

"Christ!" he hissed.

With effort he managed to straighten his leg. He bent it at the knee and straightened it again. It felt as though someone had taken a sledgehammer to his kneecap, but he would be able to walk.

Carefully he stood. Drenched and shivering, cold rain

pelting his face, he took a cautious step forward. His injured leg buckled, but he kept his balance. After a few more tentative steps he attempted a quicker, albeit lurching, pace.

Looking up from the ground, he came to an abrupt halt.

Ahead, in the middle of the road, was a lone dark shape.

15

Tabitha peeled back the pillow from the police officer's abdomen. His bleeding, she was relieved to note, had all but stopped, which likely meant the killer's knife hadn't perforated his liver, kidneys, spleen, or other vital organs. In fact, it might have spared his bowels as well. Despite the vicious sweep of the slash, it was made horizontally, not vertically, meaning the knife could have slid between the police officer's intestines, perhaps only nicking them, or even missing them altogether. And if this was the case, his injury was superficial, a flesh wound, and not fatal.

Tabitha replaced the pillow and positioned the police officer's hands atop it, so she didn't have to continue holding it in place.

She got up and padded quietly through the cabin to the bathroom. She used the toilet, then poured water into the bowl so it would flush. The mundane action made her pause. Her life was potentially in danger. She might not survive until morning. Yet still she made sure her urine didn't sit in the toilet bowl for others to see.

Back in the front room, she went to the bookcase she and Rex had moved in front of one of the windows. She studied the family photographs on the top shelf. She'd never seen a photo of Rex from his childhood, and in this one he looked unsurprisingly like a younger, miniaturized version of himself—minus the white hair, of course. In fact, she really saw the resemblance to Bobby now. Blonde, blue-eyed, thin lipped.

On the middle shelf sat several leather-bound photo albums, their spines facing outward. Tabitha lifted one free. It turned out not to be a photo album but a baby scrapbook. Taped to the first few pages was a photocopy of Rex's birth certificate, a photograph of Rex's mother in a hospital bed holding Rex, recently born into this world. The next page contained a makeshift paper pouch that contained two of Rex's baby teeth. On the page after that, a lock of golden hair. The rest of the book was filled with more cards celebrating his subsequent birthdays: ribbons presumably kept from birthday gifts; a letter Rex had written to Santa Claus, in which he stated he had been a good boy and deserved a lot of presents; a self-portrait done in crayons; and other childhood keepsakes. Amongst all of this were faded photographs annotated in neat handwriting.

Tabitha studied one photo labeled "Happy Fifth Birthday!" In it, Rex sat at the center of a table, attempting to blow out five candles atop a chocolate cake. His friends sat to either side of him, some smiling shyly for the camera, others making funny faces.

Who would have ever thought that little kid would end up flying airplanes through the sky? she thought sentimentally.

Rex had once told Tabitha that he'd always known, for as long as he could remember, that he wanted to be a pilot. So perhaps he had known this even when this picture had been taken. Perhaps when his mother, or his teacher, had asked him that age old question, "What do you want to be when you grow up?" he had confidently answered, "A pilot!"

She smiled at this, proud of him for seeking out his dreams, even as a shadow of displeasure spread within herself.

Because becoming a flight attendant had not been her dream.

Tabitha liked that her job afforded her the opportunity to travel, to see different places, and to meet new people. But the work itself was hardly glamorous.

Tabitha supposed she became a flight attendant the same way a recent college graduate with an Art degree becomes a human resources administrator or a fast-food restaurant manager: the position was available, previous experience wasn't necessary, and it paid all right.

So what *had* been her dream? she wondered.

The scary, yet truthful, answer was that she never really had one. She had never been inspired or impassioned to do any one thing with her life particularly well. She had always been content with mediocrity. Which wasn't necessarily a bad thing. The products of this mediocrity were two beautiful daughters, a loving family, great friends, and a fantastic boyfriend.

She should have been very happy.

Only she wasn't.

Because mediocrity was no longer enough.

She had started feeling this way during the divorce proceedings with Jacob. That was when it dawned on her that she was getting old. When the divorce was finalized in a few weeks' time, she would be a single mom with no house she could call her own, a ten-year-old car, and zero savings. This was not the life she had envisioned for herself. And she no longer had limitless time for the pieces of the life she *had* envisioned for herself to fall into place. She was almost forty. In another ten years or so she would be fifty.

Yes, she loved Ellie and Vanessa with all her heart and couldn't wait to watch them grow up, and, yes, she was over the moon with Rex and couldn't wait to see how their future unfolded together.

But something was missing from her life that had never been missing before.

Personal fulfillment.

She needed to know she was not simply waking up each

morning to pay the bills and to get through the day.

She needed a dream.

Swallowing hard, Tabitha closed the scrapbook and set it back on the shelf.

Her eyes fell on the policeman, and her breath hitched in her throat.

His eyes were open, and he was looking at her.

She crouched next to him. "Oh God, hi," she stammered. "Are you okay?"

He worked his mouth but didn't answer.

"Water?" she asked, but he shook his head.

He worked his mouth again. "Rex…?" he said.

"Rex is my boyfriend. But he's not here. He went to get the car. We parked way down the road and—"

"Need…t'leave."

"Yes, we know that, we're trying," she said, still rambling. "But why? Who's out there? Who attacked you?"

"Need…t'leave." He licked his dry lips. "Now."

Paul Harris knew he was cut up in a bad way. Fire burned in his stomach. He could feel copious amounts of blood drying on his skin and clothing. But his injury wasn't what frightened him. It was what was out there in the night.

It exists, he thought, cold with horror, while at the same time a part of his mind admonished himself for not accepting this conclusion years earlier, given the abundance of evidence that had piled up right in front of his nose.

In the fall of 1989, eight years after the Chapman family went missing without a trace, and two after the Peterson family followed suit, Maddy Greene, a sixty-three-year-old widowed pensioner who lived on Highway 99 five kilometers from Pavilion Lake, called the police station in a panic late one evening, saying somebody was lurking around outside her house. She changed her story when Paul arrived to investigate, saying the interloper wasn't someone but some*thing*. She came to this epiphany, she said, when she saw it pass by her kitchen window not two feet away from her glass-pressed nose. She described it to Paul as having gray or black skin, and long, skinny limbs covered with coarse hair that, in her words, "was nicely combed, like with a brush." Its height, she guessed, was roughly seven feet ("tall enough I was looking way up at it, Paul"), and although it walked on two legs like a human, its movement was jerky, its arms raised like the raptorial forearms of a praying mantis. Most surprising was her description of its face. "Hideous eyes, Paul, big like softballs, and a needle-like nose like some of those fish have, those swordfish."

Paul searched outside the house for footprints, but he found none. This wasn't necessarily saying much, as the ground had been hard and dry, and he was no expert at identifying tracks of any sort. He told Maddy that some kids from town had probably been playing a prank on her, and to lock the doors and windows and get some sleep.

Paul didn't give the incident much more thought until the following summer when Jenna and William Jannot, who lived about ten minutes down the highway from Maddy, reported that a half-dozen of their chickens had been slaughtered during the night. Chickens fall prey to foxes, bobcats, and cougars in these parts all the time. After such attacks, however, nothing usually remained of the bird except a few feathers. Yet on this occasion the carcasses of the Jannot's chickens were scattered all around the roofless coop, each one emptied of blood and featuring a well-defined puncture wound in either the neck or the hindquarters.

"Looks like you got yourself a vampire problem," Paul had told William lightheartedly.

"Ayuh, a vampire with one goddamn tooth," William had replied.

"So what do you want me to do, Will?"

"I want you to find out whoever done this, Paul. What the

hell were they using, a giant syringe?"

"It's weird, I'll admit that."

"Weird ain't the half of it, Paul. Their blood's clean gone! Jenna's scared shitless. Someone with enough screws loose to do this, who knows what they might try next? I bet ya it's that Jameson girl. She's a bit retarded, ain't she? Always walking up and down the roads at night time by herself, sometimes half-dressed and talking to the moon."

"She's got schizophrenia, Will."

"Exactly! Reason enough to do something like this."

"You're a good twenty kilometers from town. She's never come this far before."

"Maybe last night she did?"

"I'll have a word with her."

Paul never did speak to Penny Jameson. He was pretty sure the culprits were the same kids who had dressed up in a Halloween mask to scare Maddy Greene. In a small town like Lillooet, where the only things the kids had in plentitude were a lot of time and little to do, they could get very creative with the mischief they got into. Throw alcohol and drugs into the mix, along with someone who had their driver's license and access to a beat-up runaround, and nothing was off limits.

Life in the Lillooet Country continued as usual for the next while. The days were quiet and uneventful until the latest local scandal spiced things up every few months or so. Like when Alexis Dempsey, a twenty-five-year-old bank teller, was outed for moonlighting as a prostitute in Whistler Village on weekends. Or when an out-of-towner opened a sex shop on Main Street across from the supermarket (it shut down one month later largely due to the righteous efforts of crossing guard Marjorie Cooper, who sat out in front of it on a folding chair every single day it was in operation, shaming any man who dared to enter). Or when Pastor Joe at the Anglican Church had a heart attack during a Sunday morning mass, croaking in front of the fifty-person congregation that included a dozen children who were told the pastor was such a good man that God had wanted to take him before his time. Or when sycophantic Lewis Edevane, the high school biology/human anatomy teacher, broke into the house of the school's vice principal to steal her supply of anti-depressants.

But nothing else *unexplainable* happened in the remote mountain community again. Not until the spring of 1992, at any rate. It was late April, and the region had just experienced an unseasonal cold snap, along with a foot of snow. On a morning Paul had planned to spend sitting in front of the police station's fireplace with a pot of hot coffee and copies of *The Toronto Star* and *Vancouver Courier*, Billy Nubian rang up, asking Paul to come out to his property but not saying much more than that. When Paul arrived at Billy's forty-acre farm located equidistant between Lillooet and Pavilion Lake, Billy met him at the front door, where he lit up a cigarette and said, "Come around back, Paul. I want to show you something." He led Paul to the pen where he kept his goats, only now there was only a single goat in it, and it was lying on its side in the snow. "I moved the others in with the sheep so I could put this one down."

They stopped before the animal's lifeless body, and Paul frowned at the grotesque wound that disfigured its belly.

"What the hell happened to it?" he asked.

Billy flicked away his cigarette and immediately lit another. "Something spooked them in the night. Me and the wife could hear them bleating all the way up in the bedroom. I threw on a jacket and came out..." He shook his head. "I swear, Paul, I'm not making this up...but there was... something...in the pen with them."

"Something?"

Billy shrugged. "Some sort of bug thing. I know how that sounds, but..." He shrugged again. "I mean, it had these big, buggy eyes."

Paul thought of Maddy Greene's alleged trespasser and

said, "Tall and thin?"

"Yeah, I guess it was. It was crouching froglike over this goat. Like maybe it was getting ready to pick it up and carry it off or something. But yeah, I'd say it was tall and thin." Billy raised his eyebrows. "You've seen this thing before, Paul?"

"Not me. But Maddy Greene claimed to have seen it last year."

"Claimed? I ain't making this up, Paul. I ain't *claiming* anything. I saw what I saw."

"I'm not doubting that, Billy. Wrong choice of words. I believe Maddy saw it too—only, I don't think we're talking about an 'it.' What she saw were probably some kids playing a prank on her. Maybe you did too? One of them wearing some kind of mask or—?"

"Look at that goat's belly, Paul," he said, jabbing a calloused finger at it. "Torn clean open. No kids did that. Besides, I *saw* the thing, goddammit. It might've been dark out, but I saw it."

When Paul wrote up the incident report, he paraphrased what Billy had told him, mentioning only that an "unknown animal" had attacked one of his goats, along with the rest of the admittedly sparse and inconclusive facts of what happened that night.

And that was that. The world kept turning, and Lillooet went right along with it.

Eighteen-year-old Hunt Fischer was drafted by the Edmonton Oilers and, in recognition, had his mural painted on the wall of the local McDonald's PlayPlace. Lewis Edevane got into trouble again when he hosted a student party at his house that involved a copious amount of pot and alcohol. Lewis's friend and coworker in the high school's math department, Michael Finnegan, resigned after he slept with a female student a week after she graduated (they ended up marrying a few months later and divorcing a few months after that). Notoriously cranky Clyde Johnson had his tractor stolen from one of his fields (it was found two days later in a culvert without its tires and painted purple). And when Pat Florio's namesake son, Pat Jr., came out as gay in the first week of school in the fall of 1996, Father Dempsey excommunicated him from the Catholic Church (public backlash forced the priest to welcome him back into the flock in time for the following Sunday's morning mass).

On July 4, 1998, Paul had been celebrating Independence Day out at Hangman's Tree Park, named so because it was the resting place for William Armitage, who had been convicted and hanged for the murder of a fellow gold seeker in 1863. Standing amongst the revelers next to Hangman's Tree (which had long ago died and was now nothing but a six-foot-tall dead stump), Paul was eating a hot dog and listening to the cover band play CCR's "Bad Moon Rising" when his cell phone rang. It was his wife, Nancy. Eve Holleman who had a summer cabin on Pavilion Lake had called the station to report screams and gunshots coming from next door.

Paul pulled into the Ryerson's driveway half an hour later. Their potato-brown station wagon was parked in the driveway. Eve Holleman was not there to greet him. More than likely she was hiding inside her cabin with the window blinds drawn and the doors locked.

Paul put the cruiser in Park, got out, and withdrew his Glock from the holster. He had never met Rick Ryerson, or his wife, Sue, though he knew of them, as he knew of every local and summer resident in and around Lillooet. Rick was a dentist from Vancouver. He bought this property five years ago, tore down the shabby hunter's cabin that had stood on it unoccupied for years, and put up the tidy, four-bedroom cottage that Paul was approaching now. The couple had one teenage daughter.

The front door to the cabin was closed. Ignoring it, Paul moved down the side of the building. He came to a large deck that offered unobstructed views of the lake, which dazzled blue in the afternoon sunlight. He crept up the three steps, passed a gas barbecue with marble bench tops, and quietly slid open the glass patio door.

He stepped inside, holding the gun in front of him with both hands to keep it steady.

The large room featured cathedral ceilings, pastoral artwork, and expensive French country furniture—the latter of which was in complete disarray. A floor lamp with a mauve-colored shade lay on its side, next to an overturned ottoman and smashed vintage desk. A heavy oak dining table was shoved pell-mell to one side, toppling some of the chairs that had surrounded it. A mirror lay facedown on the floor on a bed of jagged pieces of loose glass.

Blood was everywhere.

There were two main stains, one on the floor near the dining table, the other in front of and on a three-seater sofa. Both had been stepped in. Crimson footprints created anarchic patterns across the floor, alluding to the bedlam that had taken place here earlier.

Trying not to gag on the sweet, metallic stench permeating the air, Paul stepped over the floor lamp and rounded a Provencal two-drawer dresser that stood incongruously in the middle of the room, as if it had been dragged there to serve as a buffer against an attacker.

"Police!" he called out in an authoritative voice, not expecting an answer and not getting one.

He spent the next ten minutes poking around each room, not touching anything. Then he returned to the back porch and called the Whistler detachment of the Royal Canadian Mounted Police. He remained outside while the forensic guys documented the crime scene before beginning the laborious task of collecting fingerprints, blood samples, and other physical evidence. By the time they wrapped up it was after dark. Most of the other lake residents had gathered out in front the cabin to rubberneck, looking scared and worried and maybe even a little excited by all the commotion.

Naturally the next day Lillooet's rumor mill went into

overdrive, and it wasn't long before the townsfolk were connecting the disappearance of Rick Ryerson and his wife and daughter to the fates of the Chapmans and Petersons. Top-secret government experiments and alien abductions were favorite topics of speculation. So too were legends from the gold mining days involving vengeful spirits and black curses and all that hocus-pocus.

One tale in particular captured everyone's imagination.

In 1904 a man named Dumb John Dagys fatally shot a Chinese miner named Ah Shing on the shores of Pavilion Lake. Six months later, after bragging about the murder during a game of poker, Dagys was arrested. According to court documents, the prosecution described Dagys as a mountain man who would show up every now and then in Lillooet with a pocketful of gold nuggets, spending all of them on booze and whores before heading back into the wilds. The general consensus at the time, and the eventual conclusion of the court, was that Dagys had discovered a goldmine amidst the mists, thick woods, and rugged terrain near Pavilion Lake—and had murdered the Chinaman, who had discovered the mine's location, to keep it secret. Dagys was hanged in March 1905, and his final words (garbled on account that he had no tongue) before the gallows trap door sprung open, were: "Anybody goes looking for my mine will wish they didn't, God have mercy on their soul."

Which begged the questions: Did Troy Chapman find Dagys' mine in '81? Did Marty Peterson find it in '87? Did Rick Ryerson find it most recently?

And did they, and their families, fall victim to Dagys' curse?

Most people Paul talked to seemed to believe this, even if they didn't come right out and say so. And with the RCMP's forensic lab report failing to unmask any terrestrial suspects, the ghost of Dumb John Dagys became the go-to natter whenever talk of the missing families came up

Until the summer of 2009.

While the rest of the world was dealing with the fall-out from the US subprime mortgage crisis, the residents of the Lillooet Country were being terrorized by an unknown creature. It was first spotted in the sky out east over Cariboo Road by Tom Eddlemon, who later described it to the local paper as something "about the size of an ape but with large transparent wings." That same week Steve Krugman snapped a photograph of what he believed to be the same creature perched on the roof of his barn (though it had been dark out, and the shape in the photo had been far from conclusive). The final encounter that eventful summer came on August 1. Before going to bed, George Long found his wife, Heather, passed out in their backyard in her pajamas and housecoat. When she came round, she claimed to have come face to face with a "half-man half-bug." The last thing she remembered was it scooping Sadie, her Jack Russell terrier, into its arms and flying off into the night (the dog has never been seen since).

And while Maddy Greene had been telling anyone who would listen of her own close encounter of the first kind for years, and most residents of Lillooet had heard through the grapevine about Jenna and William Jannot's exsanguinated chickens and Billy Nubian's eviscerated goat, it was only now that people were sitting up and listening. Because Tom Eddlemon wasn't a nutty spinster or oddball farmer. He owned and operated the busiest coffee shop in town, knew all of his customers by name, and had once dived into the Fraser River to save twelve-year-old Davy Theodossiou, who had capsized his canoe and nearly drowned.

Not to be outdone, Steve Krugman was the wealthiest man in Lillooet, thanks to his road freight transport business that operated a fleet of vehicles and employed two dozen locals. And Heather Long was a star witness as well, if only because she was considered by many—which included friends and family—to be too much of a bore to make up such a fantastical encounter.

Mr. Wang, who ran the mom-and-pop convenience store on Main Street, was the first to refer to the creature as "Mosquito Man," a sensational moniker that quickly stuck with the populace. He hired local artist, Mary Catherine Jackson, to paint a picture of the creature hovering above the moonlit town, which he hung in the shop's front window between posters advertising Coca-Cola and Lotto 649. A group of hunters led by Hank Crary put a bounty on the creature's head, and they spent countless weekends scouring the woods for it. By the time real estate agent Claude Bumiller announced that he had shot the creature—taping a tuft of its fur (which looked suspiciously like fur from a beaver pelt) in Mr. Wang's shop window—the town's anxiety had hit a fevered pitch.

Nevertheless, as summer faded into fall with no more sightings of the creature, so too did the town's enthusiasm toward it, and by winter the Mosquito Man had lost its cult status, fading back into a thing of legend, or becoming little more than a bogeyman that parents threatened their children with if they came home late for dinner or didn't go to bed on time.

Whenever talk of the Chapmans or Petersons or Ryersons came up—usually over beers at one of the town's pubs when those imbibing grew tired of bitching about their neighbors or coworkers—people were equally inclined to bring up the ghost of Dumb John Dagys as they were the Mosquito Man or Troy Chapman.

Troy had been the RCMP's original person of interest back in '81. Their thinking had been conventional. Troy got in a fight with his wife Sally and murdered her, either intentionally or unintentionally. He buried her body somewhere in the woods and went on the lam with his two boys. Rex at some point fled in fear, making his way back to town.

When the Petersons disappeared six years later, and there were no clear suspects, Troy Chapman once again became a person of interest. The RCMP speculated that Troy, and possibly his son Logan, had managed to survive the last eight years in the wilderness by living off the land, fishing, hunting, trapping. But that January and February had been the coldest on record in more than two decades, forcing Troy and Logan back to civilization. They took up residence in the Peterson's cabin—and were surprised by the family's unexpected early arrival on March 1 (most residents didn't visit the lake before the May long weekend).

This same thinking applied again in 1998. The Ryersons were the first family to the lake that year, arriving on April 3, and their atypically early arrival surprised a squatting Troy and Logan, who murdered them and once again disposed of the bodies in the woods to muddy the waters of any subsequent investigation.

Being in law enforcement, Paul knew from firsthand experience that a rational explanation existed behind every crime, no matter how well that explanation might be hidden. Which was why despite having some questions— namely why Troy and Logan never left behind any evidence of their trespassing, despite allegedly residing in both the Anderson's and Ryerson's houses for some time—Paul had always been on the same page as the Mounties when it came to the missing families.

Stupid, he thought now as he lay half dead on the floor of Rex Chapman's cabin. Because in striving for a rational explanation, he had blinded himself to the truth. *Something had been preying on the animals and people of the area, something that didn't give a rat's ass of the difference between beast and human.* His people had seen it for centuries. Maddy Greene had seen it much more recently. Billy Nubian had seen it too. And Tom Eddlemon and Steve Krugman and Heather Long.

And tonight Paul had seen it too.

The woman by the bookcase looked over at him. Her face broke into surprise at finding him alert. "Oh God, hi!" she said, hurrying to his side. "Are you okay? Water?"

He shook his head and tried to generate some saliva. "Rex...?" he said, his voice brittle and cracked.

"Rex is my boyfriend," she said. "But he's not here. He went to get the car. We parked way down the road and—"

"Need...t'leave."

"Yes, we know that. But why? Who's out there? Who attacked you?"

"Need...t'leave." He licked his lips. "Now."

Tabitha stared at the police officer, but he seemed to have used up what little strength he'd mustered. His eyes were once again closed, and he was either resting or comatose.

Leave, he'd told her.

Now, he'd told her.

Roger that, Officer, she thought. *We're out of here just as soon as my boyfriend gets back with the car, don't you worry.*

By the way, do you mind telling me what happened to you? Who cut you? And why? Because I'm pretty much in the dark right now, and it's not a nice place to be.

In fact, it's goddamn terrifying.

Tabitha checked her gold wristwatch. It was 12.53 a.m. Rex had been gone now for more than twenty minutes. He would be back shortly.

Taking a jar candle from the coffee table, she got to her feet and went to the next room. She climbed the steep staircase. The solid planks of timber that formed the steps didn't creak. The interior of the cabin was entirely quiet. Outside was a different matter. Rain continued its unabated assault on the roof, while thunder alternated between mild rumblings and cataclysmic detonations.

When she reached the top of the staircase, her eyes went immediately to Bobby's bed. For a split second she couldn't make out what she was seeing projecting from the mattress in the thick shadows before she realized it must be some kind of fort.

Were the kids inside it? Because Ellie's bed was empty—

In that same instant she noticed a small circle of light at the far end of the attic. Bobby and Ellie stood before the window, looking out.

Tabitha's stomach flipped. "Who's there?" she blurted, dashing across the attic.

Both Bobby and Ellie snapped about, looking both surprised and guilty.

"Who's out there?" Tabitha repeated, crouching before them. She set the candle on the floor and cupped Ellie's face in her hands. "Who did you see, sweetie? Who's out there?"

"No one!"

"No one? Then what are you doing? Why are you looking out the window? Did you hear something?" She looked up at the window. Without waiting for her daughter to answer, she sprang to her feet and pressed her nose to the glass. Little was visible save the black night and the slanting rain. "I can't see anything," she said.

"We were just playing a game," Ellie said.

"A game?" Tabitha said, turning from the window, all her muscles seeming to unknot simultaneously. "What game?"

"Dares," Ellie said. "Bobby dared me to look out the window. He said if I said the monster's name three times, I would see it."

"Oh, baby, why would you want to see—" She cut herself off. With a last glance at the window—now she could see her glass-caught reflection, as ethereal as that of a ghost's—she picked up the candle and said, "It's time to go. Rex went to get the Mazda. He will be back here any minute. We have to be ready."

"We're going home?" Ellie asked hopefully.

"You bet."

"What about the monster?" Bobby asked.

"There's no such thing as monsters, Bobby, remember?"

"But we almost runned it over."

"That wasn't a monster. It was just an ordinary person. And don't worry about him. Everything's going to be okay."

Tabitha led the two children back downstairs. In the front room, she helped them put on their shoes and tie their laces. The sight of their tiny shoes and their equally tiny feet caused tears to warm her eyes. *Please don't let anything happen to them. They're just children.*

"Okay, all done," she said to Bobby, lowering his foot from her lap to the floor.

He was looking at the supine police officer. "Can he come with us?" he asked.

Even in the midst of this surreal situation, Tabitha found it strange for Bobby to be talking to her without reservation, for his questions to be directed at her and not Rex.

Strange but nice.

And it was an apt question he'd asked. Were they going to take the police officer? It seemed unconscionable not to. If they left him here he would surely die from his injury, or the murderer would finish him off. Yet what if the murderer began shooting at the car as soon as Rex pulled up? There wouldn't be time to help him even if they wanted to. The safety of the kids came first and foremost above all else.

"We'll do our best," she told Bobby.

"Where's he going to fit?" Ellie asked.

"On the back seat," she said. "You two can squeeze up in the front with me."

"But we won't have seatbelts. And we might crash again."

"We won't crash again."

Lightning flashed outside, visible between the edges of the window frames and the drawn blinds. Thunder followed, a deep-bellied reverberation that climaxed in a deafening whack-boom.

"God must be really angry," Ellie said reverently.

"At us?" Bobby asked.

"At you," she said.

"But I've been good."

"He might hit you with lightning."

"Stop that, Ellie," Tabitha said.

"I want my daddy," Bobby said.

"Soon, Bobby," Tabitha said. "Soon. Just stay brave a little longer."

Which was easier said than done. One minute stretched to two. The indeterminable wait became nearly unbearable.

Rex shouldn't be taking this long. Something must have happened to him. The killer—

No.

Tabitha paced. She checked her wristwatch again. She stroked Ellie's hair. She squeezed Bobby's shoulder. She paced some more.

She paused.

Was that a car? Could she hear an engine approaching? Or was it just the storm?

She listened.

All she could hear was the machine-gun patter of rain on the roof.

Screw it.

She went to the door, flicked the deadbolt.

"Where are you going, Mommy? Ellie asked, frightened.

"Just having a quick look outside."

She opened the door and stuck her head out. Rain thrashed her face and the wind whipped her hair in front of her eyes. She couldn't see anything in the dark. Certainly no headlights.

Before she pulled her head back inside, however, she made a startling discovery.

The woman's body was gone.

Tabitha slammed the door, her heart pounding. Then she bolted the deadlock. He had been right outside! The murderer! He had taken the body!

"What's wrong, Mommy?" Ellie asked.

Tabitha realized she was trembling, and her face must have been alabaster white in the candlelight. "It's just really cold out there, sweetie," she said inanely.

"Did you see my dad?" Bobby asked.

"He's not back yet."

Her heart continued to triphammer as her mind reeled, trying to make sense of the events that seemed increasingly to be spinning out of control.

Why did the killer take Daisy's body? Was he taunting them like when he stuffed the truck keys in Tony's gut? Then again, he had been dragging the police officer into the forest before they almost hit him on the road. So he wanted the bodies of his victims. Why? To dispose of them so nobody would find them? Or was he a cannibal? Some freak straight out of *The Hills Have Eyes*?

What the hell was going on?

"He's awake!" Ellie said.

Tabitha blinked, and the room snapped back into focus. She looked at her daughter, and saw that she and Bobby were both staring at the police officer.

He was conscious again!

Tabitha knelt next to him. "Are you...?" She was going to ask, *Are you okay?* But that was a moot question when your guts were visible. "Do you want some water? Ellie, sweetie, can you go grab the water bottle? It should be on the kitchen table."

Ellie hurried off without a word.

Tabitha looked back at the police officer. His face was pasty, hollowed, his forehead and upper lip damp with perspiration. His breath came in shallow, susurrate rasps. He licked his lips and spoke a word. It was garbled, unintelligible.

"Do you have a radio?" she asked him. "We found your gun outside, but there was no radio."

He shook his head slightly.

She didn't understand why he wouldn't need a radio. Perhaps he was the only cop in town after all. "Does anyone know you're out here?" she asked.

He nodded, and her heart lifted.

"Are they coming now?"

He shook his head. "Wife..."

"Only your wife knows?"

He nodded.

"She'll get worried when you don't come back, won't she? It's late. Shouldn't she be already worried?"

He nodded again.

"So do you think someone is coming now?"

"May'b."

"Do you have a phone?"

"Dropped..."

"Rex didn't find it."

The police officer—Paul Harris—cleared his throat. "Rex? Where's Rex?"

"I told you, he went to get his car—"

Ellie came running back into the room. "Here's the water, Mommy," she said.

Tabitha took the bottle, unscrewed the cap. She poured a little bit into the police officer's open mouth. Some spilled out and over his lips. He swallowed and opened his mouth again. She poured more in. This time less dribbled out.

He licked his lips. "Thank you."

"More?"

He shook his head and his eyes slid shut.

Tabitha decided to let him rest when he mumbled something she couldn't discern.

"What?" she said, leaning closer.

"Mos...quito."

"Mosquito?" she said, baffled.

"Mosquito... Man."

"Mosquita Man!" Ellie squealed. "Is that the monster's

name?"

"Ellie, shush," Tabitha said.

"But that's what the museum woman said! Remember? She said a big mosquita was killing everybody a long time ago! Maybe it's the same monster!"

"That was just a story."

"But the monster had a big nose just like a mosquita!"

"Bar'bra," the cop said, his eyelids fluttering open.

Tabitha nodded. "We stopped by the tourist center on the way here. A tall woman with glasses—yes, Barbara—told us...this story. But what do *you* mean? Are you talking about an exterminator? Is that who attacked you?"

Paul Harris' eyelids were fluttering, as if he were having trouble keeping them open.

"Do you know who it was?" she pressed.

He nodded.

"*Who?*" she demanded. "*Who was it?*"

"Mosquito...Man."

"But does he have a *name*?"

"Story..." He turned his head so he was looking at Ellie. His lips quivered with the effort to speak. "It's true..."

"It's true!" Ellie parroted. "The story's true, Mommy!"

Tabitha was shaking her head, but before she said anything, the police officer mumbled incoherently.

"Mommy!" Ellie went on. "*Mommy!*"

"He's not making sense," she said numbly. "I don't know what he's saying."

Only Tabitha did know what he was saying, or trying to say.

And she hated the deep down part of herself that wondered whether it might be true.

16

R ex stared at the shape in the middle of the road. It was low and small, certainly nowhere near the size of a man. It hadn't been there during the walk in. Had the killer placed a rock in the middle of the road to prevent Rex from driving the Mazda back to the cabin? That didn't make sense. It would mean the killer was ahead of him on the road. And if that were so, why not just attack him before he reached the car?

A trap then? While Rex was busy moving the object, would the killer sneak out from the trees and stab him in the back?

This scenario seemed a little more plausible, and suddenly Rex felt watched. He wiped rain from his eyes and looked to the margins of the road. He could see little in the dark. Should he turn on the Maglite? He had traveled much too far for anybody lurking back at the cabin to see the light. They would have to be closer, say within a hundred feet, and if that were the case, then they were likely following Rex, and knew of his location anyway.

Rex flicked on the flashlight and shone the beam at the shape in the road—and found himself staring at some sort of alien life form. Its black face was small in comparison to its body, and its piggish eyes appeared to be scowling evilly at him.

"*Oh Jesus,*" he said, even as he realized the creature was

not something from the stars but a common North American porcupine.

Its quills, all standing on end, fanned out from its body, creating the illusion of the small face, while at the same time making the rodent seem larger and more threatening than it was.

Rex's muscles unwound with relief.

Just a porcupine.

He continued forward, giving the animal as much space as he could. It turned cumbersomely to follow his progress, clattering its teeth, or perhaps its erect quills, in warning.

"Take it easy," Rex told it, surprised to see it had a white stripe down the middle of its back, most likely to mimic the look of a skunk to help deter predators.

Less than a minute later the trees lining the road thinned, then retreated completely. Without the canopy to shelter him, the rain struck Rex's face with stinging force. Even with one hand shielding his eyes, he could barely see a few feet in front of him.

He ran the final stretch to the Mazda with his head down. The dirt road boiled around his feet. An earsplitting peal of thunder exploded above him, causing him to instinctively duck. He leapt over a pothole overflowing with water, side-stepped a long furrow, then he was at the car.

He already had his free hand in his pocket, thumb jabbing the unlock button on the remote key. The coupe's headlights and taillights winked. He yanked open the driver's side door and dropped in behind the steering wheel, slamming the door shut behind him.

Grabbing his cell phone from the glove compartment, Rex dialed 9-1-1, pressed Speaker, and set the device on his lap. He jammed the key into the ignition, turned it. The engine revved to life.

"Nine-one-one operator," a curt female voice said. "What's your emergency?"

"I'm on Pavilion Lake," he said. "There've been two murders out here. We need help."

"Pavilion Lake?" He could hear the clicks of a keyboard.

"Did you hear me? There've been two murders."

"I heard you. Now don't hang up. Is the perpetrator still around?"

"Yes!" He shifted into Drive and hit the gas. The car lurched forward.

"Can you describe the person to me?"

"I didn't really see him. But two people are dead, and a cop has been injured, badly."

"A police officer?"

He banged over a pothole, flicked on the headlights and windshield wipers. The latter thumped back and forth on full speed yet were unable to clear the rain faster than it fell.

"Yes! A cop! Send someone!"

"I already got a call started and help on the way. What's your name?"

"Rex."

"Rex, what's your last name?"

"Chapman."

"Chapman. And you said Pavilion Lake—"

"Forty minutes past Lillooet on Highway 99. We're at 5 Lake Road."

"I've got an officer on the way—"

"What?"

"I've got an officer coming, sir. If anything changes before we get there, just give us a call right back—"

Rex hung up.

17

Bobby kept his mouth shut while Ellie's mom spoke to the policeman. He was too scared to speak. Part of this was due to seeing how beat up the policeman was. Blood was even coming from his mouth! Bobby had never seen that before. He'd seen a bloody nose—like when a girl a year older than him jumped from the top of the castle in his school's playground, instead of using the slide like you're supposed to, and smashed her knee into her nose —but he's never seen a bloody mouth, and he knew that must mean the policeman was badly hurt, because the blood wouldn't be coming from his teeth but from way down inside him.

The other thing scaring Bobby was seeing how frightened Ellie's mom was. He could hear the fear in her voice, in the way she was asking questions, and she was an adult, so if she was this frightened of the monster, then it had to be super dangerous.

Which meant he could no longer pretend the monster wasn't going to get him. It probably was. And it might not just kill him, it might eat him too. He couldn't imagine what it would feel like to be eaten alive, but he knew it would hurt a lot.

And if that happened, and he was eaten alive and went to heaven, what would happen here on earth? Would everything continue as usual? Would his friends keep going to school? Miss Damond might say a prayer for him in the morning before class began. And Tom Harrity would probably miss him because they always played Superheroes at recess (and Bobby had promised to trade his Silver Surfer action figure for Tom's Ant-Man if it came with the helmet and all the other pieces). But what about everybody else? Would they even notice or care if Bobby didn't come to school again? Would someone else get to sit at his desk? Would they get rid of his nametag taped to the top of it that had taken him an entire afternoon to design? It seemed really weird *not being there*. And what would happen to all of his toys? Not just his Silver Surfer, but his Nerf N-Strike blaster and his remote control car and all of his Legos and, most important of all, his Nintendo Switch? He wouldn't need them in heaven if he could just wish for new ones. So who would get them all?

Nevertheless, what bothered Bobby the most about dying was that his mom would keep on living wherever she was without him. He wouldn't even be able to say goodbye.

Then again, maybe he could tell her from heaven that he was okay? Maybe he could send her a sign through the TV, or peek over the clouds and smile at her?

The bottom line, he decided, was that he didn't want to die yet. He liked his house and his room and Brett Huggins who lived next door and all his other friends at school. He liked having Cap'n Crunch for breakfast on Saturday mornings (he was only allowed to have plain old Shreddies or Corn Flakes the rest of the week). He liked when his dad took him to McDonald's or KFC or Burger King for a special treat. He liked Christmas and Halloween and his birthday parties. He liked eating cake and opening presents. He liked a whole lot of things he didn't want to change—

Suddenly the cabin door burst open and cold air and rain swept inside.

Along with his dad!

"Daddy!" Bobby cried, springing to his feet. He ran to his

dad, who hiked him up into his arms and gave him a big hug and a whisker kiss before setting him back down on the floor.

Ellie's mom was also on her feet. "Rex! I didn't hear the car!"

His dad hugged her next. "Driveway's thick with mud. Didn't want to get stuck."

"Nothing's out there?"

He frowned. "No. Nothing, nobody. But let's not dally. Help me with the cop." He was already moving toward the police officer. "Take his arms."

"What about Ellie and me, Dad?" Bobby asked, already forgetting about death and the afterlife and all that stuff.

"You guys stick right next to us—"

"*Where is she?*" Ellie cried suddenly. She was patting her pockets frantically.

Bobby looked at her. "Who?"

"Miss Chippy!"

Ellie's mom looked in the wooden box where the chipmunk was supposed to be. "Did you take it from there?"

"Yes!"

"I told you—"

"I didn't want her to sleep by herself!"

"She's probably upstairs," Bobby said.

"Can I borrow your flashlight? *Please?*"

Bobby handed her his keychain with the flashlight even as Ellie's mom was shaking her head. "You're not going anywhere, Ellie. There's no time—"

"But I don't want Miss Chippy to die, Mommy! I haven't even played with her yet!"

"I'm not arguing about this—"

Ellie sped from the room.

"Ellie!" her mom shouted. "Ellie, *dammit*, come back here!"

She didn't come back. Bobby heard her feet running up the stairs to the attic.

"That girl!" her mom said, scowling. "Doesn't she know

we need to—"

"Forget it," Bobby's dad said. "We'll be back in a minute. Bobby, you wait here for Ellie. Make sure she's ready to go as soon as Tabs and I return. Got it, bud?"

"Okay!" he said, happy at being treated like a big kid for once.

His dad took the policeman's legs, Ellie's mom took his arms, and together they carried him awkwardly into the night.

◆ ◆ ◆

Ellie scrambled up the staircase so quickly she bent to all fours so she didn't lose her balance and fall backward. When Rex said they were leaving, she touched her pocket, to make sure Miss Chippy was still there—and she wasn't! The zipper on the pocket was open. She had forgotten to close it earlier. Which meant Miss Chippy had fallen out. Ellie was betting it happened when she somersaulted out of the fort.

Ellie knew she was probably going to get grounded when they got home for running off to look for the chipmunk. Her mom hated it when Ellie "dawdled," especially when her mom was late or rushed. But Ellie couldn't leave Miss Chippy here by herself. They were best friends now, and best friends helped each other.

"Miss Chippy?" Ellie said, hurrying toward the two beds, sweeping Bobby's flashlight back and forth across the dusty floor. Rain pounded the roof. Thunder went off like firecrackers. Outside the window, lightning flashed, momentarily blinding her. When the dancing stars cleared from her vision, the dark seemed even darker than it had moments before.

Ellie slowed, suddenly hesitant about being up here alone. She stopped at the first bed and was about to look under it when a cold breeze blew past her face, smelling of damp and earth.

She shone the flashlight at the window.

It was open.

The tattered curtains on either side of it fluttered as if disturbed by unseen hands. Rain soaked the window ledge and the floor before it, creating a shadowy stain on the wood.

Neither she nor Bobby had opened the window.

So who did?

The wind, she thought. *The wind blew it open.*

Only it wasn't a window that opened sideways. You had to push the windowpane up.

The wind couldn't do that.

Could it?

Go back downstairs!

A squeak.

Miss Chippy!

Ellie peeked under the bed—

(*the monster lives there*)

(*I don't care!*)

—and staring right back at her was the chipmunk.

"Miss Chippy!"

She reached her arm under the bed and grabbed Miss Chippy in her hand, careful not to squeeze too tightly. The chipmunk didn't run. Miss Chippy was a good girl. Or maybe she was just too injured. Either way, Ellie had her now.

Withdrawing her arm and sitting up, she lifted the chipmunk to her face, touched noses, and said, "Silly little chippymunk! We almost left you behind!"

Ellie stuck the chipmunk in her pocket—and secured the zipper tight.

All of a sudden she heard a buzzing sound from somewhere in the attic. It reminded her of the whirling her mom's electric toothbrush made, only it was much, much louder, and angrier.

Ellie peeked up over the bed—and screamed.

Tabitha and Rex had just laid the police officer's limp body across the Mazda's back seat and were returning to the cabin when Ellie's scream cut through the night.

No! was Tabitha's first and only thought.

Anesthetized with terror, she burst past Rex and entered the cabin. Snatching the Maglite and Glock from the coffee table, holding one in each hand, she plowed through the afghan and took the steps to the attic two at a time.

She had no plan of action. When she reached the top of the staircase, she was simply going to charge straight into the killer, fighting tooth and nail to drive him away from her daughter.

Only it wasn't the killer who awaited her.

At least, not the killer she had expected.

It was a creature whose improbable reality caused her to come to an abrupt halt.

Tabitha's eyes took in the monstrous abomination all at once. Then, as if unable to accept what they were seeing, they played over it a second time in slow-motion horror.

Two compound eyes, alien and emotionless, protruded from the creature's small, round head like grotesque tumors. A pair of feathery antennae sprouted between them, probing the air. Where the mandible should have been located was a tube-like proboscis, as long and deadly looking as a rapier.

The ghastly thing—*Mosquito Man*, her mind whispered, a moniker that could have graced the neon marquee of a 1980s movie theater showing a midnight creature-feature special—stood upright on two absurdly long, thick legs. Filling the space between them was a plump, insectoid abdomen that bypassed a pelvic region to connect directly to a barrel-chested, black-furred thorax. It was from this truncated middle section that the legs originated, along with four arms that tapered into slender pinchers.

Two of those pinchers held Ellie in a secure grip.

"*Mommy!*" her daughter screamed, kicking and squirming futilely.

"Ellie...?" she said, her voice faltering in the face of the abomination that stood before her.

"*Mommy! Help me!*"

Tabitha found she could not move. The creature's eyes held her in place as securely as a tractor beam. They exhibited no evil, no gleeful malevolence. Yet it was this stone-cold indifference to her presence that made them so utterly horrifying, that stirred within her not only revulsion and fear but ineffable despair.

She was nothing but food to it.

"*Mommeeee!*"

"Baby...?" she murmured.

The creature took a herky-jerky step forward, a bassy, strumming sound emanating from somewhere deep inside its body. It raised its two free pincers before it in the prayer-like manner of a praying mantis.

"*Mom-meeeeee!*" Ellie wailed, the word disintegrating into a keening shriek.

Tabitha's paralysis shattered. She raised the pistol, aimed high for the creature's head so she didn't hit Ellie, and squeezed the trigger. The muzzle flash briefly illuminated the darkness, but the bullet missed its mark because the creature didn't even flinch.

Tabitha squeezed the trigger a second time, but realized belatedly the gun was no longer in her hand. One of the creature's pincers had knocked it free. At the same time she realized this, a jolt of pain shot through her head.

Pincer again.

So fast.

Tabitha collapsed to her knees, dazed. The creature loomed above her—

Something smashed into it, and she grasped groggily that Rex was beside her, swinging the wooden golf club. He struck the monstrous thing again, but this time it slashed back.

Rex grunted in pain.

Then the creature—*Mosquito Man*, Tabitha reminded herself deliriously—turned and scuttled across the attic to the open window, great transparent wings unfolding from its back.

Tabitha struggled to her feet and stumbled after it, still holding the flashlight, the yellow beam painting the attic in hysterical patterns.

The creature flitted through the window into the storming night, wings buzzing, whining.

"No!" Tabitha cried, slamming into the window ledge. A burst of sheet lightning backlit the thunderheads, and in the purple light she watched helplessly as the creature touched down gracefully on the ground.

Tabitha couldn't fully comprehend what had just happened. *Did the Mosquito Man, the goddamn Mosquito Man, just steal her daughter? Where was it taking her? What did it want with her?*

During a subsequent flash of lightning, she saw the creature moving into the forest, and heard Ellie's screams fading beneath the roar of the rain.

Rex gripped her shoulders, spoke to her, though she couldn't make out what he was saying.

"Tabs!" he said, shaking harder. "Tabs!"

The bubble she'd been in suddenly popped. The dumbed-down sounds and sensations she'd been experiencing snapped into crystalline clarity. The underwater-viscosity of time fast-forwarded to its normal speed. Blood pounded in her temples while fear the likes of which she had never known iced every fiber of her being.

Ellie's gone. It took her.

"You're cut!" Rex told her, brushing hair from her forehead.

"I need to find Ellie!" she cried.

"I'll go! I'll get her!"

"No—"

"Stay here! Watch Bobby! Fix that cut!"

Bobby. Bobby was still downstairs, she thought. And Rex was right. She couldn't help Ellie in the condition she was in.

"Go!" she sobbed, tears flooding her eyes. "Go get my baby."

18

Rex charged through the dark, wet forest. The Maglite illuminated glimpses of the vegetation he was trampling, but he was moving so quickly and recklessly, his visibility was so impeded by the rain, he was nevertheless getting flayed alive by branches, twigs, and other woody hindrances.

He barely noticed.

He was moving on auto-pilot, his mind on fire.

It's real! he thought wildly. *Jesus Christ, it's real!*

And not only this, he *remembered* it.

He remembered everything now.

"Take your brother, Rex, and go hide right now. You boys are good at that."

She went to the door.

"Mom!" Rex cried. "Don't leave us!"

"I have to lead him away." She pushed her dark hair from her dark eyes, which were looking at Rex but didn't seem to be seeing him.

"Hide with us," he pleaded.

Attempting a smile that trembled and became a frown, she left the cabin, closing the door behind her.

Rex turned to Logan, whose mouth was twisted in pain. "Did he have a knife?" he asked.

"It wasn't a person," Logan mumbled, and then he began sobbing.

"What?"

"I'm scared, Rex."

"What was it, Loge?"

"I don't know!"

Although Rex was the little brother, he knew he was going to have to make the decision where to hide. Logan was acting way too weird.

Upstairs under their beds was the first spot that came to his mind. But he quickly dismissed this possibility. That was the first place where people looked when they wanted to find where you were hiding.

In the chimney?

Rex grabbed Logan's hand and all but dragged him into the connecting room. He stuck his head into the fireplace's firebox and looked up. The flue was too narrow. Neither of them would fit. When he pulled his head back out, Logan had already thrown the little rug back to reveal the trap door to the root cellar. Rex and Logan had used to play down there. But then at the beginning of the summer their dad found that a family of raccoons had moved in and told them it was off limits, and they hadn't been down there since.

Logan jumped into the hole. "Come on!" he said, his head poking up above the floor.

Rex hesitated. If he went down too, who would put the rug back in place? Someone needed to, or the man who attacked their dad would easily find them (Rex couldn't believe that the person coming after them wasn't a person).

He started swinging the hatch back in place.

Logan stopped it with one of his hands. "What are you doing?"

"I need to put the rug back."

"Where are you going to hide?"

"I'll find a better spot."

Logan held his red-stained hands in front of him. "Am I losing too much blood, Rex?"

Rex shook his head. "I don't think so."

"I don't feel good."

"Just hide. Mom will be back soon."

Rex closed the hatch and pulled the rug back in place. With his heart beating so fast and loud in his chest he could hear it in his ears, he tried to think of a place to hide. In the stove? He was too big. Under the sofa? That was as bad as under the bed. In the closet? No room with the shelves. The bathroom? He could lock the door. No, the attacker would just break it down.

Outside, he decided. There were way more places to hide outside than inside.

Rex left the cabin. It was late afternoon, the sky dull and gray. The forest seemed especially quiet and still. His mind raced through all the places where he had hid before when he and Logan played Hide and Seek—

His mom screamed.

She sounded like she was near the Sanders' place, which was next door but still far away. Maybe she was going there for help? No, it was late summer, and Rex and his family were the last people remaining on the lake. She understood that. She was just leading the attacker away—

(and he caught her)

Rex grimaced. His first instinct was to go and help her, but he knew he would be too late and too small to help. His second instinct was not to hide but to run. He could try to get to the highway, and then to town. Even though nobody was on the lake, there were always cars on the highway. If he could reach it, someone would drive by and pick him up and—

His mom screamed again. It sounded like she was in great pain. This terrified Rex because he had never heard his mother in pain before. Adults, he had thought up until that point in his young life, didn't feel pain, at least not the way kids did, which was why they never cried.

But was his mom crying right then? It sounded like maybe she was, crying and screaming at the same time.

Rex ran down the driveway toward the road. The air was warm, laced with the scent of pine needles and earth and wild-

flowers. This felt out of place. Nobody should be screaming when the smell of wildflowers was in the air. Especially not his mom. She should be down at the dock with him and Loge, wearing her straw hat, reading one of her books and sipping a glass of lemonade.

When Rex reached the road, he did not turn down it toward town. He continued straight across it, crashing into the woods, in the direction he'd heard his mom screaming.

He bashed through branches and trampled saplings and small brush, barely slowing, and then he saw her in the distance, his mom, and the thing dragging her by one arm.

It was a bug.

A huge human-sized bug. But not like the ones in the old black-and-white monster movies. It was the same size as a man in a suit, but everything else about it was wrong. *Its legs and arms were too long to be human. Its waist was too skinny. Its upper body was too compact. Its head was too small. And it moved in an unnatural yet effortless and precise way. Definitely not how a human moved. More like how a man on stilts might look if captured on film and fast-forwarded.*

"Mom!" he shouted in fright.

"Rex?"

Rex kept running toward her, closing the distance. His mom's face, he could now see, was ghostly white and slack, her eyes closed. Her beige shirt was torn open and her tummy covered in blood.

The bug-thing either didn't hear him approaching or didn't care. It kept moving without looking back.

"Mom!"

"Rex?" Her eyes opened. They appeared dead. Eyes of the living dead, or of the living who knew they were going to be dead any moment. "Rex? Baby, no..."

"Stop!" he cried, coming himself to a stop a dozen feet behind the bug. "Leave my mom alone!" He scavenged a pinecone from the ground and threw it. It whizzed past the bug's head, but it got its attention. Its head turned independently of its body, just

enough so one buggy eye could look back at him.

The eye was so devoid of emotion, so utterly alien, that every-thing inside of Rex turned into a mushy soup of uncontrollable fear.

"Mom...?" he rasped, stumbling backward.

"Rex," she said, "go, get away, go..."

The bug released her arm. She fell limply onto her back.

It came for him, fast.

Rex turned and ran, careening through the trees as quickly as his legs would take him, no looking back, no slowing down. He was blind with terror. Even when he reached the road he didn't look back or slow. He just ran and kept running all the way to the highway. He didn't remember when he finally slowed to a walk, but he did at some point, because when a white pickup truck pulled up beside him he was limping on scorched feet. The win-dow was rolled down, and a man was asking him where he was going.

Rex no longer knew. He didn't even know what he was doing on the highway. The man told him to get in, he would give him a lift to town. Rex knew not to accept rides from strangers, but that didn't seem important right then. There was a coldness in-side him, a steady throbbing of terror and loss and unfamiliarity, and nothing and nobody seemed important right then, and so he got in the truck and stared silently out the window, watching the world pass by in a film of darkening despair.

Ellie screamed from somewhere ahead of Rex, tugging him back to the present. He wiped rain from his eyes, shouted back, told her he was coming.

He couldn't risk falling any further behind. If he did, Ellie was a goner. The forest stretched for millions of hectares. It could swallow an army without a trace.

He ran faster.

◆ ◆ ◆

He'd been giving chase for what must have been ten minutes now, and Ellie's plaintive screams were becoming faint and far in between. Rex tried to keep his thoughts positive, but he knew he wasn't going to be able to catch up to her. The beast was too fast. He was falling too far behind.

This understanding enraged him. He was the only person in the world that could save Ellie, her young life depended on his perseverance, and he wasn't up to the task.

Rex sagged next to a giant tree trunk, his breath coming in heaving rasps, his stomach so nauseated he thought he might throw up.

As the rain tore through the canopy and beat down upon him, he realized he could no longer hear Ellie's cries for help.

"Ellie!" he shouted, shoving himself away from the trunk in pursuit once more.

"*Help!*" came a faint cry.

"Ellie," he said to himself, almost a moan. "Ellie!" he repeated, louder.

"*Help!*" Distant, evanescent. "*Help!*"

It was a haunting and surreal experience to be running through a primeval forest in a raging thunderstorm, trying to locate a child only by her terrified screams. It was so outside the norm of daily existence Rex could scarcely believe it was happening, and for perhaps the first time in his life he understood why people who experienced something horribly uncanny often believed themselves to be sleeping and having a bad dream.

"Ellie!" he shouted.

Her reply was a distant shriek, yet different than all the others, for it also held the glassy urgency and intensity of pain.

What had the beast done to her? Rex thought frantically, at the same time wondering if "beast" was the right word to describe the ungodly thing. Because although a beast usually referred to a large, scary animal, it was an animal with a backbone. And the thing that had taken his mother thirty-eight years ago, and Ellie now, was by all appearances an invertebrate, an insect.

A mosquito.

A six-foot-tall mosquito that stands like a man.

Rex came to a halt at the base of a crag where the ground rose steeply and abruptly, and where an abundance of talus had collected from a long-ago rockslide. He turned in a circle until he was facing the scree once more.

A dead-end.

He was not about to turn back, which meant his only option was to climb the debris and see where it led him. Before he could do this, however, Ellie cried out—and it seemed her voice originated from beneath the ground.

Stymied, Rex tore through the vegetation clinging to the rocks and boulders before him...and discovered rotting slabs of timber framing the entrance to a mine.

In his excitement, Rex nearly called to Ellie again, to tell her he was coming, but he didn't, deciding it was best not to let the creature know he had discovered its lair.

Inside the mine the air was cool, moist, and stale. The blackness was stuffy and suffocating.

Rex ran his hand through his wet hair, mustered his nerves, and started into the depths of the mine, sweeping the flashlight beam ahead of him.

The passageway was roughly hewn, circular in shape, the floor strewn with loose stones. A little ways in, it angled downward, leading to a new horizontal shaft that conformed to a more rectangular shape. Here, a set of flat-bottom steel rails resting on timber ties disappeared deeper into the darkness.

Rex followed them, passing a table on which sat an ancient Edison alkaline primary battery, and a marking on the wall, made by the smoke of a carbine lamp, that read Dec. 18, 1902. Roughly fifty feet along, he came to a metal hand winch that stood at the top of a steep thirty-degree rocky stope.

He skidded down the stope, stones shifting beneath his feet. Twice he nearly fell over but managed to keep his balance. At the bottom, he hurried forward—and didn't notice the false floor until he was halfway across it.

He came to an abrupt halt. The series of timber boards beneath his feet creaked precariously. What lay below them? A hundred-foot vertical shaft? One of those booby-trapped spiked pits from an *Indiana Jones* or *Tomb Raider* film?

He took a cautious step forward, testing the strength of the boards with his foot before exerting his full weight. They flexed and creaked more but held. He took another step, then another, then he was back on solid ground.

Rex picked up his pace once again, wondering how deep the tunnels snaked. It would depend on the length of the ore vein they pursued, but they could easily meander for miles. Thankfully, there had so far only been a single, albeit zigzagging, path. Which meant he was not lost. He was on Ellie's trail. He would be able to find his way back to the surface.

He was still telling himself this when the passageway branched in two.

Of course, he thought mordantly.

Rex shone the Maglite down each passage. Both appeared nearly identical. There was no reason to choose one over the other.

"Shit," he mumbled, randomly going right.

The passageway's walls and ceiling closed quickly around him, the rock becoming increasingly jagged and cave-like. Then the tunnel came to an abrupt end. Evidently it had been an exploratory shaft that had struck out.

Rex had only taken a dozen steps back the way he had come when Ellie cried out, her voice small and distant. He resisted the impulse to call back and broke into a reckless trot to make up for lost time. Soon his lungs were heaving and his heart was pounding so quickly and painfully he wouldn't be surprised if it seized up in cardiac arrest. Nevertheless, his only concern right then was finding the poor girl. He could scarcely imagine the terror she must be experiencing. Not only had she been kidnapped by something from the mind of H.R. Giger, she was being whisked away deep into the bowels of the earth—

He tripped over a loose pile of rocks, landing hard on his hands and knees. Grunting in surprise and pain, he glanced back over his shoulder. What appeared to be a small cairn, the size of an ottoman, rose in the center of the tunnel. He'd scattered several of the stacked rocks when he'd driven his foot through it, but the pyramidal shape remained intact. His first thought, ludicrous as it might be, was that the creature had laid a trap for him. But then the flashlight beam revealed a portal in the ceiling directly above the cairn: an ore chute from a higher-level stope. The pile of rocks was not a conscience creation but the result of gravity.

Rex got back to his feet—and hesitated. The creature had wings. It would likely have no problem flying up the ore chute, even burdened as it was with Ellie's weight.

Was that where it had gone?

No, he decided. Ellie's cry had come from somewhere below him, not above.

Hadn't it?

He didn't know for certain. The enclosure of rock and earth dampened sound, making it difficult to judge the distance and direction of the source.

Besides, whether the creature went up the chute or not was a moot point. Rex didn't have wings and couldn't follow it that way even if he wanted to. There was only one direction he could go, and that was forward.

Fifty yards onward the rail tracks ended at a sharp corner where an ore cart, empty of any cargo, lay toppled on its side. Another fifty yards after this, a wall of debris blocked the passageway.

Rex experienced a moment of gut-churning defeat until he got close enough to determine there was just enough space along the left wall for him to pass. Carefully, he shimmied sideways between wall and debris, trying not to think about a cave-in and failing miserably. In fact, as his shoulders scraped the unyielding rock, and clumps of dirt fell from the ceiling to break apart over his head and shoulders, a cave-in was suddenly the *only* thing he could think about. The experience of being buried alive beneath tons of dirt, unable to move anything except your fingers and toes, and maybe not even those, taking your last few tortured breaths as the world faded around you into oblivion...

Rex stumbled free of the narrow space, doubling over, gasping for breath. He closed his eyes and felt as though he might be swaying. Yet with each passing second he felt a little bit better, and when he opened his eyes again the symptoms had passed.

He continued down the passageway, now all too aware of the shortness of his breath and the tightness in his chest and the trembling in his muscles, though he did his best to ignore these discomforts. The one sure way to have another panic attack was to think about having another panic attack.

He was so preoccupied with these thoughts, he once again didn't realize the false floor beneath him before it was too late—only this time it really was too late.

There was a loud crack-splinter, and then he was falling through the air. His feet struck the ground hard, and he fell backwards onto his butt. Pain shot through his tailbone and up his spine. The Maglite launched from his hand and clicked off upon colliding with something.

Blackness reigned.

Rex scrambled around on all fours until his hand curled

around the cylindrical barrel of the flashlight. Switching it back on—*still worked, thank God!*—he aimed the beam at the hole he'd fallen through.

He didn't think he could monkey his way back up there, which meant he would have to continue the way he had been going and hope this new shaft mirrored the direction of the one above.

Back on his feet, ignoring the dull pain pulsing in his bones, he went straight for fifty feet or so before veering left and downward. Twenty feet later he did a double take, snapping the flashlight beam back to what it had flitted over.

A skeleton.

It was small, yellowed, most likely avian. Yet a skeleton was still a skeleton, a representation and reminder of death, and his stomach soured.

Rex pressed on, though his mind remained on the bird. What had it been? A canary that had escaped a miner's cage? A crow or sparrow that had flown into the tunnel system and had gotten lost and died? He didn't know, and he told himself the bird didn't matter, shouldn't matter...but it did. There was something about its remains, something sinister, something he was missing...

Wildlife, he thought in an epiphany.

Where was all the wildlife?

Thus far, the mine had been completely barren of any such life. This was wrong, unnatural. An abandoned mine was the perfect habitat for bats, owls, rattlesnakes, rats, mice. Maybe even a mountain lion, or a black bear. So why had he not yet come across a single living animal?

It was possible the tunnels were filled with lethal concentrations of dangerous gases—methane or carbon monoxide perhaps, or hydrogen sulfide—killing trespassers not long after they entered.

Yet the more probable explanation, he believed, was that wildlife simply knew not to come down here, knew, or sensed, that it was home to an apex predator that outclassed anything else on the food chain.

The tunnel dead-ended. At least Rex thought it did, for a moment. Then he saw the square hole cut into the rock floor. He knelt at the lip of it. A wooden ladder descended into its inky depth.

He frowned. The creature didn't climb down a ladder. Its physiology would make this unlikely, comical even. *Ladders are for humans, stupid.*

Nevertheless, what option did Rex have but to descend? Turning around would lead him nowhere.

Maneuvering to his butt, his legs dangling into the hole, he tucked the Maglite beneath his left armpit and latched onto the ladder. It was bolted into the rock. He descended, keeping his left arm pressed tightly to his side so as not to drop the flashlight. It was a long way to the bottom, made more so by how slowly he seemed to be progressing. He couldn't help but think he was entering the depths of hell, a clichéd metaphor, but apt for the circumstances.

He counted forty-one rungs—perhaps the height of a three-story building—before the rock opened around him, and another ten rungs before he stepped off the last one onto solid ground.

Transferring the flashlight to his hand, he turned around, sweeping the beam through the dark—and found himself in a passageway similar to all the others. He wasn't sure what he'd been expecting, but more of the same depressed him. He was wandering blindly, irrationally hoping that the passageway he'd departed when he'd crashed through the floor would eventually meet up with wherever this one led him.

In truth, he was getting lost.

Rex was tempted to finally call Ellie's name, but he didn't. The reason for remaining silent was not only to keep his presence secret, as it had been when he'd first entered the mine, but because he now feared Ellie might not call back.

And a lack of response would be the worst possible reply.

The time for wishful thinking had long passed, and he had to be brutally honest with himself. There was no sugarcoating Ellie's predicament. This was not a movie in which the creature was going to keep her alive only for Rex to ingenuously rescue her at the last moment. It had brought her down here for one reason and one reason alone: to devour her. So if he called to her, and she didn't call back, that meant she was likely already dead, and he didn't know if he could deal with that reality right then—sometimes you're better off not knowing, isn't that what they say?—and so he kept quiet as he forged resolutely, and perhaps pointlessly, ahead.

Twenty feet on, the tunnel split.

He chose left.

Twenty more feet and it split again.

He chose right.

He came to several more crossroads and selected his path equally recklessly and randomly as he zigzagged ever deeper into the underground labyrinth.

He was no longer even pretending to keep track of the way he'd come. The lack of natural light was not only disheartening but disorientating. He was not getting lost; he *was* lost. He knew that—and in a moment of self-loathing he realized he almost secretly hoped he was lost, because then he could turn around and leave this dank tomb. He would not have to face off against the abysmal creature, an encounter no bookie worth their salt would back him to win, even armed with a pistol as he was. He would not find and rescue Ellie

(she was already dead)

but she wasn't even his kid anyway. If it were Bobby down here, he would spend his dying breaths tracking him down. But Ellie…wasn't his kid. He loved her, he thought she was a great girl, but she wasn't his. So why was he risking his life to find her? It was madness. She was gone, and Bobby was still alive. That's what mattered. *Bobby was alive.* He needed his father. So it was time Rex stopped playing hero and got the hell out of there. That was the

(cowardly)

right thing to do. Get back to the cabin, protect Bobby until the police arrived. This nightmare could all be over in a few hours. He and Bobby and Tabitha would be safe. Ellie would be gone, but the rest of them would be safe...

Rex realized he was mumbling unintelligibly and viciously to himself. He was losing it. He really was.

Stop being such a fucking pussy. You're not a coward. You never have been. Ellie's down here, and you're going to find her, and you're going to kill the abomination that's taken her.

You're going to do all of that, or you're going to die trying.

◆ ◆ ◆

Later.

Rex was deep in the earth. Very deep. The section of mine he had recently descended to was not solid rock, nor was it shored up with timber supports. It was simply compressed dirt, the walls lined with backfill. A smaller tunnel veered left. He ignored it, continuing straight on his chosen path.

Soon he came to yet another false floor. Most of the timber boards were missing. Looking down, he could see a lower, irregularly shaped stope.

He dropped onto the rubble pile. The stope led to a new subterranean corridor that was nearly twice as wide and tall as all the others he had passed through. It was also the most precarious looking, with a patchwork of stulls bracing up platforms that would have once supported miners, the series of wooden props held in place with nothing more than rusty nails and baling wire.

The ground was strewn with relics from the past. Another Edison battery, like the one he'd first seen upon entering the mine. Bits of rusted machinery of which he could make neither heads nor tails. A tobacco tin. What appeared to be a utilitarian lunchbox. A dynamite box labeled "Hercules I.C.C.C 14." A repurposed can turned into a sieve. Blasting caps, wooden ties, a pickaxe.

Further along, Rex entered another stope, different than the last, as this one was so large the flashlight beam didn't reach the far side, revealing instead only impenetrable darkness.

In fact, it wasn't a stope at all. It was a natural cavern. Swaths of the walls and ceiling were stained aqua blue by dripping water. Translucent calcite crystals as large as his fingers sprouted from the rock, alongside deposits of brilliant shiny gray galena, and buttery hued fool's gold.

Rex entered the vast space cautiously. The ground was littered with more junk the miners had left behind, including a faded newspaper from the turn of the last century with the headline proclaiming "Russia at War with Japan," and a denim jacket missing one sleeve and covered in white drops that might have been candle wax.

The flashlight beam played over another skeleton.

Not a small bird this time. The animal had once been a mature stag. A set of tined antlers were still attached to the skull, though something had happened to its legs, as only an elongated vertebrae and a partial ribcage remained of the body.

The sight, morose as it was, buoyed Rex's spirit. It meant there must be another way to get down here other than via the ladder shaft.

Which meant there was another, and likely closer, way out as well.

Two dozen paces onward the ground disappeared into a great black hole at least fifty feet wide and who knew how many across.

A subterranean sinkhole?

Struck by an idea, Rex retrieved a stone from the ground and threw it into the hole. Only it wasn't a hole. It was, as he'd suspected upon second analysis, a subterranean lake. The water, which had been as smooth as a black mirror moments before, now rippled around the spot where the stone had plopped and sunk.

He started along the lake's perimeter—and came to four more skeletons. They had once been animals the size of cougars or wolves, and they were within touching distance of one another.

Rex frowned.

Animals did not die together like that.

Not naturally, at least.

Sensing he was no longer on a wild goose chase, Rex continued along the shore of the subterranean lake—discovering more and more piles of bones. Two here, six there. They were all largish animals, with one skeleton appearing to be the remains of a bear.

The creature had not only killed a bear, it had carried it down here.

A bear for God's sake.

How the hell did it do that?

While Rex worried about this, the piles of bones multiplied rapidly, becoming so numerous they were no longer individual islands but a connected sea of white, flooding the ground as far as the flashlight beam allowed him to see.

Rex's head spun, even as an odd numbness anesthetized his terror, allowing him to think relatively calmly and clearly.

It would take decades, perhaps tens of decades, for the creature to devour this many animals. So how long had it inhabited the cavern? Had others before it called it home as well? Did those ancestors discover the cavern once the mine was abandoned? Or were they here *before* the mine? Did the miners inadvertently blast into this cavern, stirring up the proverbial hornet's nest? Was this why the mine shut down?

Were some of these bones human?

Banishing these questions from his mind—the pitch black was not the place you wanted to ask such things—Rex longed to return to the surface more than ever. He should never have come down here. He was in way over his head. Ellie was dead, and he was going to be dead very shortly too. He was going to become a meal to a prehistoric insect that had no right existing in the modern world. This was his sad fate.

Unless he turned around.

Rex's pulse quickened at the prospect. He would have to climb up and out the hole through which he had fallen earlier. He had not thought this possible before, but it had not been a matter of life and death then. Now, he sensed, it was, and if he could find his way back to the hole, he was sure he could climb out of it. He could scavenge some timber, build a rudimentary ladder. Tricky, no question, but doable. And once he was back on that upper level, it was easy sailing. Twenty minutes to the surface. Less than that. Because he would be running this time, hazards be damned, running for all he was worth to get away from this crypt and the evil it harbored.

All he had to do was turn around.

◆ ◆ ◆

He couldn't, he thought with angry despair. He simply couldn't.

He couldn't abandon Ellie if there was even the slightest chance she was still alive.

He forced himself to continue forward, toward his all too likely doom.

Ellie didn't believe that any of what was happening to her was real.

On one level she did. She knew the monster had kidnapped her. It had brought her to its underground home, and it was going to eat her, using her bones as toothpicks to clean its teeth when it was full. She knew all of this as she sat where the monster had left her, with her back against a rock wall in the perfect black, too terrified to move, listening for it to return.

But *knowing* this didn't mean she had to *believe* it. Believing was a choice. It was like pretending. You could know something was true but just pretend it wasn't. She did this all the time. Like if she was playing a game with Bobby, and she was losing, she would pretend she didn't know the score so he couldn't win. Or if she wanted to use a certain toy in the classroom at school during free time, and it was someone else's turn with it, she would pretend she forgot the rules so she could still use it and not get in trouble.

She was doing the same kind of pretending now—pretending that none of this was real, that it wasn't happening, that she would wake up and it would be one of her bad dreams.

The problem with pretending, however, was that she always *knew* when she was pretending. It was like lying. When she lied to her mom or her teacher, she knew she was lying, but just pretended she didn't know what they wanted to know.

So maybe pretending wasn't *like* lying, she decided. Maybe it *was* lying. And if that was the case, she was lying to herself right now.

The monster was real.

It was going to eat her.

Ellie felt tears spill down her cheeks. She squeezed her eyes shut tighter than they already were and pressed the balls of her hands against them, so she didn't accidentally peek and see something in the dark she didn't want to see. *I promise, God, that I'll never pretend or lie again if you send me back to my mommy right now. I'll even be nice to Bobby and stop cheating when we play games. I'll wash the dishes when my mom asks me to and I'll do all my work at school and try my hardest at everything. Please God? Is that good enough? Just send me back to my mommy with your magic. Please God? God? Are you listening? I'm still here. It's still dark. It's so dark. I hate the dark. I'm really scared God. Please send me back to my mommy.*

And then just as Ellie was giving up hope that God was listening, He appeared.

❖ ❖ ❖

Brittle femurs and cracked tibias and splintered jawbones snapped beneath each step that Rex took as he continued along the edge of the subterranean lake.

Time was playing tricks with his mind. He had only been underground for fifteen or twenty minutes, yet it felt like days; he had only been in this large chamber for a couple of minutes, yet it too felt like much longer. It was akin to those last sixty seconds in a hockey game when your team was winning by a one-goal margin and the other team had their goalie out and an extra attacker on the ice. Those sixty seconds could feel like an eternity.

How's this match going to play out, Rex? he asked himself. *You going to win or lose? There won't be a draw. That's not happening, so hope you don't lose, really hope you don't, because there'll be no rematch either. This'll be it. You'll be dead. Ellie will be dead. Nobody will ever know what happened to both of you. Nobody will believe Tabitha that the Mosquito Man got you. They'll have a good laugh over that, no doubt. You'll become a joke, a punch line at summer barbecues while people are swatting mosquitos. And after that, when you're no longer even relevant enough to be a punch line, you and Ellie will simply be gone, numbers added to the sad statistic of people who go missing and are never found. Like Mom and Dad. Like Logan. Only Loge's body did turn up, that was true, but Mom's and Dad's didn't. They didn't bleed to death beneath the cabin. They just vanished into thin air* —

Rex froze as suddenly as if he had just stepped on top of his own grave. His heart reared in his chest. The flashlight beam did not move an inch from the grisly remains directly before him.

The skeleton was different to all the others he had already become desensitized to. It was human and fully clothed. A beige cowl-neck shirt draped pointy shoulders and a flattened ribcage. A pair of flared yellow shorts outlined a butterfly-shaped pelvis and sticklike legs. Silver bangles encircled a bony wrist. Platform shoes held no feet inside them. Dark shoulder-length hair sat atop the skull like a wig. The two crusty orbits stared at him blankly if not facetiously, as if amused he wasn't in on the morbid joke that death was.

"Mom..." he said, barely aware he had spoken.

Look at you, Rexy, all grown up, she said inside his head, the tender, smiling sound of her voice forgotten to him until that moment. *My little boy, all grown up.* Her tone changed, hardened. *But you shouldn't be down here, Rexy. It's not safe.*

"Mom..." he said again, the strength leaving his body in a rush. He sank to his knees, stretching a trembling hand toward her.

I told you to go, didn't I, Rexy? Yes, I did. My little boy, my October pumpkin, I told you to run, and you did, you ran and you ran and you ran...

"Mom..." he mumbled for a third time, the backs of his fingers brushing the smooth coolness of her cheekbone. "I'm sorry, I'm so sorry. I should have stayed. I should have tried to help. But I was so young, so afraid..."

Whatever else he had to say was drowned out in a choke of sobs.

◆ ◆ ◆

Ellie mistook Rex's voice for that of God's, and when she opened her eyes in innocent relief, and saw the bright beam of the flashlight, she cried at the top of her small lungs: "God! I'm right here! I'm right here!"

◆ ◆ ◆

Rex's head snapped toward the cries of alarm emanating from somewhere in the dark directly ahead of him.

"Ellie!" he said, arcing the flashlight from side to side.

"I'm right here!"

Rex leapt to his feet and stumbled forward, careful to give his mother's remains a wide berth. Yet in his haste to reach Ellie he tripped over other bones and fell to his knees, tripped and fell and scrambled. Then he saw Ellie standing against a looming wall. She was squinting at the light blinding her eyes, and waving her hands over her head like a castaway lost at sea trying to catch the attention of a passing boat.

"Ellie!" he said when he reached her, scooping her into his arms and holding her tightly against his chest. "You're alive," he whispered into her hair. "Thank God, oh thank God."

"T-Rex?" she said, her voice muffled against his chest. It was shaky and uncertain like it got when she was all cried out after a big blow-up with her mom. "I thought *you* were God."

"*Shhh, shhh, shhh,*" he said. "We have to get out of here, okay?" He set her down and aimed the light at a patch of floor with no bones so they could see each other in the backsplash. "Where's the creature?" he asked quietly.

"I don't know! It just left me here."

Rex didn't like the sound of that. *Just left her here?* Did it understand that, as a young child, she would be too frightened to attempt to escape on her own? This seemed improbable, which meant it likely had a way to track its prey in the dark.

Was it watching them, or monitoring them, right now?

"This way." He nudged Ellie along the wall. The direction they chose didn't matter. Following it either way would lead them back to the entrance to the chamber. It might take them a little longer than following the shore of the lake, but they would not be so exposed. They would have the rock wall at their backs if the creature attacked them.

When they were halfway or so back to the entrance of the cavern, Ellie yelped and pointed.

Twenty feet away Daisy lay on her back, just as dead as she'd been on the cabin porch, the difference being her arms and legs were now stiff with rigor mortis, and three creatures sat around her body. They were just babies, Ellie's size. Their bodies appeared to be soft and fleshy, their appendages glued down with a slimy substance. Each had a proboscis plugged deep into Daisy's chest.

Ellie had begun making a sound Rex had never heard anyone make before: a mewling whine that was equal parts loathing, pity, and terror.

And then before he knew what he was doing, he was moving, closing the distance to the abominations quickly. They did not look at him, did not react in any way to his approach.

Were they too stupid to register him as a threat, just as mosquitos were too stupid to realize they were going to get swatted if they landed on your skin? Or were they simply too busy sucking up blood?

These thoughts came and went in the time it took Rex to withdraw the pistol from the waistband of his pants. He aimed three times and squeezed the trigger three times: *pop, pop, pop.*

The head of each creature—pupae?—exploded in blood and pus and goo, and their obscene bodies slumped forward onto poor Daisy's corpse.

Everything was coming together inside Rex's head at an almost nauseating pace, everything was ticking, clicking, and making sense. *It's why it guts you. No major veins or arteries in your stomach. That means no hemorrhage, no wasted blood. It guts you to incapacitate you, so it can carry you down here. At least large prey like humans. Smaller stuff—birds, rodents, chickens maybe—it just slaughters on the spot. But for something big—a human has one and a half gallons of blood inside it, a deer or bear much more—it brings it down here so it can suck away at its leisure. Not to mention offer up a blood buffet to its greedy little offspring.*

That's what happened to his mom. Probably his dad too.

And the Petersons? And the Ryersons? Were their skeletons —their leftovers—down here somewhere? The Ryersons had two girls. Were they down here? Had they been exsanguinated? Perhaps while they were still alive? Because that's another reason it gutted its prey, wasn't it? It takes a long time to die from a stomach wound, days sometimes, and as long as your heart's pumping, your blood's getting oxygen, staying fresh.

Oh Jesus—was that why Ellie wasn't *gutted? So she could be served fresh?*

These thoughts filled Rex with not only disgust but insensate rage, and right then in the heat of the moment, he almost wanted the adult creature to show its hideous face.

He wanted revenge, hot, hot revenge.

19

Tabitha was worried sick. She couldn't concentrate, couldn't sit still. Her thoughts were racing, her stomach twisted inside-out. She'd spent the last forty minutes pacing, crying, talking to herself, bemoaning ever letting Ellie out of her sight, acting like a certifiable crazy person.

The behavior wasn't helping Bobby's temperament any. When she cried, he cried. When he asked her a question, she either ignored him or snapped at him. She couldn't help herself.

Her daughter was taken. Gone. Maybe dead. Yes, maybe dead, because Rex should have been back by now. He should have been back with Ellie in his arms. Her Ellie. Her spunky little girl. Her baby.

I'm never going to see her again, am I?

It was a reasonable question, asked matter-of-factly, and it fueled her despair, and right then she hated herself. Hated herself for letting events come to this. She was Ellie's mother. She was her protector. She failed her little girl.

Tabitha sank to the sofa, curled up, and rocked and cried.

Bobby was speaking to her. She looked at him through itchy, bleary eyes. She didn't know how long she'd been crying for, only that it had been a while. She wiped her eyes and nose with the backs of her hands. She needed to pull herself together for his sake.

She tried a smile that felt like the saddest facial gesture she had ever made. "Come here, Bobby, I'm sorry, come here." She opened her arms.

Bobby seemed hesitant, but he came to her, and she drew him into her embrace.

They had never hugged before. He had always been too standoffish. His small body against hers felt so much like Ellie's, so soft and fragile and young, and she thought, *Why couldn't the creature have taken you instead?*

The thought startled her, and she shoved it promptly aside, ashamed of herself.

Why couldn't it have been me? That's what I should be asking. Why not me? It should have been me.

She began to cry again, silently this time, tears only. Bobby didn't say anything. He just held on to her. She bit her bottom lip. It continued to tremble. She tried thinking about anything but her daughter.

It was impossible. She couldn't do it.

The darkness inside her became overwhelming.

She eased Bobby aside. She tried another phony smile. "You're such a brave boy, you know that?" she said, the words coming out of her mouth before she was fully cognizant of what she was planning on saying and doing. She thought she knew. The plan was there, in her head, vague, yet taking shape quickly. "You're so brave, Bobby, and when your dad comes back, you're going to be brave for him too, okay?"

What are you doing? she thought, a niggle of panic cutting through the despair. *Don't set this in motion. Don't set this up. You might go through with it.*

She kept talking. "I want you to go upstairs and hide under the bed and stay there until your daddy returns. Can you do that for me, Bobby?"

He looked terrified at the idea. "I want to stay here with you."

"It's best you go upstairs."

"But that's where the monster got Ellie!"

Hearing her daughter's name spoken aloud broke Tabitha's heart all over again. "The monster's not coming back," she said tightly. "You'll be safe up there. Just until your daddy comes back."

"But I don't want to go!"

His refusal strengthened Tabitha's resolve to commit to her plan. She sat up straight. "We're not going to argue about this, Bobby. You do as I say."

Bobby frowned, then slid off the sofa.

She nodded. "Go on now."

He departed to the other room, and the last of her reservations went with him. She gasped, as if she had been holding her breath for the last minute or so. She covered her mouth with her fingers. She was really going to do this, wasn't she? Yes she was. She couldn't live without Ellie. She couldn't live not knowing what happened to her, or, perhaps more accurately, knowing what happened to her, because there was only one reason the creature took her.

So how are you going to do it?

The easiest method would be to hang herself. She had spent enough time since Katy Pignette's murder in morbid contemplation of just such an act, and she knew she could use the sash from her bathrobe as the ligature. Tie one end around the horizontal metal pole in the closet. Stick her head in a noose, kneel, and lean forward. The pressure on her carotid artery would cause her to black out in seconds, even if the lack of blood to her brain wouldn't kill her for another half hour.

Yet that was the problem.

Rex might return before she could die properly, or Bobby might come downstairs. Either one of them could "save" her —which would probably leave her with serious brain damage, or in a vegetative state. More than that, she simply didn't want Bobby to be the one to find her. He was five years old. After tonight, he was going to have enough issues to last him a lifetime; she wasn't going to dump anything more on him.

She'd need to do it outside, she decided. She would have to get far away from the cabin, not to mention finding a branch that was the right height and would not snap under her weight. Doing this would be uncomfortable in the storm. She would get cold and wet—

You're killing yourself! she thought indignantly. *It's the last thing you'll ever do. And you're worried about getting cold and wet?*

Tabitha stood on suddenly shaky legs. Adrenaline coursed through her veins. Every object in the room came into angelic focus. And despite being terrified right then, she found herself decidedly *excited*. She would finally be *free*.

Yes, Tabs, you damn sicko, you definitely have a bad gene inside you. More than likely, you have a whole handful of them inside you.

Moving robotically, Tabitha went to her suitcase, withdrew her bathrobe, snaked the sash free from the loops. She had bought the bathrobe at a shopping mall last June while visiting her younger sister, Ivy, in Olympia. They'd spent the morning browsing the shops for a present for Ivy's husband's upcoming birthday. They'd had coffee in a pleasant little café, and lunch at an Italian eatery, where the waiter had hit on both of them. It had been a fun weekend.

You'll never get to see Ivy again. Or Beth. Or Vanessa or Rex, for that matter...

Yes, all of that was true, but she would never see her little girl again either, and that was the harshest reality, the one she could not live with.

Tabitha left the cabin as quietly as she could. As soon as she stepped outside into the night, the storm iced her skin and chilled her to the bone. She set off in an arbitrary direction, her hands shielding her eyes from the slanting rain.

A blast of lightning stabbed the sky purple. And in that brief moment, through the silhouetted, swaying trees, she saw the vast, dark expanse of the lake, its previous calm surface now boiling with whitecaps.

She made her way toward it.

20

Moments after Rex returned to Ellie's side, a high-pitched whine filled the air.

"It's coming!" Ellie cried.

Heart thumping, Rex aimed both Maglite and pistol into the void above them.

He caught a glimpse of the creature.

It strafed right. He tracked it. Squeezed the trigger in panic.

Did he hit it?

The whining receded but didn't fade completely.

"Where is it?" Ellie cried.

"Run!" he said, barely getting the word out of his fear-shrunken lungs.

She took off ahead of him. He followed, scanning the darkness. He could still hear the whine of the creature's wings. It was either on the other side of the chamber or very high above them.

Had the bullet struck it? Was it injured? Or had the shot merely scared it off?

He shouldn't have slaughtered the pupae, he realized. They hadn't been a threat. And now there were only three rounds left in the pistol's magazine.

Ellie tripped and fell. Said "Ouch!" when her hands and knees slapped the ground. Before Rex could help her she was up and running again.

The whining increased in volume and intensity from somewhere directly in front of them.

He shouted, "Ellie! Stop!"

She skidded to a stop and whipped her head around to look at him, her loose black hair falling across her childish face. He moved in front of her and aimed the flashlight and gun straight ahead. The whining changed in pitch and direction. Confused, he aimed up, straight, right, left, up again.

Where the hell was it?

The whining stopped.

"Stay behind me," he whispered harshly.

Blinking perspiration from his eyes, Rex crept forward, keeping his back to the rock, his arms outstretched in a shooter's position, his trigger finger slick with sweat.

Don't get spooked. Don't fire again until you have a sure shot.

He heard a noise at two o'clock, a shifting of rubble, or bones.

He aimed the flashlight beam accordingly.

The man-sized insect was thirty feet away from him, standing perfectly still, its compound eyes unreadable, its antennae twitching as if smelling or tasting the air, its proboscis jutting from its face phallically. It stood erect on its two long legs. Its pinchers were raised before it, the concave jaws snipping silently at the air.

"Eat lead," he said quietly, aware of the absurdity of the comment as he squeezed the trigger.

The shot—both deafening and gratifyingly powerful—struck the thing square in the thorax. It squealed and twisted its vertebrate-esque body sideways. Its translucent wings sprang open from where they had been folded closed behind its back and buzzed frantically.

Rex fired again and again. The last two bullets both hit their mark.

Nevertheless, the creature was gaining lift fast, disappearing into the void above them once more.

Rex's ears rang hollowly. His pulse galloped. His eyes

stung with sweat.

Ellie was screaming.

He spun toward her, crouching at the same time.

"I hit it!" he said. "Now's our chance! Run!"

She clamped her mouth shut and ran.

Rex stuck right behind her.

They reached the exit to the chamber quickly. Rex's spirit soared, and he experienced the closest thing to hope since entering the mine.

They could do this. They could escape alive.

Tossing aside the now useless pistol, he scooped Ellie into his arms so they could move faster. A strange calmness fell over him as he selected without hesitation or error each tunnel leading them back the way he had come. When they reached the spot where he had fallen through the timber boards to this Dantean lower level, he hiked Ellie onto his shoulders.

"Stand up," he instructed her, transferring his hands to her ankles to support her. "Can you reach the boards?"

She was standing full height. "Yes!"

"Okay, hold on tight. I'm going to push you up higher."

He slipped his hands beneath her sneakered feet and pressed upward, like he was using the shoulder press machine at the gym. Almost immediately Ellie's weight lightened as she wormed up onto the jutting planks, her feet kicking.

Then her head peeked back over the hole. "Come too!"

"I'm coming. I just need to find—"

The words died in his mouth. Killed by the whining of wings.

Everything inside Rex wilted. He had run out of time. He was trapped and unarmed.

I don't want to die, he thought. And a split second later: *Everybody dies eventually.*

He looked up at Ellie. "You have to go without me." Standing on his tiptoes, he passed the flashlight to her. "Just keep choosing whatever tunnel leads up."

"No!" she whispered breathlessly, and in that moment he saw the beautiful woman she was going to become. "No! T-Rex! Please!"

The whining was drawing closer, shrill, like an angry dentist's drill.

"There's no time for this, Ellie!

"But—"

"Go! Get away! Go!" he said, realizing sickly that he was repeating verbatim what his mother had told him thirty-eight years earlier. "Get back to the cabin! Your mom's worried sick about you! Go!"

The mention of Tabitha clearly struck a note within her, because the fear in her face hardened into resolve. "See you later, alligator," she said, grinning expectantly.

"In a while, crocodile," he replied, swallowing hard.

Her head vanished. The light receded. Blackness cocooned him.

Exhaling deeply, resignedly—*I did my best, let it be enough*—Rex turned to face the hellish abomination approaching him in the uncompromising dark.

21

Teeth chattering and body shivering, arms folded across her chest, Tabitha stood at the start of the dock, staring out at the frothing lake.

She no longer noticed the rain slapping her face or the wind tearing at her clothing and hair. She wasn't even really seeing the lake. She was staring inward, asking questions that had eluded philosophers since the beginning of recorded history.

What's the point of it all? Why are we here? Why give us the awareness that life is fleeting, that we're going to die? Why make us love others when it's so easy to lose them?

She didn't have answers to these queries, of course. But suddenly existence seemed absurdly comical. One big joke that a higher being was having at humankind's expense.

No, not a joke, she amended, an experiment. We were nothing but curious bacteria under a God-like scientist's microscope. We were insignificant in the big picture of things and thus our individual lives were not deserving of meaning.

Because if God the Joker cared about us, if God the Scientist cared, He wouldn't make life so cruel. He wouldn't give Tabitha a husband who was a lying cheat, or a teenage daughter who hated her guts. He most certainly wouldn't have allowed a giant insect to steal away her innocent baby.

It used to make sense. Life. It used to make perfect sense.

Wake up, make the girls their lunch, drop off Ellie at school, fly the short-haul route to Olympia and back to Seattle again, smile at the passengers, serve them their snacks, pick up Ellie from the daycare, make dinner, try to engage Vanessa in talk, speak to Rex on the phone, watch some TV, go to sleep, do it all over again the next day.

Mundane, maybe, but it made *sense*. There was a purpose to it all. Being a good mother. A productive citizen. A compatible partner. All small steps, agreed, but steps that felt like they were going in the right direction.

Yet it was all bullshit, wasn't it? All a charade. A façade we imposed on life to give purpose where there was no purpose, meaning where there was no meaning.

Without Ellie, without her baby, this all became strikingly clear to her.

Thunder growled. Lightning flashed. Rain fell. Wind blew. The lake roiled.

Tabitha picked up the large stone at her feet. She had found it on the way down to the lake. It weighed at least ten pounds or more.

She carried it to the end of the dock. She stopped. Stared down at the choppy water.

Vanessa would be okay. Tabitha had life insurance and a modest nest egg. Vanessa would get that. And she would finally get her wish to live with her father. She would... graduate high school, graduate university, get a job, get married, have kids...and die too.

Jesus Christ, what a joke.

Tabitha inched forward so her toes cantilevered over the water.

She thought about the end of *Romeo and Juliet*. Romeo thinking Juliet was dead and killing himself only for Juliet to wake moments later.

What if Ellie was in fact okay?

What if she returned and found her mother dead?

This was only wishful thinking, of course. Rex had been

gone for more than an hour now. If he'd somehow caught the creature and rescued Ellie, he would have been back long ago. The fact he hadn't returned meant only two things. He was either still searching the forest for Ellie (and if this were the case, Ellie was as good as dead), or he had fallen victim to the creature himself.

Tabitha scuffed another inch forward. The weight of the stone was already causing her arms and shoulders to ache. It was either now or never.

Another inch. Only her heels remained planted on the dock.

She felt herself tipping forward, falling.

The water smashed her face. Her lungs shucked up at the coldness of it. The stone threatened to slip free from her grasp, and she gripped it more tightly.

She sank.

22

The whining stopped.

The creature had landed. Probably no more than ten feet away from Rex. He could smell a repugnant oily scent.

He didn't feel fear. He had expended all his fear.

He felt only rage. Rage that this creature had invaded his life twice now. Rage that it had killed his family and ruined his childhood. Rage that it had killed Daisy and Tony and maybe the cop back in the cabin. Rage that it had taken Ellie. Rage that it had led him to this inevitable sacrifice.

Rex heard the thing moving toward him. It didn't make much noise, but without sight, his ears, like his smell, were fine-tuned.

Come on, you fucking bug.

It came. Slowly. It knew he was there, surely. It knew it out-powered him too. So it was probably confused why he wasn't running away.

Come on.

The savage fury building inside him turned into a blood-lust.

Oh, he wanted it dead. He so wanted it dead.

Before entering the bone chamber, Rex had scavenged a stick of dynamite from one of the several wooden Hercules boxes he had come across. He now held the stick in his left hand. The absorbents and stabilizers were long past their expiry date. The stick was damp with sweated nitroglycerin. Small crystals had formed on its surface.

The dynamite was unstable as hell.

He had been crazy to be carrying it around with him. But when he'd picked it up he'd largely conceded he'd been heading to his death, and when he'd miraculously found Ellie, he'd completely forgotten about it.

He sparked the flint of his Bic lighter. A bluish flame appeared.

The creature, he saw in the anemic light, was only a few feet away from him now.

Sneaky bastard.

Rex touched the flame to the short fuse. It caught with a hiss and burned hungrily toward the blasting cap.

The creature attacked. One of its pincers arced toward his neck.

Rex's last thought was, *Figured you'd go for my gut.*

The stick of dynamite dropped from his grip and landed on the earthy ground.

His decapitated head thumped next to it a moment later.

Two shafts higher Ellie came to a fork in the tunnels. T-Rex had told her to pick tunnels that went up, so she picked the left one. She was only a few steps into it when an enormous blast shook the mine system. She stumbled forward and landed on all fours. Dirt from the ceiling fell onto her head and shoulders and back.

She couldn't fathom what had caused the blast—she had a half-formed thought of a waking dragon bellowing fire from its mouth—but she knew it wasn't a gunshot.

Maybe T-Rex had found a cannon somewhere to shoot the monster with?

She was tempted to turn around and go find him, but he'd told her that her mom was worried sick, and she most likely was. She got worried sick when Ellie went to the cereal aisle in the supermarket without telling her.

Ellie scrambled back to her feet, shook the dirt from her hair, and hurried on.

23

Constables Stephen Garlund and Karl Dunn had been thirty kilometers north of Whistler Blackcomb in the town of Pemberton, investigating a report of domestic violence (iced-up junkie who hadn't slept in days smacking around his subservient girlfriend), and thus they were the northernmost officers on nightshift when the call came over the Motorola two-way radio of multiple homicides on Pavilion Lake.

That had been ninety minutes ago. Now Garlund was navigating the big Chevy Suburban carefully down the shitty road that served the lake, trying to avoid the worst of the bumpy craters. The storm wasn't making the going any easier.

Garlund had always preferred working a one-man car. He enjoyed the freedom of driving around by himself, eating whatever he wanted, listening to whatever music he wanted, pretty much doing whatever he liked. If a bit of community relations so fancied him, he could talk to business owners or say hi to the folks at the community center without a partner getting impatient with him. If he saw a traffic violation, he could use his discretion to pursue it or not without having to justify his decision. Nevertheless, the winter season at Whistler Blackcomb was kicking off soon. The influx of skiers and snowboarders turned the small mountain community into a den of revelry and boozing, and the powers that be were experimenting with pairing up patrol officers, despite the fact this meant halving the patrol coverage.

Anyway, Garlund couldn't complain too much. Constable Karl Dunn was a good guy. Bit of a straight arrow, but easy enough to get along with. Curly blond hair, lively blue eyes, and he always seemed to be smiling, even when he was talking about nothing funny.

"So what are these rumors I'm hearing about?" Dunn asked out of the blue.

Garlund glanced at him to see if he was smiling. Sure was. Smiling on the way to the scene of multiple homicides. "What rumors?" he asked, swerving hard to avoid a flooded pothole he saw at the last moment. The windshield wipers beat back and forth hypnotically.

"Heard you bought a house in North Vancouver," Dunn said.

"Yup," Garlund said.

"You never told me."

"Never told anyone. Maybe one or two people."

"It's just that I've been your partner these past couple weeks, eight hours a day we're together, and you're going to be relocating, and you don't tell me?"

"I never told anyone anything about leaving. Maybe I won't."

"Won't leave? Why'd you buy a house then?"

Garlund shrugged. "I don't know what I'm going to do with it yet. Maybe rent it out. Maybe move. I don't know."

"Hey, you don't like me that much, that you gotta move away, just ask for a new partner."

"You are a bit nosey, Hoops." Hoops was Dunn's nickname, on account he was decent at playing basketball, especially hitting three-pointers.

"So what is it, Steve? Tired of Whistler? Bored out here?"

"I told you, I haven't decided if I'm going anywhere."

"But you're thinking about it."

Garlund shrugged again. "I like Whistler. I like my job here. It's Clara."

"What about Clara?"

"We're separating."

He frowned. "Shit! I didn't know that."

"Because I never told you. I haven't told anyone. So don't go yapping."

"Is it…a mutual thing?"

"I suppose so. You got to be young to have a one-sided breakup. When you're both fifty-two and have kids, you're too tired to get passionate about it. We just sat down and discussed it. Made sense for both of us. Decided we'd do it when the youngest, Joey, graduates high school in the spring."

"Oh man, Steve. I didn't know—I just mean, I'm surprised. You and Clara always seemed fine when I saw you together, you know?"

"We are fine. We're just not great anymore. We get on each other's nerves. We annoy each other. Being around someone for long enough, that just happens. You'll find out."

The smile returned, proud. "Jenny and me are all good."

"You've been married for how long?"

"Three years."

"Nothing bugs you about her?"

Dunn thought about it for a few seconds. "Sure, some things."

"Take all those things and multiply them by ten. And then think about how much they annoy you and multiply that by ten too. Then you'll probably know what it's like to live with her in thirty years."

"Jeez, you're a fun guy sometimes, Steve. What does Clara do that bugs you so much?"

"There're a lotta things."

"Name one."

"She's stopped brushing her teeth."

Dunn laughed, a rapid-fire burst of merriment. "What?"

"Not all the time, Hoops. But she doesn't do it two or

three times a day like she used to. Some days she'll brush them in the morning, or before bed. Some days she won't. It's annoying. How hard is it to brush your teeth?"

"How do you know she doesn't brush them?"

"I can smell her breath."

"Maybe she just has bad breath?"

"Halitosis? No, she doesn't have that. Anyway, I can tell when her toothbrush hasn't been used."

"How?"

"It's dry."

Dunn sounded surprised. "You check her toothbrush?"

"Sometimes. I think sometimes she doesn't brush her teeth just to piss me off."

"Jesus, Steve," Dunn said. "Yeah, maybe you should be getting a divorce after all, if this is where you guys are at. Shit— lookout!"

Garlund saw the child in the middle of the road too. She was lit up ghost-like in the headlights. He hit the brakes. The SUV slammed to a stop.

The little girl remained standing shock-still, her jet-black hair plastered to her head like a helmet, her eyes wide and unblinking. She wore pink jeans and a soaked-through white tee-shirt with the blue Care Bear on it.

Garlund grunted, "Where the fuck did she come from?" He threw open his door and was about to climb out when the girl ran to him instead.

"Are you a policeman?" she asked, looking at his uniform. He was dressed in his open-collar patrol jacket and dark blue trousers with gold strapping. His peaked cap was on the laptop next to him.

"I am," he said. "What are you doing out in this weather? Nevermind that, get in, quickly, you're going to catch your death." He opened the back door for her, helped her up onto the plastic seat, and gave her his jacket to drape around her shoulders like a cape. When he returned behind the wheel, he cranked up the heat in the cab, then turned to study her through the wire mesh. She held the jacket closed at her neck. Her lips were blue, and she appeared to be shivering.

"What's your name?" Dunn asked her in a friendly voice.

"Ellie," she said.

"Did you get lost somehow, Ellie?"

"Sort of," she said.

"Sort of?" Garlund said, a bit too roughly.

The girl, Ellie, looked like she might cry. "I just want to find my mom. I want to go home."

Garlund couldn't imagine there being many families on the lake in October, and he made the logical connection. "Are you Rex Chapman's kid?"

Her face brightened. "You know T-Rex?"

"No. But we got a call from him."

"He's not my dad. He's my mom's boyfriend."

"He said there's been some trouble out here?"

The girl nodded but didn't say anything more.

"There been trouble?" Garlund pressed.

"Yes," she said, looking at her lap.

"Some people been hurt?"

She nodded. "A policeman. He got cut in the stomach." She pointed to her belly.

The Chief of Police of Lillooet, Paul Harris, Garlund presumed. The man had been policing when Garlund was still a boy. They'd met on a few occasions, and Garlund had nothing bad to say about him.

"Who cut him?" Garlund asked.

"The Mosquito Man," the girl said.

He blinked. "Who?"

"He's a monster. He took me to his cave. He wanted to eat me."

Garlund and Dunn exchanged glances.

"What did he look like?" Dunn asked, still using his friendly kid voice.

"Like a mosquito!"

"He was wearing a mask?"

"No! He was a real mosquito. But big, like you."

Garlund and Dunn swapped another glance.

"I think we better get to this cabin," Dunn said.

Garlund nodded, faced forward, and put the Chevy Suburban in Drive.

Dunn continued questioning the girl. "So who's at your cabin right now, Ellie?"

"It's not mine," she said. "It's T-Rex's."

"Is he at the cabin?"

"No, he was in the cave with me." Her voice faltered. "He stayed back to fight the Mosquito Man. But he said he was going to meet up again."

"Your mom is there then?"

"Yes, and she's worried sick I'm gone."

"Because you ran away?"

"No! I told you! The Mosquita Man took me. I was looking under my bed for my chippymunk, and the monster kidnapped me. It jumped through the window and ran into the woods."

"This is serious business, Ellie," Dunn said, adopting a slightly stricter tone. "It's not time for make-believe."

"I'm not lying or pretending! I'm telling the truth! I promise!"

"Is the policeman at the cabin?" Garlund asked, glancing in the rearview mirror, but unable to see the girl.

"Yes, my mom's taking care of him."

"Is anyone else there?" Dunn asked.

"Just Bobby."

"Who's Bobby?"

"His dad is T-Rex. We're the same age but we're not friends. Why are these seats so hard?"

"So we can clean them if anybody gets sick back there."

"I'm not going to be sick."

"That's good."

"Are we almost there?"

"There's a light ahead," Garlund said. "Must be it."

He turned up a gravel driveway and parked at the end of it behind a Mazda sedan.

"Ellie," he said, "you're going to have to sit here for a minute while we go see who's inside."

"But I want to see my mommy!"

"You stay here with her, Hoops. I'll go have a quick look." Dunn nodded.

Clapping his cap on his head, Garlund got out of the SUV and went to the Mazda. He aimed the flashlight into the cab —and saw a person stretched out on the backseat. He opened the back door and recognized the man to be Paul Harris, his craggy face gaunt and pale. He clasped a pillow to his blood-ied gut.

Garlund said, "Chief? You with me?"

Harris opened his eyes but didn't say anything.

"Who did this?"

No answer.

"Paramedics will be here soon," he told Harris. "I'll be back." Outside, he unholstered his Smith and Wesson and went to the cabin. He eased open the door and peeked inside. The place was bathed in soft candlelight.

"Hello?" he called.

"Hello?" a young voice called back from somewhere else in the cabin.

"That you, Bobby?" Garlund asked.

A pause. "Who are you?"

"I'm a police officer. You just stay up there for the time being, okay?"

"Okay."

Garlund closed the door and was about to return to the SUV when he spotted a light down by the lake.

Frowning, he waved Dunn over.

The Chevy's door opened, slammed shut. Dunn dashed through the rain.

"The boy's inside," Garlund told him. "Paul Harris too. He looks bad. No other bodies I saw. Bring the girl inside and wait there until backup gets here."

"What about you?" Dunn asked.

Garlund nodded at the lake—and did a double take. The light was gone.

"I saw a light down there a second ago. A flashlight beam. I'm guessing the mom."

"Or whoever cut the cop."

Without replying, Garlund took his flashlight from his duty belt, turned it on, and picked his way down the slope through the trees. The rocky ground was mossy and slippery. At the bottom the wind blowing in off the lake reached gale-like force, sweeping his cap off his head and howling in his ears. A dock jutted over the rough water. Nobody was on it. Nobody along the shore either.

"Hello?" he called, the storm shredding his voice.

There was no reply.

He started along the dock, playing his flashlight over the weathered boards, the dark water—

Ten feet to his right. An arm. Riding the peaks and troughs of the waves.

A head too, black hair fanning around it like a lily pad.

Garlund leapt off the side of the dock. The ice-cold water came to his chest. He splashed toward the body. Reached it, flipped it over. A woman, attractive, her skin fish-belly white.

Garlund dragged her up onto shore, felt for a pulse.

She wasn't breathing.

He commenced CPR.

24

Tabitha was in a gigantic forest surrounded by towering flowers and trees the size of skyscrapers. Both rose dizzyingly into the otherworldly sky, making her feel as tiny as a bug.

No, scratch that, she thought. *I* am *a bug.*

She held out her arms to reveal strange black appendages tapering to points. She brushed her face with them, discovering she had globular eyes and a coiled proboscis.

Frantic, she glanced over her shoulder and found a pair of cerulean wings sprouting from her back—and her fear abated with the understanding she was not a mosquito but a butterfly, the latter metamorphosis somehow acceptable.

She didn't attempt to fly. She didn't know how. And so she walked on legs identical to her arms. She knew butterflies didn't walk erect on two legs, and she likely looked ridiculous, but she was moving, and that was all that mattered. She had to find her way out of this forest and get back to the log cabin. She wasn't sure why exactly, but it seemed very important she accomplish this.

Tabitha came to a huge tented maple leaf the size of a car. Something was beneath it. She could hear a *crunch-crunch-crunch*. She lifted one side of the leaf and peeked beneath.

A ladybug was sitting on her rear in a very unladybug-like way, munching on a stalk of grass. Black dots spotted glossy red wing covers. A cute black face with white patches on both cheeks looked up and smiled.

"Ellie!" Tabitha exclaimed happily.

"Mommy!"

Tabitha wanted to hug her daughter, but she didn't think she would be able to get her arms around her dome-shaped body. "What are you doing here?" she asked.

"I don't know. What are *you* doing here?"

"I don't know either," she admitted.

"Are we dead?" Ellie asked.

Tabitha had not thought of this possibility. "I don't think so."

"How do you know?"

"Why would we be dead?"

"Because you killed yourself. You jumped off the dock. Remember?"

Tabitha did remember now, and a coldness stole over her. She recalled the all-encompassing darkness. Not knowing up from down. Water entering her mouth and nose. Her throat contracting. Her eyes straining. Her lungs begging for air. Everything turning yellow, then sharp black, then pungent white, the purest color she had ever seen. Then her body going limp as a drowsy acceptance settled over her.

And Ellie speaking calmly and omnisciently to her: *Mommy, I'm safe. I'm okay. Don't die, okay? I'm coming home now. I want to see you. Don't die. Please come back, please open your eyes, please be there for me—*

Tabitha opened her eyes. Choking. Vomiting brackish water. A man pushing on her chest, then rolling her onto her side, patting her back, talking to her.

She tried to speak but only made a strangled noise.

On her second attempt she managed, "Ellie?"

"She's okay," the man said.

25

"Yuck!" Bobby said, pinching his nose closed with his fingers.

"I told you," Ellie said. "It smells like a toilet."

Bobby leaned forward hesitantly again to smell the monster-stench on Ellie's tee-shirt. He scrunched up his face. "Like a *wet* toilet. Why didn't the monster eat you?"

"I don't know. Maybe it was full? There were bones everywhere."

"Human bones?"

"Maybe."

"Were you scared?"

"A little bit. You would be too."

"Maybe."

"You would be. I promise. It was real dark too."

"When's my dad coming back?"

"He said he'd meet me here."

"Are you sure he killed the monster?"

"Pretty sure. There was a big boom. It was so loud it made me fall over."

"Sound can't make you fall over. It's invisible."

"Well, it did."

"Can I try on the policeman's jacket?"

Ellie clutched it tightly around her neck. "No. He said

only I could wear it."

"Just for a second."

"He'll get mad."

"Please?"

"It's too big for you."

"It's too big for you too!" Bobby reached for it.

Ellie shrieked. "Stop it! You're not allowed!"

Bobby gave up. He didn't want the policeman to get mad and lock him up in jail. "Do you think we're allowed downstairs now?"

"I don't know." She raised her voice. "Mr. Policeman?"

"Yeah?" a voice came back.

"Can we come down now?"

"You're better off up there."

"But we're bored!"

"Stay there!"

The policeman kept talking, and it took Bobby a moment to realize it was no longer to them. "I think my dad's back!" he said.

They both hopped off the bed and ran to the top of the stairs.

"*Ellie?*" a woman called. Her voice was so high-pitched and hyper Bobby didn't immediately recognize it as belonging to Ellie's mom.

"Mommy!" Ellie cried out. She raced down the stairs.

Bobby hesitated a moment, then followed.

When he reached the bottom, Ellie's mom was on her knees and had Ellie in a big hug, kissing her about a thousand times all over her face.

"Baby baby baby baby," she kept saying over and over again between kisses.

Ellie was giggling madly. "It tickles! Stop! It tickles!"

Bobby noticed the two policemen. They had just pushed past the afghan and entered the room. The older one was soaking wet.

Ellie's mom said, "Where's Rex, baby?"

Ellie shrugged. "He stayed back in the cave to fight the monster."

"*What?*" She looked at the policemen. "Where's Rex? Rex Chapman? He's my boyfriend. He saved my daughter." She looked back at Ellie, confused. "How did you get back here without Rex? Where is he? Where's Rex? *Where is he?*"

Tabitha listened in stunned silence to Ellie describe what occurred in the cave, myriad questions immediately demanding answers. Had Rex defeated the Mosquito Man? What was the bang that knocked Ellie to the ground? Why wasn't Rex back already? Was he injured? Lost? Dead?

Tabitha turned to the policemen. "We need to find Rex. We need to help him. He could be injured or lost or... I don't know! But we need to help him."

The older officer with the short black buzz cut and grizzled jawline said, "We don't know where this cave is. It will be light shortly. When the rain dies down—"

"There were train tracks in the cave," Ellie said. "But I didn't see a train anywhere."

Train tracks? Tabitha thought. Then, "A mine! She must mean Rex is in an old mine."

The cop nodded. "There are plenty of abandoned mines around these parts. That certainly helps. But without a map —"

"I know you don't believe her," Tabitha said, cutting him off. "But she's telling the truth about this creature. I saw it with my own eyes. It's real. It took her. And she says there's more than one. So Rex is in real danger—" The older policeman began to say something, but she spoke over him. "You don't have to believe whether the creature is real or not. It doesn't matter. But Rex is in danger. You can believe that, can't you? He's out there and he's in danger, so we can't just sit around here and do nothing until morning comes."

The younger cop—her age, maybe, and smiling sympathetically—cocked his head, as if he could hear something no one else could.

But then Tabitha heard the ambulance siren too.

The older cop said, "Excuse us for a moment."

They left the room.

◆ ◆ ◆

The paramedics—Rahul Garcia and Andy Macmillan—loaded Paul Harris onto a portable stretcher and carried him to the ambulance parked at the end of the driveway.

Andy, who was as skinny as Rahul was stocky, said to Constable Stephen Garlund, "Watch yourself, Steve. Whoever made that cut has got something big and sharp. Sick sonofabitch."

Garlund asked, "How far behind you is backup?"

"Shouldn't be too much longer."

"Better get going then."

Rahul lugged his ample weight up into the ambulance's cargo hold so he could monitor Paul Harris on the drive to Whistler Blackcomb, while Andy got behind the wheel. A few moments later the vehicle was reversing down the driveway, gumballs flashing.

Garlund turned to Dunn. "Wish I hadn't quit smoking. Could use a cigarette right now."

"You need to get inside and get dry," Dunn said.

The rain had lessened to a hard drizzle, but Garlund was already so wet he hardly noticed. "What the hell's going on here, Hoops? Cabin's all barricaded up like it's *Night of the Living Dead* or something. Girlfriend nearly drowned in the lake. Boyfriend's nowhere to be found. Little girl's running around the woods and spinning stories about a giant insect."

"I don't know what's gone down here, Steve," Dunn said, "but we're not going to find any answers standing around out here in the rain. Now c'mon—" He frowned.

Garlund heard it too.

A strange whining sound, getting louder.

26

When Tabitha finished drying off Ellie with a fluffy white towel, she draped it around her daughter's shoulders and said, "Baby? A little while ago, did you have...a feeling...that maybe something bad was going to happen to me? Like...I don't know...like maybe I was going to fall in the lake?"

Ellie frowned. "But I was in the monster's cave, remember?"

"Yes, I remember."

"So how could I know?"

She couldn't, of course. Nevertheless, Tabitha couldn't stop thinking about those eternal moments while she'd been drowning, and Ellie's voice had been in her head, telling her that she was safe, that she was coming home, that she needed Tabitha to open her eyes, to be there for her when she returned.

Had those words been the hallucinations of a dying mind? Or had Ellie really communicated to her? Had they shared some sort of mother-daughter supernatural bond?

Tabitha sighed to herself, knowing these were questions to which she would likely never find answers. "It doesn't matter, I guess, honey," she said, kissing her daughter on her ruddy cheek. "All that matters is that you're safe. And it's all over now."

"But T-Rex isn't home yet."

"We're going to find Rex, honey. First thing in the morning—"

Something crashed upstairs.

Wings whined, stopped, whined.

Ellie and Bobby cried out in unison.

Another crash.

No, God, please, no! Why? Tabitha thought in instant hysterics. Without wasting another moment, she grabbed the kids' hands and ran. She threw open the cabin's front door and all but tossed Ellie and Bobby outside ahead of her. She had no idea where they were going, only that they had to get far away—

The kids screamed.

Tabitha saw it too.

A dozen yards away one of the hellish creatures was perched on top of the young officer, its proboscis plugged deep into the man's chest, right where his heart would be, no doubt slurping up blood. The older officer was fleeing from this ghastly scene when suddenly, seemingly from nowhere, a different creature swooped down from the darkness. Its pincers snatched the cop by the shoulders and lifted him, kicking and shouting, a few feet into the air.

Someone was moaning, a sound of utter despair, and Tabitha realized belatedly it was coming from her throat.

We're not getting out of this alive, are we?

From behind her came another crash. She spun around and found one of the creatures standing in the doorway a scant two yards away.

The kids' screams jumped several octaves higher.

"Run!" Tabitha shouted to them. "Hide! Don't wait for me!"

"Mommy, no!" Ellie shrieked.

"Go! Now!"

Tabitha had never in her life placed an aggressive hand on a child, but right then she did just that, shoving Ellie and Bobby away from her with tremendous force. They lurched forward. Ellie fell flat on her face. She glanced back over her shoulder.

"Go!" Tabitha shouted. "Hide!" Without waiting to see whether they obeyed her instructions, she whirled about to face the creature once more.

It was staring straight ahead, and she couldn't tell if it was looking at her or the kids.

Probably both, she thought frenziedly. *Probably can see everywhere at once with those goddamn buggy eyes.*

"Hey!" she said, waving her hands over her head while angling slowly away from it. "Leave them alone! I'm right here!"

The creature's head swiveled on its pinched neck to look directly at her.

"Yeah, me!" she said, still angling away.

It stepped through the door, walking unashamedly upright on its two thick legs, its abdomen dangling between them like an obscene phallus.

Tabitha glanced behind her.

The farthest creature had given up trying to carry the older police officer away and had instead dropped him to the ground, where it now stood over him, stabbing him repeatedly with its pincers. The closer creature was staring at her, its blood meal forgotten.

A few feet from it, the young officer's pistol lay on the ground.

Tabitha sprinted toward it.

The creature stood.

In one fluid motion she snatched up the gun and aimed the barrel at its hideous face and triple-tapped the trigger, landing three precision shots directly between its antennae.

Before its body hit the ground she was aiming past it, down the sight.

Pop, pop, pop.

The creature atop the older policeman flew backward.

She was already turning, aiming again, finger taking up

slack in the trigger.

The final creature that had followed her through the doorway was nearly upon her, coming fast, wings whining at a fever pitch, pincers shearing the air, proboscis erect.

She fired at point-blank range.

The slug blew a large hole through the demonic thing's head. Its momentum propelled it onto its chest, directly at her feet, where its wings ceased beating and its limbs twitched robotically.

Tabitha was about to cry out in triumph when she heard a distant drone, growing louder by the second. She looked up into the night sky and realized it wasn't a fourth creature approaching.

It was an entire swarm.

Bobby saw the broken-down car through the trees. It was the one his dad had shown him the day before. He remembered the trunk, wondering if it held any treasure, and he said to Ellie, "We can hide in the trunk!"

They were both huffing and puffing and ready to fall over, and Ellie didn't even try to argue with him.

They stopped when they reached the car. Bobby lifted the trunk lid, and they climbed inside one after the other. Bobby cut his hand on a bit of sharp metal while closing the lid over them, and he bit back a cry.

It was wet and musty in the dark, cramped space. There were holes in the rusted metal too, big enough he could probably stick his arm through one and touch the ground.

Bobby thought about trying this, but decided to suck his bleeding finger instead, unbothered by the sour taste of the blood.

Ellie whispered, "Will they find us in here?"

"I don't know," he replied. "There's a lot of them now."

"I want my Mommy—"

"Shhh!" he said.

One of the monsters had landed nearby.

Bobby could hear its wings separate from all the other wings way up in the sky. They stopped beating a moment later, but he knew it was still out there. Coming for them, tiptoeing so they didn't hear it. Any second now it would open the trunk and grin down at them. They would be trapped. Two yummy human children to eat. It would gobble them up—but then maybe it would be too heavy to fly away. It would have to walk back to its cave. Maybe it would be so tired when it got there that it would go to sleep, giving him and Ellie a chance to escape. They could crawl quietly out of its tummy and fill it up with big rocks instead, so when it woke up it still thought they were inside it. And when it went to get a drink, it would fall in the water and drown because it was so heavy. Didn't his dad read him some book in which all this happened? Only the monster in the book was a wolf, and the kids it ate were goats...

"Stop!" Ellie said.

Bobby frowned, not knowing who she was speaking to.

She moved, and then he heard something else moving too, something small and quick. It was running around inside the trunk.

It brushed his hand, which he jerked back in fright.

The thing squeaked, then fell out of the trunk through one of the holes. He heard it thump against the ground. A moment later he heard it scuttling away from them, through the carpet of wet leaves.

It squeaked again—which ended abruptly.

Then Bobby heard a kind of slurping, like when he's trying to get the final few sips of a milkshake with a straw.

This didn't last long, however, and was replaced by the whining of wings.

The monster was taking off!

He listened as it flew higher and higher into the sky—and that was when he realized all the other wings weren't as loud as they were before.

"I think they're going away!" Ellie said.

"I think so too!" Bobby said.

"Should we go look?"

"I don't want to."

"But I need to go check on Miss Chippy. I found her hiding in the bathroom earlier. She got out of my pocket, and I think the monster got her."

"I think it drank her blood."

"Yeah," Ellie said glumly. "I think it did too."

Tabitha had fled into the forest when the sky filled with the sound of wings. She had not called out to either Ellie or Bobby, knowing if they responded they would reveal their location to the creatures. Instead she prayed they had found a spot to hide, and she hid too, dropping down beside a fallen tree trunk and shoving herself as far beneath it as she could. For what seemed like an eternity the only sounds were her heartbeat thudding in her ears, and the drone of wings above her. But eventually the night went quiet again, and when it did, and she was certain the last of the creatures had departed, she got to her feet and called to the kids.

"Mommy!" Ellie's voice came back, from not too far away.

Hunt hunt, eat eat, drink drink, sleep sleep. These were the instincts the creature experienced on a regular basis. But the nest had been attacked. Some of the hive had been killed. And even if the creature did not understand the concept of revenge, or the notion of justice, or experience emotions such as love and loss and hate, it nevertheless understood the new, urgent imperative ticking loudly inside its head: *de-*

fend defend.

Which required seeking out and eliminating the invaders.

So the creature continued its patrol back and forth through the night sky, the dark forest below reflected in a kaleidoscope of images on its fisheye lenses, while it used both its sight and scent to search for the invaders or those related to them.

When it could no longer detect any remaining threats, it changed course, following its brethren north. The old nest was no longer safe. They needed to find a new one. Somewhere dark, somewhere underground.

By the time the fiery reds and oranges of dawn began to light the horizon, the creature was no longer thinking any of these thoughts—it had never really been thinking them in the first place, merely acting upon them—and its primitive mind had once more reverted to its usual refrain:

Hunt hunt, eat eat, drink drink, sleep sleep.

EPILOGUE

A few months later

For the third time in seven days, Paul Harris drove out to Pavilion Lake.

He parked the aging Crown Victoria alongside the road a little distance away from the RV-like mobile command center, and the caravan of government-black SUVS used to ferry the NASA scientists and engineers back and forth each day from Lillooet, where they were staying in the scattering of modest motels that the town offered.

Paul took the brown paper bag that contained his lunch off the passenger seat and headed into the snow-mantled forest. He made his way to a well-used trail in the snow, which he followed for ten minutes until he reached Dead Man's Mine. He sat down on a log at the top of a knoll, where he liked to eat, as it provided him a clear view of the mine's entrance, as well as the white modular research habitat that looked as though it belonged in deep space rather than the icy Canadian wilderness. Two men in civilian clothes stood guard before the mine. By their posture and discipline Paul had come to the conclusion they were military.

Paul sat on the frosted log for a long while watching the snow drift silently to the ground around him. His mind wandered. Following the massacre at Rex Chapman's cabin in October, he fell into a week-long coma. When he regained consciousness, his stomach was sewn up, an IV drip was feeding him antibiotics, and according to Nancy, the RCMP had fingered a lone madman for the murders of Rex Chapman, Tony Lyons, Daisy Butterfield, as well as Constables Stephen Garlund, and Karl Dunn—the same madman, many people surmised, responsible for all of the disappearances at the lake dating back over the years.

Complete and utter bullshit, of course.

So when two Mounties came by the hospital to get a statement from Paul, he told them he didn't see his attacker, and he didn't remember a thing that happened afterward.

He never let Nancy in on the truth of what he heard and saw. Nor did he go to the press. He had planned to keep silent about the whole incident indefinitely. After all, nobody in their right mind would believe him. But more than this, you never knew to what lengths a government might go to keep matters of national security a secret—and man-sized, deadly insects were most definitely a matter of national security.

Paul wasn't a conspiracy theorist, but hell—what happened to Rex Chapman's flame, Tabitha? He'd tried tracking her down a short time after he'd been released from the hospital, knowing she would be the one person he could speak to about what they'd experienced, but she vanished into thin air. The last any of her coworkers, friends, or neighbors heard from her was a couple of days after she returned to Seattle. Abruptly, phone calls and emails went unanswered. Her house appeared deserted. Nobody knew the whereabouts of the two kids who had been with her either.

As the days stretched into weeks, and then months, Paul became a restless, haunted shadow of his former self. He tossed and turned all night in his sleep. He got headaches, stomach ulcers, joint pain. He couldn't concentrate on work. He was terrible company to be around, and so he kept mostly to himself, in his office, out of sight.

Then, out of the blue, NASA rolled into Lillooet.

Now, NASA personnel can't just show up in some dust-bowl town and not arouse suspicion from the locals, hence the story the space agency leaked to the Lillooet *Examiner*. The subterranean lake in the heart of long-abandoned Dead Man's Mine harbored a species of extremely rare coral-like formations, which were related to life forms that had existed on Earth billions of years previously. NASA wanted to study them in their natural habitat, believing they could aid in the understanding of what life might look like on other planets.

More complete and utter bullshit.

Nevertheless, Paul could no longer sit idly by. Giant insects existed. They've been killing people in his jurisdiction, right under his nose, since his first year as Chief of Police in 1981. Fifteen deaths, by his count. Fifteen deaths he didn't prevent. For his peace of mind and perhaps his sanity, he needed to know more than that these things existed. He needed to know what the hell they were, how they got so big, and whether they were going to be preying on anybody else in these parts in the near future.

And so Paul had driven out to Dead Man's Mine last Tuesday, then again on Friday, and now today, Monday. He had made no mention of the Mosquito Man—correction, Mosquito *Men*—to any of the NASA guys yet. He was simply playing the part of the bored country cop. It was why, he supposed, they put up with him nosing around and asking silly questions.

Paul was halfway through the bologna sandwich Nancy had made for him when the research habitat's airlock opened from the inside, and a man dressed in a heavy winter parka and beige khakis emerged. He lit up a cigarette.

Paul stuffed his sandwich back in the brown paper bag and picked his way through the trees.

"Howdy, Walter," he said, waving pleasantly, his breath frosting in front of his face.

"Back again, are you, Paul?" Walter Williamson said.

With his gelled hair, mousy face, and black-rimmed eye-glasses, he looked like a geekish, middle-aged astrobiologist —and that's exactly what he was, or claimed to be.

"Not much to police in a small town," Paul said. "Coming out here breaks up the doldrums. Find any more of those micro-whatdoyoucallem?"

"Microbialites," Williamson told him, sticking to the script. "Sure, we found more. Only a few freshwater lakes in the world support this kind of life. It's truly amazing."

"That's good," Paul said. "Real good. Need to know all we can about the Martians before they attack, am I right?"

Williamson chuckled.

"Anyway," Paul went on conversationally, "I'm not here today to talk about coral. My grandson's working on a science project for school. He had a few questions for me last night that I couldn't answer. And then I thought, 'Wait a sec. Walter Williamson out at the habitat is an astrobiologist. He could help!'"

Williamson raised an eyebrow. "What kind of science project is your grandson working on?"

"It's got to do with bugs."

Williamson went poker-faced. "Bugs, huh?"

"Bugs and their evolution," Paul said, rubbing his hands together to stave off the cold in his ungloved fingers.

Williamson took a thoughtful puff of his cigarette, exhaled through his nose. His gray eyes were calculating. "Sounds interesting. What kind of questions was he asking you?"

"Well, he can't really figure out why insects were so big back in the time of the dinosaurs, and why they're so small nowadays. Dragonflies apparently had wingspans of three feet! Can you believe that?"

"They were called griffinflies," Williamson said. "But to answer your son's question as to why insects are so small nowadays, it's quite simple really. Millions of years ago, the air surrounding the planet was not only warmer and moister, but contained more oxygen. This was important for insects because they don't have lungs like we do. They have an open respiratory system that diffuses oxygen through their bodies. So higher oxygen levels in the atmosphere meant more oxygen could reach their tissues, which in turn meant they could grow to very large sizes. When oxygen levels began to lessen approximately one hundred and fifty million years ago, the largest insects died off. The smaller ones remained unaffected, with many of them surviving to this day."

Paul was nodding agreeably to this line of reasoning. "I read about all that. And you know what else? Some scientists believe birds had a part to play too. Because about the time the large insects were dying off, dinosaurs were taking flight, on their way to becoming birds. As they got better at flying, they became fast and agile hunters, like birds today. Giant insects, on the other hand, remained slow and lumbering. Easy prey."

Williamson frowned. "Seems you know your stuff, Paul. Seems like you just answered your own question." He flicked away his cigarette. "How old did you say your grandson was?"

"I don't think I did say. But he's eight."

"Eight," Williamson repeated, as if impressed by the number. "Anyway, I'm freezing my ass off out here, Paul, so if you don't mind—"

"Just a sec, Walter. I have one more question, if that's all right?"

"You sure you don't already know the answer to this one too?" he asked shrewdly.

"What I'm wondering," Paul said, ignoring the remark, "is, well...you can get smaller and quicker to outclass your predators. That's one option. But there's another option too." He paused. "You can get bigger and stronger."

Williamson smiled, yet it didn't touch his eyes. If he hadn't known from the get-go that the science project talk was a farce, he certainly did now. "Bigger than griffinflies?" he said. "Those would be some damn big bugs, Paul."

"Maybe even man-sized," Paul said meaningfully. "Could you imagine something like that? A man-sized insect? A man-sized mosquito, say? You know, I have a funny idea of something like that standing on two legs just like us. Standing on two human-like legs. Like some sort of Mosquito Man. Can you picture that?"

Williamson studied Paul, his smile souring to a pucker, as though he'd just bitten into a lemon. "Why don't we cut to the chase here, Paul? What are you getting at?"

"I just..." Paul was a tough man, a proud man, a reserved man, averse to revealing his emotions. But right then he allowed his eyes to reflect the fear and confusion and turmoil that had been eating him up from the inside out these last few months. "I just need to know what in God's name those blasphemous things were, okay?"

Williamson continued to study Paul for a long moment. Paul didn't know what the man was thinking, or what words would come out of his mouth—he half expected the astrophysicist to summon the undercover soldiers to escort him back to the road—but when he spoke his voice was modulated, sympathetic: "If such creatures existed, Paul—and they don't, let's be very clear on that."

"We're clear," Paul said promptly.

"*If* they existed," Williamson continued, "there would be nothing blasphemous about them. Their gigantism would be a matter of evolution, plain and simple."

"But the way they stood—"

Williamson cut him off with a curt wave. "Insects and the rest of arthropods are covered by a more or less hardened exoskeleton. Guys like me call it a cuticle. As you can imagine, it's quite heavy. If an insect grew to be as large as you're suggesting, man-sized, the weight of its cuticle would become a problem. Its legs wouldn't be able to support its mass. It would need much thicker legs. The thing is, all insects have six legs, and if what we're talking about here is a flying insect, it wouldn't be able to get off the ground with six thick legs. You following me, Paul?"

Paul nodded, his attention laser-focused.

Williamson said, "It would probably have to settle for two thick legs."

Paul clamped his jaw tight, visualizing the creature he'd seen. "And if they weren't using the other four legs to stand on, they might evolve into…something else?"

Williamson nodded. "Appendages that could be used to attack or defend. Because while these giant arthropods would have become too large to be hunted by predatory birds, some of the bigger terrestrial animals would likely still pose a threat to them, especially during molting, when they shed their cuticle to grow."

"Pincers," Paul stated flatly.

"Those would do. Especially a lightweight variety."

Paul was silent as he processed this information. Here it was. What he came here for. What he'd so desperately sought. A scientific explanation for the physiology of the nightmare abominations. Did having this new understanding make him feel better about their existence?

Yes, in a way it did.

The creatures were not some alien life form beamed in from outer space, or some demonkin arriving on the express elevator up from the depths of hell.

They were, as Walter Williamson put it, a matter of evolution, plain and simple.

Williamson said, "I really am freezing my ass off out here, Paul. I need to get back to work."

"Right," Paul said distractedly as a huge weight seemed to melt from his shoulders. "And…thanks, Walter. I—"

"I won't be seeing you out here anymore, will I, Paul?"

"No, I don't think you will."

"That would be for the best." He turned toward the habitat.

"Walter?"

Williamson glanced back.

"Those microbialites you're studying...after you fellows leave...I'm not going to have to worry about them causing any problems around here, am I?"

"No, you're not. You have my word on that."

Nodding more to himself than to Williamson, Paul tucked his hands into the pockets of his jacket, drew a breath of pine-scented winter air into his lungs, and started back through the snow toward the police cruiser, remembering that Nancy had said she would be preparing an early supper. He was looking forward to that tremendously.

THE SLEEP EXPERIMENT

PROLOGUE

F lanked by his defense team, Dr. Roy Wallis exited the San Francisco Hall of Justice minutes after a jury had acquitted him of all the charges filed against him in his nearly month-long trial. Hundreds of boisterous demonstrators, cordoned off behind police tape, filled Bryant Street outside the austere building. Many held homemade signs proclaiming dire end-of-times warnings such as: "The RAPTURE is upon us!" and "Judgment Day is coming!" and "REPENT now for the END is near!"

Dr. Wallis stopped before a phalanx of television cameras for an impromptu and celebratory press conference. When the throng of journalists and reporters quieted down, he said into the two-dozen or so microphones thrust at him, "Walt Whitman once wrote that 'the fear of hell is little or nothing to me.' But he was Walt Whitman, so he can write whatever he damn well pleased." Wallis stroked his beard, reveling in the knowledge the world would be hanging onto his each and every word. "I'm guessing," he continued, "Walt most likely never believed that hell existed in the first place, hence his cavalier attitude." He shook a finger, as if to scorn the father of free verse. "But I, my lovely friends, I now know hell exists, and let me tell you—it scares the utter shit out of me."

Resounding silence except for the *cluck-cluck-cluck* of photographs being snapped.

Then everyone began shouting questions at once.

LAST DAY OF INSTRUCTION

Six months earlier

"**W**hy do we sleep?" Dr. Roy Wallis said, his eyes roaming the darkened auditorium inside UC Berkeley's School of Public Health, Education, and Psychology. Five hundred or so students filled the tiered gallery that fanned around him, though the stage spotlights washed most of them in black. "It seems like a silly question, doesn't it? Sleep is sleep. It's an essential part of our survival. Sleep, food, water. The Big Three you can't do without. Nevertheless, while the benefits of food and water are quite evident to us, the actual benefits of sleep have always been masked in a shroud of mystery."

He depressed the forward button of the presentation clicker in his right hand and turned slightly to confirm the image on the projection screen behind him. It depicted a sleeping person with a number of question marks above her head.

"The truth," Dr. Wallis continued, "is that nobody really knows why we sleep, even though the subject has fascinated humans for more than two millennia. The Rishis of India agonized over our states of waking consciousness and dreaming. The ancient Egyptians built temples to the goddess Isis, where devotees met with priests to engage in early forms of hypnosis and dream interpretation. The Greeks and Romans had sleep deities such as Hypnos, Somnus, and Morpheus. The Chinese philosopher, Lao Tzu, compared sleep to death. William Shakespeare characterized sleep as 'nature's soft nurse' due to its restorative nature. However, in terms of scientific understanding, the exact mechanisms of sleep remained largely mysterious until the mid-twentieth century. Researchers have since shown that neural networks grown in lab dishes exhibit stages of activity and inactivity that resemble waking and sleeping, which could mean sleep arises naturally when single neurons work together with other neurons. Indeed, this explains why even the simplest organisms show sleep-like behaviors."

Dr. Wallis clicked to the next image. A photograph of an alien-looking worm on a black background appeared behind him. "Cute, isn't he? That's Caenorhabditis elegans—a tiny worm with only three hundred and two neurons. Yet even it cycles through quiet, lethargic periods that you could argue might be sleep. Admittedly, it's not sleep as we think of the term, but that's because we have larger and more complex brains, which require deeper neural networks. More neurons joining with other neurons equals a greater period of inactivity—such as the seven or eight hours of shuteye we experience each night."

Wallis paced across the stage, stroked his beard.

"Nevertheless, even if this theory is true—neurons drive our stages of wakefulness and sleep—it still doesn't explain *why* we sleep, or what exactly is *going on* during sleep. And a lot is going on, my friends. Our bodies don't simply shut down when Mr. Sandman comes a-knocking. On the one hand, it seems our brains use this period of inactivity to take out the trash, so to speak. The brain is a huge consumer of energy, which means all those waste chemicals that are produced as part of a cell's natural activity have to get flushed out sometime. Moreover, it seems the brain also uses this downtime to reorganize and prioritize the information it has gathered during the daytime, as well as to consolidate our short-term memories into long-term ones. This explains why when you lose sleep, you tend to have problems with your attention span, working out problems, recalling certain memories, even regulating your emotions. Everything's a little out of whack."

Dr. Wallis scanned the dark veil before him. The few spectral students he could make out in the first couple of rows were watching him intently.

"Having said all of this, the human brain is an incredibly complex and powerful organ. It has more than enough computing power to get its housekeeping done while we're awake. So why shut down the entire body each night and leave us as defenseless as newborns? Is there something else going on during sleep that we don't know about? Maybe." He shrugged. "Or maybe not."

Click. A moody Neolithic scene appeared on the projection screen in which a band of fur-clad prehistoric humans hunkered inside the mouth of a cave as the setting sun bloodied the evening sky. Each burly figure gripped a stone weapon. Each set of large eyes appeared weary and watchful of the lurking dangers that night called forth.

"For our poor stone-age ancestors, it made sense for them to search for resources during the daytime when they could see best, and to hide during the nighttime when predator activity was at its peak. Yet...what do you do while hiding? If any of you have played Hide-and-Seek with an obtuse friend or sibling, you know that hiding becomes boring fast, because you're not doing much of anything. Imagine hiding in the same spot from dusk until dawn. Every night. Three-hundred-sixty-five days a year. It'd be worse than listening to a tape of Fran Drescher and Gilbert Gottfried arguing on eternal loop. So to pass the time—and as an added bonus, to conserve energy—their bodies shut down until it was time to get up and go look for food again. Such a solution applies not only to humans but pretty much every lifeform on the planet. Hell, even machines similarly 'sleep,' not to stave off boredom, of course, but to conserve energy."

Dr. Wallis paced, stroked his beard, paced some more.

"So back to my initial question of why we sleep...? Well, if you want my opinion, I believe the answer to be pathetically pedestrian. We sleep, my young friends, to pass the time and to conserve energy. All that other jazz I mentioned that goes on when the lights are out—your brain flushing waste chemicals, categorizing learning and memories—that's all ancillary, accomplished during sleep because sleep offers a convenient, not necessary, time to do so."

Click. Gone were the prehistoric humans on the projection screen, replaced by a gleaming city of glass and steel. He gestured toward the image.

"London, England. A far cry from the untamed plains and forests of ancient Eurasia, isn't it? No cave lions or bears are going to get you there. Food's not a problem either. Enter any supermarket to access aisle upon aisle of every type of food imaginable, all of which is restocked daily. Thus safety from predators and conserving our energy are no longer problems for contemporary humans. The majority of the population has evolved beyond such basic needs. So allow me to now ask you a *new* question, my inquisitive friends." He paused dramatically, acquiescing to the showman inside him. "In this enlightened day and age, do humans even *need* sleep?"

"I won't beat around the bush," Dr. Wallis said. "My answer is simple. No, I don't think humans need sleep. In fact, I think the entire human race is sleeping solely due to habit."

Chatter and uncertain laughter filled the auditorium.

Wallis waited it out for a few seconds before holding up his hands, palms forward, to command attention once more.

The mutiny died down.

Wallis depressed the forward button on the presentation clicker. The new image showed a businessman in a suit and tie seated behind a desk in a cluttered cubicle. His eyes were bloodshot, his face lined with exhaustion. A steaming cup of coffee stood next to his keyboard. "Yes, I know what you're thinking. If we don't need sleep, why do we look like this guy after an all-nighter? I'll tell you why. Because while you were out partying, your body was building up what biologists refer to as sleep pressure. That's right, that's what they call it—sleep pressure. What exactly is this sleep pressure, you ask? Well, those same biologists don't know. They've simply named something they don't yet understand. Think dark matter. We know it exists, we just don't know why. So… sleep pressure," he repeated, as if tasting the word. "Sleep pressure. Indeed, it's like a Tolkien riddle-game, isn't it? What accumulates during wakefulness and disperses during sleep? What is this metaphorical tally of hours, locked in some chamber of the brain, waiting to be wiped clean every night? And imagine…what if we could *access* it? What if we could *reprogram* it?" He smiled. "What if, my beautiful friends, we could *delete* it? Yes, delete sleep pressure. Remove forever tiredness and sleep—that colossal waste of time when we fall unconscious every night, that evolutionary anachronism that has no practical benefits for contemporary humans. Imagine if you had an extra seven or eight hours every day just how many more selfies you could post to Instagram?"

Some chuckles, though not many. The air in the auditorium sizzled with expectation.

Dr. Wallis went to the podium in the center of the stage. He played his fingers down the lapels of his tailored suit jacket. When he was sure every set of eyes in the audience were upon him, he said, "Let us consider what happened in January of 1964, my friends. A high school student in San Diego named Randy Gardner went eleven days—that is, two hundred and sixty-four hours—without sleep. Most interesting of all, near the end of the eleven days, he was not shuffling around like a zombie. To the contrary, he, among many other fascinating feats, was able to beat the researcher conducting the experiment in pinball. He also presided over a press conference in which he spoke clearly and articulately. Overall, he proved to be in excellent health."

"How long did he crash for?" a male voice in the darkness called out.

"Thank you for the segue," Wallis said. "How long did he sleep for after the eleven days? Not for as long as you would expect. A mere fourteen hours—twice the number of hours the average person sleeps today. When he woke, he was not groggy at all. He was completely refreshed. That boy is now an old man. He is still alive today, to the best of my knowledge, and time has revealed no long-term physical or psychological side-effects at all."

Silence—but not the bored kind found too often in lectures halls across academia. Rather, this silence was wound tight as catgut, ready to be plucked with a deafening revelation.

Dr. Wallis did not plan to disappoint. He said, "As amazing as Randy Gardner's eleven days of wakefulness is, it pales in comparison to several other cases of people who have defied sleep. During the First World War, a Hungarian soldier named Paul Kern was shot in the head. After recovering from the frontal lobe injury, he was no longer able to fall asleep or become drowsy. Despite doctors telling him he would not live long, he survived without sleep for another forty years, when he died from natural causes in 1955. More recently, in 2006, a few months into a new laboratory job, a man named John Alan Jordan spilled industrial-strength detergent on his skin, which contaminated his cerebral spinal fluid. Soon after, he stopped sleeping and has not been able to sleep a wink since. Likewise, a man named Al Herpin developed a similarly rare case of insomnia, though for unknown reasons. When medical professionals inspected his house, they found no bed or other sleep-related furniture, only a single rocking chair in which Herpin said he read the newspaper when he wanted to rest. To this day he remains in perfect health and doesn't seem to suffer any discomfort from his remarkable condition. There are other cases too: a woman named Ines Fernandez who hasn't slept for decades despite consulting dozens of doctors and taking thousands of different narcotics and sedatives; a Vietnamese gentleman named Thái Ngọc who hasn't slept since suffering a fever in 1973. And so on and so forth. What's most amazing is that in every case the subjects remain perfectly healthy. Ines Fernandez is still alive and ticking. Same with Thái Ngọc, who boasts of carrying two one-hundred-plus pound sacks of rice more than two miles to his house every day."

Dr. Wallis retrieved his glass of water, beaded with condensation, from the podium. He took a sip. The warm water soothed his throat.

He set it back down and said, "Call these folks evolutionary freaks, if you want, call them anything you like, if that will help you accept their extraordinary stories. But one thing they make perfectly clear is that humans don't *need* sleep to survive. We sleep because we have always slept. Because of that mysterious thing inside us all called sleep pressure…sleep pressure that perhaps one day we will be able to isolate and negate…" In the distance the sixty-one-bell carillon in Sather Tower began to chime. Wallis glanced at his wristwatch: class was finished. "Good luck on your exams everybody!" he said over the clamor of students packing their bags and making a general exodus toward the doors. Then, cheekily: "Don't stay up too late cramming!"

When Dr. Roy Wallis finished transferring his notes from the podium to his leather messenger bag, he discovered he was not alone in the auditorium. A woman remained seated in the front row of seats. With almond eyes, high cheekbones, a prominent jawline, and straight and glossy black hair, she was beautiful in a classical Asian sense. Her brown eyes sparkled when they met his. She smiled, her cheeks dimpling.

She clapped her hands lightly. "Great lecture, professor," she said. "I really enjoyed it." She stood and ascended the stairs to the stage. She was dressed cute-tomboyish in an oversized plaid shirt, loose blue jean overalls rolled up at the cuffs, and powder-blue sneakers. She stopped on the other side of the podium. "But I think you might have overlooked something."

Dr. Wallis zipped his messenger bag closed. "Oh?" he said. Penny Park was one of his brightest students. She was also one of two researchers he'd selected to assist him with the Sleep Experiment in ten days' time. She was from a low-income family in South Korea and was currently receiving a full academic scholarship. Despite having only lived in the States for three years, her English was impressively fluent. Her accent, however, needed some work, especially her pronunciation of Rs and Ls, which she consistently mixed up.

"Predators," Penny said. "You mentioned prehistoric humans needed to hide from predators during the night, and sleep resulted from hiding, something to pass the time."

"I did say that, Penny. I'm glad you were paying attention."

"Don't patronize me, professor. You know I *always* listen when you're speaking. But I was saying...okay, our ancestors, they had to hide during the night. But what about *predators*? The ones at the top of the food chain? They just hunt. They don't need to hide. So they don't need to pass the time and, according to you, they don't need to sleep. But they *do* sleep. So what you say, it doesn't make total sense. Why don't they just hunt all the time? Never go hungry?"

"You raise an excellent point, Penny," Dr. Wallis told her,

impressed with her astuteness. "Predators do indeed also experience sleep pressure. Why is this? I believe for the same reason prey animals experience it. Boredom."

"Boredom?"

"They evolved to do one thing: hunt. But hunting 24/7 would grow tiresome, for lack of a better word. Sleep provides a break from this routine. Keeps them…sane, I suppose you might say. Anyway," he added, motioning Penny toward the exit doors and falling into step beside her, "perhaps the Sleep Experiment in ten days' time will shed some much-needed light on the subject?"

"I'm so excited to be participating in the experiment. I think about it all the time."

"Me too, Penny. Me too."

She pushed through one of the double doors. Wallis flicked off the stage lights, then gave a final, nostalgic glance around the empty lecture hall, knowing he would not be back until the new fall semester in September.

"Professor?" Penny was holding one door open for him.

"Coming," he said, and joined her.

DAY 1

Monday, May 28, 2018

*I*t's like a ghost town, Dr. Roy Wallis thought as he stood at his office window, looking out onto Shattuck Avenue. Across the street, the alehouse and Thai restaurant, which were usually crowded with professors and students alike, appeared closed. The street was deserted. There were still some people around the historic campus, of course, many of them international and migrant students studying language courses, but for the most part it was... like a ghost town. Gone was the rambunctious noise of the shuffling mobs, the optimistic energy that embodied the next generation of young Americans. In its place the nearly thirteen hundred acres were unfamiliarly yet beautifully peaceful—allowing Wallis to see it almost as he had all those years ago when he was a bright-eyed tenure-track professor.

Clouds drifted in front of the sun, and Wallis caught his reflection in the glass of the window. With his slicked back undercut and his long, groomed beard, he had been compared to everyone from a lumberjack to a circus ringmaster to a hot Abe Lincoln. The latter was from a female graduate student. Admittedly, he had a lot of admirers amongst his female students. He was both embarrassed and flattered by this, given he had recently turned forty-one. Still, he wasn't trying to be some sort of "hipster professor" with the haircut and the beard. Both simply suited his face. He'd worn medium-length hair and stubble for a while, and whilst he'd liked the subtle sophistication of the stubble, he'd eventually decided a real beard had to be thick and strong and, well, manly. Consequently, he'd grown the stubble out five years back, kept his beard in meticulous condition with regular visits to his barber and daily moisturizing and oiling, and he hadn't looked back since.

Wallis turned away from the window. All tenured professors had their own office to decorate as they so pleased. Given he was now the psychology department head, he not only had his own office, but a spacious one to boot. Although not technically allowed, he'd had the institutional white walls repainted Wedgewood blue and the gray carpet replaced with a high-pile black one three years ago. The furniture was all campus surplus stuff, but he'd brought the abstract acrylic artwork—as well as a watercolor of an intense-looking Sigmund Freud smoking a cigar—and other miscellaneous items from his home. Some of his colleagues praised the personal touches; some became so inspired they spruced up their offices with their own lamps and area rugs; some never commented at all; and some openly told him they were gaudy and unacademic. Wallis didn't care what any of them thought. The space, for him, was welcoming and comforting, maximizing his productivity.

Dr. Wallis went to the mini-fridge and retrieved a bottle of water. He contemplated a beer from the six-pack of Coors Light he kept in there, but decided it was too early in the day for that. Hanging on the wall above the fridge were his medical degree from the University of Arizona and his Ph.D. summa cum laude from UCLA; a few awards he'd received in recognition of his research into circadian rhythms and narcolepsy; and two framed photographs. The first was of him posing with the great and late father of sleep medicine, Dr. William C. Dement. The second was of him and a colleague one hundred and fifty feet underground in Mammoth Cave,

Kentucky, where they'd spent two days charting their fluc-tuations in wakefulness and body temperature when freed from the regulating influence of sunlight and daily schedules —

A knock at the door startled him. Wallis frowned. Classes and exams had finished the previous week. Who would even know he was in his office?

He opened the door. "Penny?" he said. She was wearing a pair of heavy black-framed eyeglasses today that sat pre-cariously on her button nose. A long, loose purple sweater reached farther down her thighs than her shorts. Her long hair was woven into a single braid that hung forward over her shoulder. "Didn't we agree to meet at Tolman Hall?"

"I know," she said, her cheeks dimpling beneath the glasses, "but I got here early, so I thought I would walk over with you?" She pointed to one of the psychology-related cartoons taped to the door. "I like this one best. So funny." The comic depicted Goldilocks reclining on a psychiatrist's couch and telling him: "Alice is in Wonderland, Dorothy is somewhere over the rainbow, but I get trapped in a cabin with bears."

"She has it easy compared to Rapunzel."

"The girl with the long hair?"

He nodded. "I like your hair. I don't think you've worn it like that before?"

"Because when I pull it back from my face like this it makes my head look too big. Many Koreans have too large heads, did you know that?"

"No, I didn't."

"Anyway, in Korean society, a single braid means a single lady." She held up her left hand and wiggled her ring finger. "And I'm single! Thought I'd try a braid for luck."

"Well, good luck," he said. "Give me a sec and we'll head off." He collected his blazer and messenger bag from his desk, then locked up the office behind them. They took the stairs to the ground floor and exited through the main doors.

The day was humid yet overcast, with dark clouds in the distance threatening rain.

Penny Park was smiling. "Do you remember the quote you began your Sleep and Dreams course this year with, professor?" she asked.

He thought back. "No, not off the top of my head."

"'Do one thing every day that scares you,'" she said proudly.

He nodded. "Right—Eleanor Roosevelt. Thinking about getting those words of wisdom tattooed on your forehead?"

Penny laughed. "No! I was thinking about the experiment today."

"Ah," he said.

"Are you scared at all, professor?"

"There's nothing to be scared of, Penny."

"You're not even a teeny tiny bit nervous?"

Wallis hesitated. Then shrugged. "Maybe a teeny tiny bit."

Dr. Roy Wallis wasn't sure how well the Penny Park situation was going to work out.

Last month, when Wallis made the general announcement to his senior Sleep and Dreams class that he wanted to hire two students to assist him with a sleep experiment for three weeks during the summer break, ten students applied. During the first round of informal interviews he remained coy about what the experiment entailed, explaining little more than the successful applicants would need to be available eight hours a day on a rotational schedule to provide 24/7 shift coverage. This dissuaded half the students, who promptly withdrew their names from consideration. Wallis re-interviewed the remaining five applicants, explaining in more detail what their roles would involve, namely observing and recording the actions of two subjects under the influence of a stimulant gas. Two more applicants bowed out. The remaining three included Penny Park, another international student from India named Guru Rampal, and a member of the school's rowing team named Trevor Upton. Trevor was intelligent, focused, and sociable, and he would have been Wallis' first choice had his class attendance last semester been better. Two necessary qualities Wallis required of his assistants were punctuality and reliability. Which left Penny Park and Guru Rampal as the last woman/man standing.

Dr. Wallis had been confident they would both perform exceptionally, and he still believed it. The problem with Penny Park was that she was revealing herself to be a flirt. Over the last two years she'd paid him a visit during office hours a handful of times, and though she'd always demonstrated a sharp, sardonic sense of humor—you might almost call it *teasing*—he'd thought nothing of it until three weeks ago. After selecting Penny and Guru as his assistants, he'd taken them across the street from the psychology building to the alehouse for pizza and beers. Guru, it turned out, didn't eat pizza or drink alcohol and insisted he was fine sipping a glass of Coca-Cola. Penny, on the other hand, finished off most of the pitcher of regular-strength beer Wallis ordered. There are two types of drinkers. Those who can handle their booze well enough it would be difficult to tell whether they were drunk or not, and those who cannot. Penny most definitely fell into the latter category. At first her compliments were flattering: "You're actually one of the only professors that dresses *well!*" and "I know how this sounds, but you work out, right? You must work out?" But then came the blasé touches. Eventually Wallis excused himself under the pretense of using the restroom so he could sit on the other side of the table from Penny when he returned. Guru was not blind to Penny's advances and wore a big, goofy smile on his face for the next twenty minutes or so until Wallis—ignoring Penny's appeals for another pitcher of beer—requested the bill from the wait staff.

Since then Wallis had communicated with Penny via phone and email about the experiment a few times, but he'd only seen her face-to-face on the last day of classes when she'd remained after his lecture in the auditorium.

She had seemed like the old Penny Park then, as she did today...but the problem was, Wallis had had a peek behind the curtain. He knew how she felt about him. And that made him uncomfortable—and concerned.

Wallis wasn't averse to professor-student romances. Although frowned upon by some amongst academia's establishment, dating a student above the age of consent was legal and permitted in most universities. In fact, Wallis was in an off-and-on-again relationship with a former student right now.

No, what concerned him with Penny's solicitous behavior was how it might affect the Sleep Experiment. They would be working together closely on it for the next three weeks, and he would need her attention focused on the experiment, not him.

I'll play it by ear, he decided. *After all, I'm probably blowing what happened at the alehouse out of proportion. She was drunk, having a bit of fun. Nothing more to it than that.*

To say Penny Park had a crush on Dr. Wallis was a gross understatement. She was in total freaking love. And who could blame her? He was sexy, in shape, and fashionable. And not only all of this, he was her *professor* which, in a kinky kind of way, made him even sexier.

If asked, Penny would probably say it had been a case of love at first sight. She often sat in the front row of her classes because then you didn't have to deal with all the goofing around from the jocks, stoners, and "cool girls." And this was where she was sitting for the first day of Dr. Wallis' first-year psychology course. For the duration of the fifty minutes she could barely look away from him, smiling pleasantly whenever he made brief eye contact with her.

Later that week, she stopped by his office during his office hours to ask him about some of the homework questions he'd assigned. She remembered how nervous she'd been to be alone in his presence, which was odd for her. She was an extrovert, and a pretty one at that. She'd learned from an early age that she could get together with any of the boys in her grade simply by singling one out and showing him a little bit of interest. By the age of sixteen, she'd probably had close to two dozen boyfriends, most of whom she'd bored of after a week or two. She'd simply never found herself attracted to any of them in the first place.

Not like she was attracted to older men.

She'd learned why she had this fetish a year earlier from, ironically, Dr. Wallis himself. In his Developmental Psychology course, he explained that when financial and social status gains were ruled out, a young woman's interest in a mature man often came down to her relationship with her father while she'd advanced through puberty. According to Dr. Wallis, when a father is unable to deal with his daughter's burgeoning sexuality because it makes him feel uncomfortable or unsafe, he avoids her the best he can, and when this is not possible, he derides her for wearing makeup or promiscuous outfits. Unable to win his benign attention during this important stage of her development, she is forced to look elsewhere for that attention.

Indeed, this scenario described Penny Park's rocky relationship with her father to a tee. And in her case, during her teenage years, the only adults she knew well aside from her parents were her teachers—which might explain what happened in her senior year.

One evening after school, Penny had stayed late at the library to study for an upcoming test. While leaving the building, she passed her biology classroom and saw her teacher, Mr. Cho, seated at his desk, marking papers. She'd been having erotic dreams about him for nearly a year at that point, and when she'd met his wife at a school festival the week before, she found herself instantly jealous of the woman. The hag was old—older than Mr. Cho, by the looks of it—but she'd been all prim and proper with perfectly coiffed auburn-dyed hair, big doll eyes (double eyelid surgery anyone?), two-inch pumps, and an immaculate Louis Vuitton handbag. The perfect little housewife who shopped all day and whose only responsibilities in life were limited to tidying up the house and cooking for her husband.

Ever since that encounter, Penny had fantasized about stealing Mr. Cho from the woman, and so that evening while she was leaving the high school, she spontaneously and recklessly entered her teacher's classroom under the pretense of asking about the upcoming exam—all the while flaunting her sexuality, which, by eighteen years of age, had become second nature to her. When she crossed her legs and saw Mr. Cho's eyes going to the excessive amount of thigh showing beneath her short plaid skirt, she took the plunge, saying in an offhand manner, "I'm going to be in Itaewon around seven o'clock this evening. There's this little bar that's *so* fun. It's called The Railway Club, in Haebangchon. Maybe if you're nearby, you might meet me for a drink?"

Penny, of course, knew Mr. Cho would be nowhere nearby. The high school was in Jungnang-gu in the eastern suburbs of Seoul. He likely lived somewhere close by. Itaewon, on the other hand, was smack-dab in the center of the city and popular with tourists and foreign workers. Which was exactly why she'd chosen the location: it was a discreet place where two people could meet and not run into anyone else they knew.

Mr. Cho considered her offer for a long moment, and Penny was just about to blurt she'd only been kidding around, when he said, "You're too young to drink, Penny."

"I'm almost nineteen." She shrugged and smiled. "Besides, they know me at the bar. They always serve me." Which was partly true. She'd been there once after watching a live band at a nearby venue, and she hadn't had any problems ordering a drink.

"Seven o'clock, you say?" Mr. Cho said.

Penny nodded, still smiling.

"You will be with your friends?"

"No, just me."

"I might be in the area."

Penny arrived at The Railway Club fifteen minutes late and found Mr. Cho seated at a booth with a nearly empty pint of beer in front of him. When she sat down, they ordered snacks and two more beers. Penny was not a seasoned drinker, and Mr. Cho took advantage of this, plying her with beer after beer, which she happily imbibed. After an hour or so, she moved to his side of the booth so they were brushing up against each other. She rubbed his crotch through his pants, while his hand explored beneath her skirt. When she tried kissing him, he suggested they go somewhere else. He paid the bill and took her to a bawdily decorated love hotel. The only room available was dubbed "The Ramen Room," and the queen bed was actually inside a giant replica of a Styrofoam instant-ramen container.

Despite the dozen or so boys Penny had previously made out with, she'd never had intercourse before. She didn't tell Mr. Cho this, he didn't ask, and she enjoyed the experience tremendously. After he left—he told her they should walk to the train station separately—she stayed behind in the room, pleasuring herself in the two-person bathtub with an assortment of sex toys that had been stored on a shelf above the flat-screen television.

She and Mr. Cho met up on six more occasions before she graduated later that year and moved to California to begin her studies at UC Berkeley.

Despite this experience with an older man, Penny had been unable to work up the courage to proposition Dr.

Wallis that first day she'd visited his office in the autumn of 2015. She'd only been in the United States for a single month then, everything was still new and a little bit frightening, and she wasn't as confident in her skin as she'd been in South Korea. Moreover, Dr. Wallis was not a high school teacher; he was a professor at one of the most esteemed universities in the country. He had a presence and swagger that Mr. Cho could never match which, combined with his rugged good looks, likely afforded him no shortage of beautiful women.

Undaunted, however, Penny continued to visit him during his office hours most weeks over the following three years, each time telling herself this would be the day she asked him out, but she never made any headway. Being a very popular professor, he almost always had a colleague hanging out with him in his office, or a line of students at his door waiting to see him...and on those two or three occasions she'd caught him alone? Well, the moment had just never seemed right.

Then last month Dr. Wallis announced in his Sleep and Dream class that he was looking for two students to assist him over the summer hiatus with an experiment that would take place on the campus grounds. Penny immediately applied for the position and, to her exhilaration, was selected. She could recite Dr. Wallis' phone call verbatim, with him concluding, "So if this sounds like something you'd be interested in, Penny, I'd love to have you on board."

The next day Dr. Wallis invited Penny and a nerdy Indian named Guru Rampal out for pizza and beers, so they could all get to know each other better. Penny did her best to remain professional with the professor despite her running-hot libido, knowing it wasn't the right time or place to cozy up to him. Yet after a few beers this restraint went out the window—and her flirting didn't exactly go well. She was far too forward, and Dr. Wallis showed little if any interest in her advances. When she woke up the next morning, she was sure he was going to call to say he was replacing her on the experiment. But he never did.

And here I am today, she thought. *Just the two of us, walking together to Tolman Hall.*

Nevertheless, Penny wasn't going to make the same mistake twice. No more in-your-face wasted girl. She would allow her relationship with Dr. Wallis to develop organically over the next three weeks until she was confident she had won him over.

And win him over she would.

Nearly one hundred and fifty years old, the campus of the University of California Berkeley was a mosaic of classical and contemporary buildings that lined symmetrical avenues and winding pathways alike.

Tolman Hall, it could be argued, was the ugly duckling of the brood.

Constructed during the middle of the last century at the height of the Brutalist style, its exposed concrete and stark, geometric design had drawn a mixed bag of praise and criticism from the public over the decades. The Psychology Department had called it home since 1963 before moving into Berkeley Way West this year. Tolman Hall had since been deemed seismically unfit, slated for demolition, and shuttered up.

Which made it the perfect spot on campus to conduct the Sleep Experiment.

"There she is," Dr. Wallis said, looking up at the doomed building.

Penny said, "You know, after they announced they were going to knock it down, it went viral on Instagram."

"Vial?" he teased.

"*Viral.* Sorry I don't speak so perfect English like you, professor."

Wallis nodded. "I can imagine she's gone viral. You either

love her or hate her. Me personally, I have mixed feelings. She served our department well for over fifty years. But the nature of our work has changed significantly, and she's no longer state-of-the-art, is she?"

"Spooky even. Especially now, with all the doors and windows gone. Like a monster, wanting to eat us up."

"You certainly have a vivid imagination, Penny. Ah, there's Guru."

◆ ◆ ◆

Guru Rampal was leaning against a nearby tree, ankles crossed, thumbing something into his phone. He had thinning black hair which he wore in a Teddy Boys-inspired pompadour (presumably to mask the bald patch on top); dark, sleepy eyes (now covered by a pair of sunglasses); and light mocha skin. He was slim despite an incongruous belly, which his too-tight Pac-Man tee-shirt did little to hide. His beige khaki shorts were neatly pressed, his white sneakers glaringly spotless.

He had been born in a small village on the outskirts of Delhi, India, and like Penny Park, he had only been in the United States for a handful of years. He too was one of the lucky international students receiving a full-ride academic scholarship. Unlike Penny, however, he remained uninitiated to the ways of the West. Yet what he lacked in street smarts, he made up for in book smarts. In fact, he was one of the most promising students Dr. Wallis had ever had the pleasure of teaching, and he no doubt had a bright future ahead of him in whatever area of psychology he pursued, whether that be academia, industry, healthcare, or policy.

"Guru!" Penny called. She always pronounced his name *Gulu*, like the city in Uganda.

Guru glanced up from his phone. "Hi, guys!"

Dr. Wallis and Penny joined him at the tree.

"Like your shades," Penny said.

"Thanks, babe." He took them off and hooked them in his collar.

"Uh, don't call me babe, please."

"Really?"

"Really!"

Guru shrugged. "I bought them for ten dollars at Target," he said in his syllable-timed accent. "I think they give me more cool factor. Do you guys agree?"

Wallis slapped him on the shoulder. "You get any cooler, Guru, we're going to start calling you Iceman."

"Iceman," he said. "I like that. You can start calling me that right now."

Penny pointed. "Hey, are those our professional lab rats?"

Guru said, "Or in the words of George Bernard Shaw, 'human guinea pigs.'"

"That's them." Wallis checked his wristwatch. "And right on time."

The three scientists watched the Australian backpackers approach Tolman Hall, smiling and waving. They both sported deeply tanned bodies and beachy blonde hair. The woman, Sharon Nash, was dressed in a white singlet over a bikini top and cut-off jean shorts; the man, Chad Carter, wore a Billabong tee-shirt and board shorts. They walked at a leisurely pace in grungy flip-flops, as though enjoying a stroll through a park.

Whoever said stereotypes aren't true? Wallis mused. *Especially in the case of twenty-something Australians who come to California for the surf.*

In May, Wallis had placed an advertisement in the San Francisco *Chronicle* for two test subjects to participate in what he'd described as an in-patient sleep study. He was surprised by the avalanche of replies. He emailed each potential recruit a tailor-made screening test with inclusion and exclusion criteria. He settled on the two Australians for a myriad of reasons. Their BMIs were within the ideal range. They were non-smokers. Neither were taking medications, and neither had any history of pre-existing medical conditions, allergic predispositions, or anaphylactic reactions. Moreover, their answers to several questions he'd posed indicated they were Type B personalities. People in this camp tended to be more relaxed than Type A personalities, more tolerant of others and more reflective, while also displaying lower levels of anxiety and higher levels of imagination and creativity. As an added bonus, the Australians were friends but were not romantically involved.

In short, Wallis couldn't have asked for two better test subjects in an experiment that required them to be cooped up in a room together for three weeks.

Dr. Wallis greeted Chad and Sharon with firm handshakes, then introduced them to Penny and Guru.

"Mate, love the sunnies," Chad told Guru. "You moonlight as an Elvis impersonator or something?"

Guru beamed. "See, I told you guys. They *do* give me more cool factor."

Penny was eyeing Sharon's bikini top. "Were you two just at the beach?"

"Had a quick dip this morning," Sharon replied. "We were told clothing was going to be provided for us, so we didn't bother to change."

"Or bring any," Chad added.

"Or bring any," Sharon agreed.

"Clothing is most assuredly provided," Wallis told them. "Clothing and much more. You will be perfectly comfortable for the next three weeks. Come, follow me."

Berkeley Property Management had already stripped the interior of Tolman Hall bare, salvaging all the furniture, light fixtures, flooring, and cabinetry. What remained was a hollowed-out concrete block fitting of its condemned status. Tearing down the skeletal structure would have already begun had Dr. Wallis not negotiated with the property manager to postpone work until the following month, after the Sleep Experiment had concluded.

Wallis led Penny, Guru, and the two Australians into Tolman Hall's west wing and down a flight of stairs to the basement. The building still had power, and he flicked a master light switch. The old fluorescent lamps in the ceiling clunked on one after the other, bathing the windowless space in light.

"Oooh, this place is so creepy with nobody around," Penny said.

"Like an insane asylum from a movie," Guru said.

"Enough, you two," Wallis quipped, annoyed they were going to give the Australians the jitters.

"No worries," Chad said. "Shaz and me don't scare easily. As long as there's no derro living down here, we're all good."

"Derro?" Penny said.

"Derelict. You know, vagabond, bum, trash pirate, gutter rat, broke dick—"

"Yes, I understand now, thank you."

Wallis led the way among the maze of hallways. The design was rumored to have been inspired by the maze-rat experiments performed by the building's namesake, behavioral psychologist Edward Chance Tolman.

Wallis stopped next to a room with the door still intact and, next to it, a large red X spray-painted on the wall.

"X marks the spot!" Penny chirped.

"I made that," Wallis explained, "so the demolition contractors remembered not to remove anything from the room." He opened the door, stepped inside the dark cavity, and turned on the lights, which revealed a small antechamber. Ten feet in, a fabricated wall stretched from one side of the room to the other. It featured a long rectangular viewing window and another door that led to the space where the Australians would be living for the next twenty-one days. In front of the window was a table on which sat a touch panel controller the size of an iPad and a silver laptop computer.

Wallis sat down in the room's only chair. "Excited for the reveal?" he asked.

"Busting," Chad said.

"I cannot see anything," Guru complained, cupping his hands against the viewing window.

"That's because the lights aren't on, genius," Penny said.

"I am a genius, you know? My IQ is—"

"Tell someone who cares."

"Children, enough," Wallis said. To the Australians, he added, "This space used to be one of the building's largest conference rooms. I had that wall constructed for the experiment to separate this observation room from...let's call it...the sleep laboratory."

"But we won't be asleep, mate," Chad said. "So that doesn't really make sense."

"Yes, but given the nature of the experiment—it's called the Sleep Experiment, after all—I think—"

"That doesn't make sense either. Shouldn't it be called the Sleep*less* Experiment?"

Penny giggled.

Wallis smiled politely. "That doesn't exactly have the same ring to it, does it?" he remarked.

"Nah," Sharon said, somewhat nasally. "I'm with Chad on this one. Sleep lab? Nah, doesn't make sense, mate."

"You two are free to call it whatever you wish," Wallis said tersely. "But why don't we have a look?" He powered on the touch panel controller, then pressed a button on the side of it to display a lighting control page. He tapped five buttons in quick succession, which in turn powered on the five LED ceiling lights in the sleep laboratory.

"Oh em gee!" Penny said. "How cool!"

"Sweet," Chad said.

"Sweeeeet," Sharon parroted.

"That is bigger than my family home in India," Guru said, impressed. "And I have four brothers."

Dr. Wallis was glad they all approved. He had spent months applying for state and federal grants, but after consecutive rejections—citing the ethical concerns related to the experiment—he'd decided to fund everything himself. "The room is fully contained, of course," he said. "You have your own library with an eclectic mix of authors from Bronte and Atwood to Poe and King. Home theater's right next to it. There are over eighty available channels, I believe, as well as Netflix. There's also a DVD player and a good collection of movies. A small gym—"

"And a basketball court!" Penny said. "Holy moley."

Wallis nodded. It wasn't technically a court, as there were no defined sides or line markers, just enough space in front of a basketball net on a pole to shoot some hoops or have a game of one-on-one. "Kitchen's there," he continued, pointing. "The refrigerator is fully stocked. Same with the pantry. You both stated you have no food allergies. But if you want anything specific, please let me know, and I can get that for you too."

"Why're there beds?" Chad asked. "We're not supposed to be sleeping."

"You won't be sleeping." He indicated the large tank in the far end of the antechamber. It was about the size and shape of a home natural gas heating system. "That contains the gas-based stimulant. It's already being vented into the sleep laboratory. After you've breathed it in for a few minutes, you won't be able to fall asleep no matter how much you might want to. The beds are there for...personal space, I suppose you could say. You're going to have a lot of time on your hands. Even if you can't sleep, you might want a place to lie down and relax."

Sharon remained gazing at the tank. "The gas is...safe, right?"

"Of course," Wallis said. "It's been thoroughly tested."

"What's in it? I mean, what's it made up of?"

"The formula, I'm afraid, is a trade secret."

"If he told you," Penny said, "he'd have to kill you."

"What if we want to leave the room?" Chad asked. "The door's not going to be locked or anything, is it?"

"Locked? No. However, leaving the sleep laboratory is discouraged. This is a controlled experiment. All factors must be held constant except for one: the independent variable. In this case, that is both of you. If either of you were to leave that room, you would be breathing regular air, thereby introducing a second independent variable into the experiment that may affect the ultimate results of the experiment."

"To be exact, professor," Guru said, "with any human testing there are *inherent* uncontrolled variables such as age, gender, and genetic dispositions. So in the strictest sense, this is not a controlled exper—"

"Those inherent uncontrolled variables would be filtered out in further experiments, Guru," Wallis said.

"But the bottom line," Chad said, "is that we're stuck in that room for twenty-one days?"

"Correct. Which was in the Subject Information and Consent Forms you both signed," Wallis said, growing impatient. "If you are having cold feet, I need to know right now as I have an entire list of other—"

"Nah, mate," Chad said. "No cold feet." He looked at Sharon.

"I don't want to back out," she said. "We can keep traveling for another six months with the money we make."

"You heard her," Chad said. "We're not backing out. But..." He shrugged. "Say something happens? Like one of us feels sick? You'll let us leave?"

"Of course," Wallis said. "You are not prisoners. You are free to terminate the experiment at any point you wish."

"But we won't get our bonuses?"

"You get bonuses?" Penny said, surprised.

"For completing the twenty-one days," Wallis explained.

"I'm not getting a bonus. Are you, Guru?"

"No, no bonus for me," he said. "At least not that I know of."

Wallis sighed. "You two aren't the ones going twenty-one days without sleep."

Penny cocked an eyebrow at Chad. "How much is your bonus? In fact, how much are you getting paid?"

"Penny!" Wallis snapped. Seeing her startled expression, he bit back his frustration. "Penny," he said more reasonably. "This experiment is not about money. It's about science. I chose you because I thought you understood this. However, if you feel you are being unfairly compensated, I suppose we could discuss—"

"No, professor," she said, looking bashful. "You're right. This isn't about money. I'm sorry. I really don't care about... I was just..."

Wallis stood and squeezed her forearm reassuringly, which brightened her up. To the Australians, he said, "You will find a bathroom with a small shower at the very back of the sleep laboratory. It's the only section of the room we won't be able to visually observe you. Nevertheless, we'll still be able to monitor you with these." He produced two smart wristwatches from his messenger bag and handed them over. "They'll track your heartrates, stress levels, and movement. You'll find wireless chargers next to the TV. When the watch batteries are low, please charge them."

"How do we talk to you?" Sharon asked. "I mean, if we have questions about anything later on?"

"The intercom system," Wallis said. "There are six microphones installed in the ceiling, as well as a loudspeaker system. You don't need to do anything; we'll be able to hear anything you say via this tablet here. If you have a question, just ask away. One last matter. Did either of you bring your phones with you?"

"You told us not to," Chad said.

"So you didn't?"

He shook his head. "Left it with my mate."

Sharon, looking guilty, slid hers out of her pocket. "I didn't know if you were serious or not."

Wallis held out his hand. "Unfortunately, there's to be no contact with the outside world. Can't have you livestreaming the experiment on Facebook—"

"I wouldn't!"

"I'm sorry, Sharon, but I made it clear that—"

"I know. Fine." She handed him her phone. "Don't lose it."

"I'll keep it locked away in my office and return it to you the moment the experiment is completed. Now, any further questions?"

The Australians looked at each other. They exchanged hopeful smiles, which did little to mask the uncertainty wading beneath.

"All right then," Wallis said. "Let's get started."

Dr. Roy Wallis had scheduled himself to work all the shifts between two p.m. and ten p.m. He bid farewell to Penny Park and Guru Rampal, opened the laptop's word processor, then lit up a cigarette. To hell with the campus' indoor smoking bans; Tolman Hall was going to be nothing but a pile of memories and rubble in a month's time. What could a little smoke hurt?

The Australian test subjects spent their first hour in the sleep laboratory examining every corner of the room, reminding Wallis of a pair of hamsters sniffing out their new cage. Curiosity sated, they both sat down on the sofa and turned on the TV. Sharon took control of the remote but acquiesced to the home renovation program Chad wanted to watch. During a commercial she got up and fiddled around with the exercise machines. She then approached the viewing window, stopping when she came to within a few feet of it. Her side was mirrored, so she would be seeing her reflection, not Dr. Wallis.

She pushed an errant blonde bang behind her left ear. The action was hesitant, almost shy, though up until this point her personality had been far from shy. Her thick-lashed eyes swept from one side of the mirror to the other, as if seeking a spot in it she could see through. They were a light blue with a hint of spring green—the color, Wallis thought, of a tropical lagoon. Her bare lips pursed, as if she were about to say something. Instead, she waved.

Wallis tapped the Talk button on the touch panel controller and said, "Two-way mirror."

Sharon looked up at the ceiling, where his voice had come through the amplified speakers.

Chad looked up too, then returned his attention to the television.

"Now I really do feel like a test subject," Sharon said. Her voice, transmitted through the speakers in the touch panel controller, was tinny but clear. She tapped the two-way glass. The sound was sharper than it would have been had she tapped a regular window because there wasn't any framing or other support behind the glass. Wallis doubted she knew this. She had tapped for the sake of tapping it, nothing more. "Twenty-one days," she added. "No sleep. Wow."

"No sleep," Dr. Wallis agreed.

"What are Chad and me gonna do?"

"Catch up on your reading?" he suggested.

"I guess."

"The complete collection of H.P. Lovecraft is on the bookshelf. I brought it from my home library."

"He writes horror, right?"

"Horror, fantasy, science-fiction. The collection is 1600 pages, so it should eat away some of your hours."

Sharon shook her head. "Scary stuff puts me on edge. As a kid I used to get nightmares a lot...and I guess I still do."

"That's not unusual," Wallis said. "One out of every two adults experiences nightmares on occasion."

She smiled crookedly. "Right. I forgot you were a sleep doctor. Is that what I should call you? Doctor? Or doc?"

"You can call me Roy."

She appeared to think it over. "Nah, that just doesn't seem right. I like doc."

"Doc's fine then."

"Cool. So…doc…why *do* we have nightmares?"

"They're often spontaneous," Wallis told her, lighting up a fresh cigarette. "Even so, they can be caused by a variety of factors. For instance, some are caused by late-night snacks. Food increases your metabolism, signaling your brain to become more active. Some are caused by different medications, especially antidepressants and narcotics, which act on chemicals in the brain." He tapped ash into his empty paper coffee cup. "There are psychological triggers as well, such as anxiety or depression, as well as certain sleep disorders."

"What kind of sleep disorders?" she asked.

"Insomnia and sleep apnea would be the more common ones. Restless legs syndrome would be another—"

Sharon cut him off with a brisk laugh. "That sounds like something a dog looking for a hydrant might have."

Wallis smiled. "It basically manifests itself in a strong urge to move, which naturally makes it difficult, if not impossible, to fall into a deep, peaceful sleep."

"I feel pretty restless right now."

"You're in a new, unfamiliar environment. Try to relax. Soon this place will feel like home. Humans have a remarkable capacity to adapt."

"Because we have big brains, right?"

"Social brains," he amended. "We're hardwired to create, share, and pass on knowledge. This is what allows us to adjust to new situations so easily, and what differentiates us from our early ancestors, and our early ancestors from primates. But we're getting off topic, aren't we?" Dr. Wallis crushed his cigarette on the floor and made a mental note to bring an ashtray during his next shift. He tossed the butt into the coffee cup with the three others he had smoked. "Nightmares, Sharon," he finished, "are a perfectly normal part of dreaming that release pent-up emotions. I wouldn't worry too much about having them now and again. In fact, they're vital for mental health. Chad, how're you doing?"

Chad stuck a thumb in the air without looking away from the TV. "All good, mate."

"Thanks for the talk, doc," Sharon said, pushing the same errant lock of blonde hair as before back behind her ear, from where it had slipped loose. "I don't feel as lonely anymore. I think I might be chatting a lot with you over the next three weeks...if that's all right?"

"Perfectly."

"I just wish I could see you. Talking to my reflection is a trip."

Before Wallis could think of a suitable reply, Sharon wandered to the bookshelf, where she began sorting through the one hundred or so books he'd borrowed from Berkeley's Doe Library.

Wallis watched her for a little longer, then stood, stretched, and went to the bathroom down the hallway by the decommissioned elevator. All the fixtures had been removed save for, at his request, a toilet, urinal, and sink. He used the urinal, washed his hands—making another mental note to bring some toilet paper, soap, and hand towels next shift as well—and returned to the observation room.

Sharon was watching TV with Chad once more.

The next six hours went by swiftly. Wallis took nearly three pages of notes, which he was reading over when there was a knock at the door.

Guru Rampal entered the room a moment later, dressed in the same tee-shirt and khaki shorts he'd had on earlier. The sunglasses were nowhere in sight. "Good evening, professor," he said, shrugging a backpack off his shoulder and setting it on the ground next to the table.

Wallis could smell McDonald's. "Bring some late-night snacks, Guru?" he asked.

"I did not know if I was going to get hungry or not." He looked through the viewing window into the sleep laboratory. "Did anything interesting happen?"

Wallis shook his head. "Their bodies are still in sync with their natural circadian rhythms. We shouldn't expect to see any deviations from their regular behavioral patterns until they've gone at least one night without sleep." He stood. "Take my seat. You're making me nervous standing over me like that."

"Thank you, professor." He sat in the chair. "Is there anything in particular I should know before you leave?"

"No, it's all pretty straightforward," Wallis told him. "Just keep watch on our two test subjects from Down Under and record their behavior. Have a read of my notes on the laptop if you want to get a feel for what you might want to jot down. Other than that..." He shrugged. "Just don't fall asleep."

"Do not worry about that, professor. I am a night owl. Uh, what if they want to talk to me?"

"Talk to them."

"That is okay?"

"Why wouldn't it be?"

"I do not know. I guess...I have never participated in a study with human subjects."

Wallis gestured to the touch panel controller. "There's a Talk button you press if you want them to hear you, and a Listen button if you want to hear them. That's about it."

Nodding, Guru tapped his fingers on the desk.

Wallis frowned. "Is there something on your mind, Guru?"

"Do you think I should shave my head?"

Wallis blinked, caught off guard by the question. His eyes

flicked to Guru's Teddy Boys pompadour. "I like your hair," he said.

"It looks good from the front," he said, nodding. "I copied the hairstyle of a very famous pop star back home in India. But the problem is here." He bent forward and pointed to his balding crown. "Can you see?"

"A lot of men experience male-pattern hair loss."

He sat straight again. "But I am only twenty-two! If I had already found a wife, then no problem. But it will be much more difficult to find a wife when I am bald."

Wallis smiled. "You'll do just fine."

"Thank you, professor. But you have not answered my question yet. Should I shave my head? This is what all the advice online is telling me to do."

"Like I said, I like your hair. It's you. But if you're self-conscious about the thinning on top—sure, shave it off, why not? It will always grow back."

Guru sighed. "The problem is, I am not sure if I have the face for a shaved head. I am not handsome like you. I do not have strong features."

"Maybe grow some facial hair to balance things out?"

"That is another problem! I cannot! I have tried. I get a few whiskers here and here." He touched his upper lip and chin. "But that is all. And with no hair or facial hair, I fear I will look like a brown alien."

"Ladies dig brown aliens."

Guru's shoulders sagged. "You are not helping, professor. You have a very stylish head of hair, and a stylish beard to match. You do not know what I am going through."

Now it was Wallis' turn to sigh. "I'm sorry, buddy, I shouldn't be making light of this. My best advice? Go to a good barber. Not a cheap one. A good one. I can recommend you mine, if you would like? His name's Andre. He'll be able to tell you what products to use to give your hair some volume, and what cut might best suit your problem area."

Guru brightened. "Really?"

"His shop's in Union Square. You can't miss it."

"Thank you, professor! I will visit him first thing tomorrow morning!"

"You'll probably need an appointment..."

"Right. Well, I will phone him first thing tomorrow morning then."

"Now you're talking. Have a good night, Guru. And remember, any problems, any questions—check that: any *non-hair* related questions—don't hesitate to call me."

Seated in the black leather swivel chair, Guru Rampal looked around the small observation room, though there wasn't much to see. The table before him with the touch-screen panel and the laptop. A metal trolley loaded with a desktop computer and EEG equipment. And the five-hundred-or-so-liter tank that fed the stimulant gas into the sleep laboratory.

Curious, Guru got up and went to the tank. He placed a hand on the stainless steel surface. It was cool against his skin. He studied the different valves and pressure gauges but didn't dare touch any. Amphetamines and other psychostimulant drugs had to be ingested as pills or injected intravenously (or, when used recreationally, snorted as powder or inhaled as smoke). He'd never heard of any that could be evaporated into vapors and breathed in as easily as if they were oxygen. Nevertheless, if this could be done with certain anesthetics such as nitrous oxide and xenon, he supposed it had only been a matter of time before someone figured out how to do it with stimulants as well.

And not just someone, he thought. *Dr. Roy Wallis.*

My professor.

Guru was beyond excited that Dr. Wallis had chosen him to assist in his groundbreaking research. He admired the man tremendously. Over the years he'd selected every one of the professor's courses that fit his schedule, and he would continue to do so when he undertook his master's degree next spring and, eventually, his Ph.D.

To call a spade a spade, Guru was an intellectual. This was due to both genetics and hard work. According to his mother, he had been walking and talking by his first birthday. By two and a half years of age, he could count to more than one hundred. When he was five, he solved a Rubik's Cube he'd found in the school's library on his first try. In grade six, he won the school's spelling bee contest, a feat he repeated every consecutive year until he graduated.

Nevertheless, even though learning came easily to him, he did not take his gift for granted. He always pushed himself to excel that little bit more, to become that little bit better than his classmates, because he'd known that doing so was the only way he would escape the slums into which he'd been born and provide a better life for himself and his mother and his brothers.

When he was accepted as a freshman to UC Berkeley (thanks in part to a glowing letter of recommendation from the Chairman of Secondary Education in his home city of Dharamshala), his mother had urged him to pursue a degree in information technology. "Indians make very good computer programmers, Guru," she'd told him. "It is a very good job, and it pays very handsomely. I do not understand why you want to be a psychologist. Indians do not make good psychologists."

Guru, of course, disagreed that Indians did not make good psychologists, and as for why he wanted to work in the field of psychology, the answer was simple: it was what he was meant to do. His father had suffered from Alzheimer's, and his second-eldest brother was on the autistic spectrum, so Guru had spent much of his youth taking them to and from hospitals and serving as their primary caregiver. He became deeply invested in learning about their maladies, always pestering doctors and nurses with mental health questions, or cutting articles from whatever newspapers and magazines he could get his hands on. Over the years he became a veritable expert on both diseases, and when his father passed away from complications with Alzheimer's, he made the decision to devote the rest of his life to the psychology of the mind.

Guru was eager to begin this journey as soon as possible, but he still had a long road ahead of him. It would be another two years before he completed his master's degree, and four more years after that to become a chartered psychologist and gain his APA accreditation. On top of all this, he would need to spend another year or two in a fellowship program at the university to gain field experience. Only then—seven or eight years down the road—could he become a licensed clinical psychologist.

Originally Guru's dream had been to open a practice in California. However, he was now contemplating doing so in India, where he could also campaign for healthcare change at a grassroots level, for as he'd witnessed firsthand growing up, the country's healthcare was in an abysmal state of affairs. Hospitals and community organizations were understaffed and underfunded. Policies focused on curative measures rather than preventive ones. And in many of the villages and smaller towns, therapy and counseling were virtually unheard of. Yes, he would only be one voice in a population of 1.3 billion, but change always had to start somewhere—

"You there, doc?"

Jumping at the unexpected voice, Guru hurried to the touch-panel controller. "Uh, hi. This is Guru speaking."

"Elvis!" Chad said. He was standing directly before the two-way glass, grinning.

"Uh, yes, that is me." He wasn't yet comfortable using the intercom system.

"You wearing your sunnies? I can't see you in this mirror."

"My sunglasses?"

"Yeah, mate."

"No, I do not wear my sunglasses at night."

"*I wear my sunglasses at night,*" Chad sang. "*So I can, so I can…*"

Guru recognized the song and realized the joke was on him. He didn't reply.

Chad stopped singing and said, "Hey, mate, where you from? India, right?"

"Yes, that is right. From a city named Dharamshala in the state of Himachal Pradesh. You might be interested to know the Dalai Lama's residence is located there."

"No shit? Didya ever meet him?"

"When I was a boy, yes. My class visited Tsuglakhang Temple while the Dalai Lama was present so we could listen to his preaching."

"Did he do any magic?"

"Magic?" Guru frowned. "No. The Dalai Lama is but a simple Buddhist monk. He has no magical powers."

"I thought he healed people and shit?"

"No, he could not even heal himself when he became sick and required the removal of his gall bladder."

"All right, mate. I hear ya. Hey, I have a question."

"About the Dalai Lama."

"Nah, nah. Food. Got any good recipes?"

"I—no." Guru shook his head, despite the fact the Australian couldn't see him. "I am not a very good cook."

"Come on, mate. You gotta know something? We got all this food in here and neither Shaz or me know shit about cooking."

"I make a great brekky!" Sharon said, looking up from the book she was reading on her bed.

"How hard is it to make bacon and eggs?" Chad remarked.

"I can do more than that," she protested.

"Anyway, Elvis," Chad said to Guru, "give me a recipe. Something really elaborate that will help pass the fucking time in this box."

"The only dishes I prepare at home are curries. If you

would like, I could give you one of those recipes. I learned them from my mother."

"Curry, awesome! Like a vindaloo or butter chicken or something?"

"That would depend on whether you prefer it to be spicy or sweet?"

"Spicy, mate! The hotter the better."

"Do you have chili peppers?"

"We got an entire fucking supermarket in here, mate. But let me check." He went to the refrigerator. "Yup, got a whole package."

"Then check the pantry for these spices..."

Dr. Roy Wallis lived in the timeworn Clock Tower Building in San Francisco's South of Market neighborhood. Built in 1907, the brick-and-timber structure covered two city blocks at Second and Bryant Streets. It once housed the operations of the Schmidt Lithograph Company, the largest printer on the West Coast. In 1992 it underwent a facelift when visionary capitalists transformed the cavernous space into over one hundred trendy lofts, all of which featured soaring ceilings, concrete columns, and factory windows.

Wallis parked his bite-sized Audi TT in his reserved spot out back of the building and, forgoing the elevator to burn some calories, climbed the six flights of steps to the penthouse suite.

Home sweet home, he thought as he stepped through the front door into the 3,000 square-foot space. The brick walls and cathedral ceilings with their exposed steel beams were remnants of the building's industrial past, while Dr. Wallis' extensive renovations—including floor-to-ceiling windows, skylights, polished slate floors, and a black-and-gray color scheme—lifted the apartment's aesthetics into the twenty-first century.

Wallis would never have been able to afford the digs on his teaching salary. His parents, however, had been wealthy, and when they died in a yachting accident twenty years earlier, he had inherited their nearly twenty-million-dollar estate. At the time, he had been living in a modest studio apartment in SoMa, which had been a ghost town then, filled with empty warehouses festooned with smokestacks, few restaurants, and not a single grocery store. When he heard the penthouse suite in the nearby Clock Tower Building was hitting the market, he toured it out of curiosity and fell immediately in love. Not only was it airy and spacious, but it included exclusive access to the three-story Clock Tower. Wallis gave Sotheby's their asking price and moved in the next month. He had called it home ever since, and he couldn't imagine living anywhere else in the city.

Dr. Wallis hung his blazer on a wall hook, dumped his keys in a crystal dish on a table next to the door, then went to the bar, where he poured dark rum and ginger beer over ice, adding a slice of lime as garnish. He carried the highball outside to the twelve-hundred-square-foot wraparound deck, breathing the twilight air deeply. In the distance the downtown skyline glittered with lights, while the Bay Bridge appeared to magically hover above the fog-shrouded San Francisco Bay like a bejeweled necklace.

He was about to light a cigarette when his phone rang.

He withdrew it from his pocket, glanced at the screen, then answered it. "Are you downstairs stalking me?" he said. "You called as soon as I stepped in the door."

"You're standing on your deck with a Dark 'n' Stormy and admiring the night view," the female voice said.

"How did you know that?"

"I'm watching you."

Despite himself, Wallis scanned the windows of the buildings stretching away below him. "Am I that predictable?" he asked.

"As predictable as a grandfather clock."

"Is that a shot at my age?"

Brandy Clarkson laughed. "You look good for forty-one, Roy. Stop obsessing."

"I'm not obsessing."

"It's all you talked about on your birthday."

His birthday had been a month ago. Brandy had been in San Francisco, and she'd taken him to a dumpling restaurant in Chinatown, where, admittedly, he'd made a fuss about how old he was getting.

"You in town now?" he asked.

"Came for a conference tomorrow morning."

He glanced at his wristwatch: half past ten. "I can meet you at Yoshi's in twenty?"

"I'm not in the mood for jazz. I thought we could have a quiet night for a change?"

He was up for that. "You want to come over? Where are you staying?"

"The Fairmont. I'll grab an Uber and be there in fifteen."

Wallis hung up, finished his drink, then took a hot shower. He and Brandy had begun dating seven years ago, when he was thirty-four and she was twenty-one—and a student in one of his senior classes. After about three years of exclusive dating, their relationship became serious. Too serious for him, and he broke it off, much to Brandy's dismay. She moved south to Menlo Park and got a job with Facebook as a behavioral data analyst. He didn't see her again for two years until they randomly bumped into one another during happy hour at the View, a lounge on the thirty-ninth floor of the Marriot, where they had often hung out when they were a couple. They had a few drinks together, reminisced, and ended up sleeping together. Since then they'd been hooking up whenever she was in the area, which was usually once a month or so. Twenty-eight now, Brandy was more of everything—independent, confident, sophisticated—and Wallis enjoyed her infrequent company.

Nevertheless, he *was* forty-one. He couldn't keep up his

bachelor lifestyle forever, and he found himself thinking more and more about finding a proper girlfriend, someone he could spend each night with, build a future with.

He toweled off, shaved, dressed in black, and was pouring a second drink when Brandy knocked. He'd left the door unlocked and called out, "Come in!"

"Hello, my lovely!" Brandy sang, stepping inside, smiling radiantly. Holding a bottle of champagne in one hand, and a black handbag in the other, she closed the door with her tush.

"You look great," Wallis said.

"Thanks!" she said, crossing the living room, heels clicking on the slate, blonde ringlets bouncing against her shoulders, blue eyes sparkling. Flamenco-red lipstick matched the color of her dress, which clung to her breasts and hips and flaunted her long, tanned legs.

She planted a kiss on his lips.

"Mmmm," she said. "You smell good. I like that aftershave."

"You smell good too," he said. "Didn't I buy you that perfume?"

"You did indeed. Miss me?"

"I always miss you."

She pouted. "You do not. Otherwise you never would have dumped me. Here." She offered him the champagne.

"What's the occasion?" he asked, taking it and reading the label.

"Duh?" She slapped him playfully on the chest. "The first day of your big secret experiment you won't tell me anything about!"

"I mentioned it at my birthday...?"

"You did indeed, Mr. One-Too-Many-At-Dinner. And I do listen to you, Roy, believe it or not. I'm not just in this farce of a relationship for the sex."

Wallis led Brandy to the kitchen. He filled two flutes with champagne, then laid out a spread of red grapes, rye crackers, and goat cheese on the granite island.

"To the Sleep Experiment," he said, raising his glass.

Brandy tapped. "May it not be a snoozer."

"Touché," he said, sipping. The bubbly tasted light, fruity, and refreshing.

"So tell me about it," she said. "Are you hiding peas beneath a mattress in the hopes of finding your perfect princess-bride?"

"I'm studying the effects of sleep deprivation," he said simply.

She stared at him. "Is that it? That's all you're going to tell me?"

"There's not that much to it—"

"Oh, come now, Roy! You were just as cagey on your birthday! What's the big secret?"

"There is no big secret," he said. "I'm observing the behavior of two test subjects as they function without sleep." He shrugged. "And there's an experimental gas involved..."

"Here's the juicy stuff I wanted! What kind of gas?"

"A substituted amphetamine, which is to say, a class of compounds based upon the amphetamine structure."

"I didn't know you could inhale amphetamines?"

"The method is much preferable to taking pills because the subjects never miss a dose, and the gas is administered directly to the lungs, which limits systemic absorption, which limits side effects. In fact, I have so far observed zero negative central nervous system side effects in any of my clinical trials."

"*Zero* side effects? There are always side effects."

He shook his head. "Even administered in high doses, the gas has caused no neurotoxic damage to brain cells. I've only tested it on animals thus far, of course. But imagine, Brandy, if the human trials are successful—"

"You're going to have armies of meth-heads roaming the country!"

He shook his head again. "Unlike methamphetamines,

the gas doesn't act upon serotonin or dopamine neurotrans-mitters. It provides no rush or euphoria. No addiction or withdrawal. No anxiety, depression, paranoia, or psychosis. You just...don't sleep."

"Like...for how long are we talking here?"

"Days." He shrugged. "Weeks."

Brandy appeared incredulous. "Bullshit, Roy."

"As long as you're inhaling the gas, you won't sleep. It's as simple as that."

"But we *need* sleep. You, me, everybody! You can't just *not* sleep."

Dr. Wallis smiled. "That hypothesis, Brandy, is what I intend to challenge over the next twenty-one days."

Dr. Roy Wallis fielded several more questions from Brandy before steering her off the conversation and into the bedroom. Their sex was always loud, creative, and a little dangerous.

Straddling her on the bed now, Wallis peeled the red dress over her head and feathered her naval with kisses. She gripped tufts of his hair and thrust her pelvis into his. He slid his hands beneath her back and unclasped her bra—

There was a knock at the door.

Wallis straightened, wondering who it could be.

"Expecting company?" Brandy asked, smiling mischievously.

He shook his head. "Wait here."

Wallis crossed the penthouse, buttoning his shirt.

Who the hell would be coming by at this hour?

He paused at the front door. There was no peephole. He'd been planning on installing a security camera but hadn't gotten around to it.

"Hello?" he said.

"Roy? It's Brook."

Shit! he thought. Why was she here—?

They'd made plans the week before, only he'd completely forgotten about them.

Knowing he could not leave her standing on his doorstep, he opened the door and greeted her with his best smile. She smiled back.

"Hi!" she said.

"Hi," he said.

Physically, Brook Foxley was diametrically opposed to Brandy Clarkson. Her black hair was cut in a short, straight bob. Her dark eyes possessed a skittish reticence. Her pale skin looked as though it had never been touched by the sun. She had none of Brandy's curves, but her svelte figure was somehow equally feminine, and she looked stunning right then in a silk blouse, skinny jeans, and nude heels a shade or two lighter than her beaded clutch.

Personality-wise, Brook and Brandy were also opposites. Brook was watchful, reserved, playful in a friendly manner. She was not one to immediately catch your eye, but somehow she became more beautiful each time you saw her.

Brandy, in contrast, was a flirt. She flaunted her sexuality, weaponized it to her advantage. When Dr. Wallis took her out, he practically shared the date with her phone. She insisted all the messages and emails were work-related, but he never really knew for certain. And when she wasn't on her phone, she was telling him about some celebrity or Silicon Valley so-and-so she had met at a gala dinner or yacht party or glitzy function. Her life was glamorous, narcissistic, exciting...and empty. She was an outsider relentlessly searching for a way into a world to which she didn't belong and would likely never be accepted, relentlessly positioning herself to be in the right place at the right time for that Big Break to transform her life, relentlessly searching for the quickest way up the social ladder, morals and happiness and empathy for others be damned.

She was, in fact, Wallis to a tee.

"I tried calling you," Brook said, smiling uncertainly, "but your phone was off."

"The battery was low all day. It must have finally run out," he said, remaining squarely in the doorway as his mind searched madly for a way out of the mousetrap he found himself in.

Sensing something was up, Brandy's eyes flicked past him. "I hope I'm not intruding...?"

"No, not at all..." he said. "Well, actually..."

The silence that followed spoke volumes.

"I see, I'm sorry," Brook said. "I shouldn't have just stopped by... But last week we made a date for tonight. You wanted to celebrate your new experiment..."

"I know, and I did—I do—want to celebrate...with you," he said, fumbling for the right words. "It's just that I've been so busy, and the date slipped my mind—"

"What's going on out here?"

Dr. Wallis' stomach dropped at the sound of Brandy's voice. He turned to find her crossing the room wearing nothing but her lacy white lingerie.

"Oh!" Brook said, her eyes meeting Wallis' before faltering to the floor. Yet in that brief moment he read in them heartbreak—the same sensation squeezing the inside of his chest. "Goodnight," she mumbled, and retreated down the staircase.

"Brook!" he called after her.

She continued without stopping. He almost called her name again but didn't. What was the point? She wouldn't return, and even if she did, what would they talk about with Brandy standing in the living room in her thong and bra?

Brandy.

Goddammit.

Wallis stepped back inside, closed the door, then focused his frustration on his on-and-off-again fling, who now stood at the kitchen island, sipping her flute of champagne.

"What the hell did you do that for?" he snapped.

"She didn't have to leave," Brandy said. "I haven't had a threesome in, oh, far too long." She was acting nonchalant, her tone was conversational, but Wallis could tell she was pissed off, and he realized he wasn't the only one with a right to be upset.

He sighed. "Why didn't you just stay in the bedroom? I would have gotten rid of her."

"I wanted to see who you're fucking these days."

"Jesus," he said, shaking his head. He went to the bar, filled a tumbler with two fingers of rum, and swallowed the contents in one burning gulp.

Brandy asked, "Is she a student like I was?"

"No."

"She's young."

"She's thirty-three."

"Blessed with good genes. Dammit, Roy, you'll never change, will you?"

"Change?" He looked at her, surprised. "Change how? I can't see other people? We're not exclusive. You know that."

"I know, but I thought..." Her blue eyes darkened. "I thought you were changing. I thought maybe...I don't know! But we've been spending a lot of time together...I thought... Oh, fuck it!"

She stormed off to the bedroom.

Wallis poured another couple of fingers of rum.

Brandy returned a minute later, fully dressed. She snatched her handbag from the island and went straight to the door.

"Where are you going?" he asked her.

"To the hotel."

"You don't have to..."

"Goodbye, Roy." She opened the door, looked back. "You know what's sad about this? I would have been good to you. I would have made you happy."

"Brandy..."

She left, slamming the door closed behind her.

DAY 2

Tuesday, May 29, 2018

D r. Roy Wallis entered the observation room in the basement of Tolman Hall carrying his briefcase and two coffees in a pulp-fiber takeout tray. He set the tray on the table and said, "Cappuccino and vanilla latte. Your pick."

"Actually, I don't drink coffee, professor," Penny Park said. "Only tea."

"More caffeine for me then." He slumped into the second chair with a weary sigh. "I guess I could use it."

"Yeah, you look pretty tired, professor." She eyed him suspiciously. "Did you party late at a nightclub?"

"I'm too old for nightclubs, Penny. I just had a few drinks at home."

"By yourself?"

"Yes, by myself," he said, which was mostly true. After Brandy left, he'd stayed up well past midnight smoking pot and drinking his best rum and playing music way too loud. He rubbed his eyes and studied the two Australians in the sleep laboratory. Chad was lying supine on the weight bench, presumably resting between sets, while Sharon reclined in her bed, reading a book. "How've they been?"

"All good, mate," Penny said in a horrendous attempt at an Australian accent.

"My God," he said.

"Not good?"

"It's the effort that counts."

"Shaz taught me a lot of Australian expressions."

"Shaz?"

"It's her nickname."

"I know that—"

"She told me to call her that. It's what they do with names in Australia. Me, I wouldn't be Penz, because that sounds like something you write with—"

"Rather than a unit of currency."

"Ha, ha. Instead, Shaz said I'd be called Parksy. I don't know what you would be called. Probably not Royz. That sounds like the flower, which is too feminine for someone so manly as you."

"Manly as me?"

"You are a very manly man, professor. Hmmm...maybe you'd be called Wallsy? You should ask her."

"It's at the top of my list," he said. "What else did you talk about?"

"Do you know what a Map of Tassie is?"

"Yes, Penny, I do."

"Really? Prove it."

"It's an Australian colloquialism for a woman's pubic hair."

"Because the shape of Tasmania is—"

"Do you really want to spend the handover discussing this?"

"You asked what we talked about."

"I'll read your notes. Why don't you head off and relax? You've been up since the crack of dawn."

"I'm actually wide awake, professor. You know what's interesting? Chad used the bathroom at six thirty a.m."

"Why's that interesting?"

"Because that's nearly the time he would be waking up any other day. And when you wake up, you always have to pee. So it's interesting because he still had to pee at the same time, even though he didn't sleep. It means his liver is pre-programed."

"It's simply his body's endogenous, entrainable oscillation acting on its twenty-four-hour rhythms."

"Say what, professor? English isn't my first language, you know."

"His circadian clock, Penny. Endogenous means the daily rhythms are self-sustained. Entrained means they are adjusted to local environment factors such as light and temperature."

"So his circadian clock will adjust to his new environment?"

"Certainly."

"He'll start peeing at all crazy hours?"

"He'll go when he needs to. Not when his circadian clock tells him it's the usual time to do so."

"Hey professor? Can I ask you something?"

"You're not thinking about shaving your head, are you?"

"Huh?"

"Fire away."

"So this morning I was reading on my phone about sleep experiments. I had a lot of time to kill, right? Anyway, I came across a sleep experiment in the Soviet Union last century..."

Wallis smiled. "I was wondering when you or Guru were going to ask me about that."

She was referring to a paranormal legend that had been causing a stir on the internet the last few years. According to the most popular version of the tale, in the late 1940s, five political prisoners in the Soviet Union were offered their freedom if they participated in a government experiment in which they remained awake in a sealed environment for fifteen days—by breathing in an experimental gas-based stimulant.

"Because, you know," Penny said, "it sounds a lot like

what we're doing..."

"I hope our gas isn't as toxic as theirs was," he said.

"Is that a joke?"

"The Russian Sleep Experiment is a legend, Penny. Complete fiction. What we're doing is careful, calculated scientific research."

"But do you think something...so awful...could happen in real life?"

"That remaining awake for an extended period of time could lead one to insanity, self-mutilation, murder, and cannibalism? What do you think, Penny?"

"No," she answered sheepishly. "It's just that the story was so *creepy*. Maybe because I was here all by myself..."

"My advice to you, Penny? Bring in a good novel to pass the time rather than looking up nonsense on the internet."

"Yeah, right, good idea." She yawned. "Maybe I'm more tired than I thought." She collected her backpack and stood. "You work so much, professor. What do you do in your free time?"

"I have hobbies. I try to get to the gym every now and then."

"Berkeley is so empty now, right? It's strange with no one around. All my friends went home to visit their families."

"I like the quiet. It's peaceful."

Penny nodded but made no move to leave. "What I'm wondering is, maybe *we* can go out for dinner this week?"

Dr. Wallis tried not to let his surprise show. Although he'd already concluded that Penny was attracted to him, he'd never imagined she would be so bold as to ask him on out for dinner! Yes, he'd dated Brandy when she was his student, but he'd been a lot younger then. He was nearly twice Penny's age—a realization that depressed him enough to almost accept her invitation...almost.

"That would be nice, Penny," he said. "Except that I don't finish my shift until ten o'clock, by which time I'm rather exhausted. But, ah...thank you for asking."

"Yeah, no sweat," she said, her air a little too insouciant to be convincing. "I'll see you tomorrow, right?"

"Same time, same place."

She left then, easing the door closed behind her until the tongue clicked metallically in place.

Her exit was not half as dramatic as Brandy's door-slam the previous night, yet in the still basement room, the deliberately quiet action was somehow almost as emphatic.

Chad Carter didn't know for certain how long he'd been cooped up in the sleep laboratory, but he reckoned it to be about one day or so now—and it already felt like a hell of a long time. Another nineteen or twenty days seemed like a bloody lifetime.

Initially, when he and Shaz were contemplating whether to participate in this wacko experiment, three weeks hadn't sounded too bad. But of course he hadn't known then just how fucked up it would be remaining awake for hours and hours on end.

He had pulled all-nighters before, of course, on more occasions than he could count. But it was different staying up around the clock when you were shitfaced and partying, compared to when you were sober as a judge with nothing to do but watch TV or work out or stare at the fucking wall.

Man, it was hard to believe last year at this time he had been partying his ass off in Europe...and now he was a rat in a box. He'd departed Melbourne in March with his good mate from uni, Shane Eales. They landed in London, where Shane's sister, Laura, worked for some marketing company. Laura had a lot of hot friends and connections, and on their first night on the town she took them to some posh club, all red leather and velvet, which featured glass fold-down trays in the bathroom cubicles not meant for holding drinks. Every time Chad went to the Men's to take a slash, he heard snorts coming from the occupied stalls. He wouldn't have minded doing a few lines himself, but he was on a budget that didn't include blow.

Later in that evening, Kelly Osbourne, daughter of the Prince of Darkness, arrived at the pub and had countless blokes literally lining up to talk to her. Chad didn't get it. She wasn't hot. She was a spoiled rich brat. But all these guys wanted to talk to her just because she was famous by virtue of her pop?

Always the larrikin, Shane decided to chat her up during a rare moment she was alone at her table. He sat down next to her, cracked an ice breaker—and she turned her back to him. The shutdown became an ongoing joke between them for the rest of the night.

Three days later they flew Ryanair to Spain, where they spent a few nights in Barcelona before heading to Pamplona. The small city was jam-packed with foreigners due to the annual festival Hemingway made famous in that book of his. There wasn't a single bed in any hotel or hostel to be found, so the only option was to buy tents and camp out in a huge field alongside thousands of other revelers.

It wasn't hard to find Australians when you travelled. You simply followed the beer and the noise. Chad and Shane quickly hooked up with a group of about twenty fellow Aussies that had set up base around a shitty RV with a big Australian flag taped to one side, and the next few days were a haze of drinking, tossing around a rugby ball, sleeping off hangovers, barbequing, and fucking in tiny tents.

Two days before the bulls were set to run, Shaz arrived at the field by herself. She had come to Europe with a friend, but the friend had returned to Perth. Shaz was easily the hottest in the ever-expanding group of Aussies, and Chad had tried his best that night to get some action, but she wasn't game, telling him she had a boyfriend back home.

The next morning, with everyone dressed in their whites with red sashes tied around their waists, they took a chartered bus into the city. The scene was fucking nuts. Streets and balconies packed with people. Everyone running around throwing sangria on everyone else.

First order of business was to find beer, and by noon all two dozen or so Australians were smashed. Some Irish guy who'd ended up hanging out with them for much of the morning got so shit-faced he climbed a pole and leapt to his death. It wasn't intentional. Other people were leaping from the top of the pole into the locked arms of those below, sort of how rock stars belly-flop off the stage into a mosh pit of fans. The poor Irish bloke, however, jumped before anyone was paying attention to him. He landed on his head and was whisked away by paramedics. They heard later through the grapevine that he had passed away in the hospital.

Which, needless to say, was a major bummer and not exactly how you wanted to kick off a festival. But despite this, the rest of the day had come good, filled with drinking games, tapas, fights, and even conga lines. Most of those in their group passed out or returned to the field after dinner, but Chad and Shane kept partying throughout the night so they could secure spots along the fence that bordered the road which the bulls followed. Chad had planned to run, but that was before the Irish guy died, which had made the dangers of running with one-ton angry bulls a little more real and frightening.

In any event, the whole run went by ridiculously quickly, from the opening horn to the last bull charging past him lasting no more than a few minutes.

The following day the caravan of Aussies headed to Portugal, and Chad and Shaz went with them. They spent nearly three months traveling from small town to small town that lined the ocean, surfing and drinking and partying, until they broke up. The three blokes renting the RV were heading to Germany for Oktoberfest, while many of the others had already gone home or their separate ways. Sharon told Chad she wanted to see France, and for whatever reason (in the back of his mind he'd been thinking he could still get with her, boyfriend or no), he said he'd join her.

He parted ways with Shane, who was happy to check out Oktoberfest, and he and Shaz took a bus to Bordeaux, where they spent the night in an ancient, rundown hotel (same room, different beds). In the morning they rented a car and drove through the French countryside all the way to Paris, which, up until that point, might have been the highlight of the trip. The Eiffel Tower, the Arc de Triomphe, the Louvre —all that shit you saw on TV was now right around every cobble-stoned corner.

Chad and Shaz remained in Paris for a month...and maybe the romance of the city rubbed off on her, because she finally loosened up enough to make out with him one night, though she kept telling him "no" every time he tried to unbutton her jeans.

But whatever. Making out was kind of fun in itself, and the juvenile foreplay went on for another month before Sharon told him she was going to book a plane ticket to California. She didn't have much of a choice in the matter. She had to keep flying west on her around-the-world ticket. Chad's return flight to Melbourne was in three weeks' time, but he decided to fuck going home and booked a new ticket to California.

Shaz didn't exactly seem thrilled by this turn of events, and Chad figured it had something to do with her attraction for him warring with the guilt that came with cheating on her boyfriend.

Regardless, he tagged along to Cali, and they found accommodation in a house in Los Angeles, which they shared with three other Aussies and one Canadian.

LA quickly burned up whatever money they had left, so they both started looking for jobs. Sharon found work as a hostess at an Italian eatery, but Chad had a tougher time of it, eventually deciding to become a test subject for new drug trials. He participated in three clinical trials—two with the

FDA and one with a pharmaceutical giant—before he came across the advert for the Sleep Experiment, which seemed like the motherlode of test trials.

Stay awake for three weeks, get a shit load of money. What wasn't there to love?

Given the professor running the show was looking for two test subjects who knew one another but were not romantically involved, Chad convinced Shaz to apply alongside him while coaching her not to mention their on-and-off-again make-out sessions.

And now here they were.

One or two days into the experiment.

Nineteen or twenty more to go.

No mornings, noons, or nights. Nothing to provide guidance or structure to the day. Just one unending slog of *Game of Thrones, Breaking Bad,* and all the other shit playing on Netflix.

Chad lay back down on the workout bench and gripped the barbell suspended above his chest. *At least I'll be in shape when this is all over,* he thought, unracking the bar and performing the first of ten presses.

Dr. Roy Wallis was watching the Australians through the viewing window. Sharon was sitting on her bed, reading a hardback Rex Stout novel. Chad was lifting weights. He tapped the Talk button on the touch panel controller and asked, "How's everybody doing?"

Sharon glanced up sharply from the novel, apparently startled by the unexpected intrusion. "Hi, doc. You're back?"

"Enjoying the book?"

"I really like the main character, Nero Wolfe. He's a brilliant detective who solves every crime right from his living room. He never goes outside. He just stays locked up at home reading books." She smiled sweetly. "Just like me right now, I guess."

"Perhaps I should bring you some orchids to tend for?" he said, referencing one of Nero Wolfe's favorite hobbies.

"Would you? That would be terrific."

Chad finished his series of reps, then sat up on the bench. "So we survived the first day, did we?"

"Does that mean it's about breakfast time?" Sharon asked.

There was no clock in the sleep laboratory to discourage the Australians from keeping track of how long they'd been sequestered. Having them count down more than three hundred hours until the experiment's end wouldn't be a great morale booster.

Dr. Wallis tapped the Talk button again. "You've been teaching Penny some interesting slang."

"She's a quick learner!" Sharon said.

"I was hoping we could try a couple of exercises today. If you'd like to eat first, go right ahead."

"What kind of exercises?"

"The first one involves tongue-twisters."

"I love tongue-twisters! Let's do it now. I'm really not that hungry anyway."

"All right then. Nothing to it but to repeat after me..."

In total, Wallis recited six tongue-twisters, and Sharon repeated them all back with relative ease. Chad made a few more mistakes than she did, but Wallis attributed those to the complexity of the phrases, not any faltering mental capacity due to sleep deprivation.

"Excellent," he told them. "The second exercise is a little more involved. I have a blindfold with me, along with a bag of random objects—"

"Kinky, doc," Sharon said, giggling.

"I'm going to bring them to the door now. Chad, I'd like you to meet me there. You can look in the bag, but Sharon, you cannot. Understood?"

"Too easy," Chad said, already heading toward the door.

From his messenger bag, Wallis gathered a silk shoe bag with a drawstring closure that had come with a pair of loafers he'd purchased recently. He also removed a red cotton bandana with a paisley design. At the door to the sleep laboratory, he handed both items to Chad and returned to his spot at the desk.

Although the stimulant gas was odorless and tasteless, he nevertheless thought he could detect a metallic scent.

My imagination, he told himself dismissively.

He pressed the Talk button. "Chad, I'd like you to tie the bandana around Sharon's eyes."

Chad did as instructed.

"Can you see anything, Sharon?"

"Nothing."

"Good. I'd like you to stick your hand in the bag Chad is holding and withdraw a single item."

"Better be no sheep brains or anything yucky in there, doc."

"Nothing of the sort," he assured her. "They're everyday items from around my house."

"What's all this about, mate?" Chad asked.

"I'd like to know whether Sharon is experiencing any initial signs of astereognosis due to sleep deprivation—that is, whether she has any difficulty identifying objects by touch alone without any other sensory input."

"You're the life of the party, mate. But whatever floats your boat. Shaz, you ready?"

"What if I fail?" she asked.

"The good doc pushes a button and you get incinerated," Chad said.

"You can't fail," Dr. Wallis told her. "Whenever you're ready..."

Sharon stuck a hand in the shoe bag and withdrew a Rubik's Cube. She identified it right away.

"Very good," Wallis said. Globes, pyramids, and cubes

usually posed no problems. "Try again."

She set the Rubik's Cube aside and this time produced from the bag a porcelain teapot lid. She turned it over in her hand. "It's a lid of some kind."

"Can you be more specific?" Wallis asked.

"I don't know. Maybe for a teapot?"

"Excellent," he said.

"Two for two, Shaz," Chad said. "You're setting records."

"Try again," Wallis said.

This time she withdrew a novelty octopus flash drive. She frowned. "God, what's this!"

"Try to identify it using your other hand."

She switched the flash drive to her left hand. "No idea..."

"Try using both hands."

"It's a bit squishy with some...things...at one end and something sharp at the other end...but...sorry, no idea, doc."

They continued the exercise until no items remained in the shoe bag. In total, Sharon correctly identified seven out of twelve objects. She removed the blindfold.

"So does she have that astro-disease?" Chad asked.

"It's not a disease," Dr. Wallis said. "And no, her tactile recognition exhibited no observable behavioral deficit. We'll see how well you do tomorrow."

"Can't hardly wait, mate," Chad said, and went back to lifting weights.

Dr. Roy Wallis resumed his role as silent observer, and over the next several hours the only sound in the small anteroom was the clicking of the laptop keys as he filled several pages with detailed notes chronicling the Australians' behavior and emerging symptoms related to sleep loss.

Guru Rampal arrived at nine forty-five p.m., holding his phone to his ear.

Wallis blinked in surprise at the young Indian.

His head was shaved smooth.

Guru held up a finger, to indicate he wouldn't be long on the phone. Dr. Wallis lit a cigarette. Guru hadn't yet spoken a word, and Wallis would have thought he was on hold had he not been able to hear a barely audible voice on the other end of the line. When he finished his cigarette and butted it out in the ashtray he'd brought from home, and Guru had still not spoken a word, he went to the bathroom. He returned five minutes later to find Guru still listening to someone jabbering away. He was about to say something when Guru abruptly spoke a few words in Hindi, waited, spoke a few more, then hung up.

"What the hell was that all about, Guru?"

"I was speaking with my mother in India."

"She's quite the chatterbox."

"No, she hardly speaks at all."

"But you only got in a handful of words in a ten-minute conversation."

"It was a group Facebook call with my mother and four brothers. My siblings and I must speak in order, from eldest to youngest. Because I am the youngest, I always speak last. Anyway." He pointed to his bald dome. "What do you think, professor?"

"Looking good, Iceman."

Guru grinned. "Andre had a last-minute cancellation this morning, and so I visited his barber shop. He told me he could help me style my hair with mousse and other products, but it would take a lot of upkeep on my part, and my hair would only continue to thin in the future. His recommendation was to shave it all off. I was hesitant at first, but Andre is bald too, and he looks very good, which gave me greater confidence to take the plunge myself."

"I'm happy you're happy, Guru," Wallis said. "It'll certainly be easier to manage now. Maybe pick up some sunscreen the next time you're at the drugstore?"

"Good point, professor. I will get some when I go shopping for my new clothes. Yes, I am ready for a complete transformation." He sat down in the free chair and set his backpack on the floor. "May I say, professor, you are a very good dresser, you have very good taste. Would you be willing to dispense some fashion advice?"

Beguiled, Wallis studied Guru's outfit. He wore an orange tee-shirt emblazoned with an anime character from Dragon Ball Z, a pair of plaid shorts, and the same brilliant white sneakers he'd worn the day before. He looked like a poster boy for Old Navy. "My best advice?" Dr. Wallis said, wanting to tread as tactfully as possible. "The shaved head makes you appear older. Nothing wrong with that. But the graphic tees you wear are a rather youthful style. To compliment your more mature shaved head, I would recommend you dress up a bit more. Think less casual, more...urbane."

"Excellent observation, professor!" Guru said, nodding enthusiastically. "More urbane. So no more tee-shirts? Not even nice ones? I do not want to look *too* mature."

"I'm not saying wear a jacket and tie, Guru, but simply spruce things up. I'd stick with button-down shirts from now on, well-fitted, neutral colors."

"And my shorts?"

"I'd probably avoid shorts altogether, to be honest."

"Only pants. Yes, I can do that. Jeans?"

"Jeans are okay. They work for almost any age. But they shouldn't have any holes, and they should be a darker rather than lighter color."

"And my shoes?"

"Eh...you probably need to let go of all of your sneakers too."

Guru seemed distressed. "*All* of my sneakers...?"

"If you *really* need to wear sneakers, I'd go for a minimalist canvas variety. Personally, however, I'd stick with leather."

"Leather only?" Guru shook his head. "Jeez, professor. Maybe I am not ready for this new life quite yet. I feel like Tom Hanks in *Big*."

Wallis smiled. "It's heavy stuff, buddy. I feel for you. But remember, this is my advice only. You're perfectly free to continue wearing whatever you choose."

"No, professor, your advice has been very helpful."

Dr. Wallis sniffed. He glanced at Guru's backpack on the floor. "Did you bring McDonald's again?"

"I did indeed."

"Two days in a row. You might want to consider adding a healthier diet to this new lifestyle of yours too."

"I know McDonald's is not good for me. But it is the only food I can eat."

Wallis frowned. "What are you talking about?"

"My mother's cooking was the only food I ate growing up. I miss it tremendously. Since coming to America, McDonald's is the only food I have tried that I like."

"You've been here for two years!"

"Yes, I know. My diet is not enviable." He patted what Wallis had previously thought to be a beer belly but was clearly a McDonald's belly.

"You can't cook for yourself?"

"Yes, I cook at home. But when I am out, I eat McDonald's."

"There are so many great restaurants around, Guru. There's even an authentic Indian place not far from here that I'm sure—"

"On Solano Avenue? Yes, I have gone there. But the food tastes nothing like my mother's cooking—"

"Good grief!" Dr. Wallis blurted, shaking his head with incredulity. "Someday, Guru, you're going to be a very wealthy and successful man—but, brother, you're one strange duck!"

◆ ◆ ◆

Instead of returning home, Dr. Roy Wallis drove the eight miles to the neighboring city of Oakland, and then to a commercial street in Dogtown—coined so by police officers due to the unusual number of stray dogs in the area. He tooled slowly past Café Emporium where Brook worked, peering through the large street windows. He couldn't see her among the over-twenty-one crowd. He parked down the block, then returned to the dive bar. The place had a lot of personality, reminiscent of a wealthy eccentric's basement den, or perhaps an old hipster's antique shop. It was busy as usual, the bar staff pumping out Greyhounds, their marquee drink, to the thirsty throng. Wallis had tried a Greyhound once. The pour was heavy and the drink was strong, but all he could taste was the fresh grapefruit. Brook told him the bar used different grapefruit suppliers each order depending on who could provide the sweetest fruit at the time. He believed her.

Dr. Wallis squeezed in at the bar and ordered a pint of a bitter IPA. He still didn't see Brook, though there were two other bars on the premises she could be tending. He took his beer outside and chain smoked two cigarettes.

"What are you doing here?"

Wallis had been gazing across the dark, foggy bay to San Francisco's eloquent skyline on the far bank. He turned to find Brook standing behind him. Her knitted brow and crossed arms did not portend an easy reconciliation.

"Is this how you greet all your customers?" he said lightly.

"I'm serious, Roy. I don't know what you're doing here."

"I wanted to see you."

"Is a blonde bombshell going to pop out from behind a bush or tree?"

"That was rather awkward, I admit."

"Somewhat of an understatement, Roy." She glanced over her shoulder into the bar. "I have to get back to work."

"What time do you get off?"

"I'm just a simple girl, Roy. I liked you. I thought you liked me—"

"I do, Brook."

"Call me old-fashioned, but when a man and a woman like each other, and when they become intimate, they shouldn't be sleeping around with other people. Who was she anyway?" Brook shook her head. "No, I don't care. I don't want to know. I don't want to know how many women you're currently sleeping with—"

"Only her, Brook," Dr. Wallis interrupted sincerely. "We used to date, but we broke up two years ago. We just see each other casually now and then. That's it."

"That's it?" Brook repeated sardonically. "The fact you're having casual sex with your ex is actually a pretty big deal to me."

"I know, I understand," he said. "Bad choice of words. What I meant was, she's not important to me anymore. You are. I wouldn't be here if you weren't."

Something shifted in Brook's eyes. Hopeful calculation? "Are you going to see her anymore?"

"No," he said.

Brook's stiff body language relaxed. Her arms remained crossed, but she no longer seemed as though she wanted to throw the nearest drink on him. She chewed her bottom lip. "I don't know, Roy…"

"What time do you get off?"

"Not until last call tonight."

"Could you get someone to cover for you?"

"I don't know…probably…"

"Great! I'll just wait out here until you do."

"Jesus, Roy." She shook her head.

"What?" he said, grinning.

"Just—*Jesus*."

She returned inside.

◆ ◆ ◆

For the last year or so, Dr. Wallis had been coming to Café Emporium most Saturday or Sunday mornings to read the newspaper and sip a vanilla latte and occasionally nibble on a gluttonous pastry. Roughly two months ago, Brook had adopted the habit of serving his latte with a token chocolate cookie that he didn't order. He didn't give this much thought. He didn't give her much thought either. Until five weeks ago, when he glanced up from the sports section of the *Chronicle* and his eyes settled on her. She was dressed in her simple uniform of black tights and a black shirt, and she hadn't been doing anything more interesting than clearing a nearby table of dirty dishes. However, something triggered inside him. He stole several more glances in her direction before paying his bill. The next Saturday he engaged her in conversation whenever she approached his table, and before he left, he asked her to dinner. She seemed flummoxed and turned down his invitation. He persisted with a mix of stubbornness and friendly humor, and she relented. They met at a lively downtown restaurant, then watched a live show across the street at the Fox Theater. The evening couldn't have gone any better, and after a few nightcaps, Brook ended up spending the night at his place. Since then, they'd been seeing each other at least once or twice a week.

Dr. Wallis finished his beer and was thinking about going inside to order a second when Brook appeared.

"That was quick," he said.

"We're not that busy tonight," she said, though he found this hard to believe given the crowd inside. "Did you have anywhere in mind you'd like to go?"

"There's a good Spanish place over on Grace Avenue. I've been in the mood for tapas all day."

"Fine by me. But do you mind stopping by my place first so I can freshen up?"

"Sure," he said, surprised. He had never been to her place before.

It turned out Brook didn't live very far away—nor did she live in a landlocked house. She lived in a houseboat moored on the still waters of San Francisco Bay.

"Whoa!" Wallis said, taking in the squat, quaint structure on floats. "I didn't know you lived like Popeye!"

"Don't knock it, Roy. It's two-thirds the price of a single-bedroom apartment."

"I'm not knocking it. I love it."

The interior resembled that of a rustic mountain cabin: wood floors, wood walls, wood ceiling, wood cabinetry. A variety of wall hangings and throw rugs added splashes of color, while miscellaneous items—stacks of vinyl records, flowering plants, a battered guitar case leaning against a shiny black piano—lent the shoebox space a cozy, creative air.

"It's not much," Brook said, a bit self-consciously. "But it's comfortable."

"It's fantastic," Wallis said. "I feel like I'm suddenly on vacation."

"There's beer in the fridge. Help yourself. I'll have a quick shower."

"Why not just jump in the bay?"

"Funny, mister. Won't be long."

"Aye, aye, captain."

Rolling her eyes, Brook disappeared into the houseboat's only other room, closing the door behind her.

Dr. Wallis retrieved a Belgium beer from the compact fridge, twisted off the cap, and took a long sip. He was craving a cigarette but decided it wouldn't be prudent to smoke inside a house constructed entirely of hickory and oak.

Instead he studied the wall over the kitchen table. It was studded with photographs, most in simple frames, a few pinned to the wood with thumbtacks. Some were portrait shots of a man and woman Wallis suspected were Brook's parents. Others were of Brook herself: as a big-eyed, pony-tailed child; as a pretty, awkward teen; wearing a mortar-board at her college graduation; partying with girlfriends indoors, outdoors, on a lake somewhere. And in five photos she was with the same man. He was Brook's age, handsome, and fit.

Dr. Wallis frowned. He didn't often experience jealousy, but right then a greasy fire warmed his belly.

The water clunked off and stopped running through the old pipes. A minute later Brook emerged from the adjacent room wrapped in a white towel. "Not much closet space in the bedroom," she said. "The dress I want is in here." She opened a door he hadn't noticed and removed a blue dress from a rack jam-packed with hanging garments.

"Who's this?" Wallis asked, pointing at the man in the pictures.

Brook joined him in the kitchen. "Oh him," she said cavalierly. "Just an ex I sleep with every now and then."

Wallis stared at her.

She laughed. "You should see your face!"

"Who is he?" he demanded.

"My brother, Roy! *Sheesh*."

Wallis' cheeks burned with embarrassment. "I didn't notice the resemblance." He finished his beer and set the bottle on the counter. "Now that you've mentioned your ex...I don't think you've ever told me anything about him?"

"You never asked." Brook shrugged her bare, slender shoulders. "He was a wild animal keeper at the San Francisco Zoo. He was headhunted for a senior position at the San Diego Zoo." She shrugged again. "He accepted the job, I didn't want to uproot and move, so we broke up. But is he really who you want to talk about right now?"

"No," Wallis said, sliding his arms around Brook's svelte waist and kissing her on her soft lips. He became immediately aroused. He slid his hands down over her buttocks, down her firm thighs, then up them again, beneath the towel. Her breasts pressed against his chest.

"I should get dressed," she mumbled.

"No," he said.

"The neighbors can see us through the windows."

He spotted a light switch within an arm's reach and

flipped the nub, plunging them into shadows. He tugged Brook's towel loose and let it drop to the floor. Naked, she unbuckled his belt and undid the button and zipper of his slacks.

Kissing tenderly yet passionately, they shuffled through the moon-dappled boathouse to the cluttered bedroom, their bodies entwined in a slow, exotic dance.

They didn't make it to dinner.

Brook lay awake in bed that night, propped up on one elbow, watching Roy Wallis sleep. The windows and curtains were open, allowing a fresh breeze into the bedroom, as well as slices of silvered moonlight that cast Roy's strong features in a ghostly chiaroscuro effect. His bare chest rose and fell with each slow breath.

Such a handsome man, she thought, her eyes studying his straight eyebrows and thick-lashed eyes, his defined nose and chiseled cheekbones, his long and full beard. In her mind she pictured him on the cover of one of those trendy men's magazines wearing a checkered plaid shirt and suspenders with an axe resting on a shoulder.

The rugged, woodsy intellectual.

So different than her last boyfriend. Not that George Goldmark wasn't smart; he was. He was simply bland, both in appearance and personality. Standing at five-foot-ten, he was neither tall nor short. His chestnut hair, graying at the temples, was always parted on the left and brushed to the right and held in place with maximum-hold hairspray. Gray eyeglasses framing often unreadable black eyes, cleanly shaven jaw, dimpled chin. Friendly yet reserved, content to be a wallflower at a party rather than a mingler. Soft-spoken, polite, complimentary—boring.

Despite this mediocracy, Brook had cared deeply for George. He was affectionate and accommodating to her needs. He didn't take drugs or smoke cigarettes. He only drank on occasion and didn't become drunk. He was never physically or verbally abusive. He was, she supposed you could say, safe.

They had met in a Costco food court of all places. She had finished her grocery shopping and had decided to spoil herself with a berry sundae. It was a Sunday afternoon, the place was busy, and George, carrying a tray loaded with a turkey provolone sandwich, French fries, and a large soft drink, asked if he could share her table. The last thing she wanted to do was eat with a stranger, but she nodded politely. Her plan was to finish her sundae promptly and get up and go, but George didn't start chatting her up as she'd expected. Instead, he produced a crossword booklet from his pocket, opened it to a half-completed puzzle, and began working away. She relaxed a bit and took out her phone, so she was doing something too.

"A small tropical fish that is a common pet and can live in brackish water?"

"Excuse me?" she said, looking up

He repeated the crossword clue.

"A goldfish?" she suggested.

"Only five letters, third letter an L."

She was about to tell him she didn't know when she said, "Molly?"

"Ah! Thank you." He scribbled down the answer. "As a vet, you'd think I would have gotten that one."

"To be fair, most people simply flush their sick fish down the toilet rather than take them to a vet."

"They do, don't they? But I don't run a practice. I work at the zoo."

"The Oakland Zoo?" she asked.

"The San Francisco Zoo."

"I haven't been there since I was a child."

"It's a great place to spend a day with the kids. They might even learn a thing or two about the environment and conservation."

"I don't have children," she said.

"No?" he said, his eyes going to her denuded ring finger. "I'm sorry. I didn't notice…"

"Why be sorry?" She took a final spoonful of her sundae and stood. "Good luck with that," she said, indicating the crossword puzzle.

"Uh…I'm George." He stood also and stuck out his hand. She shook but didn't offer her name. "Say," he added, "I've never done anything like this before…but if you'd ever like a tour of the zoo, I'd be happy to show you around. It really is a great place to spend a day. Here, take this." He slid a business card from his wallet and passed it to her. She accepted it and cast the small print an obligatory glance.

"Thank you," she said.

She had never intended to take George Goldmark up on his offer. But the next week on one of her days off she came across his business card in a kitchen drawer where she threw all that sort of stuff, and after replaying her conversation with him in her head, she decided it couldn't hurt to call him.

He sounded delighted to hear from her and they made plans to meet at the main gates of the San Francisco Zoo at ten o'clock that morning.

The date was a pleasant change from the typical drink at a bar—there were lions and elephants and giraffes around every corner, after all—and Brook had enjoyed herself enough to accept George's invitation to dinner later in the week.

Fast forward three years and she had all but moved into his apartment building on Grand Avenue. She'd gotten to know most of his friends. She'd met his parents on several occasions. They'd adopted a cat from the animal shelter they'd named Leo. And they'd even begun talking about marriage and having children.

The relationship wasn't glamorous in any sense of the

word. It was comfortable and predictable and, yes, *safe*, and there was nothing wrong with that.

Until Brook discovered George Goldmark was a two-faced slime-ball.

A coworker at Café Emporium, Jenny Stillwater, was a divorcee constantly singing the praises of the matchmaking app Tinder. One morning when she and Brook were on the same shift she said, "I've really got to show you something, hon. Maybe I'm wrong. I *hope* I'm wrong."

She wasn't wrong.

The man in the Tinder profile Jenny showed her was calling himself George Cohen, but the photograph was definitely that of George Goldmark. According to his bio, he was single, financially secure, and looking for a serious relationship blah blah blah.

Needless to say, Brook had been devastated, but she didn't spend long feeling sorry for herself. She took off the rest of her shift, went home, and tossed all of George's stuff from the boathouse into the marina's dumpster. She refused to answer his calls, and by the time he stopped by, she'd already gotten the locks changed. He banged on the door, confused and indignant. She ignored him until he went away. He sent her a few messages over the next week, insinuating he knew why she was mad at him without admitting the reason, and insisting they could work it out. She deleted each message without replying, and eventually he stopped sending them.

That had been last autumn. Brook had gone on a date with a fitness instructor in December, and another date with a construction worker in January, but neither man had been right for her.

Then Roy Wallis came along.

To be precise, he didn't come from anywhere; he had been right under her nose in the café every weekend morning. Always smartly dressed and groomed, he was impossible not to notice. Brook often greeted him with a smile, but she never attempted to make conversation. There was something aloof about him that intimidated her, that made her tiptoe around his table when he was reading his newspaper in order not to disturb him, something that reminded her she was his waitress, his servant, and nothing more.

Which was why she had been so utterly stunned when he asked her to dinner.

Brook had mixed feelings about what happened the other day at his apartment. They'd had dinner plans, granted, but she'd never confirmed them, and by showing up at his door unannounced, she'd been intruding on his privacy. On the other hand, had she not done this, she would never have learned about the blonde woman. Roy would still be seeing her behind Brook's back, and although they'd never agreed to date each other exclusively, this was unacceptable to her.

Brook didn't play games, and she wasn't going to let herself get hurt again.

So what are you doing in bed next to him?

He'd apologized. He'd said he'd ended it with the blonde.

And you believed him?

Yes.

Roy's eyes opened, startling her.

"Not morning, is it?" he asked sleepily.

She glanced past him to the digital alarm clock on the bedside table. "Only two."

"Good," he said, slipping his arm around her back, pulling her close to him. She rested her cheek on his chest and soon his breathing assumed the deep and regular rhythm of sleep.

She closed her eyes and tried to sleep too.

DAYS 3-5

Logbook communications by Dr. Roy Wallis, Guru Chandra Rampal, and Penny Park (Exhibit A in People of the State of California v. Dr. Roy Wallis)

S ubject 1 engaged me in conversation for nearly three hours. She's teaching me Australian slang and seems to enjoy reminiscing about her country. Subject 2 did not participate in the discussions. He divides his time watching TV, lifting weights, and cooking meals. For lunch he used cookbook recipes to prepare charred leeks with anchovy dressing, turnip tartiflette, confit of salmon with drizzled dill sauce, and sticky toffee parsnip pudding for dessert (made me hungry!). While eating, the test subjects discussed their plans when the experiment concluded. Subject 2 expressed interest in moving to Hollywood, where he hoped to land some gigs as a movie extra, or even small roles with speaking lines. Subject 1 encouraged him in this endeavor, though she said nothing of accompanying him.

-Penny, Wednesday, May 30

Blood pressure, heart rate, forearm vascular resistance, and muscle sympathetic nerve activity were measured this afternoon at rest and during four stressors (sustained handgrip, maximal forearm ischemia, mental stress, and cold pressor test). Results revealed an increase in the test subjects' blood pressure and a decrease in their muscle sympathetic nerve activity. Heart rate, forearm vascular resistance, and plasma catecholamines were not significantly altered. These data suggest that while sleep deprivation increases blood pressure, it does not increase heart rate or muscle sympathetic nerve activity and thus, contrary to much literature on the subject, sleep debt likely does not potentiate an increase in cardiovascular failure.

-R.W., Wednesday, May 30

For the first two days of the experiment, the test subjects were eating or snacking in three-to-four-hour intervals. Today, for the first time, they went six hours between meals, suggesting a decrease in appetite. Also for the first time, the test subjects demonstrated signs of ataxia (subtle abnormalities in their gait, speech, and eye movement). During a series of exercises assessing their mental acumen, they displayed frustration and irritation at their results, particularly Subject 2, who ended his participation prematurely. Subject 1 remained cooperative. Declines in her abstract thinking, reasoning, and working memory were observed.

-Guru Chandra Rampal, May 30

Subjects 1 and 2 butted heads in their first argument today. Subject 1 was reading on her bed while Subject 2 was lifting weights. Subject 1 glanced at Subject 2 in apparent annoyance several times at the noise the gym equipment made when metal struck metal. Eventually she asked him to take a break. He switched to using free weights. This, however, was a short-term solution, as Subject 1 soon became equally annoyed by Subject 2's heavy breathing and grunts. This time they raised their voices at each other and traded insults. In the aftermath Subject 2 continued lifting weights. Subject 1 slammed her book shut, got off her bed, and paced the perimeter of the room. By my count, she completed sixty-one circuits before settling down to read her book again! At this point, Subject 2 had commenced watching a movie wearing headphones.

-Penny, Thursday, May 31

Subject 1 displays normal orientation, but decreased self-care and reaction time. Her mood appears depressive and her posture dysmorphic. Subject 2 also displays decreased self-care and reaction time. His answers to questions have become circumstantial and tangential. He exhibits a lack of interest and insight, and he has begun speaking with apathetic affect. Subjects have become confrontational with one another without reconciliation, guilt, or shame. Episodes of grandiosity, fragmented thinking, and memory impairment have been noted, the latter suggesting that sleep deprivation leads to a loss of connectivity between neurons in the hippocampus.

-R.W., Thursday, May 31

The test subjects went seven hours between meals today. Decreases in attention and concentration, as well as severe memory impairment, were observed. Subject 1, for instance, could not remember anything of our conversations from the day before, complaining of feeling as though she had "early Alzheimer's disease." Subject 2's lapses in memory are more severe. Notably, he could no longer perform simple math. During one exercise, in which he was tasked with counting down from one hundred by subtracting seven, he only reached seventy-two, four subtractions, before stopping and becoming upset. When I asked him why he stopped, he said he forgot what he was doing. Both subjects appear to be struggling with muscle coordination and keeping their eyes focused.

-Guru Chandra Rampal, May 31

Wow, were they moody today! They barely wanted to talk to me, and when they did, they were slack-faced, irritable, and forgetful, barely able to finish their sentences. Subject 1 continues to read regularly, though now only in small bursts, sometimes for no longer than ten minutes at a time. When not reading, she becomes agitated. On one occasion she paced the room for fourteen minutes without ever looking up from the floor. Later, she sat on the edge of her bed for fifty minutes, unmoving except for her right foot, which she tapped rapidly. Subject 2 spent the majority of the afternoon watching movies. Aside from briefly talking to me, the only other activity he performed was a solo (and lethargic) game of basketball. This is the second consecutive day he has not lifted weights. Both test subjects complained to me of feeling nauseous and have very little appetite. All they seem to be eating is citrus fruit such as tangerines and oranges.

-Penny, Friday, June 1

Electroencephalography tests were conducted on the subjects' pre-frontal cortices, as this region of the brain has a greater restorative need than others and is thus more responsive to sleep deprivation. Both subjects are right-handed and have not consumed nicotine, alcohol, or xanthine-containing beverages (coffee, tea, soft drinks) during the past week. The electrodes were positioned according to the International 10/20 System, and all electrode impedances were kept below five kilowatts. EEG data was collected from twenty monopolar derivations for five minutes with the subjects' eyes closed, in order to observe the cortex electrical activity without any external stimuli. Visual inspection was employed for the detection and elimination of possible visual artifacts, and two minutes of artifact-free data was successfully extracted from the EEG's total record. Results indicate that prolonged total sleep deprivation causes a significant power decrease in the frontal, temporal, and occipital areas of the alpha and beta frequency bands. However, temporal delta and temporal-occipital theta T6, O2, and OZ exhibited power *increases*. Traditionally, increased theta activity correlates with an increased cognitive workload and tiredness. Why it has become more pronounced during the subjects' period of continuous wakefulness, when task demands have been relatively minor, is unresolved.

-R.W., Friday, June 1

DAY 6

Saturday, June 2, 2018

S haron Nash was really starting to feel like a guinea pig. The first few days of the experiment had been a real slog with a lot of time on her hands and little to do to fill it. She spent countless hours lying down on her bed with her eyes closed, daydreaming. Sometimes she tried falling asleep, but this proved impossible. Her mind simply wouldn't shut off, and when she opened her eyes, she was always instantly alert.

Once Sharon got her head around the fact she didn't need or want sleep, and wasn't going to get it for the next however-many days, she devoted herself to reading. Growing up, she had been a bookish girl. She recalled passing a lot of summers at her family's holiday house on the Avon River outside Toodyay reading Roald Dahl, R.L. Stine, the complete *Nancy Drew* series, and even a few *Hardy Boys* books to boot if there was nothing else interesting on the bookshelf. She continued reading voraciously throughout high school —mostly Danielle Steele and J.D. Robb and other women's fiction—but this all changed during her first year at Curtin University. Her courses required so much assigned reading that little time remained to fit in recreational stuff. Add partying and dating to the mix, and she probably averaged about one paperback novel a year during her three-year sociology degree. And if she thought she might've gotten back on track while backpacking through Europe, she was dead wrong, as most of her spare time was spent meeting other backpackers, visiting famous landmarks, playing drinking games, and bar hopping. The only real downtime she had was during hungover mornings, but the last thing she felt like doing while hungover was reading.

Sharon had not wanted to participate in the Sleep Experiment. She had been perfectly content working at the Italian eatery. Although she was only being paid about a third of what she would have made an hour in Australia, the tips more than compensated for this shortfall.

Chad, however, needed cash, and he pressured her into going to the interview with him.

Admittedly, after hearing what Dr. Wallis had to say about the experiment, Sharon's reservations largely vanished. It had been approved by UC Berkeley's Committee for the Protection of Human Subjects, and according to the doc, there were no long-term repercussions to sleep deprivation. Moreover, the pay was admittedly freaking awesome, and if she budgeted wisely, the money would last her until she flew back to Australia in September.

This last thought both excited and saddened her. She'd been away from home for about a year now, and she missed her parents heaps. She was, she had to admit, a little homesick. She wouldn't even mind seeing her brat of a brother again, who was currently in his second year at Curtin.

At the same time, however, Sharon had had a total blast on her trip so far. She'd made some great friends she'd keep in touch with on social media, she'd had some wild experiences she'd likely never forget, and she knew in her heart the day she boarded the flight to Perth would be a sad one indeed.

She'd told Chad she had a boyfriend waiting for her back home, which wasn't true. But he'd been so damn hot to get in her pants those first few days they'd met in the park in

Pamplona, she'd needed to say something to get him to cool off. It wasn't that he wasn't cute or nice. He was both. He was just too much surfy testosterone dude and not enough mellow thoughtful dude, which appealed more to the book nerd inside her. Anyway, the lie worked…for a while at least. Because when she tired of Portugal and decided to check out France, and he insisted on joining her, he got all hot again… and she gave in, and they'd been making out ever since.

Well, at least until the Sleep Experiment had commenced. She understood why Dr. Wallis hadn't wanted his test subjects to be romantically involved, given how relationships can really fuck with people's heads sometimes.

Sharon didn't have to worry about this, though, because she no longer had any feelings for Chad whatsoever. Whatever attraction she'd developed for him over the last year had evaporated during their time stuck together in the sleep laboratory. In fact, he was beginning to drive her nuts. Just about everything about him now pissed her off. Like how he grunted like an ape during his workouts. Or mumbled to himself like a homeless person while he paced the room incessantly. Or bragged about his cooking, when all he did was follow a recipe in a book. The last time he fished for a compliment ("How good are the enchiladas, Shaz? Made 'em from scratch, hey!"), she wanted to throw her enchilada in his face. And she wasn't even going to get into all the TV he watched. Seriously, what a fucking couch potato! Hadn't he ever picked up a book in his life? She'd yet to see him do so.

Nevertheless, Sharon knew that as much as she was becoming fed up with Chad, her real gripe was with the Sleep Experiment itself. Because with each day that passed (or *perceived* day that passed, given there were no damn clocks or calendars anywhere), she was finding it harder and harder to cope with the mind-numbing boredom; the around-the-clock observation and the lack of privacy this entailed; and the relentless questions and tests, both physical and mental, that Dr. Wallis and his cronies put her through. Like, what was with that fucking EEG machine? Seriously, with all the electrodes stuck to her head she'd felt like a patient in an insane asylum.

Yes, she really was beginning to feel like a guinea pig.

Doesn't matter, Shaz, she told herself. *Can't be much longer until you're done with this shit. Another week maybe. Then you're home-free. You can ditch Chad and go visit Canada. Whistler-Blackcomb, mountain air, raw nature. Then home. Blue skies, the beach, Mom's lasagna and Dad's steaks on the barbie. Just a little bit longer—*

Someone was talking to her. Not Dr. Wallis or the Indian. The Asian. What was her name again? Jesus, how could she not remember her name?

The Asian—*Penny, that was it!*—kept talking in her stupid accent, pretending to be her friend in order to pick her brain...

Shut up and leave me alone! Sharon thought, refusing to look up from the book clenched tightly in her hands. *Shut up! Shut up! Shut up!*

❖ ❖ ❖

"Morning, Penny," Dr. Roy Wallis said, setting the pulp-paper tray holding the vanilla latte and green tea on the table.

Penny, today dressed completely in white, took the green tea and said, "Thank you again, professor. You are very kind to bring me a drink each day. You're definitely the most chivalrous professor I know."

"No problem, Penny," he said. "And I should compliment you on the fantastic job you've been doing this last week. I know it can't be fun waking up at whatever time you do to get here so early."

"Five o'clock, because I *always* shower in the morning."

Although this was an innocuous remark, the curl of Penny's lips and her inexplicable emphasis on "always" made it sound prurient, as though she'd wanted him to conjure a naked image of her in his mind.

Which, for a brief moment, he did.

Focusing his attention on twisting his coffee cup free from the tray, Dr. Wallis said. "I've been reading your notes, of course. They're well done."

"Thank you, professor," she said. "I've been doing my best —"

Something crashed into the viewing window.

Penny yelped. Wallis flinched, raising a forearm before his face in an instinctual gesture of defense. The reinforced glass remained undamaged. Beyond, in the middle of the sleep laboratory, Sharon was shaking a finger at Chad, her face flushed with emotion.

Dr. Wallis reached an arm across Penny—brushing the front of her chest—and jabbed the touch panel controller's Listen button.

"—disgusting!" Sharon was saying. "We have to share it for the next however long, so show a little consideration!"

"Take a chill pill, Shaz," Chad said. "It's just a little piss."

"Can't you lift the goddamn seat?"

"I never lifted the seat in the house."

"And I put up with sitting down on your piss in the middle on the night! Just because I didn't say anything then doesn't mean it was okay."

"Just wipe the seat down if it bothers you so much."

"How hard is it to aim your dick? Or is it too small to aim?"

Chad stepped toward her threateningly. "I swear, Shaz…"

While this exchange had been playing out, Dr. Wallis and Penny had swapped seats. Now Wallis pressed the Talk button and said, "Why don't you two give each other a little space?"

The Australians looked at the two-way mirror. Both were stormy-eyed and grimacing. Throwing up his hands, Chad skulked off to the lounge. He turned on the TV and clapped a set of headphones over his ears.

Sharon approached the mirror. "He's gross, doc! I mean, come on! Can you talk to him or something?"

Wallis pressed the Talk button again. "I think you made your position on the matter quite clear, Sharon," he said. "Let's first see how he responds going forward?"

"I swear," she said, fists clenching and unclenching at her sides, "if he doesn't start lifting the seat, or at least improving his aim, *I'm* going to start peeing all over the seat too!" She spun on her heels and went to her bed and picked up her book. She settled into her usual spot leaning against the headboard, facing the viewing window. After a moment she stood and pushed the bed in a counterclockwise direction. She maneuvered the headboard to about seven o'clock, then pulled the footboard until she'd turned the bed one hundred eighty degrees. She settled back into her spot leaning against the headboard—only now facing the rear of the sleep laboratory so Dr. Wallis and Penny could no longer see her face.

"Yikes..." Penny said. "She doesn't seem too happy, does she? What did she throw at us?"

"I'm not sure," Wallis said. "But it wasn't at us. It was at Chad. She missed him. Did they argue about anything else during your shift?"

"No, they didn't say anything. No, wait. Shaz spoke to me. She asked me how long they had been in the room for. Don't worry, professor, I didn't tell her."

"Was she upset?"

"More like—indifferent. It was a very brief exchange."

"Still, I wonder whether this withholding of information contributed to her outburst? She has been severely limited in what she can do each day. Limiting what she can know too is no doubt a very frustrating situation."

"Should we tell her she has only been in there for a week?"

"Absolutely not. I am simply musing out loud, Penny."

Penny nodded, then said, "She's slurring her words. Did you hear when she was talking? It wasn't super noticeable, but…is that to be expected, professor?"

"It's one of the symptoms of cerebellar ataxia, which is also responsible for the deterioration in her coordination and balance that we've been witnessing, as well as the abnormalities in her eye movement."

Penny seemed contemplative. "That teenager you mentioned in the final class of the semester," she said, "the one who stayed awake for eleven days—"

"Randy Gardner," Wallis said.

"Yeah, him—you said he showed no side effects from lack of sleep. But Shaz and Chad, they're falling all over the place, not eating, their eyes are going crazy, now they're slurring their speech—"

"I know what you're getting at, Penny," Wallis said, "and you have a right to be concerned, so let me clarify. I never said Randy Gardner showed no side effects from sleep deprivation. I merely praised his motor skills and clarity of thinking at the conclusion of his experiment. Verbal sleight of hand, I admit. But Randy Gardner most certainly experienced side effects associated with tiredness. Yet it is important to remember that all his symptoms disappeared after a good night's rest, and he suffered no long-term physical or psychological repercussions."

"Was he also a grumpybum like these two? Fighting and yelling with everybody?"

"Admittedly, no," Wallis said. "But unlike Chad and Sharon, Randy Gardner was not confined to a single room. He was permitted to venture wherever he chose. He went bowling and dined in restaurants. He interacted with other people. This would have considerably improved his state of mind." He glanced at his wristwatch. "Anyway, Penny, it's already ten past two. If you think you're getting paid overtime for hanging around past the end of your shift, think again."

"Okay, professor," she said, standing, "I know when I'm not wanted. I'll see you tomorrow!"

After Penny Park left, Dr. Wallis found himself thinking

about her. Earlier, when his arm had accidentally brushed her chest, she didn't make any effort to move back. In fact, he was quite sure she had leaned *into* his arm before he suggested they exchange seats. So what was her endgame? he wondered. Was she simply flirting with him for the sake of flirting, or did she have the more audacious goal of sleeping with him?

Smiling thinly to himself—he couldn't deny it was a good feeling to know he was still attractive to twenty-something year olds—Wallis lit a cigarette and turned to his task of observing the Australians. Over the course of the next two hours little of interest occurred. Chad binge-watched an episodic series on Netflix, while Sharon read her book, paced the room, and showered. At one point Wallis put his feet up on the desk to get comfortable. Soon his eyelids grew heavy and he had to fight to keep them open—

He snapped awake, surprised he had allowed himself to nod off. He checked his watch and discovered it was already seven o'clock in the evening. Sharon, he observed, was now watching a movie, while Chad—Chad was nowhere in the sleep laboratory.

Alarmed, Wallis sat straight.

Did he slip out while I was asleep?

Goddammit!

He smacked the Talk button. "Chad? Where are you? Sharon, where did Chad go?"

"What, mate?" an irritated voice replied. A moment later Chad's head rose above the far side of the island in the kitchen.

Dr. Wallis relaxed. "What are you doing?" he asked.

"Lying down," Chad grunted.

"On the floor?"

"What's it to you?"

His head disappeared below the island.

Wallis made a note of the incident on the laptop, monitored Chad's heartrate for the next fifteen minutes to make sure he was not somehow sleeping, then he stood and stretched, cracking his back in the process. He went to the bathroom, but afterward, instead of returning to the observation room, he decided to visit his former office for old times' sake.

When he reached the fourth floor of the old cement building, he went left, passing empty office spaces that had served the faculty and graduate students, to his corner office at the end of the corridor. Stepping inside the twilit space, nostalgia bloomed in his gut. There was nothing to look at now, but he was seeing the office in his mind's eye as it had once been. Remembering some of the students he had counseled here, the faculty with whom he had debated and socialized. The nights he had worked late, composing lectures, grading essays and exams, writing papers. This little room had been his life—and now it was a soulless husk waiting to be demolished.

Dr. Wallis went to the north-facing window and drew a finger along the ledge, leaving a line in the dust. He looked out onto rain-soaked Hearst Avenue. The traffic lights glistened wetly. Puddles reflected the sinking sun in their pockmarked surfaces.

"Why do we get old?" he mused out loud. "Why does everything have to change? Why can't we just *be*?"

Somebody was down on the sidewalk.

Wallis leaned forward until his head touched the windowpane, but the person had angled toward Tolman Hall and out of his line of sight.

He backtracked down the corridor and descended the stairs to the main floor. He looked through the glass doors that opened to the breezeway. The person wasn't out there.

And what would it matter if he or she was? he thought.

Although the campus might feel like a ghost town, it wasn't off limits by any means. Anyone was free to come and go as they pleased.

Dr. Wallis returned to the building's basement, and his

ongoing experiment.

Penny and her friend Jimmy Su sat in the inky shadows at the base of a large pine tree, the inverted cone of boughs shielding them from the light rain.

"Another one!" Penny said, using a twig to poke a beetle doing its best to move through the wet grass. "This tree must be infested with them."

"It's a pine tree," Jimmy said, "and the beetles are pine bark beetles, so your deduction is spot on, Sherlock."

Jimmy was of Taiwanese descent, but he had lived in California since he was a kid, and he was about as Californian as you could get, with the gym body, the blond streak through his otherwise black hair, and the nose and tongue and helix piercings.

He and Penny had been friends since orientation week, and given he'd never once hit on her, she suspected he was gay, though he never admitted to this and she never asked. Because whether he was or not didn't matter to her. She simply liked having a guy friend she could hang out with every now and then.

Ever since he'd started his part-time summer job as an assistant to an arborist, however, he'd been acting a little weird. He would stop before random trees, for instance, place his hands against their trunks and close his eyes, like he was speaking telepathically to them. He would also bombard her with all sorts of stupid tree facts. Not five minutes ago he told her the pine sheltering them from the rain was one of more than a hundred different species in the genus *Pinus*, which were divvied up based upon their types of leaves, cones, and seeds, and—hold onto your hats, people! —they had once been the favorite snack of duckbilled dinosaurs.

Needless to say, she was looking forward to getting the

old Jimmy back at the end of the summer.

Poking the beetle with the twig again, Penny said, "How do you know this thing's a pine bark beetle? It looks like any other beetle to me."

"It's a pine bark beetle," Jimmy assured her.

She squashed it beneath her heel.

"Hey! What the hell did you do that for?"

"I hate beetles. Besides, they're killing this tree."

"We don't know that for certain. Most pine beetles live in dead or dying hosts, which means there's a good chance the tree is already rotting."

Penny looked up at the towering pine. "Looks pretty healthy to me."

"You can't tell if it's sick just by looking at it. Bet if we peeled off a bit of its bark, the cambium layer would be brown and dry—"

"Holy God," she said, slapping her forehead. "Is this what my life has become?"

Jimmy frowned. "What's wrong with being knowledgeable about trees? You do realize that without them animal life would cease to exist?"

"Yeah, yeah," she said. "And I also realize it's time I get some more friends."

"Great! I wish you had more friends too. Then maybe it would be someone else other than me sitting out here cold and wet. What *are* we doing anyway?"

"I told you. Waiting for Dr. Wallis."

"Yeah, you want to jump his bones. But do you really think stalking him like this is the best way to go about it?"

"I'm not stalking him!" she said indignantly.

"You're sitting under a tree at night, drunk, waiting for him to stroll past unaware. That sounds like stalking to me. Why can't you just go into Tolman Hall and meet him? You two work together, after all."

"Because Guru's going to be arriving any minute to do the handover."

"So?"

"So, I don't want him around when I make another—"

She cut herself off. She had been about to say *make another move*, but she hadn't told Jimmy Dr. Wallis had already rejected her this morning. She was too embarrassed. The rebuff had stung, and it had continued stinging all day.

Even so, the more she'd thought about what had occurred, the more she became certain the only reason Dr. Wallis turned her down was because he was her professor. He was trying to keep to some moral high ground. But of course he secretly wanted her. He was forty-one. She was hot and young. No way he would say no again if she ditched the talking and simply presented herself to him, ready and willing.

Which was why she'd invited Jimmy up to her apartment earlier (he lived on the second floor in the same building) for a few drinks. The plan was to make it look as though she had been out partying all evening with a bunch of friends and had decided spur-of-the-moment to stop by Tolman Hall on her way home to say hi.

Penny took another swill of the vodka and orange juice from Jimmy's little silver flask, and she almost barfed it back up.

"Whoa!" Jimmy said. "You okay?"

Her eyes watering, she nodded.

"Take a deep breath..."

She swallowed the acid biting her throat and took a deep breath. "Whew..." she said, taking another breath.

"Maybe this isn't such a good idea right now," he said. "We've had a lot to drink. Maybe come back tomorrow—"

"*Shhhh!*" Penny said, spotting Guru crossing the breezeway toward the old building's front entrance. "There's baldy! Won't be much longer now."

Dr. Wallis checked his wristwatch when Guru entered the

observation room: 9:45 p.m. Guru's head was as bald as ever, and he was dressed smartly in one of his new outfits, which consisted of a pink button-down shirt, navy jeans, and a pair of burgundy leather loafers sans socks.

"I'm digging your style, my man!" Wallis told him. "You look just like me on my day off."

"You flatter me, professor," Guru replied sincerely. "I owe all of my good fortune to you."

"Good fortune? Have you found a suitable wife already?"

"No, not yet, though I am sure it will not be long now." He held up his backpack. "Can you smell it?"

Dr. Wallis sniffed. "I smell something, but it's not McDonald's."

"Not today! Look at this!" He set his backpack on the table and produced a paper bag with the Chipotle logo on it. "I present to you—Chipotle!" He pronounced the restaurant chain's name *Chee-pol-til*.

"It's called *Chee-poht-lay*, Guru."

"You've heard of it?"

Wallis raised his eyebrows. "*Are you mad?* It's one of the most popular fast-food joints in the country. You haven't heard of Chipotle before today?"

"No, never. I have never paid close attention to restaurants. But when I went for a walk this morning, and I saw Chee-poht-lay, I thought to myself, *Professor Wallis is right. I need to improve my diet.* So I went inside and ordered a burrito bowl, and much to my astonishment and delight, I was allowed to select all of my own ingredients!"

"That's how they work, Guru. Sort of like a Mexican Subway."

"Subway? What is Subway? Ah! I got you there, professor! Of course I know Subway. But a big American sandwich never sounded appealing to me."

"But a big American burger did?"

"No, I only ordered the chicken nuggets from McDonald's."

"*Every* day?"

"Yes, every day. But now I have discovered Chee-poht-lay, and I will never return to McDonald's again."

"All right, I gotta get out of here, Guru, you're blowing my mind." Wallis stood and collected his messenger bag. "Chad and Sharon have been quiet for most of the day. They had an argument earlier. You can read about it in my notes. Looks like they've put their differences behind them. But if anything happens, you have my number."

"Do not worry about me, professor. I can hold down the fort."

It had stopped raining, and the night was cool and wet, smelling of earth and rain. Dr. Wallis started east along Bayard Rustin Way when he heard heels clapping the pavement behind him.

"Professor!"

He turned to find Penny Park hurrying after him, sporting red pumps and a three-quarter-length jacket.

"Penny?" he said, surprised. "What are you doing here? You don't start until the morning."

"Of course I know that, professor," she said, coming to stand next to him. "I came here to see you!"

Dr. Wallis couldn't smell alcohol on her breath, but he could see it in her eyes, and hear it in the slippery way she was speaking.

"You look dressed to go out," he commented.

"I *have* been out. With my friend, Jimmy, and some others. But I got bored."

"So you came to see me?"

"Yes." She batted her fake eyelashes and took his arm. "Was that bad?"

Wallis looked past her but saw nobody else nearby. He looked back at Penny. She was smiling expectantly at him.

"Penny, I can't go anywhere with you."

She sulked. "Why not?"

"I'm your professor."

"So? Professors are allowed to go out with their students. I'm twenty-one."

"It's not appropriate."

"Who's going to care!" she said. "Nobody's even going to see us! Nobody's around Berkeley right now."

Dr. Wallis actually found himself considering her words. Then: *No—no way!*

Penny, perhaps sensing his hesitation, pressed: "Come on, professor. We'll go somewhere small and quiet."

"Sorry, Penny," he said. "Not tonight."

"It will be *fuuuunnnnnn*," she said softly, rocking forward on her toes to lean against him.

"No, Penny," he said decisively. "I'm going to call you an Uber."

"Awwww..." She hiccupped.

"How much have you had to drink?" he asked.

"Not much," she said. "And you can't call me an Uber."

He frowned. "Why not?"

"I don't trust them. You know how many girls go missing in them."

"They're just as safe as taxis."

"I don't trust taxis either."

"Then how did you get here?" He didn't think the bus, dressed how she was.

"Jimmy dropped me off."

Wallis' frown deepened. "How did you expect to get home then?"

She hiccupped again. "C'mon, professor. Let's go have fun!"

"I'll drive you home."

"But I want to go out!"

"Penny, you either let me drive you home, or you hang out here with Guru all night. Your choice."

"Oh, God! Fine! Where's your car?"

Wallis led her to where he had parked on nearby Crescent Lawn.

"An Audi!" Penny said. "What are you, rich or something, professor?"

"I don't have kids to spend all my money." He immediately regretted the remark.

Penny seized on the opening and said, "So you're not married, right?"

"No," he said simply.

"Girlfriend?"

"In the car, Penny."

He pressed Unlock on the remote key, then slid in behind the wheel and closed the door. Penny climbed in shotgun, her door thudding closed a moment after his.

"Sporty!" she said.

"What's your address?"

"You don't have to put it into the GPS. I'll just tell you. Turn left on Oxford Street."

Dr. Wallis followed the instructions, his car the only one tooling through the night.

"So," he said, thinking of a safe topic to discuss.

"So?" she repeated mischievously.

The girl's incorrigible! he thought.

"I don't think I've ever asked you," he said. "What are your plans after you graduate next year? Workwise," he added quickly, so she didn't think he was propositioning her for marriage or something else equally ludicrous.

"I want to be a K-Pop star." She sighed. "But I'm not a great singer, so I don't think that's happening. Realistically? Something that lets me travel. I want to see Paris and London and Taiwan and Laos. I want to travel the world."

"You're in the wrong major then," he remarked.

"Psychology, you mean?" She smiled. "Oh my, professor. That's not my major. International affairs is."

Wallis glanced at her. "But you were in every one of my

classes last semester. That must have eaten up most of your electives?"

"*All* of them. Want to know a secret?"

He wasn't sure he did, but he waited expectantly.

"I was in your first-year psych class too," she said. "You probably don't remember because that class was huge, like five hundred people."

He didn't remember.

"I really liked it," she went on. "I mean, I only took it because it was one of those first-year classes every freshman takes. But, well, I developed a bit of a crush on you."

Wallis gripped the steering wheel more tightly. "Where am I turning?" They were approaching Bancroft Way.

"Next street turn right."

"Durrant?"

"Yeah, go straight on it for two blocks. Anyway, that was my secret."

"Right. Well, thanks for telling me, Penny. I'm, uh, flattered."

"Now it's your turn," she said. "Tell *me* a secret."

"I don't think so."

"Why not?"

"I don't have any."

She laughed. "Right! Everybody has a secret. Okay, stop! We're here."

Wallis tapped the brakes. "Here?"

She pointed out his window to a red, brown, and silver six-story student building. Above the double-door entrance freestanding letters spelled: VARSITY.

"That's where you live? It's less than a mile from Tolman Hall!"

"You don't have to tell me, professor."

"What I mean is, you could have walked."

"In heels? No, thanks! Besides," she said, turning to face him, "I like being in your car."

"You should get some rest, Penny," he said.

"Do you want to come in?"

"No."

"Just for a little bit." She touched his arm.

"No."

"Why not?" She leaned closer, the throat of her jacket opening to reveal her cleavage in her low-cut dress.

"You're too forward for your own good," he said.

"I like getting what I want." She leaned ever closer.

"Penny, you need to go," he told her.

Her lips pressed against his. She kissed him forcefully, and he found himself kissing her back. She rested a hand against his chest, then attempted to relocate her body over the center console to straddle him. This proved too difficult in the cramped space, and she settled for sliding her hand down to his groin—

"Penny," he said, his voice husky. He gripped her wrist. Her eyes were inches from his, glistening, wild, alive. "You should get some rest."

He was sure she would protest, and he was steeling himself for an argument, but she simply slumped back into her seat. With a subtle smile, she said, "See you tomorrow, professor," and got out of the car and closed the door.

Dr. Wallis watched her until she entered the building, and only then did he wonder if it had been Penny he'd spotted earlier from the window of his old office.

"Jesus Christ," he said in conflicted bemusement. He put the Audi in gear and headed home.

He didn't go home.

He wouldn't have been able to sleep. Instead, he stopped by The Hideaway, a pirate-themed pub in San Francisco's Fillmore District. The place might be decked out in Caribbean kitsch, but it was open late, always loud, and it boasted the largest selection of rum in the country.

Dr. Wallis managed to score a recently vacated stool at the bar, and he was promptly greeted by Julio, the always-smiling proprietor and head bartender, who was probably the only person in the state more passionate about rum than he was.

"Yo ho ho, Roy," Julio greeted him, speaking loudly to be heard above the chatter. "What's it going to be tonight? Your regular, or do you feel like continuing your voyage?"

The voyage he was referring to involved Wallis drinking his way through all one-hundred or so drinks on the menu. He was about halfway there, having already tried everything from colonial tavern tipples to Prohibition-era Havana creations to complex ten-ingredient tiki cocktails.

"What's next on the voyage?" he asked.

"I don't believe you've had a Rum Flip yet? Whole egg, Demerara, freshly grated nutmeg, and of course a hand-picked premium rum."

"Dinner and drink in one. Sounds good, brother."

Julio went off to build the drink, and Wallis took out his phone. He opened the messenger app. The last text was from Brook thanking him for dinner the night before. He'd replied with a thumbs-up emoticon. It had seemed appropriate at the time, but now it seemed uninspired, underwhelming, and even a bit dickish, considering he'd also spent the night on her houseboat.

This interpretation was no doubt fueled by guilt due to the bizarre encounter with Penny, but he nevertheless typed:

Had a great time too. You looked spectacular. When are we going to do it again?

He set his phone down. The woman on the stool to his left said something to him.

"Excuse me?" he said. She was roughly thirty, dirty blonde, and had one hell of a rack.

"Rascal, scoundrel, villain, or knave. Which one are you?"

"All rolled into one," he replied.

386

She raised her elaborate cocktail in appreciation.

Julio returned then with a yellow concoction that looked like something you would drink on Christmas morning.

Dr. Wallis took a sip. "Excellent as expected, my man," he said.

Julio bowed with a flourish, identified the rum he'd used, and returned to serving other customers.

"Come here often?" the blonde asked.

"Where have I heard that before?"

"A girlfriend of mine recommended this place to me for the atmosphere." A smile lifted her lips. "She should have recommended it for the men."

Wallis studied the woman more closely. Her tight, knee-length green dress and gold stilettos straddled a fine line between slutty and elegant. However, her jewelry seemed real, and her makeup wasn't over the top...and he couldn't yet decide whether she was into him, or a lady of the night looking to offer her services.

"Is your girlfriend here with you?" he asked.

"I'm alone."

Dr. Wallis was chewing on this when his phone chimed and vibrated.

"Excuse me," he said, opening the messenger app.

The text was from Brook:

Hi Roy. I didn't work tonight. I made spaghetti and a salad earlier. If you want to come by, there are plenty of leftovers. But I understand if you've just got off work and are tired... Please let me know.

Wallis smiled to himself. Typical Brook: genuine, timorous, polite.

He felt worse than ever for what happened with Penny... and for the thought in the back of his mind that perhaps he should buy the woman next to him a drink.

He stood. "Unfortunately, business calls."

"Business...or pleasure?" the woman asked.

Wallis hesitated. "It was nice meeting you."

She extended a bony hand. "I'm Liz."

"Roy," he said, shaking.

"Maybe I'll see you around here, Roy?"

"It's one of my favorite hangouts."

"Lucky girl," she said, her eyes flicking momentarily to his phone in his hand.

"No, lucky me," he said, taking his leave then, and thinking, *Luckier than I deserve.*

DAY 7

Sunday, June 3, 2018

D r. Wallis was having the dream that had stalked him throughout his childhood, adolescence, and adult life. He was seven or eight years old, walking down a street bustling with tourists and lined with dozens of kiosks all selling similar-looking jewelry, shot glasses, coffee mugs, and cheap magnets. A huge cruise ship, docked at port, loomed in the background like a modern-day castle.

Roy couldn't see what was following him, but he knew it was there. It was always there, and it always caught up to him. This was the reason for the cold terror in his gut: the inevitability and inescapability of his fate. The thing had caught him a thousand times before, and it would catch him another thousand times in the future.

Still, he continued to weave his way through the cheerful crowd, continued to look back over his shoulder for his unseen pursuer, continued to fight the tears brimming in his eyes. He had an almost overwhelming urge to approach one of the police officers in their meticulous uniforms directing traffic. He didn't because he had approached one before, in a previous dream, and the police officer had been unable to help him and had, in fact, only slowed him down, expediting his pursuer's arrival.

Roy started to run. He bumped into strangers and

knocked over tacky souvenirs from tables and called for his mom and dad, but they couldn't help him either. They were dead. They had died here in the Bahamas. The capsized yacht had been discovered floating twenty nautical miles off Paradise Island by local fishermen. Their bodies were never found. This tragic event might not have occurred until Roy was a sophomore at UCLA, and he himself had never before visited any of the islands or cays in the archipelago, but chronology and logic mattered little to one's slumbering mind.

The throngs of tourists and locals thinned around him, and before he knew it he was alone on the street. On one corner rose the huge Roman Catholic church he used to go to on Sundays with his parents. He hurried through the gaping entrance into the structure's cavernous belly. The interior was not as he remembered it. No pews spanned the hardwood floors. Great swaths of uninhibited ivy climbed the stone walls and smothered the stained-glass windows. Chunks of missing ceiling and roof created great big skylights opening to the blue expanse above.

For some reason people had abandoned this church, leaving it to weather and fall apart, and God had abandoned it in turn.

Which meant there would be no safety for him here. He had to go. He had to find someplace better to hide—

He was too late.

The doors to the church no longer led outside. They led only to blackness.

"No," he whimpered, and a part of him knew he had spoken that same word out loud in the bed where his adult self slept.

The blackness beckoned him, and he moved toward it, unable to disobey. When he reached the doors, Roy could sense the size of the demon in the abyss beyond. He had only ever experienced it in spatial terms. Never a face or a body. No malevolent eyes or pointy teeth. It was only big. Monolithic. Making him in comparison feel no larger than a pebble at the base of a mountain—

Dr. Wallis jerked upright in bed, swallowing back bile that had risen in his throat.

Bright sunlight seared his eyes. He squinted until they adjusted and he made out Brook's bedroom. That feeling he always experienced when waking in a woman's bed— that he was in a place that wasn't his own, and maybe one where he shouldn't be—encapsulated him now. Yet this was lessened by another feeling: one of carefreeness. Nightmare be damned, it was simply nice to be waking in Brook's bedroom. The warmth of the sun's morning rays slanting through the porthole windows. The strawberry scent of her sheets. The gentle rock of the houseboat on the calm bay waters. All the natural wood and eclectic knickknacks, which created the illusion of waking up in a beloved childhood tree fort.

Wiping beads of sweat from his forehead and dismissing any lingering dream-fear, Dr. Wallis called, "Brook?"

She didn't answer.

The houseboat wasn't big, and he couldn't hear water running, which meant she had likely gone somewhere.

He pushed aside the covers and hunted down his clothes, which he'd expected to find strewn all over the floor, but which he found folded neatly on the seat of a corner rocking chair.

Brook had left a note written on a small piece of pink paper atop them:

Another Saturday, another morning shift. Before I knew you, I always used to look forward to seeing you when you came in for your vanilla latte. Now what do I have to look forward to?

Help yourself to anything you'd like. Call me later.

xoxo

Wallis checked that his phone and keys were in his

blazer pockets, then he left, making sure the door locked behind him. The morning was sunny and cool, the air crisp and moist with sea fog, and he felt absolutely dynamic. He spotted a bakery café across the street and realized he was famished, having eaten none of Brook's spaghetti the night before. He checked his wristwatch and found that it was almost nine o'clock. Rarely did he sleep in so late.

Wallis sat down at the bakery and ordered sourdough waffles with fresh whipped cream, seasonal fruit, powdered sugar, and maple syrup. Afterward he ordered a second coffee to go and detoured through a park redolent with the smells of eucalyptus trees and wild fennel. When he reached his car, he saw a slip of paper pinched beneath one of the wipers. For the briefest of moments, he thought Brook had left him another sweet note. He plucked free the parking ticket, which cited him eighty-three dollars for parking in a red zone.

Crunching it into a ball in his fist, he tossed it in the Audi's center console (*which Penny had tried to climb to straddle you, big boy*, he recalled with real contrition), then got behind the wheel. He had nearly five hours to kill before his shift at Tolman Hall commenced. Instead of driving home, he detoured to a boutique jewelry atelier a few blocks from his apartment where he had purchased a number of his custom-made rings and belt buckles. Inside the small, industrial space, focused spotlights hammered light onto silver pendants, stackable jeweled rings, necklaces, and numerous other creations by local metalsmiths and artisans.

"Roy!" Beverley St. Clair, the artist-in-residence, greeted him from behind the glass counter. White hair cropped and spiky, leathery skin tanned from the sun, she wore a pair of tortoiseshell Ben Franklin bifocals and about twenty pounds of silver around her neck. She had designed the gold signet ring engraved with his family crest that currently adorned the third finger on his right hand. "Wonderful to see you again," she added, her Eastern European accent always making him think of Count Vlad.

"Morning, Bev," he said, stopping before the counter.

"What sort of ring inspires your visit today? You know, you have so many calaveras, I have always believed a king lion design would suit you magnificently. Large, one hundred fifteen grams of solid silver. Diamond or ruby eye socket inserts. Or perhaps aquamarine for something fresh?"

"Actually, Bev, I'm not looking for anything for myself today."

"Oh?" she said, arching an inquiring eyebrow.

"Something for a lady friend of mine." He held up his hands, intuiting what she was thinking. "Not a diamond. In fact, nothing too flashy or glitzy. Let's say—unassuming yet tasteful. Can you help me out with that?"

"Most definitely, Roy. Most definitely. Just a moment while I get my sketchpad."

"You're finally here!" Penny said as soon as Dr. Wallis entered the observation room. "Things are crazy!"

He set the hot drinks he'd brought on the table and looked through the one-way mirror—and found himself face-to-face with Chad. The Australian seemed to be in some sort of distress. His eyes stared at his reflection with haunted concern, the way one might upon finding the face of a stranger staring back. He held both hands to his head, slowly running them over and through his wavy (and unwashed) blond hair. Sharon was pacing the perimeter of the room, her eyes glued to the floor.

"What's going on with him?" Wallis asked, concerned.

"He says mushrooms are growing from his head."

"Mushrooms?" Wallis nodded. "He's hallucinating. This is not to be unexpected."

"This is normal?"

"Sleep deprivation exceeding forty-eight hours is considered unethical today by the prudish wing of academia, so there's not exactly a treasure-trove of information on the effects of extreme sleep-loss. But the studies I've read concerning individuals suffering from extreme insomnia all reported visual distortions, illusions, somatosensory changes, and, yes, in some cases, frank hallucinations, even in cases of people with no history of psychiatric illness."

"What we're doing is *unethical*?" Penny asked, apparently surprised by his a priori statement.

"Come now, Penny!" Dr. Wallis chastised. "We're depriving two individuals of sleep for potentially twenty-one days. We're not going to win the Noble Peace Prize. But when you're pushing the boundaries of scientific study, ethical matters are not always black and white. There's a lot of gray." He pressed the touch panel controller Talk button. "Chad? How are you doing, buddy?"

"Mushrooms are growing from my head, mate!"

"Why do you think that?"

"Shaz told me."

Wallis' eyes went to Sharon. She was passing in front of the exercise equipment, her eyes still downcast.

"I don't see any mushrooms," he said.

"You sure, mate? I can *feel* them."

"No, I don't see any. I think Sharon is simply trying to stir you up."

A hopeful look. "You think?"

Sharon's circuit took her directly behind Chad. She mumbled, "Outta the way, mushroom-head!"

"See!" Chad cried, his hands once more furiously probing his hair.

"There are no mushrooms, Chad!" Wallis said firmly. "Do you trust me?"

His brow knit. "I—I don't know."

"Do you trust Sharon?"

"Hell no!"

"Then you trust me more than Sharon?"

"Yeah, I guess."

"Then believe me when I tell you there are absolutely no mushrooms growing out of your head. You are perfectly healthy."

Sharon, now passing the kitchen, cackled: "Your head's rotting, and you got mushrooms growing out of it!"

Chad whirled on her. "Shut the fuck up, mate!" he exploded, his hands balling into fists. "The doc says there are no mushrooms, you're full of bullshit, so shut the fuck up!" He started toward her.

"Chad!" Dr. Wallis said. "Do you want to end your participation in this experiment?"

His whirled to face the mirror, eyes wide. "End it?"

"You can leave right now. We'll continue with Sharon only."

"Leave? You mean, no more gas?"

"No more gas. You can go home."

His face ghosted. "No! I—I want to stay. Shit, I'm sorry, doc."

"You'll keep your temper in check?"

"Yeah, no problem, mate, I promise."

"Good," Wallis said. "That's good, Chad. Now why don't you go watch a movie. Put on your headphones. Relax."

"Yeah, I think I'll do that..."

He went to the lounge, put on a DVD of *Beverly Hills Cops*, dropped onto the sofa, and clapped the headphones over his ears. Sharon continued to pace the room, though now she was ignoring him.

Dr. Wallis sank back in his chair, pensive.

Penny said, "This is getting weird, professor."

"Seven days without sleep is quite an achievement, Penny. Only a few more days to go to surpass the Guinness World Records champ Randy Gardner."

"You mean that guy, Randy Gardner...no one's ever beaten his eleven days?"

"In fact, several people have. Guinness, however, stopped

certifying attempts at his record, believing that going too long without sleep could be dangerous to one's health."

Penny was quiet as that sunk in.

"Their reticence is nonsense, Penny," Wallis assured her. "Unfounded in science. After Randy Gardner's experiment concluded, he was taken to a naval hospital where he slept peacefully for fourteen hours straight. Although the scientists monitoring his brain signals discovered his percentage of REM sleep was abnormally high, this returned to normal in a matter of days."

Penny nodded but said, "Chad and Shaz are a lot worse than they were yesterday."

Wallis shrugged. "Chad had a mild hallucination, Penny. It is nothing to be too concerned about."

"Shaz hasn't stopped pacing my entire shift. Eight hours. She just walks in circles."

Wallis frowned. "She didn't stop once?"

"No."

"Did they eat anything today?"

"Only oranges. We're going to need to get some more."

Wallis contemplated this.

Penny said, "I don't know if they're going to make it two more weeks, professor. I don't even know if they're going to make it *one* more week."

"They very well might not."

"But how will we know when to end the experiment?"

"We'll know when Chad or Sharon tell us they want to end the experiment," he said curtly. "And you heard Chad just now. He wants to keep going."

Dr. Roy Wallis watched in fascination while Chad re-enacted scene after scene from the 1984 film, *Beverly Hills Cops*. In each he recited the dialogue of Eddie Murphy's character, Axel Foley, word for word.

He'd been doing this for the last hour.

"Look, cuz, don't even try it okay...?" Chad was saying now as he played out the scene in which Axel Foley confronted a wealthy art gallery owner and his thug in an exclusive men's club. "Get the fuck away from me, man," he said to the imaginary thug before performing some comical martial arts shit, adding all his own sound effects.

"Shut up!" Sharon shrieked suddenly and dramatically. For most of Dr. Wallis' shift she'd been sitting on the edge of her bed, her back to Chad, holding her hands over her ears and tapping her foot. "You're talking too much! Shut up! Just shut up!"

Chad seemed nonplussed. "I'm rehearsing, mate. Big role coming up. Gotta nail it."

"You're not a movie star!" she wailed. "You're nobody!"

"After I land this role, Shaz, everybody's gonna know who I am!"

She stood and faced him. "What's your name?"

"My name?" He shrugged. "Eddie."

Sharon cackled. "Eddie, right! Like Eddie Murphy?"

"Yeah, so?"

"He's black!"

"So?"

"Are you black, you dipshit? Look at your arms!"

Chad held his arms before him.

"They look black to you?" she said.

"Yeah, mate. What's your deal?"

"Your name's Chad! You're a white Aussie wanker with no job—unless you call this experiment a job—and no future prospects in acting! Don't believe me?" She snagged his wallet from the table separating their two beds. "Driver's license, right. I don't see a black wanker looking back at me. I see you. And, surprise, surprise, his name's not Eddie Murphy. It's Chad Turner."

Chad marched over and snatched the wallet from her hand. He flipped open the plastic sleeve with the driver's license and studied the identification closely. Different emotions rippled across his face. Then he stuffed the wallet in the pocket of his track pants. "Eddie's my *acting* name, Shaz. A lot of actors have acting names. You think *Spacey* is Kevin Spacey's real name, you fucktard?"

"Actors might change their names, but they don't change their race—"

"Don't know what you're yabbering on about—"

"You're not black! You're white! You're white! You're white! You stupid goddamn mushroom-head—"

Chad swung at her. She ducked, and his fist bounced off the top of her forehead.

Dr. Wallis smacked the Talk button. "Chad! Leave her be!"

Ignoring the instruction, Chad scrambled for Sharon, who retreated to the kitchen, where she kept the island between herself and Chad. She was screaming and laughing at the same time. Chad was seething and feinting left and right.

"Chad!" Wallis bellowed, shooting to his feet, wondering whether he was going to need to enter the sleep laboratory and physically intervene. "Chad!" A lightbulb: "Eddie!" he said. "Eddie Murphy!"

Chad swung his head toward the two-way mirror, his expression a mix of rage and bewilderment. "Who's that?"

Wallis' mind raced. "Your manager, Eddie. Your talent manager. Now you leave that woman alone."

Chad shook his head. "She's a fucking spaz, a shit-talking spaz. She called me—"

"You want to work in Hollywood again, Eddie?"

"What'd you mean?"

"You touch a woman, every major studio and director worth their salt is going to blacklist you. They don't tolerate that type of behavior. Not one bit."

Chad looked at Sharon, who was grinning wickedly at him, almost daring him to attack her. He snorted, then spat on the ground. "You're not worth it, Shaz. You're not gonna derail my career." He looked back at the two-way mirror and scratched his chin. "What was I doing?"

"Rehearsing," Wallis told him. "For your role in *Beverly Hills Cops*. The Harwood Club scene."

"Ah, righty-o." Chad grinned, his dark disposition immediately abandoned. "How was I doing?"

"You're very talented, Eddie. The role's as good as yours."

"I better keep rehearsing then—"

"Why don't you give it a break for now? Put on a movie perhaps?"

"Nah, don't feel like that." He raised his arms above his head and sniffed his pits. "Think I might have a shower. I stink. Can't go into an audition like this."

"Excellent idea," Wallis said. Chad's last shower had been three days earlier.

Whistling a tune—and completely ignoring Sharon—he grabbed a fresh set of clothing from the wardrobe, went to the bathroom in the back of the sleep laboratory, and closed the door behind him.

"He's crazy!" Sharon said, looking directly at the two-way mirror, her gaze so focused and intense for a moment Dr. Wallis had the uncanny feeling she was somehow seeing him beyond her reflection. "You locked me up with a crazy, doc!"

"How are you feeling, Sharon?" he asked her.

"Can't remember crap. Feel like a goldfish in a tiny, stupid bowl."

"Can you recall what you ate for lunch today?"

She glanced at the kitchen. "What?"

"Nothing," Wallis said. "You haven't eaten anything all day."

"Not hungry."

"You need to eat, Sharon."

She looked back at the mirror with those x-ray eyes. "We going crazy, doc?"

"Of course not," he said. "You both are performing exceptionally."

"Doesn't feel like we are. Feels like we're going crazy."

"What exactly do you mean?"

"Feels like there's somebody else inside my head. Somebody who wants to do the talking and everything."

Dr. Wallis leaned forward. "Does this person have a name?"

Sharon approached the viewing window. She stopped directly before it, less than a foot away. This close he could see that her eyes were dancing left and right. Her blonde hair fell around her oily face in tangled clumps. She glanced over her shoulder at the bathroom, then back at the mirror. She whispered, "I need to talk to you, doc."

"Why are you whispering?" he asked her.

"I don't want *him* to hear," she said.

"Chad?"

She nodded.

Wallis turned down the volume of the loudspeakers in the sleep laboratory so his voice too was barely more audible than a whisper. "He won't be able to hear anything now."

Sharon, her eyes dancing faster than ever, said, "He's faking."

"Faking what?"

"I don't trust him. He's *spying* on me."

"Spying? How so?"

"Like, I catch him watching me. Like, I'll look up from my book, and I'll catch him."

"What does he do then?"

"He looks away."

"Have you mentioned this to him? Perhaps tell him it makes you uncomfortable and you would like him to stop —"

"He *wants* something."

Wallis frowned. There was a violent inference to that statement. "What do you think he wants, Sharon?"

She smiled. "What do *you* think he wants, doc?"

The water in the bathroom stopped running. Sharon pressed a finger to her lips. After a long moment of silence, she whispered, "He's listening to us right now."

For a surreal moment Wallis became caught up in Sharon's paranoia and believed that Chad was not in the bathroom drying off but crouched with his ear pressed to the door, listening to them talk about him.

Nonsense.

He pressed the Talk button to reassure her of this conclusion, but before he spoke, Sharon went to her bed, picked up her book, and began reading. Chad emerged from the bathroom a minute later. His hair was wet but not brushed, his clothes fresh, though he wore no socks. He tossed his dirty clothes in the hamper by the bathroom door, then went to the lounge. He glanced at Sharon as he passed her bed. She remained intently focused on her book. He spent some time perusing the stacks of DVDs before selecting John Carpenter's *The Thing*. He clapped his headphones over his ears and slumped down on the sofa.

Sharon continued reading her book.

That night Dr. Roy Wallis stopped by The Hideaway on his way home from Tolman Hall. He continued his mixological voyage with two new rum libations and found himself both desiring and dreading a run-in with Liz of the tight green dress and gold stilettos. When he didn't find her at the bar—or during a very roundabout trek to the bathroom and back—he decided she wasn't there and that this was for the best.

At home he built a Dark 'n' Stormy but only took one sip before climbing into bed with all his clothes on and falling into a deep, dreamless slumber.

DAYS 8-9

Logbook communications by Dr. Roy Wallis, Guru Chandra Rampal, and Penny Park (Exhibit A in People of the State of California v. Dr. Roy Wallis)

S ubject 1 initiated conversation with me today while Subject 2 was watching a movie wearing headphones. She refused to speak, instead using a pencil and pad to communicate. She reaffirmed her concern that Subject 2 was spying on her and had some sort of nefarious intention in store for her. However, when I asked if she wanted to end her participation in the experiment, she emphatically opposed leaving the sleep laboratory, appearing determined to complete the twenty-one days. Later, she complained of insects in her hair, noises that I couldn't hear, and a smell like burning food. She described the sleep laboratory as a magical, ever-changing forest, filled with creatures that speak to her and a meandering path that unfolds before her in whichever way she wants to go. I wonder if it is this forest and path she is seeing when she paces the room for hours on end?

-Penny, Monday, June 4

Significant changes in both subjects were observed today, including increased psychomotor activity, emotional liability, accelerated speech, and inappropriate smiling. Subjects have begun to exhibit paranoia, cognitive disorganization, and psychotic symptoms including auditory, tactile, and olfactory hallucinations of varying degrees.

-R.W., Monday, June 4

Subject 2 has become fully immersed in the vivid and sustained hallucination that he is the actor Eddie Murphy. He repeatedly performs scenes from the actor's films and bits from his stand-up comedy routines, effectively adopting the actor's mannerisms and manner of oral expression. The test subjects have not spoken to one another during my shift. Subject 1 mumbles to herself and is prone to interchangeable bouts of laughter or crying, nervousness, and excessive excitability. She has also displayed perplexing and concerning behavior such as throwing objects around the room, spitting on herself, and pulling down her pants. She continues to experience instances of paranoia. Although she believes Subject 2 to be spying on her, I have observed no evidence of this. Contrary, it is Subject 1 who frequently and fervently glances at Subject 2. Neither have eaten any food for more than eighteen hours.

-Guru Chandra Rampal, Monday, June 4

Physical examinations today documented weight loss, pupillary dilation, lacrimation, rhinorrhea, fever, and sweating in both subjects. Other changes noted were variances in body temperatures, decreased thyroid hormones, increased metabolic rates, high pulse rates, high plasma norepinephrine levels, an elevated triiodothyronine-thyroxine ratio, and an increase of an enzyme which mediates thermogenesis by brown adipose tissue. The changes in body temperatures are attributable to excessive heat loss and an elevated thermoregulatory set point, both of which increase thermoregulatory load, while the other changes can be interpreted as responses to this increased load. These data indicate sleep serves a thermoregulatory function in humans and suggests continued total sleep deprivation can result in flu-like symptoms.

    -R.W., Tuesday, June 5

DAY 10

Wednesday, June 6, 2018

C had was becoming worried.

He'd been working so hard memorizing his lines, feeding the right amount of emotion into them, really embodying the character of Axel Foley, the street-smart Detroit cop trying to solve the murder of his friend... and now it could all be for naught if fucking mushrooms started sprouting from his head.

Martin Brest would never cast him with fruiting fungi all over his face, and the role of the lifetime, the role that would catapult him to stardom, would go to some other actor.

Chad ran his fingertips over his forehead for the hundredth time, feeling for the bump he'd noticed earlier.

There it was, over his left eye, right between his hairline and his eyebrow.

He applied pressure. The bump mushed a bit, or at least he thought it did.

Was there even a bump there?

Yeah, there was. The mushroom wasn't big yet, but it was there all right, and it could pop up fully grown at any time, just like the fuckers did after a heavy rainfall.

Chad was tempted to check himself out in the two-way mirror, but he didn't want the professor or his two fruitloop assistants asking him what he was doing. They might call up

Martin Brest and tell the director Chad wasn't fit to make it to the casting call.

He rubbed the bump again and noticed Shaz watching him.

"What the fuck you looking at?" he asked her.

She quickly returned her attention to her book.

Chad glowered at her for another few seconds, then turned his back to both her and the observation window.

He continued rubbing the bump on his forehead.

Sharon tried to focus on the Dean Koontz novel open on her lap, but the words weren't making any sense. They hadn't been for a long time, but she kept staring at them and turning pages so everyone spying on her would think she was okay.

But she was definitely not okay.

Not only was she hot all the time lately, like she had a fever, she was getting a pretty bad sore throat that made it painful to swallow. Her stomach wasn't great either. It felt bloated and full even though she couldn't recall the last time she had eaten anything of substance.

When she had been sick as a kid, her mom would stay home from work to take care of her, making her chicken noodle soup and letting her have ice-cold cans of her dad's Canada Dry ginger ale. At nighttime, she would tuck Sharon in beneath her bedcovers and apply Vicks VapoRub to her chest and read to her until she fell asleep.

Sharon missed her mom and her dad and her brother so much, but she knew she would not be able to see any of them again until the Sleep Experiment finished. She simply had to deal with the fever and sore throat and bloated stomach until Dr. Wallis told her she was free to leave.

You're not a prisoner, Shaz. Just tell him you want to go. He'll let you.

Yeah, right. As soon as I step out of the sleep laboratory, I'll fall asleep. And who knows what he'll do to me then. I'll probably wake up strapped to a table with my stomach cut open.

Why would he want to cut your stomach open?

To see what's inside me.

What's inside you?

"Shut up!" Sharon shouted abruptly, launching the paperback novel across the room. She leapt off the bed and began pacing.

Someone was speaking to her. The Indian. Asking what was wrong.

"Leave me alone!" she shrieked, grabbing an avocado from the basket on the kitchen counter and smashing it against the ground. It kept its pear shape. She crushed it with her heel. The green skin split and the fleshy golden meat squished out from both sides of the fruit like lumpy mucus. The big seed rolled across the floor, stopping at the base of the oven.

The destruction made Sharon laugh, and when she laughed, she stopped thinking about missing her family and what was growing inside her and all that other stuff she didn't want to think about.

A few minutes later, sitting stone-faced on the kitchen floor, the fever and other symptoms returned, the feeling of being spied on returned, the darkness of her thoughts returned.

All worse than before.

She wept.

Guru checked the gold-plated Casio wristwatch his

mother had gifted him upon his acceptance to the University of California. It was 5:45 a.m. Another fifteen minutes to the end of his shift. He yawned. It was getting harder and harder to remain awake throughout the night. Neither Chad nor Sharon spoke to him anymore. In fact, they didn't do much of anything lately. Chad sat on the weight bench or the sofa staring at a middle distance, while Sharon sat on her bed staring at whatever book was open on her lap, sometimes not turning the page for extended periods of time. Every now and then they'd do something noteworthy. Chad would jump up and begin rehearsing a scene from *Beverly Hills Cops*. Sharon would spontaneously crack up laughing or crying, like she'd done earlier in the morning. But for the most part they just sat around doing nothing, which meant Guru was just sitting around watching them doing nothing.

For eight long hours.

Nevertheless, while Guru and Penny might have been reduced to little more than babysitters, Dr. Wallis was still conducting important cognitive tests on the Australians, bolstering his research into the effects of the stimulant gas on human subjects, and Guru remained proud to be a part of the experiment.

He heard footsteps approaching. A moment later the door to the observation room opened and Penny appeared dressed in one of her eccentric mix-and-match outfits that made Guru think of how a six year old might dress a Barbie doll. She was smiling and seemed to be in a spunky mood.

"Morning, Guru!" She rubbed his smooth head. "I wish for a new Lamborghini."

"*I* wish you would stop doing that to me every morning."

She skipped to the observation window. "How're our little rats doing?"

"Unfortunately, Sharon had another meltdown earlier."

"I really mean it," she went on, as if she hadn't heard him. "They're just like rats, aren't they? Put a person in a room for a long time with nothing to do, and they lose what makes them human. They just sit around like dumb rats. Why do we think we're so special?"

"You sound as though you might be having an existential crisis."

She turned to look at him. "Why do you talk like that?"

He frowned. "Like what?"

"So formal all the time. And so fast. Your speech pattern —way too fast. Gobble, gobble, gobble. You need to slow down."

"*You* are giving *me* speech advice? You cannot even pronounce my name properly."

"Gulu?"

"It is Guru! Guor-*roo*!"

"That's what I said. And what kind of name is Guru anyway? Isn't 'guru' a common noun?"

"'Guru' is a Sanskrit term for a teacher of a certain field."

"So, like, you're some kind of teacher?"

"I am not a guru, Penny. Guru is simply my name, just as Violet or Rose can be a woman's name without any connotation to the flowers."

"I bet you're a *sex* guru."

Guru stood. "I think I will be leaving now."

"But we haven't done the handover yet!"

"Yes, well, if you will be serious for once—"

Penny dropped in the now vacated chair. "Actually, I don't care about the handover," she said, putting her sneakered feet up on the desk. "I need to ask you a question."

"Yes?" he asked, eyeing her feet disapprovingly.

"Do you know where the professor lives?"

Guru blinked. "Dr. Wallis?"

"What other professor would I be talking about?"

"Why do you want to know where he lives?"

"I'm just curious, that's all."

"I am sorry. I do not know."

"But you can find out online, right?"

"Why would you think that?"

"Because you're Indian, and Indians are really good at computers and stuff."

Guru rolled his eyes. "You sound like my mother. And Indians are no better at IT than any other race. There are just more of us—"

"I'm kidding!" she said, cutting him off. "But you *are* good with computers, right?"

"I am no computer guru."

"Oh God, please shoot me. You are *so* not funny so don't try to be."

Guru's smile vanished. He thought it had been a pretty good joke.

"So come on," Penny pressed. "Can you help me out or what?"

"I think we should respect Dr. Wallis' privacy."

"Aww, I knew you would be a huge nerd about it." She dropped her feet to the ground and swiveled the chair so her back was to him. "See you tomorrow, *nerd*."

Guru was surprised by the venom in her tone. He contemplated the predicament for a moment, then said, "Have you searched for Dr. Wallis on social media sites?"

Penny spun around. "Yeah, of course. He has a LinkedIn account, but I can't see any of his personal information because the account is private."

Guru shrugged. "Given we already have his phone number, we could try a reverse lookup," he said. "If Google has ever crawled his number on a publicly accessible webpage, we might be able to pull it up, as well as any information related to it, such as an address..."

Penny cracked a smile. "Then let's do it!"

Dr. Roy Wallis hadn't seen Brook since the night he'd slept over in her boathouse, and he was looking forward to their date this evening tremendously. After showering, he dressed in a simple monochrome outfit along with a pair of wool loungers with cream soles. He stepped through a spray of cologne, then added some pomade to his hair and worked a dab of cedarwood balm into his beard. In the living room, he played background music on the stereo, adjusted the lighting to a pleasing ambience, built a Dark 'n' Stormy, then went to the wraparound deck for a cigarette. He was about to light up when the doorbell rang. He returned the smoke to the pack, carried his drink inside, and opened the front door.

Brook, channeling a 1920s debutante with a long pearl necklace and beaded dress in bold Art Deco colors, looked ravishing.

"Welcome, my dear," Wallis said, kissing her on the cheek.

"My, don't you smell nice," she said. "Woody."

"Remind you of home?"

"Does my houseboat smell *that* much of wood?"

"No, it smells *only* of wood. Drink? I have a great California Syrah I've been saving for just such an occasion."

"Sounds lovely."

Dr. Wallis poured her a glass of the single-vineyard wine in the kitchen, then said, "Come on, I want to show you something." He led her to the clock tower room, then looked at her heels. "Are you going to be able to climb three stories in those?"

"Three stories?" She frowned at the staircase. "Don't tell me this place has *three more* levels?"

"No, only this tower."

"Tower—?"

He took her hand and led her up the powder-coated steel staircase. She seemed pleasantly surprised by the man-cave-esque first level with its pool table, pinball machines, and city views through the four large picture windows. She oohed and aahed over the second-level library/office/garden solarium. But it was the third level—where star- and moonlight filtered through the four giant clock faces, setting the room aglow in an eldritch light—that took her breath away.

"Oh, Roy, I love it!" she said, peeking through a clear pane of glass in the east-looking clock face. "I feel like a princess in her own fairy-tale castle!"

"I'm glad you like it," he said, topping up his drink at his second bar. "It's what sold me on the place twenty years ago."

"If you don't mind my asking, Roy...how can you afford such an apartment? I mean, I know professors get paid well, but this must have cost millions..."

"I received a large inheritance when my parents passed away. I had to spend some of the money on something. Real estate seemed a good bet."

"Oh, Roy," she said, expressing regret. "I'm so sorry...I knew I shouldn't have asked—"

Dr. Wallis pulled her close and kissed her on the lips. They continued kissing for several long seconds until he stepped back to give his libido some space. He wanted to enjoy the evening with Brook, not rush right to the hanky-panky.

They returned to the main floor and set about preparing dinner. Wallis had stopped by the local supermarket that morning to pick up the ingredients to make a caprese salad, bruschetta, and the simple yet classic pasta carbonara. His enjoyment of cooking didn't extend to baking desserts, however, and he'd opted to purchase a tiramisu cake rather than attempt to bake one from scratch.

They were finishing up their meal on the deck when his doorbell rang.

Wallis flashed immediately and horribly back to the evening with Brandy nearly two weeks before when Brook had come by unexpectedly.

Could it now be Brandy at the door in some karmic twist of fate?

"Excuse me," he said, dabbing his lips with a napkin and standing. Unable to offer Brook any explanation, he promptly returned inside and went to the front door, trepidation expanding in his chest with each step.

He gripped the doorknob, paused a beat, then pulled open the door, hoping for the best, which right then would have been anybody but Brandy.

It was Penny Park, all K-popped up in an oversized sweater, frilly scarf, and miniskirt.

Dr. Wallis blinked. "Penny?" he said, careful not to raise his voice too loudly. He looked past her, saw nobody else. "What are you doing here?"

"I wanted to hang out." She smiled. "You free, professor?"

"How did you get my address?" he demanded.

"Not too hard if you know your way around online."

Wallis restrained a surge of anger at the blatant invasion of his privacy. "This isn't a good time, Penny," he said simply.

"Come *on*, professor," she said playfully. "I mean, I'm not drunk tonight. I'll behave."

"This is *not* a good time, Penny," he repeated meaningfully.

Comprehension flickered in her eyes, and she peered into the apartment, drawing a connection between the bottle of wine on the kitchen island, the mood lighting, and the background music.

Her face darkened.

"Go home," he added gently. "We'll talk tomorrow."

For a terrible moment Wallis thought Penny might burst into tears, or worse, throw some sort of scorned lover's temper-tantrum. Thankfully, she merely hurried down the stairs.

Badly shaken, he returned to the deck. Brook had not touched any more of her food and was standing by the railing that bordered the deck, gazing out at the night.

"It was my assistant from school," he explained. "She wanted to update me on the experiment."

Brook turned. "At close to midnight?"

Wallis scratched his head. "Look, it's bizarre. I don't really know what to make of it."

"She knows where you live?"

"I'm baffled, Brook. I swear, she's never been by before, and there's nothing going on between us." He couldn't believe he was speaking these words, feeding Brook such a cliché defense, but he nevertheless added: "She's my *assistant*, for Christ's sake! She's twenty-one."

"I think I should go," Brook said tightly.

"Brook, no—hold on! Look, she has a crush on me, okay? That I know. She's made it pretty clear. But there's nothing between us! I swear to you, nothing!"

Brook studied him for a long moment, then, in a disconcertingly blasé tone, she said, "Okay, Roy. I believe you. I don't know what's going on, and I don't think you're telling me everything, but I believe you're not romantically involved with this assistant of yours. Still, I can't stay tonight. I'm sorry."

She marched past him and went inside. Wallis followed, at a loss for what to say or do to right the situation.

"Brook..." he said lamely when she opened the front door to leave.

She didn't reply. The door swung shut behind her.

After a long moment of thoughtful silence, Wallis returned to the deck to finish his dinner—and smashed his pasta-laden dish on the slate tiles, followed shortly by his Dark 'n' Stormy.

DAY 11

Thursday, June 7, 2018

D r. Roy Wallis did not bring Penny Park a green tea the following morning. He set his vanilla latte on the desk and got straight to business. "How were they?" he asked, looking through the viewing window. Chad sat on the workout bench, slumped forward, his head held in his hands. Sharon was nowhere to be seen.

"Is Sharon in the bathroom?" he inquired.

"Yup," Penny said, not looking at him. She was wearing a denim jacket over some sort of multi-colored court jester's shirt. Jovial, however, she was not. More like royally pissed.

Dr. Wallis didn't appreciate the attitude. He'd done nothing wrong the night before. She was the one who'd tracked down where he lived and busted up his date.

"How long has she been in there?" he asked.

"A couple hours."

"*A couple hours?*"

"They're bad," Penny said. "Like, really bad. Way worse than yesterday." She finally glanced up at him, but instead of the anger he'd expected to find in her eyes, there was only concern. "We made them sick, professor," she continued. "And I think we need to end the experiment."

Dr. Wallis straightened in shock. "*End it?* Penny, we can't end—"

She cut him off. "These last few days, I haven't been comfortable with the experiment. I've been worried about Chad and Shaz. Now I'm *really* worried about them. What we're doing, stealing their sleep, it isn't right. You said this yourself—"

"The experiment was approved by the university's Institutional Review Board. Chad and Sharon both provided written informed consent. Most importantly, they've displayed no willingness to end—"

"Stop it!" Penny cried. "Stop talking and listen to me, okay? Chad and Shaz are not well. Look at them! Watch them! See for yourself."

Dr. Wallis and Penny Park observed the two Australians for the next twenty minutes. Chad remained on the weight bench holding his head in his hands. When Wallis coaxed him into conversation, his replies were curt and slurred, and he complained of dizziness, nausea, and the "fucker of all fucking headaches." When Sharon returned from the bathroom, she appeared gaunt, clammy, and unsteady on her feet. She curled into a ball on her bed and wrapped her arms around her knees in an effort to stop her body from trembling. She refused to speak at all.

Dr. Wallis tried once more. "Sharon?" he said. "I would like to perform another EEG. Would that be acceptable?"

When she didn't reply, he got up and rolled the metal cart with the EEG equipment into the sleep laboratory.

Neither Australian paid him any attention.

He stopped next to Sharon's bed.

"Sharon?" he said in a clinical voice. "Open your eyes please."

She cracked them open. They were red and watery. "What?"

"Remember this machine?"

She looked at the EEG equipment. "No."

"We used it a few days ago."

"What does it do?"

"It will help me find out what's bothering you. Sit up please."

She didn't respond for a long moment. Then slowly, like an old woman suffering osteoarthritis, she sat up, shoulders rolled forward.

"I'm going to place this on your head now," he said, picking up the electrode headband. After smearing some gel on her forehead, he slid the headband in place so the smooth side of the metal discs were in contact with her scalp, and the adhesive ground patch was behind her ear. "We're all set. You can lean back against the bed's headboard, if you'd like?"

She only closed her eyes.

Dr. Wallis adjusted the photic stimulator so the lamp was directed at Sharon's face, flicked on the amplifier, and began recording her brainwaves.

While Penny Park watched Dr. Wallis perform the EEG on Sharon, the questions that had consumed her thoughts all morning returned:

Who was that woman he'd been with last night? Is she prettier than me? Is she some big-shot professor too? Are they dating? Can I compete?

Penny totally regretted going to the professor's house last night. She'd made such a fool of herself. She cringed each time she recalled the disapproving look in his eyes when he found her on his doorstep, and how he'd sent her home like she was nothing but a silly little schoolgirl.

She was furious with him for making her feel as lousy and worthless as she did. She wanted to hurt him the way he'd hurt her, which was why she'd taken so much satisfaction in telling him the Sleep Experiment had to end. The dismay on his face had been priceless! But she was not motivated to end the experiment by her embarrassment and jealousy alone.

Sharon and Chad really were sick, and they really did need medical attention.

When Penny had taken over for Guru at six a.m., the Australians were their normal sedentary selves. By midmorning, however, Sharon began sweating and shivering, while Chad swatted at invisible objects and mumbling gibberish. By noon Sharon had curled into a fetal position on her bed where she rocked and moaned and sobbed, and Chad could hardly stand for a few minutes without losing his balance and falling over, looking for all the world like a drunk after an all-night binge.

Penny had nearly called Dr. Wallis then, to tell him about the Australians' rapid decline in health, but her pride did not allow this. She didn't want to show weakness. She didn't want him to view her once again as a silly little schoolgirl, for despite her anger with him, she still craved his respect.

So she stuck out the last two hours on her own, checking her wristwatch every ten minutes, silently urging the hands to move faster.

Dr. Wallis, Penny noticed now, was removing the electrodes from Sharon's head.

The EEG test was done.

Penny knew the professor was going to try to spin his findings in the best possible light and insist everything was okey-dokey. She would like to believe this, because deep down she really didn't want the Sleep Experiment to end, as that would mean her relationship with Dr. Wallis, however rocky, would end also.

But what she wanted didn't matter anymore.

It's not about me, she told herself, realizing how selfishly she'd been behaving lately. *It's about Chad and Shaz. It's about doing what's right for them.*

"The electrical activity in Sharon's brain is exceedingly abnormal," Dr. Wallis admitted to Penny when he returned to the observation room. "It's similar to what you might expect to observe in someone with epilepsy, and very severe epilepsy at that, multiple seizures a day."

"See!" Penny said, appearing vindicated. "She's sick! Something's not right in her brain. She needs to see a doctor...a medical doctor."

"Bah!" Wallis said, brushing these concerns aside with a wave. "You're overreacting."

Penny seemed taken aback. "You're not going to do anything to help them?"

"What can we do right now, Penny?"

"For starters, professor, we shut off the gas and take them to the hospital."

Wallis blinked in surprise. "You were serious about wanting to end the experiment?" He shook his head vigorously. "Where is the scientist in you, Penny? We do not shy away from the unknown; we embrace it."

"Not at the expense of two people's health, professor."

"Penny, Penny, Penny," he said, alarmed at her flip of allegiance to him. "Does this newfound moral compass of yours...have something to do with last night?"

"No! God! They're *sick* in there!"

"They may be, but simply letting Chad and Sharon out of the sleep laboratory is no magic solution, I'm afraid. They won't instantly and miraculously recover. In fact, their symptoms may worsen."

Penny frowned. "What do you mean? You don't *know* for certain? The stimulant gas, professor...you've tested it before, right?"

"Of course I have, Penny. Extensively. On mice."

"On *mice*? Only mice? And what happened to the mice?"

"They didn't sleep, naturally," he told her. "And then, unfortunately, they died."

"Died!" she cried, shooting to her feet.

"Penny, calm down."

"But what if Chad and Shaz *die*?"

"Humans aren't mice, Penny! They'll be fine. I'll reduce the amount of gas being vented into the room each day," he lied, giving her a chance to come back to his team. "We'll wean them off it during the last week of the experiment."

"No! No way, professor! This has to end." She took her phone from her pocket.

"Who are you calling?" he demanded.

"Guru."

"Guru? Why?"

"So he can talk some sense into you—"

Dr. Wallis grabbed her phone and stuck it in his blazer pocket, steeling his nerves for what he now was convinced had to be done. Penny had left him little choice. Her mind was set in opposition to him. She could no longer be trusted to do his bidding and keep her mouth shut. She had become an existential threat to the experiment. "You're not calling Guru, Penny," he said, "so stop being such a melodramatic twat."

Penny stiffened as if he'd slapped her. The cloudy confusion and hurt in her eyes quickly focused into sharp fear as she read his intention on his face.

"Professor...?" she said, back-stepping toward the door.

"Why couldn't you have been a good girl, Penny? Why couldn't you have simply nodded your head and gone along with me, Penny? I don't want to do this. I really don't."

"Professor...?" Her back bumped into the door. She turned—fast. Got the door open, but that was all before Wallis grabbed her from behind and swung her about. She cried out in alarm. He shoved her to the floor and fell on top of her.

She screamed.

Dr. Wallis covered her mouth with one hand. The scream became a strangled muffle. She writhed back and forth beneath him and swatted his sides with her hands. He worked his weight forward until his knees pinned her biceps to the floor. Tears smarted her eyes and her body shuddered as she sobbed into his palm. With his free hand, he pinched her nostrils closed.

Her eyes bulged. She went wild, bucking her hips and thrashing her head from side to side and biting his skin.

Wallis didn't watch her die. He wasn't a sick man. He was an ambitious man, and he couldn't allow anybody to sabotage his life's work.

Not when I'm so close to uncovering the truth behind the human condition.

So he lowered his lips to her ear and told her in a soothing tone that her suffering would soon be over, that she would no longer feel any pain, that she would be at peace.

Wallis continued telling Penny Park this for a good minute after she had stopped moving.

At nine thirty p.m. Dr. Roy Wallis left the observation room and waited out front Tolman Hall for Guru to arrive for his ten o'clock shift. Swollen storm clouds robbed the night sky of the moon and stars. Rain fell in a steady drizzle, and a nippy wind rustled the wet leaves of the nearby trees. Dr. Wallis chained smoked and tried not to think too much about Penny, or the work ahead of him to dispose of her body. When he spotted Guru approaching through the dark, he crushed out the smoke beneath his heel and met the Indian in the middle of the breezeway.

"Professor?" Guru said, surprised to see him outside. "What are you doing out here?"

"Nice night, isn't it?" Wallis said. "I like it when it rains. Everything is clean and fresh."

"I like rain too, but not so much when I have to walk through it."

"At least you don't have to worry about it messing with your do anymore."

"That is true, professor. I continue to reap the rewards of my transformation."

"You don't have a car?"

"I do not even have a driver's license. Should we go inside? It is rather chilly."

"Here's the thing," Wallis said, stroking his beard. "I'm not sure the best way to break this to you, buddy, so I'll just spit it out. The Sleep Experiment is over."

Guru's eyebrows arched. "Over? Did something happen to —"

"The Australians are fine. But since your last shift their conditions deteriorated demonstrably, and I decided, in the interest of their health, to take them off the gas."

Guru's shoulders slumped as he digested this information. He looked like a lost puppy dog that had been kicked in the side. "I should have expected this. Their health had been declining for days. Have they begun to reacclimatize?"

"They're still in the basement. Once I turned off the gas, and the air in the sleep laboratory approximated the ambient air in the building, they quickly fell asleep in their beds. I suspect when they wake sometime tomorrow their symptoms will have decreased significantly, if not have resolved all together."

Guru sighed. "Well, this is unfortunate. I was enjoying assisting with the experiment very much. I am sad it has come to a premature end."

"Look on the bright side, my man. The experiment lasted eleven days. We tied the Guinness Record. That should be something to celebrate." Dr. Wallis clapped him on the shoulder. "Your contribution has been greatly appreciated. Go enjoy the rest of your summer. Of course, you'll be compensated for the full twenty-one days, so don't worry about that. Just email me your bank details, and I'll wire the money tomorrow."

"You are too generous, professor." Guru stuck out his hand awkwardly. "I must thank you for this experience. I will not forget it."

Dr. Wallis shook. "I hope to see you in a few of my classes next semester."

Guru frowned when he noticed the compression bandage wrapped around Wallis' right hand, which hid the teeth marks on his palm.

"Spilled some hot coffee on it," Wallis said by way of explanation. "Nothing to worry about. You take care now."

DAY 12

Friday, June 8

D
r. Roy Wallis spent the next several hours observing the Australians and recording notes as usual. Cloistering himself in the small observation room 24/7 for the foreseeable future was not going to be ideal, but he would put up with the discomfort in the name of his research. He would purchase an inflatable mattress to sleep on, and he would eat most of his meals at the nearby cafés and restaurants in downtown Berkeley. He would have to return home to shower and shave, but that shouldn't cause any problems. The Australians had displayed no desire to leave the sleep laboratory. All would be fine.

At two o'clock in the morning, Wallis walked through the wet night to his car and parked it out front Tolman Hall. He returned to the empty basement room where he had stored Penny's body and carried it under the cover of darkness to his car, where he laid it across the tiny backseat.

Slipping behind the wheel, he pressed the ignition button and spent some time plugging his destination into the GPS system. A minute later he was about to put the transmission in gear when a knock on his window made him jump. He peered out to see the round face of campus police officer Roger Henn. He was smiling beneath his waxed Monopoly Man mustache, so Dr. Wallis didn't think he'd seen

Penny's body. Moreover, the Audi TT was a two-door coupe, and the backside windows were little more than tiny triangles, which made it very difficult to see into the backseat. Still, Wallis played it safe and got out of the car.

"Rodge, my man," he said, digging his cigarettes from his pocket and leading the bigger man away from the car.

"How ya doing, doc?" Roger Henn said. His ball cap—stamped with *POLICE: University of California*—was pulled low over his forehead, the bill keeping his bright blue eyes in shadows. He had the ruddy cheeks and nose of a seasoned drinker, and he smelled strongly of spearmint gum.

"I'm good, my friend. Catch any students making out in the bushes tonight?"

"Pepper sprayed the shit out of them."

They laughed. Wallis lit a cigarette.

"So how's that experiment of yours going?" Roger Henn asked. "What you doing down there anyway?"

"Oh, you know, what all scientists do. Run rats through mazes and mess with effervescent test tubes."

"While cackling evilly and striking dramatic poses."

"Exactly." Doing his best imitation of Gene Wilder in *Young Frankenstein*, Wallis spread his hands and said, "*It's alive!*"

They laughed again.

"So how are you, Rodge?" Dr. Wallis asked. "Quiet night?"

"We got an interesting feller back at the station on remand," Henn said. "Says he's a pickpocket, and you gotta hear how he allegedly spends his weekends. Takes his local train to San Francisco International Airport Saturday morning, dipping all the way. At the airport, buys a pack of envelopes and stamps and posts what he calls his 'takings' back to his home address. Then he dips some more around the departures lounge before taking a cheap flight to Phoenix, Santa Fe, fucking Topeka—wherever he feels like sightseeing for a day or two, still dipping and posting the cash back, so none of his ill-gotten gains are on him if he ever gets busted.

And he says he never does 'cause if anyone ever notices they've been pickpocketed, he drops the wallet instantly and points it out to the person, like a Good Samaritan. Says he's lost count of how many people fucking thank him."

Dr. Wallis tapped ash from his cigarette. "So how'd he get caught tonight?"

"DUI."

"Ah, yes. The bane of the midnight shift patrolman. Speaking of which, how does a cop get stuck on graveyard duty anyway?"

Henn shrugged his beefy shoulders. "We got a shift bid policy. Patrol officers bid by seniority."

"But you're what? Thirty-five? Thirty-six? You must have a fair bit of seniority under your belt?"

"Thirty-seven, and yeah I do. But I don't mind the dark side. Less nuisance report calls, and most of the other cops, being more junior, are less cynical about life than the guys on the other shifts. But shit." He yawned. "I do get tired sometimes."

"Because what you're doing isn't natural, Rodge. Humans are diurnal. We're not meant to stay up all night and sleep in the day. It works against our circadian clock."

"That's right, you're the Sleep Doctor. Got any recommendations how to make me feel less tired?"

"Sure, get enough sleep."

"Easier said than done. You ever try sleeping in the daytime?"

"Your brain can be tricked into going to sleep under the right conditions. Get some blackout shades for your bedroom, or an eye mask. Earplugs too for when your neighbor decides to weed whack or mow in the middle of your night."

"Yeah, I might try that, doc. Neighbor has a dog that never shuts up."

"You can try changing out your lights as well. Get some low-wattage ones. Maybe even red ones."

"Shit, no! I ain't gonna turn my house into a brothel."

"You asked for my advice."

"I'll stick with the eye mask and ear plugs."

Dr. Wallis shredded his cigarette beneath his toe. "All right, Rodge. It's been fun, but I have to get home myself. Have a good night."

Roger Henn continued his patrol east along Hearst Avenue, and Wallis returned to the Audi, pleased at how calm he'd remained while speaking to a police officer with Penny's body hidden a dozen feet away.

Making a U-turn, Wallis left Berkeley and drove west along I-580. Thirty minutes later, just past the prison where Johnny Cash recorded an album live, he continued west along Sir Francis Drake Boulevard to Samuel P. Taylor State Park.

He had been an outdoorsman in his younger days, and he'd discovered the park quite by accident a dozen years ago while driving to Point Reyes National Seashore. It quickly became a favorite place of his to spend a solitary weekend camping, hiking, and mountain biking. He couldn't remember the last time he'd come out this way, but it must have been more than five years ago now.

The park, as Wallis recalled the lore, was named for a man named Samuel Penfield Taylor, who hit it big during the California Gold Rush and used some of his gold to buy a parcel of land along Lagunitas Creek, where he built the first paper mill on the Pacific Coast. When a stretch of the North Pacific Coast Railroad was constructed nearby, the ever-entrepreneurial Taylor built a resort alongside the tracks catering to city-weary San Franciscans. After Taylor died, the State of California took possession of his property for non-payment of taxes, and he became immortalized as the modern-day park's namesake.

Dr. Wallis parked the Audi about a mile west of the Camp Taylor entrance, in a pullout on the side of the road. At this hour there were no other cars. He removed Penny's body from the backseat. Thankfully rigor mortis had yet to affect her muscles, and he flopped her body over his shoulder like a bag of potatoes.

Across the road, he knew, were trails leading up to Devil's Gulch. He had no intention of following trails. Instead, he started west off the beaten path into the old-growth forest.

The towering redwoods blocked any celestial light penetrating the clouds from reaching the ground, but the torch app on his phone served well to illuminate his way. Despite the fact he was in good shape and Penny's body was thin and light, the trek was not easy. Steep hills and winding creeks impeded his progress, while a light fog shrouded roots and rocks, causing him to stumble on more than one occasion. After ten minutes he was panting and sweating. After another ten minutes he stopped to catch his breath. However, this was not the occasion to be lazy or sloppy. The deeper into the forest he brought the corpse, the better.

In the end, he pressed on for what must have been another thirty minutes before deciding he had gone far enough. He dumped Penny's body onto the leaf litter with a sigh of relief. He wiped sweat from his forehead and eyes and shook the numbness out of his shoulders and arms. Then he withdrew the hunting knife he had collected from his home on the way to the park. He'd only used it before to cut rope and clean fish. Tonight's activity would be very different, and for a moment he worried he didn't have the stomach to decapitate Penny. But he knew it was a necessary horror. He didn't own a shovel, and he hadn't been about to go purchasing one in the middle of the night. Even if he found somewhere that sold them well past the witching hour, he would have to use cash to avoid leaving a paper trail, and the transaction would be suspicious as hell. The clerk would remember him and could potentially provide his description to the police. He supposed he could have waited until morning and popped by Home Depot. But the store had CCTV cameras, and being caught red-handed on camera was worse than any eye-witness account.

Besides, he didn't need a shovel. The park was full of carnivorous wildlife. Black bears, cougars, gray foxes, and bobcats were all opportunistic predators that would jump at a free meal. And Penny in the belly of a bear was better than Penny buried beneath the ground, where, if ever discovered, her remains could be identified.

The problem was her head.

It was too big for any animal to consume, and even if the elements and decomposition reduced it to a whitewashed skull over time, forensic technology could reconstruct her face.

So he had to dispose of it properly.

Crouching, Dr. Wallis commenced the gut-churning job of detaching Penny's glossy-haired cranium from her body. The five-and-a-half-inch serrated steel blade made relatively easy work of this, even when it came to severing her cervical vertebra, though he get did get blood all over his hands.

Standing, Wallis thought he might be sick. But a few deep breaths stayed his nausea.

He picked up Penny's head by the locks and made his way back to one of the creeks he had passed earlier. He set the head on the bank, then waded into the water to test its depth. It came nearly to his shoulders at the deepest point, which would be good enough. He scrubbed the blood from his hands, then returned to the bank. Bacteria in the gut and chest of a deceased person will eventually create enough gas to float a submerged body back to the surface of any body of water. You didn't have this problem with a head though. Still, to be safe, Wallis stuffed Penny's mouth with small river rocks. Then he lobbed the ghastly thing into the middle of the creek.

It sank promptly out of sight, and Dr. Wallis continued to his car, satisfied with a job well done.

He returned to his penthouse apartment just as dawn was painting the rain-scrubbed sky amber, apricot, and vermillion. He showered and changed and was planning to head out to purchase the necessities he would require in the coming days, but the sight of his king bed was too tempting.

Just for an hour, he told himself in a moment of weakness, flopping down on top of the duvet.

During the latest REM stage of his comatose-like slumber, he dreamed it was daytime in Samuel P. Taylor State Park, the forest still and silent. He was hurrying through the shadows cast by the giant coastal redwoods, glancing back over his shoulder for his unseen pursuer, when a thick fog materialized from nowhere, and within it, a decrepit stone church sprouting from the rotted-out stump of a felled tree. The stone walls were cracked and crumbling in places, and a trail of white smoke, nearly indistinguishable from the fog, wafted from a chimney.

He crept into the hybrid structure through a gap in the jagged stump. The interior was much larger than should have been possible, and he hurried across the nave and took refuge beneath the cloth-draped altar. Yet even as he hid, the air was shifting and thickening, a darkness was gathering, and when he worked up the courage to peek out from beneath the altar cloth, he found himself suspended in an abyss so vast it would reduce even the tallest redwoods to toothpicks. He was not alone, for the amorphous, monolithic demon now shared the darkness with him, and he knew his time was almost up—

Dr. Wallis snapped awake with a breathless gasp. Night filled the bedroom windows, disorienting him. It had been morning when he'd lain down. Surely he hadn't slept all day?

He sat up and checked his wristwatch. It was eight-thirty p.m.

"Fuck," he mumbled. Then, like a zap from a live wire, he recalled his middle of the night excursion, and what he'd done to Penny's body, and he cursed again in remorse.

Wallis went to the bathroom, splashed cold water over his face, brushed his teeth, then returned to the bedroom. He collected his phone and was heading to the front door when he saw on the display that he had missed a call from Brook.

He paused in the living room, conflicted. He rang her back.

She picked up on the second ring. "Hey," she said, sounding neither upbeat nor upset to hear from him. Had it only been the day before yesterday when she had been over and Penny had paid the unannounced visit? That seemed like an eternity ago.

"Hi," he said, trying to sound more chipper than he felt. "Missed a call from you."

"I'm sorry, I shouldn't have disturbed you while you're working—"

"I'm not working right now," he said promptly. He had to get back to Tolman Hall, he knew. The Sleep Experiment had been unsupervised for more than eighteen hours now. Yet...he was depressed and anxious, and the sound of Brook's voice was familiar and comforting. He wanted to see her. He wanted to experience the normalcy that her company would offer, even if it was a false normalcy, for the murder of Penny was going to be a stain on his conscience for a long time to come. "What are you doing?" he asked.

"Sipping a glass of wine and looking out at the bay."

"Sounds nice."

A pause. Then: "Would be nicer if you were here with me."

He didn't reply.

"Roy?"

"I was just thinking... Have you eaten?"

"Yes, but I could eat again, something light."

"How about that izakaya restaurant on San Pablo Avenue. That's not too far from your place."

"We'll need reservations."

"I know the owner. He should be able to squeeze us in. Say, half hour?"

◆ ◆ ◆

With the Audi's top down, Dr. Wallis sped across the San Francisco-Oakland Bay Bridge, enjoying the roar of the wind in his ears and the great black expanse of night sky overhead. The moon shone bright and full amongst the scattering of stars.

He parked in downtown Oakland and walked the few blocks to the izakaya. He remained anxious and on edge, worried Brook was going to read in his eyes what he'd done. This was nonsense, of course, just his guilt distorting his judgement, and he told himself to get his shit together.

The hostess—an Asian woman channeling an Edo-period ninja with her headband, loose black clothing, and slippered feet—led him to a corner table. Brook hadn't arrived yet, and he took the opportunity to order a drink. The restaurant didn't stock rum, so he settled for a twelve-ounce carafe of sake. David, the owner, came out from the kitchen to say hello. They'd gotten to know each other on a small-talk basis by virtue of the sheer number of times Wallis had patronized the establishment over the years.

When the waitress brought the sake, David returned to the kitchen and Wallis ordered a second carafe before he had even touched the first. The waitress, God bless her, didn't bat an eye.

The izakaya restaurant was dark, minimalist, and not very large. All the tables were occupied with middle-aged well-to-dos enjoying a night out without the kids. The smells of deep-fried tempura and teriyaki sauce and grilled pork belly aromatized the air, and Wallis realized he hadn't eaten since yesterday afternoon.

Brook arrived ten minutes later in strappy sandals and a sleek cocktail dress. The waitress had cleared the carafe he had polished off, so only one remained on the table, albeit half-full.

"Sorry I'm late," she said, after they kissed and sat. "I couldn't decide what to wear."

"You look great," he said.

"You always look great."

"It's easy when all you have to do is throw on a jacket."

Dr. Wallis poured Brook a cup of sake, then ordered another bottle, along with some house-made pickles, edamame, mushroom tempura, and beef skewers.

"Cheers," he said, tapping cups and drinking.

"So I just want to get this out of the way first," Brook said. "I'm not mad about the other night. I probably overreacted a little by going home. I can hardly blame your assistant for having a crush on you. *I* have a crush on you. It was just that..."

"You don't have to explain anything, Brook," he said. "And you might be happy to know, I've dismissed her from the experiment."

"You dismissed her? Oh my, Roy, you didn't have to do that!"

"Yes, I did. It was completely inappropriate for her to come by my house like she did. She looked up my address online somehow. That's borderline stalking."

"Well...as long as *you* think it was the right thing to do, and it had nothing to do with my reaction."

"It was the right thing to do," he assured her. "However, I'm going to have to pick up her eight hours, which means I won't be available much if at all until the experiment concludes."

"Which is, what, another week?"

Dr. Wallis had told Brook the duration of the Sleep Experiment was twenty-one days, as he had told Guru and Penny and the Australians, but the reality was it would last as long as was necessary to either prove or disprove his revolutionary premise.

Regardless of this, he said, "Yes, another week."

She pouted with put-upon exaggeration. "What am I going to do without you?"

"Hey, I got you something. Close your eyes."

"Really?" Smiling, she closed her eyes.

"Hold out your hand."

She stuck her hand out, palm upward. "Okay."

Wallis produced from his jacket pocket the ring Beverley St. Clair had made for him. He tried slipping it over Brook's middle finger. The fit was a little tight, so he slipped it over her ring finger instead.

"All right," he said.

Brook opened her eyes, which lit up in delight when she saw the ring. "Oh Roy!" she said, holding her hand before her face to admire the piece of jewelry. "It's lovely! It really is."

The ring was sterling silver with a green quartz. On the bottom left corner of the gemstone, as if perched on the edge of a leaf, was an eighteen-karat rose gold ladybug.

"I wasn't sure of your size..."

"It's perfect." She took his hand in both of hers and squeezed it affectionately. "Thank you, Roy. I don't think I'll ever take it off."

The waitress arrived with the third carafe of sake and the food. Dr. Wallis ordered several more dishes, which he ate almost exclusively over the next hour or so. During the leisurely meal, he and Brook spoke about everything under the sun. Their conversation was easygoing and pleasant. They had a natural synergy. They liked the same things. They had a similar sense of humor. What Wallis enjoyed most about spending time with Brook, however, was the way she always put his mind at peace. Her life was simple, which made her simple by extension, but in a desirable way. This was why, he believed, she had cast such a spell over him. She had no pretenses. She didn't play games. She had no grand aspirations in life and didn't desire to have any. She had her job, which she liked; she had her friends, the ones he had met down to earth and genuine; she had her silly little houseboat, which she adored; she had her health.

She lived *in* the moment, not for some greater moment, and he found himself not only enchanted by this paradigm, but envious of it too.

"So they're saying we're going to be getting a month's worth of rain in the next week," Brook was telling him now, taking the last edamame from the dish and delicately sucking the soybeans from the salty pod. "Three storms in seven days. Can you believe that?"

"We talking winter-level storms here?" he asked her.

"Not that heavy, but it will be raining nearly nonstop."

"Good thing I'll be cooped up inside Tolman Hall."

"I'd love to see it."

"Better be quick. It's going to be torn down later this summer."

"I mean your experiment."

Wallis blinked in surprise. "Really?"

"Sure. Can I?"

"There's nothing to see. It's just two people sequestered in a room."

"I know you don't like talking about it much, Roy, but I really would like to see it. I'm a mess if I don't get my eight hours of sleep each night. And your guinea pigs have gone two weeks?"

Wallis hedged. "I don't know, Brook...I'm not exactly running a freak show, a penny a peek."

"I won't interfere or anything, I promise. Didn't you say there was a two-way mirror? So they won't even see me."

"When did you want to come by?"

"We're not doing anything right now."

Wallis contemplated this as he chugged what remained of the sake.

"All right then," he decided, dabbing his bearded lips with a serviette. "Let's do it."

◆ ◆ ◆

"Jesus H. Christ!" Dr. Wallis exclaimed as soon as they stepped inside the observation room.

"Oh my God... Is that?" Brook spun away and made a retching sound.

Wallis couldn't take his eyes away from the viewing window. One or both of the Australians had torn hundreds of pages from the books in the library and plastered them to the two-way glass with their feces. Their work was so thorough he couldn't see into the sleep laboratory at all.

He hit the Talk button on the touch panel controller. "Hey, guys...?" he said, a singsong intonation to the question.

They didn't answer.

Brook came to stand beside him. She didn't speak

"Chad?" he tried again. "Sharon? What's going on in there?"

He heard susurrate whispers and witchy laughter.

"Roy...?" Brook said, her voice careful.

"This is absolutely unprecedented," he told her.

"Is it a joke? Why would they...do this?"

"They've been experiencing mild hallucinations. This must be some sort of extension of their distorted perception."

"Like they saw something in their reflections they didn't like so they covered up the mirror?"

Wallis thought of Chad's hallucination that mushrooms were growing from his head and nodded.

"I don't like it, Roy," she added. "Should we...I don't know...should we get them help?"

"*No*," he said harshly as he experienced a sickening sense of déjà vu. Nevertheless, he quickly dismissed any notion that he would have to serve Brook the same fate as Penny. Brook wasn't impulsive or disloyal or motivated by self-interest. She would never go behind his back to the Board of

Trustees. "I mean, not right away," he added. "I'll keep watch on them for a bit, let them outside to get some fresh air, give them some time to clear their heads."

"You think that's all they need? What they've done is..."

"I'm ninety-five percent sure it's all they need, Brook. Maybe I'll even take them for ice cream?" He smiled. "Anyway, if for whatever reason they don't shape up, I'll drive them over to Alta Bates Summit myself. Their health, of course, is of the utmost importance."

"You don't want me to stick around with you until you know for sure that everything is okay...?"

"Everything *is* okay, Brook." He smiled again, only this time it was a little tighter. "Trust me. I've been spending eight hours a day with these guys for the last two weeks. I know them inside out. They just need to be let out of the room for a while. Now why don't I drive you home? It's late, and you have work tomorrow morning, don't you?"

"Well, okay then. I guess...well, I won't be seeing you for another week, will I?"

Dr. Wallis kissed her on the cheek and led her from the observation room. "Hopefully we can find time before that. Maybe you could even come back in a couple of days to see the Australians when they're back to their boring old selves reading books and watching TV?"

"Yes, I would like that." They started up the stairs to the main floor. "Thank you for the lovely evening, Roy." She glanced over her shoulder the way they had come, laughing. "I mean, it *was* really lovely...up until *that*."

"You're getting off easy," he said, laughing too. "I'm the one who's going to have to figure out how to clean it all up."

DAY 13

Saturday, June 9

Sharon was happy they could no longer see her. All their spying had been driving her crazy. Her hands smelled like crap, the entire sleep observatory smelled like crap, but the privacy was worth it. She felt giddy with the success of what she and Chad had done...giddy and *free*.

They can't see me! They can't see me! They can't see me!

A series of giggles escaped her mouth.

Chad, across the room, looked at her. She thought he was going to start yelling like he always did, but instead he giggled too.

She scampered toward him on all fours.

"They can't see us!" she whispered.

"Fuck them!" he said.

They both broke into titters.

"Chad...?" she said quietly.

"Yeah...?" he said.

"Can you hear the voices...?"

"Yeah..."

"But they're not coming from the speakers..."

"No..."

"They're coming from inside me..."

"Me too..."

"They want me to...do stuff..."

"Me too…"

"They want…out…"

"I know…"

"Should we let them…?"

He began laughing then, his fouled hands clamped over his mouth, and after a moment of watching him, she joined in.

❖ ❖ ❖

Chad and Sharon refused to communicate with Dr. Wallis, and all he could hear via the microphones in the ceiling of the sleep laboratory was shuffled movement and the occasional rustle of secretive laughter.

He didn't know if they still wore the smartwatches he'd given them, but the devices were either turned off or out of batteries because the touch panel controller was no longer displaying their heartrates or blood pressure.

He pressed Talk once again, but this time he said, "Guys? I'm coming in, okay? Just to make sure everything is okay."

Laughter.

Dr. Wallis went to the door to the sleep laboratory.

It didn't budge.

He tried the handle again, realized the door was blocked from the other side, and threw his shoulder into it.

No good.

What the hell had they moved in front of it?

He returned to the desk and sat down. Although frustrated he could no longer visually observe what was going on in there, he was also brimming with excitement.

The Sleep Experiment had entered the next phase.

❖ ❖ ❖

At 1:43 that morning, Sharon began to scream.

◆ ◆ ◆

By 3:00 a.m., her screaming and crying had stopped.

◆ ◆ ◆

Half an hour later, after repeated attempts at communication with the two Australians, Dr. Wallis made a call.

"Professor?" Guru Rampal said, sounding sleepy.

"I need you come to Tolman Hall. Right now."

As soon as Guru Rampal stepped into the observation room, he stopped flat-footed as if he'd run smack into a wall. "Yikes!" he said, staring at the violated viewing window. "*What have they done?*"

Dr. Wallis stood and offered Guru the chair. "Sit down, Guru. We need to have a talk."

He sat down, frowning. "Have I done something wrong, professor?"

"No, this concerns the Sleep Experiment. Details that you don't know, and that you need to know, if you are to help me."

"What would you like me to do?"

"You are a bright young man, Guru. You must understand that no great progress is ever made without sacrifice."

"Yes, I do understand that, professor. I myself made a great sacrifice to leave India and my family to study in America."

Wallis nodded. "I too have sacrificed much—a social life, marriage, children—all in the name of my work. The last ten years I've been consumed with a theory that, if proven correct, will change the world forever. Success is tantalizingly close. But it all hangs on the success of the Sleep Experiment."

"But you said you ended the experiment, professor?"

Wallis stroked his beard. "When I was a child, Guru, my parents took me to church every Sunday morning. I remember the services well. They always began with a procession down the aisle. The big old Hammond organ would blast out rusty notes while the altar boy, carrying a giant cross, would lead the slow-moving line. Following him came the candle bearers and the priest and finally the deacon with the Gospel Book. The congregation would join them in a hymn. Although it was played in the upbeat major key, and meant to be joyous, and everybody gave it their best falsetto, I was always confused by the verses. They implied that Satan wasn't trapped in a fiery lake in the middle of the earth like I'd believed up until that point in my young life. He was, in fact, loose upon the world, leading an invisible army of demons. When I asked my mother about this, she quoted the Scriptures, telling me, 'Satan has desired to have you.' This is what Jesus told his apostle Peter in the Garden of Gethsemane, because Peter was prepared to fight bravely for Jesus against flesh and blood enemies, but he was unprepared to meet Satan on the battlefield of the heart and mind. And that's where Satan and his minions will get you, I learned that day, where he will always get you, wherever and whenever he wants, perhaps without you ever even knowing. In the heart and mind." Wallis lit up a cigarette. "Growing up, the inexorableness of this concept terrified me. In fact, to this day, I still have dreams that play to these fears. My point here? It was this simple statement—'Satan has desired to have you'—that set the course of my life. It's what got me interested in psychology." He pondered this for a long moment. "You see, Guru, my parents died when I was only a little younger than you," he continued. "They were sailing in the Bahamas when pirates attacked them, if you can believe that. Fucking pirates. The swine boarded my parents' yacht, stole everything of value, then sent my parents overboard.

That's what the local police believe happened, at any rate, and I don't have any reason to doubt them. I went to a dark place after that, I won't lie. A very dark place. I didn't care if I lived or died. I had suicidal thoughts. Once, when I was driving down the freeway, I had a nearly irresistible urge to swerve my car into oncoming traffic with no thought for the others I would kill in the process of killing myself—and it was that moment I realized Satan had already gotten me." Wallis took a long, hard drag, exhaling smoke through his nostrils. "I turned my life around then. I did my best to banish the darkness inside me. I changed my major to psychology to understand better why people did some of the awful things they did, to help them if I could. Nevertheless, it was the science of sleep that proved to be my true calling. I joined the wave of researchers endeavoring to uncover what went on in our brains when we slept. Before the 1950s, everyone thought sleep was a passive activity, but then electroencephalographs changed the game, revealing that our brains have a clear four-stage routine that repeats over and over until we wake at the end of a bout of REM, our minds full of melting clocks and impossible places and faces we can't remember."

"Here is an interesting fact, professor," Guru said. "One of the first researchers to study REM found that he could predict when an infant would wake by watching the movements of its eyes beneath its eyelids."

Dr. Wallis nodded, twisting his cigarette out in the ashtray. "A party trick to liven up any Tupperware party, no doubt. Now, here's an equally interesting fact: every single creature you can strap electrodes to and keep up past their bedtimes—birds, seals, cats, hamsters, dolphins, you name it—all experience this four-stage routine when they sleep."

"Hamsters dream when they sleep?"

"Dream and a lot more, brother. Golden hamsters wake from hibernation—just to nap. So something pretty damn significant—essential, I would say—goes on when the lights are out. The question is, what? What the hell is going on during sleep that is so vital to every creature's survival?"

"May I remind you, professor, that in your Sleep and Dream class, you argued that we sleep out of habit. We sleep, to paraphrase you, because we have always slept."

"That certainly makes an interesting talking point, doesn't it? Not to mention packs my lecture halls with inquisitive young minds. But do I believe this?" Wallis began to pace in the small observation room, his hands clasped behind his back. "Ten years ago—during the summer of 2008—I conducted my first sleep deprivation experiments on mice. At the time, most of this research was being conducted on fruit flies due to the fact they're much cheaper and easier to maintain. But the benefit of mice is that they can be hooked up to an EEG machine. In the experiments, I stimulated the mice just as they were about to enter a bout of REM, causing an escalation of sleep pressure. Later, when I let the mice sleep undisturbed, I isolated any that were displaying odd behavior and dug into their genomes. Eventually I discovered they all shared a mutation in a specific gene. Their EEGs revealed an unusual number of high-amplitude sleep waves, suggesting they were unable to rid themselves of their sleep pressure and were consequently living a life of snoozy exhaustion. Although I have never been able to understand the full relationship between the mutated gene and sleep pressure, my research ultimately allowed me to engineer a preliminary version of the stimulant gas—which changed everything."

Guru was leaning forward in his chair. "What do you mean it changed everything, professor?"

"Control mice exposed to traditional sleep deprivation lived for anywhere between eleven and thirty-two days. No anatomical cause of death was ever identified; they simply dropped dead, which I speculate was due to stress or organ failure. The mice exposed to the stimulant gas, however, all died within fourteen days, and they didn't merely drop dead. They died extremely horrible deaths."

"I must ask how a mouse can die horribly, professor?"

"During the initial five or six days of the experiment, they behaved similarly to the control mice. They experienced a loss of appetite while their energy expenditures doubled baseline values, which resulted in rapid weight loss and a debilitated appearance. All to be expected. But then, between ten and fourteen days, they began spontaneously attacking one another with tooth and nail. These were not minor skirmishes due to tiredness, Guru. They were fights to the death—fights beyond death. Because whenever one mouse died, the survivors would attack its corpse for no apparent reason. Chew out its eyes, gnaw off its feet and tail, eviscerate its gut and remove its innards. Behavior antithetical to mice, and indeed to all animals, save for perhaps the most depraved of our species. And then when only a final mouse remained, it would turn on itself, performing acts of self-mutation until it was incapacitated by mortal injury." Dr. Wallis paused theatrically. "*That*, my friend, is how a mouse can die horribly."

"But if the control mice behaved normally until they died of natural causes," Guru said, "why would the mice under the influence of the stimulant gas act so bizarrely?"

"I asked myself that same question on a daily basis for months on end," Wallis said. "Until one morning the answer stumbled onto my lap. I had been out for breakfast when a priest sat down at the table next to mine. Soon he was joined by another man, a friend perhaps, or another priest not wearing his collar. In any event, they engaged in a theological discussion I had no interest in overhearing but could not help but listen to given their close proximity to me. I did not stick around for my usual second cup of coffee, and as I returned home, I began thinking about all the Sundays I had spent in church as a child. The song the congregation used to sing came to me. My mother quoting the Scriptures, warning me that Satan has desired to have us, and that the way he would get us was in our hearts—"

"And *minds*," Guru said meaningfully. "Do not tell me you believe the mice under the stimulant gas were *possessed*, professor?"

"Possessed?" Dr. Wallis shrugged. "I am no longer a religious person, Guru, but I suppose 'possessed' is an adequate description of what happened to those mice, because what is possession other than the expression of a chaotic mind? And this is my point, my young friend. Every living organism—from tiny multicellular bacteria and viruses to mammals and human beings—we're all chaos wrapped in order. In other words, we've all been born with madness inside us, though it's kept in check by innate, fixed-pattern behavior."

"You mean instinct?" he said.

"Exactly, Guru. Instinct—the instruction booklet on how to act sane, if you will. Because imagine if a lioness had no maternal instinct to raise her cubs? Or if a newly hatched sea turtle had no instinct to run to the ocean and relative safety? Or if a marsupial, upon being born, had no instinct to climb into its mother's pouch? Indeed, without instinct a spider would never know how to spin a web. A bird would not know how to build a nest or hunt for worms. A bear would not hibernate during winter and likely starve to death. A dog would not shake water from its coat and likely fall ill. Without instinct, you see, existence would be chaos."

"But what of us? Humans? We are not puppets of instinct —"

"Of course we are, Guru!" Wallis said. "Fear, anger, love. Instinct rules almost every moment of our lives. But you are right in one regard. With our complex brains, and our capacity for reason and free-will, we're in the rare position in the animal kingdom to sneak a peek behind Mother Nature's curtain to get a taste of the madness bubbling inside us. Because let me tell you, buddy, instinct has never told someone to jump off a bridge, or drive a van into a group of shoppers, or kidnap and torture a child. That's the crazy inside us talking, the madness, unfettered by instinct."

Guru's expression was a mask of studious disbelief. "Even if this is true, professor, even if nature is balanced on a knife-edge between chaos and order, I still do not understand what this has to do with the mice and the stimulant gas?"

"Because instinct was not Mother Nature's only tool to provide us sanity. She had one more powerful trick up her sleeve."

Comprehension dawned in his eyes. "*Sleep...?*"

"Why does every biological lifeform experience sleep pressure? Why do we have a failsafe in the form of micro-sleep to guarantee we will nod off even when we try our hardest not to? What are our brains doing for a third of our lives that is so important and requires so much juice that, at the end of each day, they essentially render us unconscious and paralyzed? What evolutionary advantage is worth the risk of the brain taking itself mostly offline for a good chunk of each day? I'll tell you what, my good friend. Our brains are doing their damned best to keep the madness inside us at bay. It's true. I've witnessed firsthand what happens during the total and prolonged absence of sleep and microsleep. Yes, admittedly only in mice thus far, but now..." He looked at the feces-smeared viewing window.

Guru looked too, and he gasped. "Chad and Shaz, they are not sleeping like you said?"

"No, Guru, they are not."

"They have...peeked behind Mother Nature's curtain?"

Dr. Wallis nodded. "And they need our help."

"Chad, Sharon, I'm coming in," Dr. Roy Wallis said.

He didn't expect an answer and didn't get one.

To Guru: "We're going to have to bust the door in."

"What about the viewing window?" he said. "Would it not be easier to break that?"

"Easier, yes, but then the stimulant gas would contaminate the antechamber. Now, on the count of three, you and I are going to shove this door open. Ready?"

They shoved. Something sounding like metal on concrete squealed from the other side of the door.

"Keep pushing!" Dr. Wallis said.

Inch by inch the door cracked open until Wallis could see that the large seven-hundred-liter refrigerator lay on its side in front of it.

"A little more," he grunted. And then: "Okay, that should do it." He studied the narrow space they'd created between the door and the frame. It would be a tight fit. "I'll go first."

With his back flush with the door, Wallis placed his right knee on what was now the top of the toppled fridge and allowed himself to fall sideways. His upper body cleared the narrow space, and then it was simply a matter of dragging his legs through after him. He stood, dusted off his hands, and surveyed the room.

"Oh, shit," he said.

Dr. Roy Wallis approached the middle of the sleep laboratory, which smelled ten times worse than the filthiest restroom he had ever had the misfortune of visiting. Chad was crouched in a far corner, near the lounge, watching him with eyes that almost seemed to shine with an inner glow. But it was Sharon who Dr. Wallis was focused on. She lay on her bed, on her side, naked from the waist down. Across the center of her forehead either she or Chad had carved a straight incision from temple to temple, which had bled tremendously, painting much of her face red.

Her eyes, like Chad's, seemed to shine catlike, though whereas his were guarded and watchful, hers were intense and manic, conjuring the image of a woman in the final few minutes of childbirth.

"What the *fuuuuck*?" Guru said from behind him.

"Sharon?" Dr. Wallis said. "Did you cut yourself? Or did Chad?"

Her lips curled into a smile.

"Where's the knife?" he pressed.

"There it is, professor," Guru said, pointing.

A steak knife, stainless steel blade and black plastic handle covered in blood, lay on the floor ten feet away from the bed.

"Go get it," Wallis said. "Don't startle Chad."

Guru went to the knife slowly, his eyes never leaving Chad. When he reached the knife, he crouched—and hesitated. "Are you sure I should touch this, professor? It is evidence."

"If you leave it there, Guru, either Chad or Sharon might use it again—to do something worse."

Guru picked up the knife and stood. "What now?" he asked.

"Take it to the observation room and bring back the first-aid kit."

Guru did as he was told, and Dr. Wallis returned his attention to Sharon. The incision across her forehead was deep but not excessively so. It most definitely required stitches, but this was not a service he could offer. Her hands, he noted, were smeared with dried excrement and blood, the latter leading him to believe she had been the one who did the cutting.

"Why'd you cut yourself, Sharon?" he asked her.

Her smile returned, the corners of her mouth twitching upward in a sinister rictus. Wallis did not like that smile one bit. He looked back to the door. Guru was squeezing through the crack to reenter the sleep laboratory. He scrambled over the fridge and came to the bed.

"Here you go, professor," he said, handing Wallis the bright red first-aid kit. "What should I do now?"

"Get some warm soapy water from the sink and bring it over."

Dr. Wallis unzipped the kit and set it on the bed. By the time he had snapped on a pair of blue Nitrile gloves, Guru had returned with a glass of soapy water and a roll of paper towel.

"This might sting a little, Sharon," he said.

"Okay, doc," she replied, her voice as dry as the rustle of October leaves, her manic blue-green eyes never leaving his.

Wallis wetted some paper towel and gently dabbed the long incision. Sharon didn't flinch.

"Does it hurt?" he asked her.

"I like you touching me, doc."

Wallis paused for only a moment before he resumed cleaning the incision, which he then misted with antiseptic spray and smeared with a liberal amount of antibiotic cream. He placed four small Band-Aids perpendicularly over the cut in the hopes of holding it together in the absence of sutures. He wrapped her head with the same compression bandage he'd used on his hand. He then used more paper towel and water to wipe the dried blood from her forehead, face, and neck.

"That's about the best we can do for now," he said, studying his handiwork. "How does the bandage feel? It's not too tight, is it?"

"All good, doc," she said. "But what about my tummy?"

She wore one of the nearly two dozen identical navy sweatshirts he'd purchased for her. He'd been so focused on her forehead he hadn't realized the sweatshirt was saturated with blood.

"Can I take a look?" he asked her.

Sharon sat up in the bed and raised the oversized garment —it was clearly one he'd purchased for Chad—to just below her breasts.

A second gaping incision divided her taut stomach an inch above her belly button. Blood, much of it still wet, smeared her lower abdomen, pubis, and inner thighs.

Guru inhaled. Wallis swore.

"Guru," he said tightly, "go get me some more water."

When the Indian returned, Wallis used nearly the entire roll of paper towel to clean the incision and surrounding skin. The wound was still bleeding, but there was nothing he could do about that.

"Do you like touching me there, doc?" Sharon asked abruptly.

Wallis was wiping down her left inner thigh. "I can think of a myriad of other activities I would prefer to be performing right now, believe it or not."

"*I* like it when you touch me there. You don't have to use the gloves."

"Guru, pass me the antiseptic spray, then go get her a fresh set of clothes."

Dr. Wallis sterilized the incision, taped it closed with the largest Band-Aides available, and looped the compression bandage several times around her torso.

"Do you need help changing," he asked her when Guru brought him the clothing, "or can you manage yourself?"

Sharon pulled the sweatshirt swiftly over her head so she sat on the bed stark naked.

"You're going to need to stand up," he told her, holding out his hand in assistance.

She took it and stood with little trouble despite her injuries. Guru passed him a pair of white underwear. He crouched before her. "Lift your left foot," he said. She lifted it. "Right foot." She lifted it. He pulled the underwear up an over her thighs. The band snapped snugly around her waist. He repeated the same procedure with the sweatpants. "Do you want to wear a bra?"

"No," she said simply.

"Arms up."

She raised them in the air, and he pulled the sleeves of the sweatshirt over each, then lowered the neck hole over her head, careful to avoid touching her forehead.

"You can sit back down," he told her.

"Can we dance?" she asked him.

"We're not dancing."

"Please, mate? I *wanna* dance."

Dr. Wallis packed up the first-aid kit, then requested Guru's help to return the refrigerator to its upright position. On small wheels, it was easy enough to push back into its place in the kitchen. "Collect the rest of the knives from the cutlery drawer," he told Guru, "and wait for me in the antechamber. I'll be there in a minute."

Wallis went to the viewing window, crinkling his nose in distaste at the smell and sight of it. He peeled free three stained pages from the two-way mirror and rubbed the surface clean with what remained of the paper towel.

He turned to find both Australians watching him with their strangely gleaming eyes. Chad had joined Sharon in smiling at him.

"I believe this small portal to be a fair compromise," Wallis announced loudly. "You both have more privacy than before, yet we are still able to look in here every now and then to check up on you."

Neither of them spoke.

"You are both extremely malnourished and need to eat. If you would like anything specific not provided for already, please let me know."

They began to giggle—awful, high-pitched batty sounds as unnerving as fingernails drawn down a blackboard.

"At least drink water to stay hydrated," he added. "It's essential for your health."

Now the giggles became full-throated, hyena-like, hysterical.

Dr. Wallis returned to the observation room.

"What time is it, professor?" Guru asked. "Am I asleep? Because I feel as though I am trapped in a nightmare."

And it's only going to get worse, my friend, Dr. Wallis thought, but didn't say.

They were in the observation room, Guru slumped in the chair, as if exhausted, Wallis sitting partially on the table, his arms folded across his chest.

"Why would Sharon do that to herself? No, you do not have to explain, professor. I know why. It is the madness." His shoulders sank. "How can this be?"

"The proof is right in front of you, Guru. They've gone insane. Or they're very, very close to the tipping point."

"Should we not try to help them? Should we—"

"It's too late for that. They're beyond the point of help."

"But we cannot just sit here and let them go insane—or go *more* insane."

"That's exactly what we have to do."

"But professor! They are not lab animals. They are humans!"

"I'm well aware of that fact, Guru. But you have to think of the greater good here. Over the next couple of days the evidence we document will be invaluable. Think about it. We will have demonstrated that you, me, the entire human race, *all animal life*, is essentially mad."

"Is this something we *want* to make known to the world?"

"Of course! It may seem like a pessimistic revelation at first glance, but it is in fact quite the contrary. We once thought the universe was ordered because it appeared to run on a set of rules that we termed the laws of physics. But quantum theory has shown us that these laws, at their core, are actually random and unpredictable. Chaotic. However, far from diminishing our view of the universe, this knowledge has enlightened it tremendously. We now know matter can essentially be in an infinite number of places at any given time. We know it is possible there are many universes, or a multiverse. We know that when subatomic particles disappear they reappear somewhere else, which sounds preposterous but is a proven fact and one day might lead to the tantalizing prospect of time travel. And speaking of the future, in the coming century mastering quantum theory will enable us to master matter itself. We'll create metamaterials with new properties not found in nature, and quantum computers that operate at millions of times the speeds of computers today. Invisibility, my man. Teleportation. Space elevators. Limitless energy. Advances in biotechnology and medicine we can't even begin to comprehend."

"What are you saying, professor?"

"I'm saying, Guru, that no scientific discovery has ever set us backward. Imagine the new fields of psychology our research will open up, the new fields of quantum theory applied to the *mind*. Jesus, our research may set in motion the steps to one day crack the code of consciousness—and with that, *reality itself*. Can you dig that, my man? *Can you dig it?*"

"Oh my, professor. This is almost too much for me to process."

"What matters, Guru, what matters right in this moment, is that while it's unfortunate what's happening to Chad and Sharon, certainly, it's for the greater good. Remember—no great progress is made without sacrifice. You told me you understood that?"

"I do, professor, I do." His face dropped. "Oh my..."

"Penny could not grasp the big picture. She was too close-minded. Which is why I had to dismiss her from the experiment. But you're not like her, buddy. I know that. I've always known that. You're a scientist at heart. The search for knowledge and truth is in your genes. So you're not going to make the same mistake she did, are you? You're not going to walk away from what will arguably become one of the greatest intellectual triumphs in the history of human civilization, are you?"

Nearly a full minute of silent contemplation followed this grandiose statement, but then the tormented indecision in Guru's expression hardened into a fierce resolve.

"No, professor," he said finally. "I am not."

DAY 14

Sunday, June 10

D r. Roy Wallis left Tolman Hall at 7:00 a.m. to purchase a pair of air mattresses, pillows, sleeping bags, and any other necessities he and Guru might need in the coming days. He was pleased with his decision to bring the young Indian into the know. Not only did Guru take the around-the-clock pressure off Wallis, but it was simply a great relief to finally confess to someone the true purpose of the Sleep Experiment, and with this, the theory he had been working on for much of the last decade.

On the walk to the Audi, Dr. Wallis bristled with life. Everything about the day seemed fresh and wonderful: the magenta and coral dawn sky; the warm rays of the waking sun; the scent of grass and, beneath this, nutmeg and cloves, which was probably the organic herbicide the campus employed to control the weeds in the block-pavement walkways.

You're so, so close, buddy, he was thinking excitedly. *Another day, perhaps two, to discover if your theory will be proven correct.*

And if so... Well, the implications simply could not be understated. Overnight *Roy Wallis* would become a household name, spoken in the same sentences as Newton, Einstein, Tesla, Galileo, Aristotle.

It was all a little unreal right then. But he'd get his head around it.

He would thrive in the spotlight. He was born for it.

◆ ◆ ◆

Dr. Wallis' voice echoed inside Guru's mind:

We're all chaos wrapped in order.

Guru shivered.

Did he believe this extraordinary claim? Really, truly believe it?

If anyone other than Dr. Wallis had told him this, the answer would have been an emphatic no. But the professor was one of the world's foremost experts on the science of sleep. He knew what he was talking about.

Moreover, Guru had witnessed the changes in Chad and Sharon himself. They were going mad before his eyes.

We're all chaos wrapped in order.

Guru was not a spiritual man. When he pondered the vastness of the universe and the wonders of the natural world and the mysteries of consciousness, he did not search for a divine power to give meaning and purpose to it all. He accepted a material world that could be understood through the logical reasoning of science.

Consequently, even if he did believe Dr. Wallis' extraordinary claim—and he thought perhaps he did—he did not necessarily share the professor's description of the chaos as some sort of 'demon.' However, whatever it was, the chaos in question was clearly not benign.

It was dark, twisted, wicked.

Just look at what it had done to the Australians.

Guilt and shame filled Guru at the thought of the raving lunatics Chad and Sharon had become. When the experiment concluded, they would be carted off to a mental institution where they would spend the rest of their days in straightjackets. This image was all the more terrible when

Guru contrasted it with the smiling, healthy, easy-going people they had been less than two weeks before. Sharon especially. She had been so friendly to him, so inquisitive, always smiling and asking him questions.

And look at her now...all cut up and mad as a hatter.

Nevertheless, nothing could be done about this. The damage to her mind had already been inflicted. There was no rewind button.

If Dr. Wallis and Guru walked away now, Chad and Sharon's sacrifices would be for naught.

So the professor was right. There was only one course of action available to them.

They had to see what they'd started through to the end.

After tossing everything he'd purchased from a Target in West Oakland into the small trunk of the Audi, Dr. Wallis slid behind the wheel, stuck the key in the ignition...but didn't put the car in Drive. His libido was revved up with blinkers on. It had been more than a week now since he'd slept with Brook, and after that whole episode with Sharon stripping in front of him, he was having a tough time getting sex off his mind, and he knew it would soon begin affecting his ability to work and concentrate.

Dr. Wallis didn't like the term "sex addict." It sounded dirty and unbecoming of someone of his position in society. Not that the clinical designation of "hypersexual disorder" was a much better alternative. Nevertheless, Wallis couldn't deny that he was addicted to sex. He didn't have the cravings as bad as some people did, but he thought about sex—and engaged in it—a lot more than most.

The addiction began when he was a young man of twenty-two, shortly after his parents were murdered in the Bahamas. Sex, he discovered, helped to numb the pain of their loss. At first he was paying for one or two prostitutes a week, but it wasn't long before he was blowing two grand every other night in strip clubs. The next step in his disillusioned pursuit of happiness was the local sex club scene. Even when Brandy came into the picture a few years later, he spent most nights he wasn't with her with other women. The thrill of everything that came before the sex—the flirting, the conversation, the drinking, the dancing, the thoughts of *will we or won't we?*—filled him with adrenaline and became almost as important as the sex itself. Orgies, BDSM parties, swinging, exhibitionism, dogging, he'd done it all—and was always searching for more extreme and exciting iterations of sex. Brandy never knew of his nighttime doppelgänger, of course. He supposed it hadn't been fair to have strung her along in a dead-end relationship for as long as he had, because no matter how much he liked her as a person, he had become detached from the emotional value of sex and relationships in general. She had offered him a sense of belonging and nurturing, which he'd so desperately desired, she had made him feel wanted, which he'd so desperately needed, yet despite all of this...it inevitably amounted to a false intimacy. He had a hole in his stomach, and he had a compulsive need to fill that hole, and one woman was never going to be enough.

The unfortunate situation was repeating itself with Brook now. He enjoyed spending time with her, and he enjoyed the attention she gave him, and the serenity she exuded, but in the back of his mind he was already preparing for when he would have to cast her aside and move on.

Brushing these thoughts aside, Dr. Wallis drove to an upmarket twenty-four-hour bordello in Oakland's Financial District. It was not one of the seedy brothels posing as a massage parlor you could find all over any city. To the contrary, it was an invitation-only establishment that served a very select list of clientele.

Wedged between a bank and a nail salon, the bordello resembled an old European hotel, and for tax purposes it in fact doubled as a boutique short-stay hotel. Wallis entered through the front door into a small, dimly lit lobby filled with plants where a receptionist he didn't recognize welcomed him with a smile.

"Good morning," she said. "Are you looking for a room for the night?"

"No, I am not," he said.

"Have you been here before?"

"I have."

"May I have your name?"

He told her, she entered it into the computer, then said, "It's very nice to see you again, Mr. Wallis. Would you follow me?"

She led him to a private waiting lounge that resembled an elegant Victorian men's bar. There were more plants here, while portraits of abstract female nudes in muted colors decorated the walls. A few minutes later the madam of the house, who Wallis did recognize, appeared with three primped women in skimpy yet elegant clothing.

"Hello, Roy," the madam said, shaking his hand. Unlike the prostitutes, she was dressed in regular clothing and cute sneakers. "How are you, darling?"

"Just fine, Janet."

"Which one of these lovely girls would you care to join you this morning? If you'd like to spend some time in private with each to get to know—"

"Not today," he said.

"Of course. Girls?"

Obediently, they took their leave.

"So who will it be, Roy?" Janet asked.

Dr. Wallis had been with the African before, the Asian was too overly augmented for his liking, so he decided on the Scandinavian.

"Excellent," Janet said. "She's only been with us for a month or so now, but everybody loves her. She's part of the family. Cash or credit?"

Dr. Wallis paid with a credit card for a thirty-minute booking. The madame placed the girl's cut into a folder of the sort restaurants use for the bill, handed it to Wallis, then picked up a telephone. "Vivian, darling? Thirty minutes with Roy." She hung up and said, "You have a very special time now, and please come back soon."

She left the waiting room and the Scandinavian returned shortly thereafter.

"Hi!" she said brightly. "I believe you have something for me?"

Wallis handed her the folder, and she led him deeper into the house, which quickly morphed from Victorian to Greek décor. Her room featured four corner columns, a hot tub, and a statue of Venus.

"Shower's right in there," she said, indicating a door that led to a marble bathroom. "I'll be right back."

Wallis had a hot shower and returned to the bedroom with a white towel around his waist.

Vivian held a box in her arms and was neatly arranging an assortment of condoms, toys, and lubricants on a small table.

"Have you been here before?" she asked, smiling at him.

"Yes," he said, obliging the small talk. "Janet mentioned you're new?"

She nodded. "This is my first month…in the business."

Dr. Wallis put her in her early thirties, which meant she was late to prostitution.

"I was in sports medicine," she said.

"What led to the change in profession?"

"The money."

He nodded.

"What do you do, Roy?"

"I dabble in psychology."

"Is that so? Have you met Lisa before?"

"I don't believe I have."

"She's been here for about a year now. She used to work as

a licensed psychologist. She once told me she felt as though she helped more people here than she had at her previous practice."

"I can imagine," he said, making a show to glance at his wristwatch. "In any event, and in the interest of expediency, the faster we drop the charade and fuck, the better for me, as I have somewhere rather important I need to get back to."

◆ ◆ ◆

Dr. Wallis returned to the observation room in the basement of Tolman Hall at 9:15 a.m.

"They've behaved?" he asked, going immediately to the small portal and surveying the sleep laboratory. Chad sat in the same corner he'd been in earlier, only now he was facing it, his back to the viewing window. Sharon was lying on her side on her bed, in a slightly fetal position.

Guru nodded. "They have hardly moved since you left."

"Good," Wallis said, grateful he had not missed anything. "Now come step outside with me for a moment." In the hallway where he'd left the two large Target bags, he added, "Take one of those, my friend, and choose a room where you would like to set up."

Guru retrieved a bag and said, "Which room do *you* want, professor?"

"Doesn't matter to me." He poked his head into the room adjacent to the sleep laboratory. "This will do fine."

"I will go this way a little then." Guru started down the corridor, sticking his head into one room after another before stopping at the fourth one down. "I like this one."

A chill feathered the nape of Wallis' neck. Guru had selected the same room where he'd stored Penny's body.

"Make yourself at home," he said with a forced smile. "Mattresses have an in-built pump, but give me a call if you need a hand."

Dr. Wallis unpacked and inflated his own mattress, unrolled his sleeping bag on top of it—and stared at the bed longingly. He hadn't slept all night, and the Australians weren't doing much of anything right now. Perhaps he could squeeze in a couple of hours...?

◆ ◆ ◆

Brook never did too much of anything on her days off from work. She began the mornings with a homemade breakfast after which, Karl the Fog permitting, she would embark on a forty-five-minute walk along the bay. At the end of the walk she would often stop by the library to browse the head librarian's recommendations. Back home it would be something simple for lunch, then the outstanding chores (cleaning, laundry, emptying the septic tank if it was full), then...well, it would be time to start preparing dinner, and where did the day go?

Today Brook had spent the morning puttering around the marina and feeding and watering her plants, and now she was in the kitchen, making a half dozen devilled eggs...and thinking about Roy.

In fact, she hadn't been able to stop thinking about him and his Sleep Experiment ever since returning from the university campus the night before. That the two young people Roy was employing would smear their own excrement over that window was not only mindboggling but terribly worrisome. They were clearly not in a very healthy state of mind.

Roy had appeared shocked at what they'd done, but he'd quickly brushed it aside as no big deal.

Why?

Had he been downplaying their behavior for her benefit, or had he come to expect such conduct from them? Was psychosis a side-effect of remaining awake for a substantial period of time? And if so, had Roy's Sleep Experiment been sanctioned by the proper authorities? Because it was hard to imagine how any ethics review board would sign off on an experiment that drove the test subjects crazy.

Then again, this certainly wouldn't be the first experiment involving human test subjects to cross ethical red lines. Brook, as an avid reader, could cite all sorts of examples off the top of her head. The physician who'd developed the smallpox vaccine deliberately exposing children to the deadly disease to advance his research. Project MKUltra, a CIA-sponsored research initiative, plying unwitting Canadian and American citizens with LSD and other mind-altering drugs in an effort to develop chemicals that could be used in clandestine operations. Nurses at the University of California employing cruel and unusual techniques to study blood pressure and blood flow in newborns as young as one day old. The Imperial Japanese Army's covert biological and chemical warfare research experiment, Unit 731, in which scientists removed the organs and amputated the limbs of Chinese and Russian prisoners to study blood loss. A South African army colonel and psychologist who was convinced he could cure homosexuality via electric shock therapy. The chief surgeon at San Quentin State Prison performing testicle transplants on living inmates using the genitals of executed prisoners, and in some cases, goats and boars. The United States Army releasing millions of infected mosquitos in Georgia and Florida to observe whether the insects could spread yellow fever and dengue fever. And, of course, everything that was revealed during the Nuremberg trials concerning Nazi experiments on Jews, POWs, Romani, and other persecuted groups.

Brook shook her head at these thoughts as she sliced another egg in half lengthwise. It was ridiculous to compare Roy to the Imperial Japanese Army or to the Nazis. He wasn't committing crimes against humanity; he was merely keeping two test subjects awake for an extended period of time with that mysterious gas of his.

Besides, who was she, a waitress, to question UC Berkeley's Chair of Psychology? Roy knew the laws and codes that governed his work better than anybody. He would not skirt them. She simply had to trust in him.

Brook focused on the culinary task before her. She dumped the yolk from each hard-boiled egg into a small bowl and added mayonnaise, Dijon mustard, apple cider vinegar, and salt and pepper. She stirred the mixture into a creamy paste and scooped a spoonful of it onto each egg white. She placed the finished deviled eggs in the refrigerator, made herself a tea, and then went to sit on the sheltered deck out front of the boathouse. She gazed out at the menacing storm clouds and the slanting rain pockmarking the bay, but her mind was a million miles away.

She was thinking about Roy again.

He'd told her he'd dismissed one of his assistants. Was this truly the case? Perhaps she had not been let go but had instead quit. Perhaps she'd disagreed with the direction the experiment had been heading?

Who cares, Brook? What's gotten into you?

She didn't know. She simply felt as though something was...wrong.

In any event, Roy was working double shifts. Which meant he was now spending sixteen hours a day in that dingy little basement room.

It would be extremely boring.

And lonely.

Brook sipped the tea without tasting it. A raft of fluffy white clouds eased in front of the sun, stealing the brightness from the sky.

I should make him something for dinner, she thought. *Bring it over for him later in the afternoon.*

He would appreciate the food and the company.

And she would get a second look at this experiment of his.

Dr. Roy Wallis shot upward out of sleep. All was dark and quiet. His heart was beating quickly in fear of a dream that he couldn't remember. He was about to get up and go to the observation room to check on Guru and the Australians when he felt an itch at the back of his skull. Frowning, he reached a hand behind his head to scratch it—and discovered a small protrusion in the little valley where the occipital bone met the cervical spine. He probed it with his fingers. It was hard and unyielding. Concerned, he picked at it until he felt blood smear his fingertips. He knew this wasn't doing him any good, but he couldn't stop himself.

When all the skin was removed, he realized the protrusion was made of metal.

A zipper, he thought a moment later.

He gripped the slider between his index finger and thumb and pulled upward. It moved slowly along the parallel rows of teeth, creating a Y-shaped channel in his skin in its wake.

The zipper terminated at the very top of his skull. Still unable to stop himself, he slid his bloodied fingers beneath the dangling flaps of skin and peeled them forward. The skin came free easily, almost like the shell off a hard-boiled egg.

Fascinated, repulsed, and alarmed, he stared at the folded clumps of hair and skin cupped in his hands, which also included his shapeless face—

"Professor?"

Dr. Wallis opened his eyes. For an awful moment he thought he was in a prison cell. Then he made out Guru crouched above him, aglow from the hallway light.

He sat up quickly. "Has something happened?" he demanded.

"No...not exactly. But that may be the problem."

"What the hell are you talking about, man?"

Before Guru could answer, Wallis was on his feet and hurrying to the observation room. He peered through the portal in the viewing window.

Chad remained seated in the same corner as before, his back to Wallis. Sharon was not on her bed.

"Where's Sharon?" he asked, even as his eyes went to the closed door at the back of the room.

"She went to the bathroom nearly two hours ago," Guru said. "She has not come out."

"*Two* hours ago?" He glanced at his wristwatch. It was 10:13 p.m. "I've been asleep all day!"

"I did not want to wake you..."

Dr. Wallis sniffed. Then he saw the brown paper bag with Chipotle branding sitting on the desk. "You left them unsupervised to get food?"

"I would never do that, professor. I ordered Uber Eats. There is a steak burrito in there for you."

Famished, Wallis dug out the burrito, tore away the aluminum foil wrap, and sank his teeth into it.

Guru smiled. "Is it not delicious?"

"Pretty damn good," he said around a full mouth. "Now you say Sharon's been in the bathroom for two hours?"

"Yes, roughly."

"Have you tried communicating with her?"

"She doesn't answer."

Dr. Wallis swallowed, licked some adobo sauce from his fingers, and pressed the Talk button on the touch panel controller. "Sharon? How you doing?"

No answer.

"Sharon?"

Nothing.

Wallis turned to Guru, his concern growing. "Why didn't you wake me earlier?"

"I did not think there was anything to be concerned about, professor. If she was cutting herself again, I would have...heard her."

Wallis nodded but didn't mention the possibility she could be in there hanging from the shower head.

Suddenly no longer hungry, he set the burrito down on

the table, wiped his mouth and beard with a paper napkin, and said, "I'm going to check on her."

◆ ◆ ◆

The sleep laboratory still reeked powerfully of excrement and body odor, and beneath this, the sweet scent of blood.

As Dr. Wallis crossed the room, he noticed Chad turning to keep his back to him.

He stopped. "Chad?"

The Australian made a phlegmy, broken sound.

Giggling?

Wallis said, "How about turning around for me, brother?"

He went very still.

"Chad, buddy?"

When the Australian refused to respond, Wallis decided to deal with him later. He continued to the bathroom and rapped his knuckles on the door.

"Sharon?" he said. "It's Dr. Wallis."

Giggles—though unlike Chad's, these were deceptively childlike.

"What are you doing in there?"

More childlike giggles.

"I'm going to come in."

"No!" Sharon screeched suddenly.

Dr. Wallis pushed the door inward. It moved two inches before slamming back shut. She had her back or feet to it.

"Why don't you want me to come in?" he asked her.

"I don't want to leave!" Her voice was raspy, frightened yet excited, like a gasper's voice during erotic asphyxiation.

"You don't want to leave the bathroom, or the sleep laboratory?"

"The sleep lab!"

"Don't worry about that, Sharon. I have no intention of making you leave the sleep laboratory. Why would I do that?"

"I've been bad."

"What have you done?"

Giggling.

"Sharon?"

Mumbling, as though she were talking to someone.

"I don't care what you've done, Sharon," he said. "But I'm coming in whether you like it or not. I suggest moving away from the door."

He didn't hear her move.

He threw his shoulder into the door.

It barely budged.

"Sharon?"

Laughter now, high-pitched and impetuous.

"All right then," Dr. Wallis said. "You've left me no choice. I'm going to have to turn off the gas."

"No!" she screeched.

"Then let me in."

Sobbing—or was it more laughter?

This was accompanied by lethargic, laborious movement.

He waited until he heard nothing more, then tried the door again.

It swung inward easily.

Dr. Wallis had been expecting a macabre scene, but what he found defied anything he had imagined.

Blood covered the floor, perhaps an inch-deep where it had pooled in the recess around the drain, which was plugged with...chunks of flesh. Sharon sat slumped against the toilet, her elbows hooked over the seat, keeping her upright. She resembled a cross between a woman who'd had five too many tequila shots and one who'd survived—barely—a rabid wild animal attack.

"My Lord, Sharon," Wallis breathed, fighting to keep the burrito down.

The tension bandages that had been around Sharon's

head and stomach now lay on the floor in the spilled blood, which had turned them bright crimson. The incision across her abdomen was much larger than before, revealing glistening white hints of her bottom ribs. Her gastrointestinal tract had spilled (or been pulled) onto her lap, a messy pile of wormy spaghetti. Her small intestine, Wallis noted in horror, was digesting food before his eyes, muscles contracting and fluids flowing behind the thin pink membrane. Even in the enormity of the moment, he wondered how this could be possible when she had not eaten in days—until he realized what she was digesting must be her own flesh.

"Hi, doc," Sharon said, her brazenly glowing eyes meeting his, and her mouth creeping into a smile.

"What have you done to yourself?"

"I'm letting it out."

"Letting *what* out?"

Sharon commenced that godawful giggling—only it was more harrowing than before because the sweetness had left it, leaving behind only a bitter cackle. Her eyes remained locked on his, impossibly bright and alert. Then she coughed, a fine red mist spraying the air before her. A sustained round of coughing followed, sending thick rivulets of blood trickling over her lower lip and down her chin and neck.

Yet her health was no longer of concern to Dr. Wallis. His inner scientist, detached and clinical and craving answers, had taken over. "What is it, Sharon?" he demanded. "What's inside you?"

The smile returned. "I think you know, doc."

He thought he did too, and he cursed himself for not bringing the EEG machine with him. He needed to see inside her head. He needed evidence of *what* was inside her head.

"Guru!" he shouted over his shoulder. "Bring the EEG in here! Now!"

"Want me to show you, doc?" Sharon asked.

"What?" Wallis snapped, returning his attention to her.

"Want me to show you what's inside me?"

"No, don't! Just wait... Just wait, goddammit!"

Dr. Wallis heard the door to the sleep laboratory open and then the clatter of the cart carrying the EEG equipment.

"Look, doc. *Look.*"

"Guru! Hurry!"

Sharon reached a hand into the cavity in her gut that had once held her gastrointestinal tract. Screaming—though in what sounded as much ecstasy as pain—she shoved it upward and beneath her ribcage.

"Sharon, no!" Wallis yelled, lurching forward to stop her. His foot slipped in the pool of blood and he fell to the floor. His head cracked against the tiles. A darkness washed over him in pounding waves, though he fought to remain conscious.

Nevertheless, he could do little more than watch in slow-motion despair as Sharon's wrist and forearm followed her hand deeper into her innards with the sloppy slurping of two virgins kissing.

All at once her body stiffened. Spasmed. She yanked her arm out of her stomach triumphantly.

Dr. Wallis had managed to prop himself up on an elbow, though he knew he could no longer stave off the darkness.

The last thing he saw before passing out was Sharon holding her still-beating heart before her in a clawed fist.

Dr. Wallis' phone, which the professor had left on the table in the observation room, was ringing. Guru ignored it. He was frozen in terror as he listened to what was happening at the far end of the sleep laboratory. He could only see the broad backside of Dr. Wallis as he stood inside the bathroom door, but he could hear everything clearly.

What have you done to yourself?

I'm letting it out.

Letting what out?

Guru's blood went cold at Sharon's words, because he knew what she wanted to let out, even if he couldn't fully accept the reality of the possibility.

This cannot be happening, he thought. *Demons do not exist —*

"Guru!" Dr. Wallis' voice blasted through the intercom. "Bring the EEG in here! Now!"

Guru raced to the corner, grabbed the metal cart with one hand while opening the door to the sleep laboratory with the other. He backpedaled through it, dragging the cart behind him.

"Guru!" Dr. Wallis shouted. "Hurry!"

Guru swung the cart around in a circle, so it was now in front of him. He pushed it toward the bathroom as fast as he could.

Just as he reached the door, Dr. Wallis slipped in blood coating the floor and went down hard.

"Professor!" Guru said, leaving the cart and rushing to his aid.

Yet when he saw Sharon slumped next to the toilet, sliced open and holding her heart in her hand, he hit an invisible wall. He watched as she convulsed a final time, her heart sliding from her blood-greased hand and dropping to the floor with a wet, fat sound.

Wheezing on air that was suddenly sauna-dry, Guru tore his eyes away from the ghastly corpse and knelt next to Dr. Wallis. With trembling fingers, he checked the professor's pulse and was immensely relieved to find it beating fast and strong.

His first thought: *Call an ambulance.*

His second thought: *Call the police.*

He dashed back to the observation room, grabbed his phone from his bag, was about to dial 9-1-1—but hesitated.

There was no emergency.

Sharon was dead. No paramedic could bring her back to

life. Dr. Wallis had suffered a bump to the head but was breathing. He'd come around soon—and be furious with Guru if he panicked now and called for help.

He needed to calm down and *think*.

Stuffing his phone in his pocket, Guru went to the adjacent room and brought Dr. Wallis' air mattress to the antechamber. Then he reentered the sleep laboratory. Chad was sitting on the floor by the TV, his back to the room. How he could remain indifferent to all that was happening, Guru couldn't fathom, but it didn't matter right then.

He went to the bathroom. Keeping his eyes averted from Sharon's body, and careful not to step in the puddle of crimson-black blood, he gripped the professor's wrists and dragged him back to the antechamber, a streak of red marking their progress.

Breathing heavily—Dr. Wallis had been much heavier than Guru would have imagined—he hooked his hands beneath the professor's body and rolled him up and onto the air mattress.

Guru wobbled over to the chair and dropped down into it, the events of the last few minutes finally sinking in.

Sharon was dead by her own hand, and he had defiled the suicide scene.

Was this a crime?

He hadn't called 9-1-1.

Was this a crime too—?

Guru heard approaching footsteps in the hallway. The police! He leapt to his feet, ready to flee, but there was nowhere to go. Trapped! He spun toward the door, bracing for a SWAT team to bust through it, assault rifles locked and loaded—

"Hello?" someone said at the same time a knock sounded.

A moment later the door opened and a pale-skinned woman with short black hair and dark eyes peeked into the room.

Guru swallowed. "Who—who are you?" he managed.

"I'm Brook. Roy's friend. You must be—" Her eyes nearly

doubled in size when she saw Dr. Wallis, covered in blood, sprawled atop the air mattress. "Roy!"

When Dr. Roy Wallis returned to the world of the living, he found himself lying on his back on his air mattress in the observation room. He sat up, groaning as an icy needle poked his brain.

"Professor!" Guru exclaimed, appearing next to him. "He's awake! Ma'am, he's awake!"

Ma'am?

Dr. Wallis sensed movement from the other half of the antechamber, and a moment later Brook was crouching next to the air mattress, her face tight with concern, her eyes red and wet, as if she'd been crying.

"Roy," she said, taking his hand gently in hers. "Don't move too much. You have an awful gash on your head."

He pulled his hand free and touched the left side of his head, discovering a large Band-Aid taped to his temple. He winced as the icy needle poked a little deeper.

"What...?" He was about to ask what happened, but the gruesome images of Sharon's self-mutilation came flooding back in vivid glory. "What are you doing here, Brook?" he asked instead.

"I tried calling you a little while ago," she said, "and again on my way over here, but you didn't answer your phone. I, well, I thought you would be hungry, and I just wanted to bring you some food!" A sob escaped her then, and she turned away while she collected herself.

"It's okay," he told her. "Take a deep breath—"

"It's not okay!" she said. "Your assistant told me she's dead! The girl working for you! That's her blood on you! She's in that room back there, and she's dead!"

Dr. Wallis glared at Guru, wondering why he couldn't have kept his fucking mouth shut. Nevertheless, he realized the Indian would have been hard-pressed to explain why Wallis looked as though he had just spent the evening partying with Jeffrey Dahmer.

Buying himself time to wheel out a plausible explanation for Sharon's death (telling Brook the girl had torn her beating heart from her chest was simply not an option), he said, "His name's Guru, and—"

"*Why's she dead, Roy?* How did she die? What in God's name is going on here?"

"She committed suicide," he told her.

"But all that *blood*."

"She slit her wrists." It was the best he could come up with. "I slipped in the blood when I was trying to help her."

"Why did she—"

Wallis cut her off. "I'd like to change," he said. "I'll explain everything after that."

Brook rubbed her eyes. "I'll go get some clean clothes from your place—"

"No," he said, not wanting her to leave his sight in the event she did something foolish like call the police. "One of Chad's tracksuits should fit me."

Despite protests from both Guru and Brook, Wallis lumbered to his feet. A spell of dizziness almost made him fall backward onto his ass, but it passed after a few disorienting seconds. He entered the sleep laboratory, feeling more sure-footed with each step. Chad, he noticed immediately, sat facing the same corner as before. He had pulled the sweatshirt's hood up over his head, and with his slumped shoulders, he resembled a beggar on a street corner unable to face the world.

He was no threat. Not right then.

At the wardrobe, Wallis withdrew a pair of boxers, sweatpants, and a sweatshirt. He stripped off his bloodied clothes and glanced momentarily at the bathroom. He would have liked a shower, but he wasn't going to start messing around moving Sharon's body with Brook in the next room. He pulled on the fresh clothes and returned to the antechamber, feeling slightly better.

Guru was pacing anxiously. Brook stood by the door, her arms folded across her chest, staring at the floor.

"You shouldn't have come here," he told her.

She looked up. "What happened to that girl, Roy? Why did she kill herself?"

"She was having hallucinations. She—"

"It was that gas, wasn't it? Your assistant told me—"

"His name's Guru."

"Guru told me the gas made them go crazy. So why, Roy? Why didn't you stop this experiment if you knew what was happening to them, if you knew—"

"I *didn't* know," he snapped. He closed his eyes for a moment against the flare-up of pain in his head. "I didn't know she was going to kill herself," he added more reasonably, despite the statement being a bold-faced lie. "She was hallucinating, yes, but that's to be expected in severe cases of sleep debt. It's been well documented."

"And *that*?" Brook said, waving her hand at the feces-splattered viewing window. "Was that to be expected? That's just...sick. And the young man in there, is he hallucinating too? Is he going to kill himself too? Because he's just sitting in the corner staring at the wall. That's not normal, Roy!"

"Of course it's atypical behavior. He's gone fourteen days without sleep, Brook. *Fourteen days*. We're in uncharted territory here. Regardless, from this moment onward, I'm going to keep an eye on his every waking minute to make sure he doesn't...do anything rash."

"You're continuing the experiment?" she said, aghast.

"It's nearly over. Just another day or so and—"

She was shaking her head. "I can't believe I'm hearing this!"

"Hearing what, Brook?" Dr. Wallis asked calmly, though her melodramatics were beginning to piss him off.

"That girl is dead, Roy! Your experiment killed her! We've got to call the police."

Wallis clenched his jaw. "We *will* call the police, Brook," he said. "*After* the experiment has concluded. One more day —"

"What's so important about this experiment, Roy?" she demanded. "What's so important about it that it's obscured your values and decency?"

Dr. Wallis considered explaining everything in detail to her as he had to Guru. But he found he couldn't be bothered. Besides, Brook wasn't an intellectual like Guru. She wouldn't appreciate the magnitude of his revelation. She wouldn't be able to get her pedestrian mind around the fact that no great progress was made without sacrifice. That the lives of one, two, a dozen individuals meant nothing in the grand scheme of things. Across the globe thousands of people were dying every hour due to old age, disease, accidents, and plain old stupidity. So who gave a shit if one or two more joined them? One or two more dying not in vain but in the name of knowledge—knowledge that would change the world forever? They should be honored to serve humanity so, and anybody who could not understand this was, as far as Wallis was concerned, a simpleton who had no purpose existing themselves.

He tried a smile. "One more day, Brook," he said. "That's all I'm asking. One more—"

She threw her hands in the air. "You're crazy, Roy! This experiment has made you crazy too! Those aren't lab rats in there! They're people."

"You have two options, Brook," he said in a perfectly reasonable tone to contrast her hysterics. "You can stay here and calm down while I check on Chad and make sure he's all right, or you can leave and call the police and royally fuck everything up."

Brook glared at him for a very long moment, her dark eyes smoldering even as her face struggled for aplomb. Then she opened the door to leave.

"Aw, fuck, Brook," Wallis mumbled under his breath, sincerely wishing she hadn't called his bluff. As she stepped into the hallway, he snagged her by the shoulder and pulled her back into the antechamber.

She whirled in surprise. "Let go of—"

Dr. Wallis drove his fist into her jaw.

◆ ◆ ◆

"Professor!" Guru cried.

Dr. Wallis looked at him. "I couldn't let her go to the police, buddy," he said. "You know that."

Guru clapped his hands against the sides of his bald head in an absurd imitation of the figure in Munch's *The Scream*. "This is too much for me. Too much."

Dr. Wallis stepped over Brook's body and gripped Guru by his forearms and shook him hard. "You know how important this is, Guru! You know what's on the line here! Don't wimp out, man!"

"I know, but..." He tore his arms free and backed away. "We will go to prison."

"No, we won't," Wallis said, encouraged that his assistant was thinking in terms of the practical rather than the ethical, because the practical, at least, could be appealed to with reason. "Look," he added. "I just need to hook Chad up to the EEG machine. After I get the evidence I need..." He shrugged. "That's it. We won't need him anymore. Not that he's going to last much longer. He's going to take his life just as Sharon did. So how are we culpable? We didn't force their hands. They did what they did to themselves."

"But we *allowed* it, professor."

"Bah! No one will know that. Just yesterday, did you believe they were suicidal?"

Guru frowned. "They were experiencing hallucinations and—"

"Yes, yes, but did you think they were suicidal?"

"No," he said simply.

"No," Wallis repeated. "Their final decline, their descent into madness, happened quickly. Literally overnight. So we simply...fudge some of the facts."

"Fudge some of the facts?"

"I get what I need from Chad's head, then you and I go out for dinner to celebrate the conclusion of the experiment. We turn off the gas and leave Chad and Sharon to catch up on some much-needed rest. And when we return in the morning...they've done what they've done. They've done it in our absence. Some side effect of coming off the gas. I don't know. I'll spin it in scientific terms. The bottom line is, the experiment was all above board on our watch. We couldn't have foreseen what was to happen to them, and we weren't around to prevent it."

"You want us to lie," he stated.

"Shiva, Krishna, and fucking Christ, Guru! Don't be like the rest of them, my man. Lie? If you want to call it that. I call it a pretty near representation of what happened, fudged a little to cross the T's and dot the I's. And what's wrong with that? You want to wallow in ethics? How about philosophical consequentialism then? Judging whether something is right by what its consequences are. And I'd say, given what the consequences of the Sleep Experiment will be, we are pretty damn square in the right."

"What about her?" Guru looked at Brook.

Dr. Wallis looked too. Brook was sprawled on the floor where she had fallen. Truth be told, he wasn't quite sure what he was going to do with her yet. He couldn't dispose of her as he had Penny. He was her boyfriend. He had met some of her friends. Most of the staff at Café Emporium knew they were dating. He would be the first and perhaps only suspect if she went missing. And two people close to him disappearing within a matter of days? No, offing Brook was out of the question. "I'll talk to her," he told Guru. "When she hears everything I have to say, she'll come around. She might not be happy about Chad and Sharon's deaths, but she loves me. She'll—she'll keep quiet for me," he added, hoping he'd spoken with more conviction than he'd felt.

Then, realizing the hypocrisy of his words with Brook lying limp as a noodle on the floor, the right side of her jaw already turning ballet slipper pink, Dr. Wallis knelt next to her body and carefully—lovingly—moved her onto the air mattress, where you could almost imagine she was sleeping peacefully.

Dr. Wallis turned to Guru expectantly.

"Let's finish this, brother."

◆ ◆ ◆

They entered the sleep laboratory together.

"Chad, how you doing over there?" Wallis asked.

The Australian didn't react to his voice.

"You've been pretty quiet, buddy."

No response.

Dr. Wallis stopped when he was directly behind Chad, who reeked of body odor and something else that made Wallis think of rotting wood. He motioned Guru, who was pushing the metal cart with the EEG equipment, to join him. "So this is the deal, Chad," he said. "We're going to do one of the tests on you with the computer and the headband, and then we'll leave you alone after that. You can keep sitting how you are. You don't even have to turn around. But you're going to need to pull off the hoody." He retrieved the electrode gel from the cart. "You might not remember how this works, he continued, "but it doesn't hurt at all. The gel might be a little cold, but that's it. Ready?"

Dr. Wallis pulled back Chad's hoodie.

The Australian twisted about with a venomous hiss.

Wallis gagged and heard Guru retch behind him.

Chad had no face.

He'd peeled away every inch of visible skin to reveal the harvest-colored stew of fat, muscle, and connective tissue beneath. In some places along his jaw he'd gouged his flesh so deeply that his mandible, wet and white, peeked through.

Where his lively blue eyes had been were hollow pools of black and blood. Where his nose had been was a mucus-encrusted hole. Where his lips had been were bleeding gums and a hideous rictus grin.

None of the missing organs lay discarded on the ground before him, which meant they'd most likely been ingested.

"My God," Wallis breathed, and even as he stared in shock at the monster before him, he found himself wondering whether Chad had torn away his face in an effort to rid himself of the hallucinatory mushrooms he'd believed to be growing there, or whether he, like Sharon, had been trying to let whatever was inside of him out.

Guru was saying something quickly in Hindi, maybe a prayer.

Ignoring him, Dr. Wallis said, "It's okay, Chad. You're okay. We're not going to hurt you." He tossed the electrode gel back onto the cart, as there would no longer be a need for a liquid agent given Chad no longer had any skin on his forehead. He picked up the headband. "Remember, pal, this isn't going to hurt."

Bending forward, holding the headband before him with outstretched arms, Wallis lowered it over Chad's head as if crowning a mutilated monarch.

With amazing speed, the Australian's hands gripped Dr. Wallis' wrists, and in the next instant Wallis found himself corkscrewing through the air. He struck the floor with bone-jarring force and rolled several feet before coming to a rest.

A dazed assessment of his body confirmed it to be in working order, and he quickly sat up.

Guru was backing away from Chad the way you would from a German Shepherd foaming at the mouth. "How—how —how did he do that?" he stammered.

"Just keep moving to the fucking door," Wallis told him.

Getting to his feet, and never turning his back to the Australian, he followed.

"That was impossible!" Guru said. "He would need the strength of five men to throw you the way he did!"

"Not impossible, my good friend," Dr. Wallis said, his eyes alight with excitement now that they were safely back in the observation room. "It *happened*."

"But *how*?"

"An educated guess? Adrenaline."

"Adrenaline? Surely—"

"Adrenaline, enzymes, proteins, endorphins, our emotions. When the body's entire stress response is activated, most people are capable of lifting six or seven times their own body weight. The young woman who heaves the car off her father after it slipped off the carjack onto him. The man who tears a caved-in door from his crashed vehicle in order to rescue his wife. Such cases of superhuman strength are not unheard of."

"But we were not threatening Chad. He—"

"He might not have known that. He no longer has eyes to see with."

"What are we to do then? He clearly will not let us hook him up to the EEG machine, let alone remain cooperative for the duration of the tests."

"No, not in his present state," Wallis agreed. "But I have an idea."

Dr. Roy Wallis explained his plan to Guru Rampal, who reluctantly acquiesced to help him carry it out. Then he transferred Brook to Sharon's bed in the sleep laboratory, so the

Indian could keep her contained if she were to regain consciousness while Wallis was gone. "If she comes around," he instructed, "don't let her out of that room, no matter what she says."

"Just please hurry, professor," Guru said.

Nodding, Dr. Wallis left Tolman Hall. The week-long storm thrashing the Bay Area remained in full swing. Slanting rain fell in icy curtains, while the howling wind whipped the branches of the nearby trees into a frenzy of flapping leaves. Thunder cracked loudly, followed by a burst of forked lightning.

Wallis' colleagues in the English Department would call this pathetic fallacy; he called it a pain in the fucking ass.

Head bowed, he hurried along Bayard Rustin Way to his car, then drove with his windshield-wipers thumping to Lawrence Berkeley National Laboratory, which was nestled high in the hills above the campus.

At the summit he passed through the main gate and followed the snaking road among the cluster of buildings. On a pleasant day he would have had distant views of the San Francisco Bay, but right then he couldn't see anything outside the twin tunnels the Audi's headlights punched in the darkness.

He parked illegally out front of Building 33 and dashed through the rain to the entrance. He swiped his keycard and stepped inside the lobby, his presence activating the computer-controlled lighting system.

Supported by the US Department of Energy, and managed by the University of California, Berkeley Lab conducted unclassified research across a wide range of scientific disciplines. They studied everything from the infinitesimal scale of subatomic particles to the infinite expanse of the universe. Building 33, aka the General Purpose Lab, had been designed to facilitate research between scientists from every walk of life.

Dr. Wallis took the stairs to the third floor, then passed

all sorts of customized wet and dry labs before coming to his own lab. He swiped his keycard and entered the small space. Although he had euthanized all of his mice some time ago, he hadn't yet returned the vivarium in which he'd kept them, the freestanding biosafety cabinet he'd used while handling them, any of the expensive research equipment cluttering his workstations—or, most significantly, the small pharmacy of drugs he kept in a locked cabinet.

He went to the cabinet now, unlocked it, and stuffed his jacket pockets with several syringes and vials of Vecuronium, a neuromuscular blocking agent he'd used to keep his mice still during certain experiments or surgery. It was also part of the three-drug cocktail used to execute death-row convicts in Tennessee, Virginia, and other states yet to abolish the death penalty.

Dr. Wallis locked the cabinet again and was about to leave the lab when someone called out, "Hello?"

Wallis froze.

However, remaining put and hoping the person went away seemed like wishful thinking, and so he stepped out of the lab, pulled closed the door, and said, "Hello?"

He heard the squawk of rubber soles on the polished flooring, and then a middle-aged woman dressed in a tracksuit not unlike his own appeared from around a corner. With her mop of rust-gray hair, doughy face, and rotund physique, you wouldn't be blamed for mistaking her for a school crossing-guard on the cusp of retirement. However, like many in academia who prioritized mind over body, her eyes were sharp, clear, and inquisitive.

"Roy!" she said, throwing wide her stubby arms. "I was wondering who might be here at this hour!"

"I was wondering the same thing, June," Wallis said, forcing a smile. June Scarborough was a fellow psychologist completing a Ph.D. dissertation on the complexity of squirrel behavior. She and her undergraduate helpers had spent the better part of the last two years armed with nuts and stopwatches and camcorders while they stalked fox squir-rels around the campus. Dr. Wallis had run into her often last semester as she'd zeroed in on a population of squirrels liv-ing near Berkeley Way West.

"I forgot my work laptop here yesterday," she explained, slapping her forehead. "Stupid me! Because I'm heading to Colorado tomorrow with the hubby and kids to spend a week at my brother-in-law's cabin. It's a perfect opportunity for me to study tassel-eared squirrels, which are native to the southern Rocky Mountains."

"Can't separate work and pleasure, huh?"

"My work *is* pleasure, Roy! I love the furry little critters more than anything else save my kids...and even that com-parison is pretty darn close. Have you ever wondered why a squirrel rotates a nut between its front paws the way it does?"

"Can't say it's ever crossed my mind."

"It's considering a number of factors such as the nut's per-ishability and nutritional value, as well as the availability of food at that time in the presence or absence of competitors —all of this to make the critical decision of whether it eats the nut right then and there, or buries it for later. Isn't that just fascinating? Squirrels are solving complex problems right under our noses, and most people are never the wiser."

"Guess their behavior isn't so...nutty...after all."

"Oh Roy!" June said, clapping her belly like jolly old St. Nick. "Anywho! Enough about squirrels. What brings you here at close to midnight?"

"Same reason as you." He shrugged. "I had to pick up some work notes."

"Were they written in invisible ink on invisible paper?"

Dr. Wallis realized what she meant; he was empty handed. "May as well have been," he said, "because they weren't here. Must be over in my office. Guess I'm going a bit senile in my old age."

"I'll let you get to it then. I have to get home to bed

myself."

"Enjoy Colorado."

An earsplitting clap of thunder erupted in the sky almost directly overhead.

"Oh my, this storm is really something, isn't it? Don't catch your death out there, Roy!"

"Toodles, June," he said, and headed for the stairs.

Brook sat up slowly, wondering where she was and why she hurt so much. She wrinkled her nose at a rude stench that reminded her of her septic tank, only she wasn't on her houseboat. She was in the basement of—

Roy hit me.

Brook touched her jaw and found it swollen and numb. A sharper pain needled her gums, and when she probed the location with her tongue, she discovered one of her teeth had been knocked loose.

"You bastard," she mumbled. "You *hit* me."

She forced herself to her feet. After a moment of unsteady lightheadedness, she looked around the room. It was like a hodgepodge of Ikea display rooms all merged into one: bedroom, dining room, living room, kitchen, gym.

At the back, the door to the bathroom was slightly ajar, and she could see part of a tanned leg resting in a whole lot of blood.

The girl.

Dead.

Swallowing tightly, Brook turned toward the front of the room. Next to the big window obscured with crap and paper was the door to the antechamber.

She went to it, gripped the handle, and pushed.

It barely moved.

She pushed again, got it open an inch, but then it slammed shut.

Someone was leaning against it.

"Let me out, Roy!" Brook shouted, banging on the door with her open hand.

"I am sorry! I cannot!" came the reply.

It wasn't Roy; it was his assistant, Guru.

She leaned her shoulder into the door, but the Indian remained firm in his resistance.

"Guru?" she said. "Is that you?"

"Yes," he said.

"Why are you blocking the door?"

"Dr. Wallis told me you cannot leave."

"Is Roy there?"

"Not at the moment."

A pocket of hope opened inside her. "You have to let me out, Guru! Please? Before he returns."

"I cannot. He told me—"

"This is kidnapping!"

"I am sorry, ma'am, but—"

"There's a dead girl in here with me, Guru!"

Suddenly wondering where the other test subject was, she scanned the room and spotted him in a far quadrant behind the weight equipment, seated on the floor, facing the corner.

What's he doing?

And how long until he comes after me?

Brook banged the door again.

"Let me out of here, Guru! Please!"

"I am sorry but Dr. Wallis—"

"Screw him!" she blurted. "He's lost it! Can't you see that? His experiment has warped his mind!"

Guru didn't reply, and she shrieked in frustration. Then she paced, cold fear and hot rage warring inside her. Roy had hit her—*hit her*—and now he was keeping her locked up like an animal. How could this be the same man she'd cared so deeply for? How could she have been so completely fooled by him?

❖ ❖ ❖

Dr. Wallis didn't park in his typical spot along University Drive, because while he usually enjoyed the five-minute walk to Tolman Hall, he was already wet and cold and didn't look forward to getting any wetter or colder. Instead he drove directly to Tolman Hall and pulled into one of three handicapped spaces directly out front of the suspended breezeway.

He was about to enter the building when he noticed a flashlight beam bobbing through the storm toward him.

"For fuck's sake," he mumbled, recognizing who it was.

"Hiya, Dr. Wallis!" Roger Henn greeted, holding a black umbrella in one hand, the flashlight in the other. He wore a loose black rain poncho over his uniform. POLICE was stenciled across his chest in white letters. His short hair was tousled, his Monopoly Man mustache waxed, and his cheeks as ruddy as ever. "Ain't this weather something?"

"It's not raining under here, Rodge."

"Ah, righty-o." He lowered the umbrella, collapsed the ribs, and stamped the metal ferrule on the ground to shake water from the nylon canopy. His boyish eyes twinkled as they gave Dr. Wallis the up-and-down. "Lookit you, doctor," he said with a good-natured smile. "I ain't never seen you dressed so…normal. You're usually all spiffed up—in a good way. What you doing running around in this weather?"

"Had to get some notes from my office."

Unlike June Scarborough, Roger Henn didn't notice or question where the notes were. Instead he nodded generously and said, "I hear ya, I hear ya. So how's that experiment of yours going? I haven't seen you out and about in must be days now."

"I've been back and forth," Wallis said. "And the experiment is going just fine, thanks." Then, realizing he could make Roger Henn an unwitting witness in the story he and

Guru would inevitably have to spin to the police, he added, "Actually, Rodge, the experiment is just about wrapped up, to be honest. We've had a major breakthrough tonight. My assistant and I are about to go out to celebrate."

Henn grinned. "You and that cute little Chinese thing?"

"She's South Korean," Wallis corrected. "And no. Me and the bald little Indian thing."

"Ah, shucks, that'd be too bad, doc. She's a real hottie, ain't she? I haven't seen her around lately either. She always used to say hi to me in that funny accent of hers."

"She...ah...parted ways with the experiment a few days ago."

Henn frowned. "Is that so? How come?"

A rumble of thunder climaxed with a resounding explosion, causing both men to duck their heads and eye the heavens warily. Lightning flashed, branching into jagged steps.

"Jee-zeus!" Roger Henn said. "And I gotta work in this shit. So the Chinese girl's gone, huh?"

"Unfortunately, yes," Wallis said. "Her mother is sick—in Seoul. Penny returned to Korea to be with her."

"Sick as in *dying* sick? That's a real shame. Real shame. Didya bang her?"

Dr. Wallis blinked. "Excuse me?"

"Didya bang her before she left?"

"No, I did not. She was one of my students."

"I'm just asking, 'cause, word is, you don't have any problem with the ladies."

"That's the word, huh?" Wallis said, wondering who the security guard was networking with to gather such information. "Anyway, Rodge, I have to get back to work. A few details to tidy up before Guru and I hit the town."

"Sure, no problem. Wish I wasn't stuck here working, else I'd join ya. You and me, we could clean up, you know what I'm saying? I've had some luck with the divorced crowd myself. Seems they're not so picky once they got kids and wrinkles."

"You'd be right up their alley, Rodge. Just don't take no for an answer."

"Don't take no, I hear ya. By the way, doc, what exactly *is* the experiment you're wrapping up anyway? You've never told me nothing about it."

"And so it must remain that way for now, my friend. But I'm sure you'll be hearing about it soon enough."

Brook eyed one of the tubular steel chairs at the kitchen table. She picked it up, carried it to the front of the room, and launched it through the viewing window amidst a shower of shattering glass.

The assistant, Guru, appeared on the other side of the now paneless window.

"What are you doing!" he cried. "You cannot do this! Stop!"

Brook went to the nearest bed, removed the neatly made (and likely unused) duvet, and wrapped it around her right arm. She returned to the window and used her now-padded arm to clear the jagged triangles of glass jutting up from the frame.

"Stop this!" Guru said, waving his hands above his head as if this act alone would dissuade her.

"Get out of the way!" she said, tossing the duvet over the horizontal strip along the bottom of the frame.

"Stop!" Guru said, seizing the duvet and trying to pull it clear.

"Don't!" she said, grabbing her side of cover. "Let go of it!"

"You cannot do this!"

They played tug of war for a few seconds until she released her grip. With no counteracting force to offset his pulling, Guru flew onto his butt.

Go! she thought. *Now's your chance!*

Planting her hands on the windowsill—ignoring the

sharp bites in her palms from small, unseen pieces of glass—
Brook leapt over it as if it were a pommel horse and rushed
toward the door.

◆ ◆ ◆

Inside Tolman Hall, Dr. Wallis shook as much rainwater
from his beard and clothes as he could, then he went to the
basement. When he heard Guru yelling, he broke into a run.
He threw open the door to the observation room—and col-
lided into Brook.

She bounced off him, stumbling backward a few steps.

"What the hell's going on?" he demanded.

"You are back!" Guru exclaimed. He was sprawled on the
floor several feet away, his expression one of immeasurable
relief. "She was about to escape!"

Brook pointed her finger at Wallis. "Get out of my way,
Roy," she said, her words sounding mushed and slow. The
pink bruise on her right jaw had swollen and turned an angry
red. Her expression resembled that of a cornered beast: wary
yet dangerous.

"I can't do that right now, Brook."

"*Let me go!*" she screamed, spittle flying from her mouth.

"I will, Brook, of course, I will," he reassured her. "But not
until the experiment has concluded."

Her body was stiff yet at the ready, as if she were considering charging past him. Her breathing came in labored
heaves. "You don't have to do this."

"Do what?"

She didn't answer, and he didn't like what that silence
implied. If she believed he had it in him to kill her, she would
never keep quiet for him, ever.

"Do what, Brook?" he repeated, smiling.

"Holding me here," she said, seeming to intuit his thinking and changing the narrative. "You don't have to hold me
here. I'm not going to...tell anybody anything."

"You already mentioned going to the police."

"As an option. But if that's not...what you think should be done, then...let's talk."

"This isn't the time to talk, Brook." He lowered his voice. "I don't know if you've noticed our friend Chad in the other room, but he's not in the best of health. I'm not sure how much time he has left, and I really need to get a look inside his head before he expires."

"Roy! Please!"

"After, Brook. We'll talk after. I need to help Chad right now. Now go back into the sleep laboratory.

"No."

Dr. Wallis stepped toward her. "Let's not repeat what happened earlier," he said meaningfully.

Her eyes went to his clenched fists—and the fight seemed to leave her. Shoulders sagging, she turned and entered the sleep laboratory.

"Block the door," Wallis instructed Guru, then followed her into the room, closing the door behind him.

Brook stood in the kitchen.

"Back of the room," he told her.

"I'm not going to go anywhere—"

"Back of the fucking room, Brook. *Now.*"

She went to the back of the room, her stride sure if not defiant. He watched her until she reached the far wall. Then he crossed the room to where Chad was seated on the floor facing the same corner he'd been facing for the past twenty-four hours.

Dr. Wallis' pulse had quickened, and he could feel sweat slicking the palms of his hands. What he was about to attempt was anything but guaranteed to succeed. He had the advantage, certainly. Chad was blind. Nevertheless, as soon as the needle pierced the Australian's skin, the advantage would be lost. Which meant Wallis would have to inject him quickly, then put space between them until the paralytic drug took effect.

You screw this up, man, you're going to have someone with the strength of a gorilla bashing in your skull.

I won't screw it up.

Dr. Wallis stopped behind Chad. From his left jacket pocket, he produced a syringe he'd collected from his lab, and from his right jacket pocket, a vial of Vecuronium. Both the metal band around the top of the vial and the over-seal read: "Warning: Paralyzing Agent."

Holding the syringe in his hand like a pencil, the needle pointing upward, he pulled back the plunger. He plugged the needle into the rubber top of the vial and depressed the plunger, filling the vial with air to prevent a vacuum from forming. He turned the vial upside-down, then pulled the plunger as far back as it would go, thinking, *Going to be one big dose, Chad, my man. One doozy of a dose, in fact.*

Under normal circumstances—say a doctor prepping a patient for surgery—he or she would inject the drug into the patient intravenously. Dr. Wallis clearly did not have the luxury of this option. Instead, he would inject the drug straight into Chad's spinal column. This would destroy the nerve cells along his spine and induce permanent paralysis—which, of course, was exactly what Wallis wanted.

Crouching, Wallis judged where Chad's spinal cord would be beneath the sweatshirt, counted to three in his head, then jabbed the needle and depressed the plunger.

Chad shot to his feet, caterwauling in unholy rage.

Dr. Wallis scuttled away, preparing himself for any eventuality. Chad flared his arms blindly, lurching at unseen assailants, the hoodie slipping free of his head. Then, spinning in a circle like a dog trying to catch its tail, he unsuccessfully probed for the needle protruding from his back.

He soon slowed, then stumbled. He dropped to his knees, then his side. He stopped moving completely.

That's when Brook began to scream.

"What did you do to him? Look at his face! *What did you do to him?*"

"I didn't do that!" Dr. Wallis told her. "He did it to himself!"

"*He doesn't have a face!*"

"Brook! Listen to me! I didn't do that—"

"It's doesn't matter. It was your drugs that did that."

She sank to her butt, dropped her head into her lap, and sobbed.

Trying his best to ignore her, Wallis wheeled the cart with the EEG machine next to where Chad had fallen. He rolled the Australian onto his back and slid the electrode headband over the pulpy mess that was his forehead. He clicked on the amplifier, which boosted the electrical signals produced by the millions of nerve cells in Chad's brain, then pulled up a chair to study the wave patterns appearing on the monitor.

Guru was speaking via the intercom, asking if everything was all right. Dr. Wallis had no idea how long he had been staring unmoving at the monitor, but he was no longer seeing the data on the screen. He was thinking about all the wonderful ways in which his life was about to forever change.

"Professor, can you hear me?"

Dr. Wallis snapped back to the moment, feeling as giddy as a boy on Christmas morning. "Guru, my beautiful friend, get your butt in here!" he said with a huge smile.

Brook, he noticed, had raised her head from her lap in curiosity at the sudden commotion.

"It's over, Brook," he told her, his smile growing. "We did it."

"What are you talking about, Roy?"

The door opened and Guru entered.

"Get over here, brother."

Guru looked apprehensively at Brook.

"She's not going to go anywhere," Wallis told him. "She's going to want to hear what I have to say. I mean it. She's really going to want to hear what I have to say." He opened his arms wide. "So get on over here and give me a hug."

Guru frowned. "Professor?"

"Jesus Christ, man!" Wallis went to the Indian and lifted him off the ground in a bear hug, turning in a circle while laughing. When he set Guru down, he rubbed the Indian's bald head affectionately. "You stayed with me, man. You. Stayed. With. Me." He slapped Guru on the shoulder, perhaps with too much gusto, because Guru nearly fell over.

"What's going on, Roy?" Brook asked.

"Neuroscience 101," Dr. Wallis said, slipping easily into lecture mode. "Our brain cells—aka neurons—communicate with each other via electrical signals and are always active, even when we're asleep, and it's this communication that's at the root of all our thoughts, emotions, and behaviors. Essentially, what you think of as 'consciousness' is actually an ever-changing concert of electrical impulses. Brook's brain, mine, Guru's, they all have about one hundred billion of these neurons. An EEG"—he waved at the equipment on the cart—"tracks this neural activity. Picture yourself dropping a pebble into the middle of a still pond and the ripples it would make on the water. Now picture the pebble as a neuron and the pond as the surface of the brain and the ripples as brainwaves. You with me, Brook?"

She nodded.

"Good, now listen up, both of you, because this is the important stuff. Instead of dropping a single pebble into the pond, imagine yourself dropping an entire handful. You'd get a whole lot of overlapping ripples. This is similar to what happens when you have multiple neurons firing off synchronized electrical pulses: you get a whole lot of overlapping brainwaves. An EEG detects these brainwaves and divides them into different bandwidths measured in Hertz. Slow delta bands are less than 4 Hz. Theta bands are anywhere between 4 to 8 Hz. Alpha bands range from 8 to 12 Hz. Beta bands, the most abundant during our normal state of waking, are between 14 and 30 Hz, and gamma bands, the fastest, are between 30 and 80 Hz. Together the brainwaves, or bandwidths, create our continuous spectrum of consciousness, always reacting and changing according to what we're doing and feeling. When slower ones dominate, we feel tired and sluggish. When higher ones dominate, we feel hyper-alert. So all those funny lines that appeared on that computer screen during Chad's EEG? They're his brainwaves, his consciousness. And much as a fortune teller reads tea leaves to gain insight into the natural world, I read these bandwidths to gain insight into Chad's mind."

"And...?" Guru asked eagerly.

"After I filtered out all of the artifacts and extraneous information, I discovered an entire spectrum of...shadow... brainwaves, I suppose you might call them, although they all possessed different amplitudes and frequencies than the originals."

Guru and Brook stared at him like deer caught in headlights.

"*Shadow brainwaves!*" he repeated, doing his damnedest to keep his composure despite the high he was riding.

"I have no idea what that means," Brook said.

"It means, my lovely, lovely darling," Dr. Wallis said, grinning wider than ever, "that residing within Chad's brain are two distinct consciousnesses."

"Impossible!" Guru blurted immediately.

"No, it is not, my good man. The proof is in the pudding, right over there on that computer."

"Two consciousnesses?" Brook said. "You mean like Dr. Jekyll and Mr. Hyde?"

"Not at all," Wallis said. "I'm not talking about a common dissociative identity disorder. There are literally *two distinct consciousnesses* inside him. Two people in one. Or, given what I suspect to be at the root of our beings, one person and one demon."

Brook shot to her feet. "What are you talking about, Roy? This is ridiculous!"

"Don't be so quick to judge, my darling, when there is still so much you have yet to understand."

Wallis explained.

He repeated to her everything he'd told Guru the day before. The mice with the mutated genes that led to the development of the stimulant gas. The significance of microsleep, or the lack thereof, and how absolute sleep deprivation turned the mice into murderous cannibals. And ultimately his theory that all biological lifeforms are born with madness inside them, kept in check only by instinct and sleep.

Brook interrupted him about a thousand times, but when he finally got it all out, her skepticism had been replaced with studious contemplation. Even better news, she no longer appeared as though she were in fear of her life. In fact, he began to wonder if he could win her over after all.

"Let me get this straight, Roy," she said now. "You mentioned *demon* earlier. That's the word you used. One person, one demon inside that young man. Are you suggesting this... madness...inside us is a *demon*?"

"A demon. The devil. Hell itself. Whatever tickles your fancy. They're all suitable metaphors for, yes, the madness within us, which I believe to be responsible for the evil we perform."

She looked at Chad, then quickly looked away again, the tone of her skin draining to the color of winter. "And it was this madness that caused him to do that to himself—"

Wallis' eyes bulged.

◆ ◆ ◆

Chad was sitting up.

Which, given the dosage of Vecuronium that Dr. Wallis had injected into him—*into his spinal column no less*—should have been very much impossible.

Wallis withdrew another syringe and vial from his jacket pocket and filled the syringe even as he crossed the room. As he approached Chad, he slowed to a stealthy walk, knowing the Australian still had his hearing. Very quietly, he crouched in front of Chad, waving his hand before the young man's ruined face. The Australian didn't react.

Dr. Wallis wasn't going to take any chances this time.

He hovered the needle directly before the Australian's heart.

"No!" Brook cried—too late.

Wallis had already plunged the needle into Chad's heart. He inhaled sharply—a terrible dry and rattling sound—but did little else. Then he slumped backward and lay still.

"You said this was over, Roy!" Brook cried. "You said—"

"It should have been over, Brook. I gave him ten times the regular dose of that drug directly into his spine. It should have..." He didn't finish this sentence for fear of alienating her further, but he thought, *It should have paralyzed every muscle in his body, even those used for breathing, which in the absence of ventilatory support, would have led to asphyxiation.*

"It should have what, Roy?"

"Nothing."

"It should have killed him?"

"Look at him, Brook!" he snapped. "You think he was going to survive regardless? You think he would have *wanted* to survive?"

She turned her back to him, and to hell if she wasn't crying again.

Dr. Wallis stood and went to the door.

"Where are you going, professor?" Guru asked him.

"To turn off the gas."

When Dr. Roy Wallis returned to the sleep laboratory after shutting off the stimulant gas, he said, "It's over now, Brook. For good."

She wiped tears from her eyes and took a deep breath. "Okay."

"Okay?" he said.

"Yes," she said.

"What does 'okay' mean?"

"It means...I'm okay with...everything."

Dr. Wallis studied her closely. He couldn't decide whether she was speaking honestly or only telling him what he wanted to hear. Probably the latter.

"So what do you think we should do now?" he asked her.

"I think... What do *you* want to do?"

"Guru and I had plans to go out and celebrate. Right, buddy?"

Guru nodded with reticence.

"Celebrate," Brook repeated.

"I know what you're thinking, Brook. How could we celebrate when we have two dead bodies on our hands?"

"Your experiment has been a great success, Roy. It will no doubt change the world, or how we perceive the world. But, yes, you're right. There are two dead people down here." Her voice choked on the words *dead people*, yet she pressed on. "We can't ignore that fact. The police won't ignore that fact either, despite the experiment's success. But you and your assistant have plans to *celebrate*?"

"I hear what you're saying, Brook. Loud and clear. So let me explain. Less than twenty-four hours ago, Chad and Sharon were in fine health. They were experiencing hallucinations and such, but they were in fine *physical* health. Sharon took her life only this morning. I was sleeping. Guru woke me. I was too late to save her. And calling the police would not have saved Chad either. He had already done what he'd done to himself. I wasn't aware of this at the time because he had his hoodie on. But he'd already done it."

"You knew what you were going to find, didn't you, Roy?" she said. "You knew about the so-called shadow consciousness?"

"Yes."

"Was it present in your mice?"

"Yes."

"And that wasn't good enough for you? You had to trial the gas on humans?"

"We're getting off topic here, Brook," he said tersely. "What I'm trying to say is that if I'd shut down the experiment after Sharon's death, and called the police, we wouldn't be discussing this legal gray area right now. Sharon had signed a consent form. She knew there would be risks participating in the experiment. Unfortunately, she succumbed to one of those risks."

"But she didn't know the extent of the risks, did she? She didn't know what happened to the mice, did she?"

"Just finish hearing me out, Brook. If I'd shut down the experiment, if I'd called the police, I wouldn't have recorded Chad's brainwaves, and the experiment would have been for nothing. Chad and Sharon would have died for nothing. So, really, all I'm guilty of, if I'm guilty of anything, is not reporting Sharon's death right away. I'm not even sure that's a crime. But why wade through murky legal waters at all?" He held up a hand. "Imagine this scenario. Chad and Sharon are still alive. They've...crossed over, for lack of a better expression...but they're still alive and haven't harmed themselves.

I conduct the EEG on Chad, the experiment concludes, I turn off the gas, and we all go out and celebrate, you, me, Guru. When I return in the morning, I find the Australians in their current states. They reacted badly to coming off the gas when I wasn't present. They tripped out and performed these horrific acts of self-harm when I wasn't present. I can't be held accountable for that. Nobody gets fucked over. End of story."

Brook was silent.

Guru was looking at his shoes.

"All we'd really be doing, Brook," Dr. Wallis pressed, "is postponing calling the police. Considering the implications of the Sleep Experiment, don't you think postponing calling the police for a few hours is justifiable? I mean, I've just fucking proven that a second, repressed consciousness resides within every member of humankind—"

"Did you hear that?" Brook said.

Dr. Wallis looked at Chad.

"I swear," she added, "I heard him say something."

"I heard him too, professor," Guru said.

"Impossible!" Wallis crossed the room and stopped before Chad. The Australian looked just as dead as ever. True, Wallis had never checked his pulse after injecting the paralytic drug into his heart, but there was no way anybody could have survived that.

There was no way anybody could have survived the paralytic drug injected in their spine either.

A cold ball of unease forming in his gut, Dr. Wallis checked Chad's wrist for a pulse. He couldn't find one—

"Ache."

Wallis sprang back in surprise.

"See!" Brook said.

"*How?*" Wallis hissed.

"What did he say, professor?" Guru asked.

"I—I don't know. 'Ache,' I think."

"*Ache?*" Brook said. "Oh God, he's in pain!"

Heart pounding, Dr. Wallis crept closer to Chad's body. "Chad?" he said. "Buddy?"

"Aaaaaaaache…" He spoke the word without moving the lipless, crusty hole that had once been his mouth.

"This is impossible," Wallis said. "It's simply impossible."

"*Aaaaaaaaache…*"

"Help him, Roy!" Brook cried.

Wallis realized Chad was still wearing the electrode headband. He slapped the keyboard to wake the monitor. Chad's brainwaves appeared on the screen, only now…

"My God," he breathed.

Guru appeared next to him. "What is it, professor?"

"It can't be…"

"*What is it?*"

"It appears his shadow consciousness isn't a shadow anymore. It's his *only* consciousness."

Abruptly Chad began convulsing, as if suffering a major seizure.

"Help him!" Brook cried.

"Don't touch him!" Wallis ordered.

Abruptly, Chad let loose a scream so loud and shrill it sounded utterly inhuman. His head flailed back and forth. The cords in his neck stood out like knotted ropes. His hands clenched and unclenched while his body spasmed. Thick, sludgy blood oozed from his eye sockets and nose cavity.

Then the seizure, if that's what it was, ceased. The Australian went still.

"Look!" Guru said, pointing to the monitor.

The fast scribbling patterns of Chad's shadow beta brainwaves, indicative of an active cortex and an intense state of attention, had transitioned to slower, low-frequency shadow theta waves.

In the next moment, the brainwaves flat-lined.

"He died!" Guru said.

"At the very moment he fell asleep," Dr. Wallis marveled. "Fascinating!"

"Is he dead for certain this time?"

Dr. Wallis toed Chad's body. "Seems like it."

"What did you mean, professor, when you said his shadow consciousness was his *only* consciousness?"

"Exactly that, Guru. The person Chad had once been had died, and all that remained was the demon within him."

"Could that be why the drugs did not have the anticipated effects on him?"

"I'd bet the farm on it. And I'd also bet he—or *it*—wasn't saying 'ache.' It was saying 'wake.'" It somehow knew we'd turned off the gas, and it knew it had to remain awake or else..."

They both looked at Chad's body again.

"So the demon *took him over*," Guru said, appearing appalled at this possibility. "It *possessed* him."

Wallis nodded. "It makes one wonder whether all those cases of demon possessions and exorcisms over the centuries weren't total bullshit. Perhaps the victims were in fact suffering from severe cases of total sleep deprivation..."

"Oh my, professor," Guru said, shaking his head. "This is not good. This is not good at all. We have opened Pandora's Box! When others learn of this discovery, when they too begin to play God...what if these demons *get loose and take over*? Not only a few individuals, but the entire human race?"

Dr. Wallis grinned. "Sort of sums up the Book of Revelations pretty nicely, doesn't it?"

"I do not joke, professor! *What have we done?*"

"Calm down, man! What are you freaking out about? We haven't opened the gates of hell. We've simply located where they are. Can you grasp that? We're not villains! *We're heroes!*"

The door connecting the sleep laboratory and observation room banged closed.

Brook had fled.

Dr. Roy Wallis gave chase, stopping when the narrow hallway opened up before the inoperable elevator and the bathrooms. The primary staircase was tucked away out of sight to the left of the elevator, easy to miss. Conversely, the secondary staircase was around the corner to the right. The layout was disorienting, and during the early days of the Sleep Experiment, he had mistakenly taken the emergency staircase on a number of occasions—mistakenly because it brought you to the loading dock on the ground floor rather than the building's main entrance.

Dr. Wallis had no way of knowing which way Brook had gone, and so he randomly chose the primary staircase. He emerged in the peach- and avocado-colored lobby. It was deserted. A glance through one of the four glass entrance doors that gave to the breezeway didn't reveal Brook fleeing into the night, which meant she had likely become disoriented herself and had taken the secondary staircase.

Wallis went west down the dark hallways, and much to his relief, he discovered the silhouetted shape of Brook in one branching corridor, coming his way.

Spotting him, she cried out in surprise, put on the brakes, and reversed, slipping out of sight through a doorway that led back to the secondary staircase.

Wallis followed hot on her heels, ascending the steps two at a time, his eyes already adjusting to the gloom. Although he couldn't see her, he could hear her shoes slapping the cement steps above him, indicating she had bypassed the first floor. When he reached the second floor, he paused to listen. He made out her footsteps fleeing down a distant hallway. Knowing he could lose her amongst the maze of corridors, he resumed his pursuit, sprinting full speed, and he soon had her in his sights once more. She was fifty feet ahead of him, racing east down the long hallway that spanned the breezeway and connected the psychology and education departments.

She swung left and out of sight. He reached the same spot five seconds later and followed her into the library. Although the wooden cubicles and tables and chairs had all been removed, for whatever reason the demolition contractors had left behind the steel bookstacks.

Through the empty shelving—the books had long-ago been transferred to the Gardner Stacks and the Social Research Library—Dr. Wallis glimpsed Brook climbing the staircase to the mezzanine.

And he knew he had her, as those stairs were the only way up or down.

Slowing to catch his breath, he said, "Stop this, Brook! What the hell are you doing? I thought you *understood*? I thought you were going to play ball?"

"Leave me alone!" she shouted from above him. "Go away!"

He ascended the stairs. "I haven't given up on you, Brook," he lied. "We can still work this out. Just come back to the basement with me."

"Go away, Roy! I've called the police! They're on their way!"

A jolt of fear shot through him before he told himself she was bluffing. Her phone hadn't been on her when he'd transferred her, unconscious, from the air mattress to Sharon's bed. Which meant it had likely been in her handbag on the table in the observation room. And unless she'd had the presence of mind to grab it when she'd fled the sleep laboratory —which he doubted, because why not simply take her entire handbag, which would have been easier and faster—he had nothing to worry about.

When he reached the top of the staircase, Wallis spotted Brook at the far end of the aisle dividing seven or eight rows of stacks, swinging her head left and right, knowing she had nowhere left to go.

He started down the aisle toward her.

"Why are you doing this, Roy?"

"Doing what, Brook? You're the one running around like a chicken with its head chopped off."

"Please let me go."

"Come back to the basement with me."

She dashed to her right, and by the time he reached where she had been standing, she had put the full length of the steel shelf between them.

He started down the row; she started up the parallel one.

They met in the middle of the stack with only the steel shelving separating them.

They were so close to one another he could see the perspiration beading her shadowed face and the fear swimming in her eyes.

"Where's your phone, Brook?"

She didn't say anything.

"Didn't you say you called the police?"

She stepped left. He stepped left also.

She stepped right. He stepped right.

"Nowhere to go, Brook."

"I loved you, Roy."

"Did you?"

"Why are you doing this?"

"All I'm doing, Brook, is preventing you from sabotaging my life's work."

"I haven't done anything!"

"It's not what you've done. It's what you're going to do. You're going to betray me."

"I'm not, Roy. I just want to go home."

"If I let you leave, you're going to go back to your little boathouse, snuggle up in bed, and forget you ever stopped by here this evening?"

"Yes!"

"Bullshit!"

He feinted left, as if to sprint around the bookstack. She stumbled right, yet when she realized he wasn't coming for her, she went no further.

Slowly, confidently, he walked back down his row so he stood opposite her once more.

"How long are you going to keep this up, Brook?"

"I was wrong, Roy. I shouldn't have questioned you. You couldn't have saved Chad. I understand that now. I'm on your side."

"Good," he said. "Come back to the basement with me then."

"Why?"

"So I can keep an eye on you."

"For how long?"

Dr. Wallis clenched his jaw. The charade was up. They both knew the other's real intentions. They were simply wasting time.

Wallis dashed to the left, deciding the only way to end this would be to chase her down, even it if took him a dozen loops around the shelving.

Brook ran right, but instead of rounding the end of the stack and coming up the other side, she scissor-stepped over the stanchion handrail that ran along the edge of the mezzanine.

"Brook!" he shouted, believing she would jump.

She didn't. She lowered herself so she hung from her hands from the edge of the balcony, reducing the distance between her feet and the floor below.

She let go as he lunged for her.

She landed with a pained grunt, and even as he was deciding whether to do as she had done, or return to the staircase, she was scrambling to her feet and fleeing once more.

"Shit!" he said, and ran to the stairs.

Guru Rampal knew he had made a grave mistake.

He should have done the right thing after Sharon had killed herself and called the police. By going along with Dr. Wallis' plan to keep her death under wraps until the experiment concluded, he had committed himself to a path that, at every unexpected turn, had proved very difficult to leave no matter how much he'd wanted to.

And, ultimately, look where it had led him.

Sharon dead.

Chad dead.

Brook...

Yes, what of the pretty woman Brook?

If Dr. Wallis caught her, he wasn't going to sit her down for a stern talking to. He had punched her in the face. He had imprisoned her against her will.

If he caught her...he wasn't going to sit her down for a stern talking to, no...and he wasn't going to let her go either.

He was going to kill her.

Guru couldn't believe he was entertaining such a thought, but after everything that had happened over the last few hours, he knew it to be the truth.

You can't let him do this!

No, he couldn't.

Guru began racking his brain for options.

When Brook reached the hallway spanning the breezeway, she knew she had two options: run or hide.

Her instinct was to run, but reason insisted Roy would catch her. He was faster than her; he knew the building better.

Besides, even if she managed to find her way outside, where would she go? Her car was parked a block away. Nobody was around to help her.

Her mind had processed all these thoughts in less than a second, and it offered up its counsel just as quickly:

Hide then.

She ducked into the second room on the left of the hall-way.

It was empty but dark.

She went to the corner to the left of the door where the shadows seemed thickest.

She waited.

When Dr. Roy Wallis emerged from the library, he expected to see Brook sprinting down the long hallway, back-tracking to the building's entrance.

Yet it was empty.

He listened. Didn't hear her footsteps.

Which wasn't right.

Sound carried in the old cement structure, almost as though it were a giant echo chamber. Given she hadn't gotten that much of a head start on him, he should still be able to hear her, whichever way she'd gone.

Unless she'd decided to go to ground.

Dr. Wallis started down the hallway, slowly, to mask his approach. Six classrooms lined each side of the corridor. He entered the first one on the left. Rain pelted the large windows that faced Hearst Avenue. Although his eyes had adjusted to the lack of light, they couldn't probe the thick shadows that had pooled in the far corners of the room. Only when he'd moved all the way to the center of the room was he satisfied it was empty. He returned to the hallway and entered the first room on the right.

Empty too.

A greasy sensation built in his gut as he worried that Brook may have somehow given him the slip, that she was already outside, on her way to the police to blow the lid off the Sleep Experiment before he could tie up all the loose ends and hammer out a plausible story.

Bitch! he thought, spangles of red creeping into his vision. *Should have finished her off when I had the chance!*

He returned to the hallway and entered the second room on the left. A deafening clap of thunder shook the sky, and had Wallis not instinctively flinched and turned his head, he might not have seen Brook slinking out the door behind him.

He hurried quickly yet quietly after her, and he managed to close the distance between them to less than five feet before she either heard or sensed him.

Glancing over her shoulder, her eyes flashed wide and she issued a high-pitched yelp. She picked up her speed, no longer concerned about stealth—but it was too late.

His right hand snagged the back of her blouse, dragging her to a halt. She spun, swinging her arms. He got his own arms around her. She yelled and twisted and kicked her feet so ferociously he could barely hold on to her.

"Stop it, Brook!"

"Let me go!"

"Stop it!"

He launched her sideways. She bounced off the cement wall and crumpled to her hands and knees. Towering over her, he gripped fistfuls of her blouse and hiked her to her feet.

"Two choices, Brook," he snarled, his face inches from hers. "You walk with me back to the basement, nice and civil, or I knock the sense out of you one more time and drag you by the hair. What's it going to be?"

Guru was in the sleep laboratory seated on Chad's bed with his head held in his hands when Dr. Wallis marched Brook through the door.

"Thanks for the help, buddy," Wallis remarked sardonically.

Guru looked up. "I was waiting for you to return, professor. I wanted to tell you—you cannot do this." His eyes flicked momentarily to Brook.

"Can't do what?" Wallis asked.

Suddenly and comically, Guru produced a steak knife that had been stuck in the waistband of his pants against the small of his back. He held it before him in a shaking hand.

"What the hell is that?" Wallis demanded.

"Do not harm her, professor!"

"Put the goddamn knife away."

"Let her go!"

Dr. Wallis considered the situation, then said, "You're fucking up, my man. But I'm going to offer you a way out."

Guru frowned. "What do you mean?"

"Kill her with that knife."

"*What?*"

"She's going to tell the police on us—"

"I am not—"

"Shut up, Brook!" Wallis shouted, glaring at her until she broke eye contact. To Guru: "She's going to tell the police on us. Try to pin Chad and Sharon's deaths on us."

"But we did nothing..."

"That's exactly it, buddy. We did *nothing* after Sharon died. We continued the experiment with Chad. The cops aren't going to look too favorably on that. But when you kill Brook, we no longer have that problem. We'll come back tomorrow and discover the three bodies."

"Three?"

"Just like I told you earlier. The experiment concluded. We turned off the gas. We went out to celebrate. Now—here's the new twist. Brook comes by to monitor the Australians for us while they sleep off the gas. They begin behaving oddly. She goes in to check on them and they kill her, then they kill themselves. It's even better than the original story!"

After this declaration, a momentous silence filled the sleep laboratory. Then Brook began to cry. Guru shook his head frantically.

"No, professor," he said, waving the knife. "We cannot! We cannot!"

"We have no choice!"

"That is murder!"

"Jesus, Guru, do you want to go to prison?"

"This cannot be happening. How did you talk me into any of this in the first place?"

"I'll hold her down. All you have to do is cover her face with a pillow. Then it'll be over—"

A bloodcurdling, filthy sound erupted from the other side of the sleep laboratory.

Chad was sitting up.

And laughing.

Dr. Roy Wallis stared at the faceless abomination in disbelief.

It was impossible, utterly impossible, that Chad could be alive. *I watched him die! I witnessed his brainwaves flatline!*

But there he was, sitting up.

And laughing.

At us?

Chad pushed himself to his feet then, not in the lumbering manner of the rotting undead, but in the easy, graceful way of a virile twenty-two year old in perfect health.

"What are you?" Wallis demanded as reality seemed to fade around him in a hot wave of melting light. "*What are you?*"

"I. Think. You. Know."

Although Chad's lipless mouth didn't appear to move, the slow, mushy words most definitely originated from within the permanent rictus.

Dr. Wallis shuffled backward a step. Guru and Brook seemed rooted to the floor in wide-eyed, slack-jawed shock.

"*What are you?*" Wallis demanded once more, ashamed by the naked fear in his voice.

"You," the thing that was Chad rasped. "The deepest animal part of you...that you hide from...in your beds." He stepped forward, sightless yet surefooted. "What you sedate into silence...every night." Another step. "We are *you*."

Issuing a low, fragile whimper, Guru bolted for the door.

The Chad-thing moved incredibly fast. It rushed across the room, crashing blindly into Sharon's bed. It fell to its knees atop the mattress but regained its feet with barely a second lost.

It reached Guru just as he opened the door, seizing the Indian from behind and throwing him back into the sleep laboratory as if he weighed little more than a rag doll.

Guru must have soared a good fifteen feet through the air before crashing into the refrigerator. The steak knife clattered away from him across the floor.

The Chad-thing cocked its head to one side.

Listening, Wallis thought.

Guru seemed to understand this too as he clamped his trembling mouth closed in a desperate effort to suppress any unwanted sounds.

The Chad-thing moved toward the kitchen.

It passed within a foot of Dr. Wallis, who summoned all his willpower to remain still and silent.

Brook, he noticed, was a bloodless white statute.

The Chad-thing continued moving toward the last sound it heard.

Eyes bulging, Guru raised his hands in the slow, cautious manner of a man who had a gun pointed at him, then pressed them over his mouth.

The Chad-thing cocked its head to the left, then to the right.

In the face of the approaching nightmare, Guru's bladder

gave out. The groin area of his beige khaki trousers darkened, then the legs, and then urine was leaking out of his left cuff, spraying the floor.

The Chad-thing zeroed in on the noise.

It grabbed Guru by the head and lifted him high enough his feet dangled in the air.

Guru was screaming now, and Dr. Wallis thought it was in terror before realizing it was in pain, for the Chad-thing had dug its thumbs into Guru's eye sockets as if they were the finger holes of a ten-pin bowling ball.

Blood gushed down the Indian's cheeks like bright red tears.

Backing away from the gruesome scene as silently as possible, Wallis slipped unnoticed from the sleep laboratory.

Brook had gotten her shit together enough to follow him, and together they hurried through the observation room. Yet as soon as Dr. Wallis opened the door to the hallway, he heard the Chad-thing wail, followed by a loud commotion.

It had heard the door open.

It was coming.

"Run!" Brook shouted from behind him, shoving him through the door.

Wallis ran for all he was worth. He didn't hesitate when he came to the defunct elevator. He blew straight past it and made a hard right to reach the main staircase. Moments later he reached the ground floor. He shoved open one of the glass doors and shot through it. In his haste and panic, however, he tripped over his own feet and toppled forward, his knees and palms skinning the wet pavement before his body rolled twice. But then he was back on his feet, bee-lining toward his car, thanking God he had parked in one of the disability spots right out front of the building.

Digging the remote key from his pocket, he jabbed the

unlock button, whipped open the Audi's driver's side door, and slid inside. At the same time the passenger side door opened, and Brook jumped in next to him.

Both doors thudded closed moments before the Chad-thing burst through them into the storming night.

Dr. Wallis reached for the push-button ignition, but before he pressed it, Brook seized his wrist.

She was shaking her head: no.

Wallis looked past her to the Chad-thing.

It was moving in their direction, but it seemed aimless now, as if it had lost their scent.

Our sound, Wallis amended.

He nodded so Brook knew he understood the meaning of her head shake, though he kept his hand hovering near the push-button, ready to press it in a heartbeat.

The Chad-thing banged blindly into the Audi. It raged against the roof with its fists, then began making its way around the trunk. It moved down Dr. Wallis' side of the car and stopped next to his window. It stood there for a dreadfully long moment, silent, no doubt listening for movement with its super-human hearing, which seemed matched only by its super-human strength. Wallis didn't understand the physiology behind these amazing feats, and he realized the Sleep Experiment had not reached its conclusion. In fact, it had only just begun.

There's so much to learn about these...demon souls.

So much to learn about...us.

The Demon Soul—for that was now how Dr. Wallis thought of the Chad-thing—turned quickly so it was facing Hearst Avenue.

Wallis saw a flashlight beam arcing through the dark some fifty feet away.

Brook saw it too and gasped.

Hearing her, the creature turned back to the car, bending over to peer into the driver's side window with its empty, bloody eye sockets.

Wallis didn't flex a muscle. Didn't dare to breathe. A bead of perspiration slid down his brow and into his left eye, stinging it.

He didn't blink.

"Roy?" the distant voice of Roger Henn called. "That you?"

The Demon Soul vanished from the window, reappearing a moment later moving in a quick gait on all fours toward the police officer.

"No!" Brook breathed, and tried to smack the car horn.

Wallis grabbed her hand and said, "*What the fuck are you doing?*"

"It's going to kill him!"

"Better him than us!"

"Roy, no! Enough!"

When she couldn't yank her hand free from his grip, she screamed.

The Demon Soul, Dr. Wallis saw in alarm, stopped to look back at the car.

"Hey, who's there?" Roger Henn called, picking up his pace. The curtain of rain and inky darkness clearly obscured his vision, and he didn't see the creature until he was nearly on top of it. Skidding to a stop, he said, "Whoa—oh boy! *What?*"

Brook slapped the horn.

The Demon Soul paid the sharp *honk!* no notice. It sprang toward Roger Henn. The big cop, nimble for his girth, dodged the attack, tearing his pistol free from its holster.

"Freeze!" he shouted, aiming the weapon at the creature. Then, almost as an afterthought: "Police!"

Thunder exploded. A detonation of lightning shredded the night sky, casting a stroboscopic effect over the unfolding action. The Demon Soul scrambled forward. Henn fired two shots at point-blank range, the twin rounds dropping the creature to the ground.

Brook threw open her door. Wallis reached in front of her and pulled the door shut again.

"Let me go!" she shrieked.

"*Quiet!*" he hissed.

"Roy?" Henn called, close enough to now recognize the Audi. "*Roy?*" he repeated, his voice several octaves higher than usual. "What the fuck is going on? *What happened to this guy?*"

"Help!" Brook yelled. "Help me!"

Wallis punched her in the mouth. She slumped against the door, blood leaking from her lips, but still holding onto consciousness. He punched her again, this time in the nose, and heard her nasal cartilage crunch. She went slack.

"Out of the car, Roy!" Police Officer Roger Henn shouted. "I can see you! Leave that woman alone!"

But all Roger Henn could think was, *I shot that man, I killed him, goddammit I killed him!* And in concert with this, *What happened to him? He had no face! It looked like it'd been chewed off!*

"Hear me, Roy? Come out of the car with your hands where I can—*Jesus!*"

Henn stared dumbfounded as the guy with no face and two .40 caliber rounds in his chest pushed himself to his knees, then his feet.

Henn raised the Glock 22, but the man's Lazarus-act had filled his veins with ice and slowed his reflexes. Before he could squeeze off another round, the man was on him, tackling him to the ground, clawing and biting him with a strength and ferocity that defied comprehension.

Dr. Wallis jabbed the ignition button, put the Audi into reverse, and swung out of the parking spot. He shifted to first and stepped on the gas. His first thought was to speed away down Hearst Avenue. In the same instant, however, he changed his mind and swerved left toward the Demon Soul. Lit up in the stark white light of the LED headlights, it was hunched over Roger Henn's unmoving body, throwing fist-fuls of the cop's innards into the air as one might throw rice or confetti at a wedding.

Dr. Wallis realized he was screaming uncontrollably as the Audi barreled down on the monstrosity.

Hearing the vehicle approach, it leapt to its feet.

Wallis shut his eyes as the three-thousand pounds of German engineering plowed into the Demon Soul, launching it up the hood and over the roof.

Slamming the brakes, he opened his eyes to find the windshield spider-webbed and bloodied.

He glanced in the rearview mirror and saw the creature lying on the pavement awash in the hellish red glow of the car's taillights.

It twitched.

Wallis shifted into reverse, floored the accelerator. The tires squealed.

The Audi jumped, once, twice.

Whud! Whud!

Wallis stamped the brakes.

Lying on the pavement in front of the car now, lit up once more in the headlights, the Demon Soul was a bloody lump of flesh and blood.

A bloody *unmoving* lump of flesh and blood.

Brook stirred, and maybe moaned, but the darkness remained impenetrable, cloaking her thoughts in a black fog.

Dimly she knew she was in the passenger's seat of Roy's car. Understood her life was in danger, from both Roy and the poor Australian, or whatever it was that the poor Australian had become. Yet she couldn't seem to clear her mind or move her body...and then, from a place very far away, someone spoke her name.

She moved her mouth, formed a word, though what it was she wasn't sure.

"Brook?"

The voice was closer now.

"Roy...?" she managed.

"Brook?"

She forced open her eyes. This set off bright lances of agony inside her skull. She could see little more than dark shapes, though she could hear the steady, angry drone of the rain falling on the roof of the car.

Cool, wet air. Hands shaking her shoulder.

Someone had opened her door.

It was Roy, soaking wet, his hair plastered to his skull, rain streaking his face.

He hit me—again.

She touched her face. It felt numb, like it belonged to a different person. Yet there was sharp pain as well.

"Wherezhe...?" she asked, finding it extremely difficult to work her lips. She tasted slippery blood.

"It's dead," Roy said, holding out his hand for her.

"Dead...?"

"Come on," he said.

"Where...?"

She couldn't complete the sentence and simply took his hand. He all but lifted her from the car until she stood on jellied legs. She teetered against his chest and felt his arms encircle her body in an embrace. The rain hammered her head and splashed the ground at her feet.

You have to get away.

Yet she didn't know how to go about achieving this feat.

She couldn't think clearly, could barely stand, let alone fight him off her. "The policeman...?" she said.

"It's going to be okay," Roy said soothingly, and kissed her on the forehead.

His arms moved up her back and wrapped around her head, and she didn't like this, it wasn't right, wasn't how you hugged someone—

"*Roy...?*"

His arms flexed and twisted.

The next thing Brook knew she was flat on the ground, staring at Roy's cap-toe Oxfords. She tried to get up, couldn't. Her right arm was pinned beneath her, but it wouldn't move. She felt no pain, but she found it was becoming increasingly difficult to breathe, and this sent a wild panic through her.

Roy crouched. Although she couldn't see his face, she could hear his voice.

"It's okay, Brook. It won't be long now. Everything's okay."

What have you done to me, you bastard? What have you done to me? WHAT HAVE YOU DONE?

She was still screaming these silent questions inside her head when she died from asphyxiation two minutes later.

EPILOGUE

D
r. Roy Wallis scavenged Sharon's bloody tension bandages from the floor of the sleep laboratory and dumped them, along with the used syringes and empty vials of Vecuronium, through the iron grates of a rainwater gutter on Shattuck Avenue. Next he went to Chad's body and wrapped his arms around it, to transfer the Australian's blood to his clothes.

Then he called the police.

Within minutes, three squad cars and an ambulance, gumballs flashing, screeched to a halt in front of Tolman Hall. Half a dozen officers secured the scene. Paramedics attended to the victims and confirmed there were no survivors. The senior cop grilled Dr. Wallis on what happened. When Wallis refused to make a statement without his attorney present, he was hauled off to the Berkeley Police Department Jail Facility, questioned some more by a pair of detectives, and eventually arrested and booked.

After being fingerprinted and photographed, Wallis said, "I have the right to one phone call."

The guard shrugged. "Make it quick."

Wallis used the telephone on the guard's desk to call his personal attorney.

"Don?" he said, turning away from the guard. "It's Roy Wallis."

"Roy," Don Finke said, a note of concern in his voice. "A

call at this hour can't be good news."

"I've been arrested," he said. "They're holding me at the Berkeley Police Department Jail Facility, and I really don't want to sit around here for any longer than I have to."

"Don't sweat it, Roy. Don't sweat it at all. I'll have you out of there in no time."

There was no longer a municipal courthouse in the City of Berkeley, so midmorning Dr. Wallis was driven to the Superior Court in Oakland for his arraignment, during which he pleaded not guilty. The district attorney, a fussy, gaunt man named Edward Prince, did his damnedest to fight Wallis' bail request, while Don Finke argued that Dr. Wallis was a reputable university professor and stalwart of the community and no flight risk. In the end, after more than twenty minutes of back-and-forth, the presiding judge ruled, "Bail is granted in the sum of five hundred thousand dollars."

Three days later district attorney Edward Prince charged Dr. Wallis with five counts of involuntary manslaughter, just as the Sleep Experiment was becoming a bona fide international phenomenon. On a purely criminal level, the experiment involved a mass murder that had claimed the lives of five people. Given the self-mutilations and violent deaths involved, it rivaled the sensationalism of the 1969 Tate murders. Add to this Dr. Wallis' public claims that the killer, Chad Carter, had been possessed by a madness that resided at the core of all of humanity, a madness largely kept in check only by the miraculous powers of sleep—well, you had a media blitzkrieg the likes of which had not been witnessed in recent history.

While the vast majority of the public believed Dr. Wallis to be running some sort of publicity hoax, this didn't stop his name from entering the daily lexicon of every major newscaster and talk show host in America, or the phrase "Demon Souls" from becoming one of the top trending hashtags across social media sites the world over.

Indeed, the buildup to what became dubbed the latest and greatest "Trial of the Century" could not be understated, and the criminal case against Dr. Roy Wallis commenced to global fanfare four months later on October 14, 2018. It was heard in the San Francisco Hall of Justice complex. The granite-clad building housed the Sheriff's Department, the County Jail, as well as various municipal courts, and until recently it served as the location of the Office of the Chief Medical Examiner. The courtroom selected for the trial featured paneled oak walls, a coffered ceiling, and linoleum flooring. Hanging on the wall at the front of the room, behind the imposing mahogany bench, was the seal of the jurisdiction, bookended by the flags of the federal and state governments. Adjacent to the bench was the currently empty witness stand, as well as desks behind which the court clerk and court reporter were seated. Against the left-hand wall was the jury box, occupied by the twelve jurors, six men, six women, all white.

For the last three weeks they had patiently listened to accusations and counter-accusations and expert testimony by more than two dozen witnesses, which included the chief of forensic pathology at the coroner's office, SFPD detectives in the robbery homicide division, various doctors, a toxicologist, a narcotics expert, a computer forensics examiner, and a physician specializing in internal medicine. And today, the final day of the trial, they would hear the prosecution's and defense's closing arguments.

Dr. Wallis sat at the defense table, handsome, composed, and meticulously dressed in a black tailored suit and matching silk tie. Ever since he had become a household name, there had been nearly as much discussion in the media regarding his looks, his style—and even his beard—as there had been about his guilt or innocence, or his Demon Soul theory. He had amassed a legion of female fans from as far away as New Zealand and Japan who mailed him over a thousand letters a week, in which he often found racy photographs and propositions of marriage. On several occasions during the trial women had catcalled to him from the packed gallery, prompting the presiding judge to twice clear the courtroom and once threaten to close it to the public for the remainder of the proceedings.

Nevertheless, not everybody who came to watch the criminal case against Dr. Wallis supported him. Some displayed neither adoration nor sympathy, but enmity and expectation. They despised him for his wealth and his attractiveness and the cult-like status he had garnered, and they wanted nothing more than to see him cut down to size.

At nine o'clock sharp, the uniformed bailiff called the court to order.

Everybody rose as Judge Amanda Callahan, clad in plain black robes, entered the courtroom and took her seat behind the bench. At her prompting, District Attorney Edward Prince went to the lectern between the two counsel tables and addressed the jury. He had proven himself to be a skilled and able prosecutor, and in simple, broad strokes, he outlined the State's case against Dr. Roy Wallis. He argued that Dr. Wallis was a dangerously ambitious man who had put the success of the Sleep Experiment above all else. When the two test subjects began to demonstrate severe mental and physical deterioration, far from ending the experiment, or even temporarily suspending it, he continued full steam ahead, consequences be damned.

Edward Prince concluded his address by saying, "The events set in motion four months ago are now at a close. On June 14 crimes of ghastly proportions were committed. On that day a young girl ripped her heart from her chest and a young man murdered three other people in brutal fashion before his own life was taken—five lives squandered and gone forever. The questions that had been on everybody's mind from coast to coast, and indeed across the world, were, *How could this have ever been allowed to happen? And who should be held accountable?* Well, those questions have come to rest right here in this courtroom, and it's fallen to you as members of this jury to answer them.

"Based on the evidence presented to you over these last three weeks, based on what you've heard and seen, the answers are clear. The tragedy should never have been allowed to happen, and the defendant, Dr. Roy Wallis, must be held accountable, for he is guilty of criminal gross negligence.

"Everyone in this courtroom agrees that Dr. Roy Wallis, as the person in charge of the notorious Sleep Experiment, is responsible for the deaths of the five unfortunate victims. This is not up for debate. The defense believes it. The State believes it. Sharon Nash's life didn't have to end on a bathroom floor with her heart clutched in her hand. Brook Foxley didn't have to die slowly and terrifyingly from asphyxiation due to a broken neck. Officer Roger Henn, a husband and father of two boys, didn't have to lose his life to Chad Carter, his intestines torn from his stomach.

"So this case isn't about whether Dr. Roy Wallis is responsible for the massacre or not. This case is about whether his conduct during the Sleep Experiment constitutes not just negligence but *criminal* negligence—and the State submits to you, ladies and gentlemen, that it most certainly does.

"You have heard several instructions from the judge over the course of the trial. The State would like to refresh your memory on a couple of them.

"The first is the character instruction that stated you *may* consider the character of the defendant in assessing his guilt or innocence. The defense will have you believe Dr. Roy Wallis is an upstanding citizen, a respected university professor and scientist, and an all-around good guy. However, do not forget the witness testimonies that described him as an alcoholic, a serial womanizer, a playboy who lives in a multi-million-dollar penthouse, and a delusional megalomaniac whose ambition has no limit.

"Another instruction the State would like you to remember referred to callous disregard of human life. The judge put the definition of *callous* in parentheses, because it was important for you to make the distinction as to whether the deaths of the five victims were the result of simple negligence, or negligence so gross, wanton, and culpable as to show a *callous disregard of human life*. The State would now like to remind you the definition of callous is "showing or having an insensitive and cruel disregard for others," and this would most certainly encompass the cruel disregard present in this case. Fourteen days of cruel disregard, in fact.

"In successfully tried cases of involuntary manslaughter against motorists under the influence of drugs or alcohol—the most common case of involuntary manslaughter heard by the courts—the killings happen in a flash." He snapped his fingers for emphasis. "It's momentary. In the case against Dr. Roy Wallis, on the other hand, the deaths of the five victims weren't momentary, nor did they occur in a momentary lapse. The defendant had fourteen days to end the experiment, *fourteen days*, which was the time it took for two young people to literally lose their minds while under his supervision. It was in his power all along to stop the Sleep Experiment when it began spiraling out of control, but he never did so. The defense would like you to believe that Dr. Roy Wallis had no forewarning that Chad Carter or Sharon Nash would become dangers to themselves or to others. But how can you possibly believe this claim? The day before the massacre they covered the viewing window into the sleep laboratory with their own feces—*covered the window with their own feces*. Now, I might not be an acclaimed psychology professor—but I don't need to be—to deduce that these people needed help. Help that Dr. Wallis denied them for fourteen long days."

Edward Prince walked toward the jury box.

"Everyone is entitled to what we refer to as self-evident truths: life, liberty, and the pursuit of happiness. Chad Carter, Sharon Nash, Guru Rampal, Brook Foxley, and Roger Henn had a right to life, to experience joy and love and disappointment that comes with life too, to grow old and die peacefully...but because of Dr. Roy Wallis' callous disregard of human life, because of his blind and reckless ambition, their lives, liberties, and pursuits of happiness were stolen from them.

"Don't be fooled into thinking the defendant should get a pass because his scientific research was special or noble, or because he shed a new insight into the human condition. Even if his claims of so-called Demon Souls are ever independently verified, he still shouldn't get a pass. You must make the same decision about Dr. Roy Wallis' callous reckless actions as you would about anyone else's. It doesn't matter if you believe he had good intentions in undertaking his experiment. That's a sentencing issue. That's not a guilt/innocence issue."

Edward Prince spread his arms.

"So when it's all said and done, Chad, Sharon, Guru, Brook, and Roger didn't have to die how they died. They shouldn't have died how they died. Dr. Roy Wallis should have ended the notorious Sleep Experiment well before it reached its bloody conclusion. The fact he didn't displays not just negligent conduct on his part but *criminally* negligent conduct that is gross, willful, wanton, and culpable.

"Thus the State asks you to find the defendant guilty of involuntary manslaughter based on all of the circumstances presented here. Ladies and gentlemen of the jury, the decision is in your hands. Thank you."

You could hear a pin drop in the courtroom as the scrawny Edward Prince returned to his seat behind the prosecution table. Dr. Wallis averted his eyes from the jurors, for the faces he had come to know so well the last three weeks now appeared cold and unfriendly.

Judge Amanda Callahan said, "Mr. Wilks, are you going to close for the defense?"

"I am, Your Honor, may it please the Court."

Stephen Wilks, a former judge himself, was a short, portly man with a receding hairline, out-of-fashion red muttonchops, and heavy eyeglasses that seemed to magnify the size of his eyeballs behind the lenses. Dressed in an unassuming tweed suit and scuffed loafers, he ambled to the lectern. He shuffled through his papers, then looked up, blinking, as if awed by his formal surroundings. At first glance he was the antithesis of the flashy defense attorneys usually retained by wealthy defendants accused of felonies, yet he was one of the most respected criminal lawyers in the country. He held the impressive record of never having lost a major case in his career, which was why Dr. Wallis had chosen him to lead his defense team.

"Five people are dead and somebody must pay," Stephen Wilks began, pushing his eyeglasses up the bridge of his nose. "You heard it from the witnesses, and you heard it from most of Mr. Prince's closing argument. Right to life. Right to grow old. Five people dead; someone must pay. Dr. Roy Wallis must pay. Well, on one level, the defendant will pay. He'll pay for the rest of his life, but that's not what this case is about. It's about whether you the jury can find beyond a reasonable doubt that the deaths of the five victims were the direct result of criminal negligence on the part of Dr. Wallis, criminal negligence that was so gross and wanton and culpable as to show callous disregard for human life.

"So let's look at what facts the State has used to argue that Dr. Wallis acted with callous disregard for the lives of the victims, what they think they have proven beyond a reasonable doubt. Their main argument is that Dr. Wallis did not stop the experiment early enough. However, the Court has instructed you time and time again that the fact the defendant did not end the experiment sooner, in and of itself, is not enough to justify a conviction of involuntary manslaughter. It doesn't show Dr. Wallis had a callous disregard for his test subjects' wellbeing. Thanks to the meticulous notes recorded by the defendant and his two assistants, we've had access and insight into the hour-by-hour functioning of his test subjects' minds. And, yes, while some of their symptoms might seem alarming to you, particularly as they approached the end of the Sleep Experiment, there were zero red flags indicating they posed dangers to themselves or to others. Dr. Wallis didn't know they would snap to the extent they did. After all, he didn't expose them to torture. He simply deprived them of sleep. He didn't know what the full repercussions of this would entail—for that was the exact purpose of the experiment!"

Stephen Wilks scratched his head, and for a moment he seemed to have lost his train of thought. But then just as the jury members began fiddling uncomfortably in the silence, he said, "The act of not knowing, ladies and gentlemen, is an involuntary act. You don't intentionally not know something because then it isn't something you don't know. It's something you're ignoring. If you ignore something, that's different than not knowing it. Dr. Wallis didn't ignore any red flags in his test subjects. He simply didn't know what was going to happen. And although the act of not knowing is an involuntary act, it doesn't meet the standard of involuntary manslaughter because it doesn't prove criminal negligence.

"Now, when events *did* make a turn for the worse, and it was clear the test subjects *did* become a danger to themselves and others, if—*if*—Dr. Wallis had done nothing at this point, then I would not be arguing before you in his defense, because he most certainly would be guilty of criminal negligence. But this is not what happened at all. As soon as Guru Rampal informed him that he was concerned about Sharon Nash, Dr. Wallis attempted to help her. Unfortunately, by that time, there was nothing he could do. So he immediately terminated the experiment, shutting off the gas, and went to assess the other test subject, who suddenly and inexplicably attacked Guru Rampal. At this point did Dr. Wallis run? No, he did not. According to his own testimony, he valiantly wrestled Chad off Guru, suffering a nasty gash to his head, and blacked out. When he came to a short time later, he found his assistant Guru Rampal dead, his girlfriend Brook Foxley dead, and Chad Carter savagely attacking Roger Henn. Again, did he run or hide? No, he did nothing of the sort, and although he was not able to save Mr. Henn, his actions could not be described as anything but heroic."

Stephen Wilks ambled from the lectern to the jury box and smiled timidly at the men and women seated there. "Please don't be swayed by the gruesome way in which the four victims perished," he said. "Their deaths are in every way a tragedy, but not every tragedy is a crime. Allow me a moment to read some of the judge's instruction to you." He produced a piece of paper from his pocket. "*If you find that the facts are susceptible to two different interpretations, one of which is consistent with the innocence of the defendant, you cannot arbitrarily adopt the interpretation which incriminates the defendant. Instead, the interpretation more favorable to the defendant should be adopted unless it is untenable, under all the circumstances. The evidence must not only be consistent with guilt, but it must be inconsistent with every reasonable hypothesis of innocence.*"

Stephen Wilks tucked the paper away.

"So you see, ladies and gentlemen," he said, "the action of keeping two individuals awake with a stimulant gas is simply not enough to warrant a conviction of involuntary manslaughter. Yes, there are five dead individuals. Yes, Dr. Wallis, as their supervisor, is responsible for those deaths. He has never denied this. But the question at hand is whether a criminal, a felon, stands before you. If you are unsure of your position on this, even in the slightest bit, then the State has not proven beyond a reasonable doubt that Dr. Roy Wallis is guilty of callous disregard of life, and you must rule in his favor. And he *is* innocent, ladies and gentlemen, for if the State had shown that he knew Chad Carter and Sharon Nash were a danger to themselves and to others, and continued with the experiment, then that would have been involuntary manslaughter. Heck, I'd be happy to argue the case that it was *voluntary* manslaughter. Yet, to the contrary, the State did *not* prove this at all, and so I ask of you to understand that, despite whatever you think of the Sleep Experiment, or Dr. Wallis himself, he is not a criminal, and there is only one verdict you can possibly reach. Not guilty."

The jury was out for four hours. Dr. Roy Wallis watched as they filed back into the courtroom. Although he remained outwardly calm, he felt as though a nest of snakes were slithering inside his stomach. A guilty verdict, while not the end of his life, would be devastating. He could not afford to spend the next five years in prison. He had so much work yet to do!

Judge Amanda Callahan asked, "Has the jury reached a verdict?"

"We have, Your Honor." The jury foreman held up a piece of paper pinched between his fingers.

"Would the bailiff get the verdict, please?"

The bailiff went to the juror, took the piece of paper, and passed it to the judge. She opened it, read the contents, then looked up. "The jury finds the defendant not guilty."

Pandemonium resulted. The spectators in the gallery shot to their feet, with everyone talking at once, many applauding and cheering, others shouting profanities.

Outside the Hall of Justice, Dr. Wallis stopped before a

phalanx of television cameras for an impromptu and cele-bratory press conference. When the throng of journalists and reporters quieted down, he said into the two-dozen or so microphones thrust at him, "Walt Whitman once wrote that 'the fear of hell is little or nothing to me.' But he was Walt Whitman, so he can write whatever he damn well pleased." Wallis stroked his beard, reveling in the knowledge the world would be hanging onto his each and every word. "I'm guessing," he continued, "Walt most likely never be-lieved that hell existed in the first place, hence his cavalier attitude." He shook a finger, as if to scorn the father of free verse. "But I, my lovely friends, I now know hell exists, and let me tell you—it scares the utter shit out of me."

Resounding silence except for the *cluck-cluck-cluck* of photographs being snapped.

Then everyone began shouting questions at once.

"Will you perform another sleep experiment in the future, professor?"

"Do you plan to make your complete research available to the public?"

"What would you like to say to your doubters?"

"Are you going to apologize to the families of the deceased?"

"Do you know where Penny Park is?"

"Do you have plans to sell the stimulant gas to pharmaceutical companies?"

Ignoring the bedlam, Dr. Wallis followed the path his de-fense team cleaved through the crowd to a waiting black SUV. He climbed into the backseat, closed the door, and frowned at the driver in the front seat.

"Who are you?" he demanded.

"I'm your driver today, sir," the gray-haired man replied.

"Where's Raoul?"

"Sick."

"Sick?"

"He called in sick today, and I was given the gig."

"Do you know where my apartment building is?"

"The Clock Tower Building, sir. I live only a few blocks away from it."

Demonstrators were slapping the windows and roof of the SUV, so Dr. Wallis said, "Get a move on then."

The driver rolled away from the curb. Once the vehicle cleared the crowd, Wallis noticed a palpable quiet to the streets, and it wasn't until they passed a busy bar—at 11:45 in the morning—that he realized the quiet was because of him. The city—hell, the country, more like it—had ground to a halt as people in their living rooms and offices, at work and at play, had gathered to watch on their televisions and their phones as his verdict was read.

Dr. Wallis googled himself on his phone and read the headlines from a half dozen leading newspapers:

Jury Clears Dr. Roy Wallis of Involuntary Manslaughter
Spellbound Nation Divided on Sleep Doctor Verdict
No Justice!
Not Guilty!
Jury Stunner: Wallis Walks
Demon Soul Doctor Free!

As Dr. Wallis skimmed the lead story in *The New York Times*, however, his smile became a frown. The journalist was clearly a biased hack, as the piece was a hit job on Wallis. It labeled him a murderer who escaped justice, while lambasting his Demon Soul theory as the "fantasy role-play of a delusional megalomaniac."

Scowling, Dr. Wallis shoved his phone back into his pocket. He shouldn't be surprised by the coverage. The press had been largely critical of him the entire trial, too close-minded—and frightened—to believe the evidence he'd put before them.

We'll see who has the last laugh, assholes, he thought, already anticipating his second sleep experiment, which he'd livestream to the masses. *Let them see with their own eyes what we are and what we become when sleep is banished and the gates of hell are thrown wide open.*

Wallis was so engrossed in his thoughts he didn't realize they'd arrived at the Clock Tower Building until a mob of reporters and journalists surrounded the SUV, cameras and microphones at the ready.

"Get me as close to the front door as possible," he grunted.

"Yes, sir," the driver said.

Inching through the excited crowd, the SUV eventually stopped directly before the building's front entrance. As soon as Dr. Wallis stepped out of the vehicle, microphones were shoved in his face, everyone shouting questions over everyone else.

Ignoring the bedlam, he quickly entered the building, closing the glass door securely behind him so none of the jackasses could follow him inside.

Straightening his blazer and smoothing his tie, he studied himself in the annualized steel elevator doors, deciding he looked damned good.

When the doors opened, he took the cab to the top floor and let himself into his penthouse apartment. The first thing he did was put CNN on the large TV in the living room. With the news anchor talking about Wallis and the Sleep Experiment in the background, he went to the bar and made a Dark 'n' Stormy. He watched a bit of the coverage, but when the white-haired nerd continued to belittle his life's work, he decided to go to the wraparound deck for a cigarette.

He froze when he noticed the glass in the door to the deck had been broken.

"That was me," a male voice said from behind him.

Dr. Wallis spun around as a man emerged from the clock tower room. With slicked-back black hair and a haggard face, he looked like someone who had spent more than his fair share of time in smoky bars. He wore blue jeans and a black leather jacket over a denim shirt a slightly lighter shade than his pants. He was thin yet clearly no lightweight as cords of muscle stood out like knotted ropes in his neck.

"Who the fuck are you?" Wallis demanded, his voice brash and unafraid even as his pulse spiked and his insides hollowed. Nobody was okay with finding a stranger in their home—let alone an armed stranger, as the man gripped a baseball bat in his right hand.

"Bill," the man said. "I'm Bill."

"What are you doing in my house, Bill?"

"I'm here to kill you, Roy."

Wallis' throat tightened to the size of a straw. He swallowed hard. "Why would you want to do that?"

"Let me introduce myself properly, Roy. I'm Bill *Foxley*."

Dr. Wallis' eyes widened, and that hollow feeling inside him intensified tenfold.

"Hey look," he said, holding up his hands, "I didn't kill Brook. That was Chad Carter—"

"I don't care if it was you who broke my sister's neck, or that psycho patient of yours. The fact is she's dead, and she wouldn't be if it wasn't for you and your fucked-up experiment—"

Wallis threw his Dark 'n' Stormy at Bill and bolted toward the front door. He heard the man coming after him, knew he wouldn't get the door open before the baseball bat hit a homerun with the back of his head, so he whirled about midstride.

Deflecting a blow from the bat with his forearms, Wallis threw a punch, striking Bill in the jaw, staggering him. Even so, he knew he was outmatched unless he found a weapon. He turned, intending to make a break for the first level of the clock tower, where he could grab a pool cue—but came face to face with a second assailant.

He immediately knew the person was Bill Foxley's brother—the resemblance was reflected in their smarmy faces and their wiry physiologies—but even as he processed this, the man was swinging a bat.

The polished wood cracked Dr. Wallis squarely on the forehead. Pain exploded behind his eyes in a fireworks of chaotic light. He was unconscious before he hit the floor.

Dr. Wallis came around to trumpets of pain blasting from ear to ear. Despite the white haze that engulfed his thoughts and vision, he realized he was seated in a chair, his hands secured with rope behind his back.

Blinking salty tears from his eyes, he saw Bill pacing before him in the kitchen, a glass of whiskey in his hand.

Bill noticed him rousing and said, "About fucking time."

"I have money," Dr. Wallis mumbled, his thoughts still muddled but quickened with fear. "Look around. I have a lot of money. How much do you want?"

"Money?" Bill laughed mirthlessly. "I don't want your money, hotshot. I want my sister back. But since I can't have that, I want revenge."

And Wallis knew Bill could not be bought; the man was going to murder him.

"Please!" he said, straining violently at his restraints. "Brook's death wasn't my fault. I was just acquitted of—"

Arms slipped around his head from behind.

The second brother.

Bill nodded slowly, and before Dr. Wallis could protest, his head snapped violently to the left. He slumped forward in the chair, the rope around his wrists preventing him falling forward onto his face. His breathing came in sharp, ragged gasps. He knew his upper cervical spine had been fractured, and he would die shortly from asphyxiation, just as Brook had died on the asphalt of the breezeway. Even as this morbid irony registered, he thought with indignant fury, YOU CAN'T DO THIS TO ME! I'M DOCTOR ROY WALLIS! *I'M FAMOUS NOW!*

The last thing the famous Dr. Roy Wallis heard in his life was Brook's brother telling him in a sanctimonious voice, "Good night, doctor. Sleep tight."

AFTERWORD

Thank you for taking the time to read the book! If you enjoyed it, a brief review would be hugely appreciated. You can click straight to the review page here:

World's Scariest Legends: Volume 1 - Amazon Review Page

Best,
Jeremy

ABOUT THE AUTHOR

Jeremy Bates

 USA TODAY and #1 AMAZON bestselling author Jeremy Bates has published more than twenty novels and novellas, which have been translated into several languages, optioned for film and TV, and downloaded more than one million times. Midwest Book Review compares his work to "Stephen King, Joe Lansdale, and other masters of the art." He has won both an Australian Shadows Award and a Canadian Arthur Ellis Award. He was also a finalist in the Goodreads Choice Awards, the only major book awards decided by readers. The novels in the "World's Scariest Places" series are set in real locations and include Suicide Forest in Japan, The Catacombs in Paris, Helltown in Ohio, Island of the Dolls in Mexico, and Mountain of the Dead in Russia. The novels in the "World's Scariest Legends" series are based on real legends and include Mosquito Man and The Sleep Experiment. You can check out any of these places or legends on the web. Also, visit JEREMYBATESBOOKS.COM to receive Black Canyon, WINNER of The Lou Allin Memorial Award.